Beauty, danger, passion . . . the small town of
Arundel, North Carolina, has them all—
in Jude Deveraux's thrilling novel
of romantic suspense

First Impressions

"An entertaining read . . . the surprise ending is a fun
fillip for longtime fans."

—*Booklist*

"An adventurous tale spiced with both humor and danger. Deveraux strikes again!"

—*Romantic Times Book Club*

"Enjoyable romantic suspense. . . . A delightful romantic
thriller."

—Harriet Klausner

"A must read for all Jude Deveraux fans. . . . As usual,
Deveraux has written a story full of interesting fact
mixed with fiction that keeps us turning the pages."

—*The Best Reviews*

*Turn the page to read more critical acclaim for
Jude Deveraux's beloved bestselling novels. . . .*

WILD ORCHIDS

"A not-to-be-missed novel . . . that will keep you on the edge of your chair."

—*Rendezvous*

"[Deveraux] does a superb job of building up to her chilling conclusion."

—*Publishers Weekly*

THE MULBERRY TREE

"Deveraux's touch is gold. . . . Irresistible."

—*Publishers Weekly*

"Mystery, romance, and good cooking converge."

—*People*

THE SUMMERHOUSE

"Marvelously compelling reading. . . . Deeply satisfying."

—*Houston Chronicle*

"Entertaining summer reading."

—*The Port St. Lucie News*

TEMPTATION

"Filled with excitement, action, and insight. . . . A non-stop thriller."

—Harriet Klausner, Barnesandnoble.com

"Deveraux['s] lively pace and happy endings . . . will keep readers turning pages."

—*Publishers Weekly*

Jude Deveraux

First Impressions

Pocket Books

New York   London   Toronto   Sydney   New Delhi

Pocket Books
An Imprint of Simon & Schuster, Inc.
1230 Avenue of the Americas
New York, NY 10020

This book is a work of fiction. Any references to historical events, real people, or real places are used fictitiously. Other names, characters, places, and events are products of the author's imagination, and any resemblance to actual events or places or persons, living or dead, is entirely coincidental.

This Pocket Books paperback edition April 2016

POCKET and colophon are registered trademarks of Simon & Schuster, Inc.

For information about special discounts for bulk purchases, please contact Simon & Schuster Special Sales at 1-866-506-1949 or business@simonandschuster.com.

The Simon & Schuster Speakers Bureau can bring authors to your live event. For more information or to book an event, contact the Simon & Schuster Speakers Bureau at 1-866-248-3049 or visit our website at www.simonspeakers.com.

Manufactured in the United States of America

10 9 8 7 6 5 4 3 2 1

ISBN 978-1-5011-3135-6
ISBN 978-1-4165-0008-7 (ebook)

This book is for Brenda and Judith.

"I want her to be my age," Brenda said. "And I want her to find a fabulous man and to have an adventure."

"And funny," Judith said. "I want the book to have a lot of laughter in it."

Hope you guys like it.

Prologue

The moment he saw the smirk on Bill's face, Jared knew he was going to be given a job he wouldn't like. So what did a man have to do to finally be able to choose his own assignments? he thought for the thousandth time. Get shot? Naw, he'd done that three times. How about getting kidnapped? That had happened twice. Hey! How about being home so seldom that his wife leaves him for some other guy, a used car salesman who is now the father of their three kids? Nope. That had happened too. So how about getting too old for the field? Too late. At forty-nine, Jared felt that he'd reached that age about six years ago.

"Don't look at me like that," Bill said, holding his office door open for Jared to enter.

Groaning, Jared put on a pronounced limp as he hobbled toward the chair opposite Bill's overloaded desk, WILLIAM TEASDALE on a plaque in front. Sticking his leg out stiffly in front of him, he ostentatiously rubbed his knee, as though he were in great pain.

"You can cut it out," Bill said as he sat down behind his desk. "I have no sympathy for you, and even if I did, I couldn't let you out of this one." He picked up a folder, then looked across the top of it at Jared. "Most agents are glad to get out in the field. Why not you?"

Jared leaned back in his chair. "Where should I begin? With pain? I was in the hospital for three weeks after the last job. And life. I like living. And then there's—"

"Got a new girlfriend?" Bill asked, his eyes narrowed.

Jared gave a bit of a grin. "Yeah. Nice girl. I'd like to see her sometimes."

"She's a reformed what?"

"Stripper," Jared mumbled, giving Bill a sheepish grin. "So sue me. After a wife like Patsy—"

"Spare me," Bill said, and once again he was the boss. "We need somebody to find out something, and you can do it. Remember that agent we found out had been a spy for the last fifteen years?"

"Yeah," Jared said, bitterness in his voice. He'd worked with the man about ten years ago, and had filed a report saying that something wasn't right about the guy, but he didn't know what. No one paid any attention. A few months ago, they'd found out that the agent was a spy and that he'd been feeding information to his mother country for years. "So what did you find out from him?"

"Nothing. Suicide before we could get to him."

"Please tell me that you don't want me to travel to wherever he was from, go undercover, and find out—"

"No," Bill said, waving his hand. "Nothing like that. The truth is that we can't figure out what his last big project was. He knew we were coming about ten minutes before we got there, so he had time to destroy a lot of evidence. But we found disks hidden under the floors, and a list of names inside a lightbulb. He had time to get rid of it all, so why didn't he destroy it?"

"But he didn't," Jared said, feeling the old wave of curiosity well up inside of him and trying hard to suppress it. Why? was the question that had caused most of the problems in his life. Even after a case was considered cold, Jared's "why" often made him continue. "What did he do?"

"He wadded up several pieces of paper into tiny balls and swallowed them."

"I bet somebody had fun retrieving them."

"Yeah," Bill said with a half smile. "We lost most of what went down him, but forensics managed to get a name and part of a Social Security number." He pushed a clear plastic folder across the desk, and Jared picked it up. Inside was a small piece of paper that seemed to have some writing on it, but Jared couldn't make it out.

"Eden Palmer," Bill said. "That name and a few numbers were the only things the crime lab could recover."

"Who's he?"

"Her. As far as we can figure out, she's nobody." He pulled a piece of paper from the folder in front of him. "She's forty-five, had a baby when she was eighteen, no husband then and not one since. She worked at one low-level job after another until her kid started college, then she went back to school and got a degree." He looked at the paper. "A couple of years after she graduated, Eden Palmer moved to New York, where she worked in a publishing house. When we first heard about her, she didn't know it, but an old woman she knew had died and left her a house in eastern North Carolina. The lawyer taking care of the case was looking for her, but we fixed it so he was delayed in finding her. We wanted to find out about her first." Putting the papers down, he stared at Jared.

"So how did she get connected to somebody who's been spying on the U.S. for umpteen years?"

"We have no idea." He was still looking at Jared, as though he expected him to figure out something.

"Maybe it was personal," Jared said. "Maybe the guy was in love with her. Or is she too ugly for that?"

Bill unclipped a photo from the file and pushed it across the desk.

"Not bad," Jared said, looking at the photo. It was her driver's license picture, so Jared figured she was actually three times that good looking. He studied the picture and the information. She was short, only five three, her eyesight was good, and she was an organ donor. Limp, blondish hair with a bit of curl in it surrounded blue eyes, a small nose, and a pretty mouth. She looked tired and unhappy in the photo. Probably had to wait in line for three hours, he thought. He gave the picture back to Bill. "So where do I come in?"

"We need you to find out what or who she knows."

Jared blinked a couple of times. Bill had said that only he, Jared, could do this, but this was a job for a rookie, not a senior agent. They could bring her in for questioning and find out what she knew. Probably something that she didn't know she knew. That wouldn't be too difficult. Where had she been in the last few years? Carried any packages for anyone? Jared almost smiled at the last thought, then he glanced at Bill's intense stare. What was he missing?

It hit him all at once: they wanted him to seduce the information out of her. Cozy up to a lonely spinster, then ask her what she knew. "Oh, no, you don't. I will risk my *life* for the agency, but I don't kiss for it."

"But James Bond—"

"Was a made-up character," Jared said, ignoring Bill's smirk. "James Bond doesn't really exist. He—" Jared ran his hand over his eyes, calmed himself, then looked at Bill. "I respectfully request that I not be given this assignment. Sir."

Leaning back against his chair, Bill folded his hands over his well-toned stomach. "Look, Jared, old friend, this case has us baffled. We don't want to haul her in here and scare her into telling us whatever she knows. If she knows anything, that is. And, as you said, maybe this was personal. This woman lived in New York for a while, so maybe she met this guy"—he glanced at the paper—"Roger Applegate—good American name, huh?—in New York. Maybe he met her, liked her, maybe they fell in love. Maybe he was planning to retire and marry her. Maybe when he knew that he'd been found out, his only thought was of protecting her name. He didn't seem to care if we investigated the criminals whose names were on the disks, but maybe he did care that we didn't involve the love of his life in something sordid. On the other hand, maybe this Ms. Palmer had no idea this man had a crush on her. He was a mousy-looking little thing who nobody noticed, so maybe Ms. Palmer was the secret object of his affection and she never knew about his great love for her."

"Or maybe she knows everything," Jared said tiredly. "And maybe you want me to find out one way or the other."

"You always were heavy in the brains department," Bill said, smiling.

Jared gave a sigh. In all his years in the agency, he'd tried hard to never get personally involved with the people connected to his investigations. Emotions kept you from seeing things clearly. But now, if he was understanding this, he was being asked to get to know this woman in a personal way and find out what she knew. She wasn't some underworld figure, wasn't a reformed anything. She was a— He looked at Bill. "She go to church?"

"Every Sunday."

Jared groaned. "But she did have a child out of wedlock." There was hope in his voice.

"She was seventeen and walking home from choir practice when a man leaped on her. Her parents kicked her out when she came up pregnant."

Jared looked like he was going to cry. "Lord! A persecuted heroine. Tragic happenings to an innocent," Jared said, his mouth a tight line. "Deliver me!" He glared at Bill, but Bill just grinned. Jared knew that he'd been chosen because of his age and his looks. He had dark hair, dark blue eyes, and a body kept trim by years spent in a gym. If he drank gallons of beer and ate lots of doughnuts, could he get fat in about four days? "So who left her the house?"

Bill leafed through the papers in the folder. "Alice Augusta Farrington. Born rich, but her druggie son spent everything. At least he had the courtesy to die before his mother did, so she had a few years of peace. She left the house and what was left of her fortune to our Ms. Palmer."

"How did our perfect heroine meet the rich old broad?"

"Seems the old gal took her in when Ms. Palmer

was just a kid and pregnant. She, the old one that is, wanted someone to sort out all the papers in her attic. The house was built in"—he glanced down— "about 1720 by one of the ancestors of the old woman's. Ms. Palmer spent years cataloging the family papers."

"Another virtue and another talent," Jared said with a grimace. "Truly an angel. Let me guess, Ms. Palmer and her kid stayed for years, beloved by all."

"She stayed until her daughter was five years old, then left in the middle of the night." Bill looked at Jared hard. "The old woman's son was a registered sex offender. Little kids. Girls, boys, he didn't care which. We have no way of knowing, but we figure he went after Ms. Palmer's daughter, and she left her comfortable home in a hurry."

Jared looked away for a moment. He really hated people who hurt children. He looked back at Bill. "Okay, so she's not had an easy life. A lot of us haven't. But it sounds to me as though she's been enough places and seen enough that she could have met this guy Applegate. Maybe if you just *ask* her what she knows she'd tell you. Maybe—"

"Remember Tess Brewster?"

"Sure," Jared said, his jaw muscle working. "But what do you mean, remember?"

"About a month ago, we started making some discreet inquiries about Ms. Palmer. New York turned up nothing. Neither did the town where she was born. But we moved Tess into Arundel, that's where the old house is. We rented a place for

Tess down the road from the one Ms. Palmer has inherited. Well, last week Tess was killed in a hit-and-run. We investigated as quietly as we could; it looks like it was a professional job."

Jared sighed. He'd liked Tess. She could drink any man under the table, and she'd been a good agent. "Do you think it's the house or the angelic Ms. Palmer?"

"We don't know, but we're sure something's there. One of the two is being watched very closely, and that's one reason we need *you*."

"I see. *I* have managed to keep my mug out of the paper."

"Yeah, for the most part, you've been hidden from public view. Tess—"

"Was easily recognized. Her face was all over the papers for about six weeks when she testified against that mobster." Jared's head came up. "Maybe he—"

"Maybe that hoodlum she testified against killed her? He died two years ago, and we don't think he was powerful enough or beloved enough that anyone would risk killing a federal agent on his behalf. And why wait seven years? No, we think someone recognized Tess for what she was and she was killed so she wouldn't find out what Ms. Palmer knows—or what's in that house."

Jared felt that Bill knew more than he was telling, and he doubted if anyone really thought the woman was innocent. "Do you have any idea *what* this Palmer woman knows? Is it someone's name? Or is it information? Or is it something that she has? Maybe she knows what's buried in the back-yard."

Bill lifted a file box from the floor onto his desk. "This is full of info about her. Everything we could find. Tess made two reports before she was mur-dered but found out nothing. I'll tell you what, you take that box home, read it over the weekend, then tell me what you think on Monday. If you agree to do it, fine. If you don't, then that's fine too."

Jared had worked with Bill for too many years to fall for that. If he knew Bill—and he did—a new identity was already waiting for him. Jared reached for the file box. "What's my cover?" he asked.

Bill tried to keep from smiling but failed. "We rented the house next door to her. It's just a fishing cabin that used to belong to the old woman, but she had to sell it to pay her son's debts. Between drugs and lawyers, he cost her millions. You're to be a retired policeman, out early on account of your knee, your wife of twenty-six years has just died, and you've rented this house in the middle of nowhere so you can go fishing and hunting and forget all your troubles. You need something to cry on her shoulder about. Women like that."

Jared bit his tongue to keep quiet. Bill had been married to the same woman for thirty-five years and liked to think that he knew all about women and marriage. The truth was that his wife spent nearly half the year in another state living with her never-married sister, who was rumored to be a real hellion. There was a lot of laughing speculation as to what Bill's wife got up to when she was with her sister.

"If this woman hasn't been told yet that she's inherited this house, how do you know that she won't sell it sight unseen? What makes you so sure she'll move away from the city lights to go to the wilds of rural North Carolina?"

He looked at Jared. "The truth is that we think this woman knows something and it has to do with that house. If she sells the house right away, then our theory is shot, but if she quits her job, runs out on her pregnant daughter, and jumps on the first plane to Arundel, it's possible that she's in a hurry because she knows something."

Jared took the box off Bill's desk. "So when do I leave?"

Grinning, Bill opened his desk drawer and withdrew a set of keys. "A three-quarter-ton, four-wheel drive, dark blue Chevy pickup awaits you in parking space number eighty-one. It's full of fishing gear and whatever Susie in accounting ordered for you from the L. L. Bean catalog. There's a marked map on the passenger seat and a key to the house on the ring. It's late, so you can stop in a motel tonight and read every word about Ms. Palmer before you meet her."

Jared hated that Bill knew him so well that he'd arranged all this before he'd been consulted. "What's my name to be this time?"

"We were kind to you and let you keep your first name. I hear you complained that you didn't like the last name we gave you. What was it again?"

"Elroy Coldheart," Jared said with a grimace. Kathy in the records department had let him know that she was interested if he was, but he wasn't. The next time he saw her, she'd handed him his new passport with a smile. It wasn't until later that he saw the name.

"This time you're named Jared McBride. Whatever did you do to Kathy to make her come up with the name of *McBride*?" Bill was chuckling, but he was also curious. He wanted to know everything that went on in his department.

Jared didn't answer. Lugging the big file box, he left the room smiling. He wasn't going to tell Bill anything. His only thought was to get this assignment over and done with as quickly as possible.

Chapter One

"M om? Mom? Are you all right?" Melissa looked at her mother with concern. She'd brought in the mail and put it on the hall table, then went to get herself something to eat. She was five months pregnant, and she could eat the legs off a table. Her mother had come in from work and picked up the mail, opening a letter from what looked to be a law firm. Melissa hoped it was nothing bad. "Mom?" Her words were muffled by the peanut butter sandwich in her mouth. She'd been tempted to add grape jelly but was afraid her husband would smell the jelly on her breath. Stuart was adamant that she didn't gain too much weight during pregnancy, so at dinner Melissa ate steamed vegetables and broiled meat. It was just during the day, while he was at work at the prestigious accounting firm, that she indulged in chocolate and shrimp—together.

"Mom!" Melissa said loudly. "What in the world is wrong with you?"

Eden sat down on the little sofa by the hall table. The sofa had been a rickety piece of junk when she'd seen it in a small, out-of-the-way shop in a district that Melissa's husband didn't want them to visit. Eden had known right away it was Hepplewhite. She and Melissa had tied the sofa onto the roof of the station wagon and taken it home. It had taken Eden six weekends to repair, refinish, and upholster it. "Aren't you clever?" Stuart had said in his haughty way, as though Eden were of a lower class than he was. She'd had to grit her teeth, as she always did when she dealt with her son-in-law. Melissa loved him, but Eden had never been able to figure out why.

"Mrs. Farrington left me her house."

"Mrs. Farrington?" Melissa asked, looking at the clock. She had seventeen and a half minutes before Stuart came home. Was that enough time to make herself another sandwich?

"Go on," Eden said, knowing her daughter's mind. "I'll cover for you."

"I shouldn't. Really, I shouldn't. Dinner will be soon and—"

"It's grilled chicken breasts, steamed broccoli, roast potatoes, and sugarless Jell-O for dessert. Very good for you. Not a calorie in any of it."

Melissa opened her mouth, then scurried off to the kitchen, her mother behind her. She was slathering peanut butter on bread when Eden walked into the room, the letter open before her. "Who's Mrs. Farrington?"

"You remember her, don't you, dear? We lived with her until you were five."

"Oh, yeah. I do remember her. Sort of. Very old. And a long time ago you mentioned a man. Was he her son?"

Eden didn't bother to suppress the shiver that ran over her body. "Yes, her son. Dreadful man. It seems that he died some time ago. Before Mrs. Farrington did."

"You didn't keep in touch with her?" Melissa was pouring chocolate syrup into her milk. It was a good thing that Stuart never opened the refrigerator or he'd see the forbidden things that Eden bought for her daughter. No, Stuart was the type who believed food should be eaten at a table and served to him by someone else, preferably his wife. He didn't go rummaging in the refrigerator looking for something to eat.

"No," Eden said tightly. "After we left I had nothing to do with her. Not that she..." She broke off. What happened was not something she wanted to have to explain to her daughter. I didn't want that pedophile of a son of hers to know where I was, she could have said, but didn't. "No, we didn't keep in touch."

Many times over the years she'd wondered what had happened to dear Mrs. Farrington, and Eden often felt a wave of guilt run through her when she thought about that sweet woman being left alone with her evil son. But then Eden would look at her daughter and know that she'd done the right thing in running away and never looking back. She glanced at the clock. "You now have approximately two and three-quarter minutes before the master returns, so you'd better drink that and clean out your glass."

"Mother," Melissa said primly, "Stuart isn't like that. He's a kind and loving man and I love him...ery uch." The last words were muffled, as her mouth was full.

"Yes, he's wonderful," Eden said, then cut herself off when she heard the sarcasm in her voice. It was tough to think how she'd tried to raise her daughter to be an independent woman, only to see her marry a control freak like Stuart. To Eden's mind, Stuart was all show. For all his talk of having a great future before him, he'd willingly moved into Eden's apartment "for a few weeks," as he'd said just before the wedding. "Until I get a place for us. A little farther uptown." Stuart had made Eden's generous offer seem as though it were worth nothing, and she'd had to resist the urge to defend herself. But that was two years ago, and now nothing Stuart said bothered her. He and Melissa were still in Eden's small apartment, still letting her cook for them and letting her take care of most of the household chores. Months ago, Eden had decided she'd had enough and was going to evict them. She'd built up her courage to the point where she didn't care if they had to live on the street for a while. It might do them some good. Teach them some lessons. But then Melissa had announced she was pregnant and that was that. Eden could still remember the smirk on Stuart's face when Melissa made the announcement. It was as though he'd known what Eden had been thinking and he'd calculated the pregnancy just so she couldn't throw them out. "You don't mind, do you, Mom?" Melissa had said. "It was an accident. We meant to have children, but we wanted to wait until we had a place of our own. But with Stuart on the verge of a promotion, it doesn't make sense to buy something small and dreary when in just a few weeks we'll be able to afford something grand and glorious."

Since her daughter had married, Eden often wondered if Melissa had become a marionette. "Small and dreary" and "grand and glorious" were Stuart's words, not Melissa's.

Eden took a seat on a bar stool at the kitchen island and read the letter again. "Mrs. Farrington had no other heirs, so she left me everything."

"How nice for you," Melissa said. "Any money?"

Eden kept her head down, but she felt the blood rush up the back of her neck. Anger did that to a person. There was fear in Melissa's voice, and Eden well knew what caused it: Stuart. For all that Melissa told Eden at least three times a day how much she loved her husband, the truth was that after two years of marriage she'd come to know him well. If he found out that Eden had inherited a lot of money, there would be problems.

"No money," Eden said cheerfully and tried not to hear her daughter's sigh of relief. "Just a falling-down old house. You remember it, don't you?"

"A Victorian monstrosity, wasn't it?"

Eden started to correct her daughter and say that the house had been built before George Washington's Mount Vernon, but she didn't want Melissa to tell Stuart that. He might see money in a house that old. Melissa hadn't yet learned that she didn't have to tell her husband everything that went through her mind. "More or less," Eden said, still looking at the letter. She was to go to a lawyer's office in North Carolina as soon as possible to sign the papers and take possession of the house. They're probably worried that the roof's about to cave in, she thought, but said nothing as she folded the letter and put it back in the envelope.

"What will you do with an old house like that?" Melissa asked, her eyes wide.

Eden knew that her daughter was afraid for her mother to leave. They'd rarely been apart since Melissa's birth twenty-seven years ago. "Sell it," Eden said quickly. "And use the money to buy my grandson a house in the country. With a copper beech tree in the backyard."

Smiling, Melissa relaxed, then hurriedly drank the rest of her chocolate milk when she heard the front door start to open. She washed the glass in seconds, so she was ready to turn and greet her husband when he walked into the kitchen. Stuart was tall, thin, and handsome. Melissa's eyes lit up when she saw him.

Eden gave her son-in-law a nod, then slipped out of the kitchen to go to her bedroom and close the door. For a moment she leaned against the door, closed her eyes, and remembered back to that summer when she'd been pregnant with Melissa. Eden had been just seventeen years old, just out of high school, when she'd been walking home from church choir practice one night. She'd been leaped on by a man, thrown down, and...She'd never been able to remember much of what happened after that. When it was over, she dragged herself up, pulled her skirt down, and staggered home. She'd wanted to call the police, but her parents had refused. They didn't want their family to be the object of gossip; they didn't want people to know what Eden had done. "But I didn't do anything," she'd cried. A few weeks later, when she'd started throwing up from morning sickness, her parents told her to get out of their house. Nothing Eden said could sway them. She'd packed one suitcase, taken the $300 her parents had grudgingly given her, and got on a bus going east. She ended up in North Carolina, a state she'd never been in, but it was beautiful and she loved the old houses and the flat fields.

She'd tried to get a job, but there wasn't much work to be had, and no work for a girl who was by then obviously pregnant. When she'd applied at the newspaper office in Arundel, a man had taken pity on her. He was looking at the job application she'd filled out. "You didn't misspell one word," he said, teasing her. Eden was hot, tired, hungry, and wishing she'd never been born. All she could do was look at him. Was he going to grade her application?

He looked her up and down for a moment, then said, "Let me guess about you. It's something I'm good at. Decent family, church every Sunday, good grades in school, wrestled with the high school football quarterback on the backseat of a car, and now the two of you've run away together. Or did he leave you somewhere along the way?"

Eden was too tired to play games. He'd probably eaten more for lunch than she'd had in the last two days. "Religious fanatic parents who spent my childhood telling me I was a sinner. Top of the top grades in school, but then if I went below an A plus I got the belt, buckle first. No quarterback, just a rapist on a dark night. When I came up pregnant, my parents threw me out. I now have fifteen dollars to my name, no place to live, nothing to live on. I've been looking hard at the local train tracks."

The man blinked at her a couple of times, then picked up his telephone and pushed a memory button. "Gracey? Henry here. I'm sending over a young woman. Feed her and let her have that bed in the back, will you? She needs food and rest, then I'm going to send her out to Alice's." He paused, listening. "Yeah, I know Alice is a pain in the neck, but, trust me on this, this girl can handle her. Compared to what she's been through, Alice will seem like a dream."

Somehow, Eden managed to get out of the chair

and make it to the door without fainting. Rage at the injustice of what had happened to her had kept her going, but now that someone had shown her some kindness, she feared she might collapse. The man didn't help her up or walk her to the door. Maybe he'd guessed that Eden's pride would get her there on her own. It wasn't easy to be proud when you hadn't had a bath in over a week, but she managed it.

Eden was almost run over by a pickup as she made her way across the road to Gracey's Restaurant. A tall, wiry woman, her gray hair in a bun at the back of her neck, came out to put her arm around Eden. "Honey, you're worse than Henry told me you were."

Three hours later, after Eden had eaten more than Gracey had ever seen a person eat at one sitting, Eden climbed into bed and didn't get out until the next morning. It was Sunday when Gracey drove Eden out to meet Mrs. Alice Augusta Farrington, who lived in an old house across a bridge, just outside downtown.

Eden had always loved history, and she'd loved any movie that was set in a historical context. That was good, since her parents didn't allow her to watch any movie that had been made after 1959. Their opinion was that the 1960s were the beginning of the end of Godliness in America. When Eden got out of Gracey's car and looked up at the old house, she knew that she was looking at the genuine article. This wasn't a house "built in the Colonial style." This was a Colonial house. She'd never seen Colonial Williamsburg, but she thought this house would fit in there.

"Ghastly old place, isn't it?" Gracey said. "I tell Alice that she ought to bulldoze it and build herself a nice brick ranch style."

Eden looked at Gracey to see if she was kidding. The older woman's eyes were twinkling. Eden smiled.

"Just checking," Gracey said, smiling back. "We like old houses around here."

Eden looked up at the house. Seven bays across the front, a full porch on the ground level. There were some truly big trees on each side of the house, and she wondered if they'd been planted when the house was built.

Alice Augusta Farrington was so small that she made Eden feel big—which wasn't easy, since Eden was small herself. But Mrs. Farrington was about four-eleven and couldn't have weighed more than ninety pounds. "What she lacks in size, she makes up for in spirit," Gracey had said on the way out to the house, when she told Eden about the Farrington family. They'd built the house back in the early 1700s and had held on to it ever since. To Mrs. Farrington's mind, that made her American royalty. "DAR ha!" she'd say. "Upstarts. Go through a couple of books, find out their ancestors stowed away on a ship, and think they're worth something. Now, my ancestors..." Mrs. Farrington would then be off and running with stories about her ancestors having been aristocracy in England. "And they would be aristocracy in America if that idiot George Washington hadn't turned down being crowned king. I'd be a duchess now. What was *wrong* with that man?!"

Gracey said that no one knew if Mrs. Farrington was kidding or not, but it didn't matter, as she never expected an answer. "She likes to talk and just likes for others to listen." Eden had spent a lot of her life listening to her father pontificate about what he thought God was thinking, so she was good at listening.

When the house came into sight, Gracey told her that the outside might go unpainted for twenty years at a time, but the roof was always kept in perfect repair, because otherwise, it might leak on her precious papers. It was a local legend that every piece of paper the Farrington family had ever owned was still in that house. Receipts, recipes, diaries, letters—lots of letters—all of them were still there.

But even after what Gracey had told her, Eden wasn't prepared for her first sight of the interior. The huge, high-ceilinged center hallway was so full of furniture that a person could hardly walk. The walls were lined at least two pieces deep. A tall desk stood in front of a huge cabinet. A long table was pressed against a wall, covered in what looked to be stacks of old letters wrapped in faded pink ribbon, then smaller tables were set on top of the letters. Tables, cabinets, chairs, couches—every surface was covered with papers. Some were in boxes, some in trunks, many of them loose. Eden's eyes widened when she saw a hatbox that resembled one she'd seen in a book on antiques. Eighteenth century?

"Alice," Gracey said to the tiny Mrs. Farrington. "I found her for you."

Mrs. Farrington looked Eden up and down and obviously found her wanting. "This little thing? Too weak. And is that a child in her stomach? Am I to start running a shelter for wayward girls now?"

Gracey ignored the last question. "Henry Walters—you know, old Lester's youngest son—researched her, and she's from a good family. She's twenty-three years old and her young husband was killed in a horrible accident while defending his family. She was so overcome with grief that she ran away from home. Her family is searching for her, but she begged Henry to let her find her own place in the world, so she can make it on her own. She wants the job, and she can do it. She has a degree in American history from Vassar. When her baby is born, she will, of course, return to her loving family. You won't be bothered with anything as burdensome as a child."

Eden's mouth was hanging open as she stared at Gracey. What incredible lies! She turned back to look at Mrs. Farrington. Should she tell her the truth and risk losing the job—whatever it was? Eden hoped she wasn't being offered the job of trying to clean this house. The dust on that furniture could be carbon-dated.

Mrs. Farrington was looking at Eden in speculation. "Family throw you out when you got pregnant?"

"Yes, ma'am," Eden said, her eyes looking into the old woman's. They were small black eyes, glistening with life and vitality. Old body; young spirit.

"How old are you really?" Mrs. Farrington asked.

Behind the older woman, Gracey was vigorously shaking her head at Eden not to tell the truth.

"Seventeen," Eden answered.

Mrs. Farrington turned so quickly that she caught Gracey shaking her head, disgusted that Eden hadn't lied. "Your whole family are liars," Mrs. Farrington said, without animosity in her voice, then she left the room, leaving Gracey and Eden alone.

Gracey wasn't offended by Mrs. Farrington's remarks. In fact, she was smiling broadly. She pushed Eden to follow Mrs. Farrington. "Go on."

"But she didn't say I was hired," Eden said. "Maybe—"

"Believe me, if you *weren't* hired, Alice Farrington would have told you. She likes you."

"Likes me?"

"She didn't say one hateful thing to you. It may be a first. Now go on, I have to go bake the pies for tomorrow."

Gracey made it all the way to her car outside before Eden recovered enough to hurry after her. "But what is the job?" Eden called from the porch. Her suitcase was on the ground. "What am I supposed to *do*?"

"Oh," Gracey said with a wave of her hand as she got into her car. "Make a list of all those papers."

"A list?" Eden asked, not understanding what she meant.

"Like in the library." Gracey shut her car door and started the engine.

Eden watched her until the trees hid her from view. "Like the library?" she whispered. Then her head came up. "Cataloging? She wants me to catalog that mess in there?" In high school she'd worked in the library, so she had an idea of what was involved in such an undertaking. Were the other rooms of the house as full as the central hall? If so, making even an inventory would take a very long time. Years, even.

Eden looked out at the lawn in front of her. The house sat in a little oasis of greenery, surrounded on three sides by acre upon acre of farmers' fields. On the fourth side was a wide, deep creek, probably where the original owners moored their ships. On the right side of the house was what looked to be a vegetable garden, with flowers mixed in with the peas. To the back was what could be an orchard. It was all as messy as the interior. Taking a breath, Eden smelled the air. Fresh air, shade trees, fresh fruits and vegetables. In an instant, she made a decision. She was going to do the best job of cataloging that anyone had ever done, so that Mrs. Farrington would let her stay for the next several years. And Eden was going to raise her child here in this idyllic spot.

Smiling, she went back into the house.

"Can you cook?" Mrs. Farrington's voice came from somewhere in the back of the house.

"Not at all," Eden called back, feeling quite happy.

"That's something else you'll have to learn," came the voice.

Smiling, Eden went in search of the kitchen. She was willing to bet there were cookbooks somewhere in the house. "Probably Martha Washington's original cookbook," she said as she made her way through the stacks of furniture to find the kitchen. Turning the corner, she gasped. The kitchen was a huge room with lots and lots of cabinets—and every one of them was so full of papers that the doors wouldn't close. On one countertop was a foot square that held a few dishes, a skillet, and a pot. Eden had an idea that was all the cookware that Mrs. Farrington used.

Now, leaning against her bedroom door, Eden smiled in memory. Yes, that was all the cookware that Mrs. Farrington had used, but later Eden found whole sets of dishes hidden away inside the cabinets. Her daughter's first years were spent in that wonderful old house. Her baby dishes had been from the 1920s, and her silverware had been real, with English hallmarks.

It was the silverware that sparked the "clearing of the wealth" as Mrs. Farrington called it. Casually, Eden had remarked that the silver must be worth a fortune. "Then we have to hide it!" Mrs. Farrington had said quickly, her voice almost panicky. At first Eden had stiffened with pride. Did Mrs. Farrington think she was a thief? She calmed when she realized that if Mrs. Farrington had thought she was a thief she wouldn't be telling her, Eden, to do the hiding. It wasn't until Henry from the newspaper office came to visit that Eden understood.

"He's out," Henry had said. Mrs. Farrington turned pale and sat down. Seeing her sit made Eden worry, because Mrs. Farrington never sat down.

"I knew it was close, but I thought I'd have more time," Mrs. Farrington whispered.

After Henry left, Eden didn't ask any questions, but Mrs. Farrington told her. She had one child, "a son so worthless he shouldn't be allowed to live" is how she stated it. Eden didn't ask questions, but she assumed that "out" meant out of jail. For the next three weeks, the two women hid things. Anything that was valuable, they hid. They pried up floorboards and shoved in silver teapots. They cut a hole behind the lath and plaster and dropped spoons down into the walls. They buried plastic boxes of things in the garden. Young Melissa, a year old by then, loved the game, and they caught her just as she was shoving Mrs. Farrington's reading glasses into a mouse hole in the baseboard.

But Alester Farrington didn't show up then. He didn't show up until Melissa was five—and that's when Eden found out why he'd been locked up. He was a pedophile. But she didn't know it that first night.

The night her son returned home, Mrs. Farrington woke Eden, whispering in a way that made her sound like a crazy person. "They told me he'd changed. They said there was no more danger."

Puzzled, Eden had allowed Mrs. Farrington to pull her into the next room, Melissa's room. In the dark, silhouetted by the night-light, Alester Farrington was standing over the child's bed. Just standing there and watching Melissa sleep. In an instant, Eden understood everything. Mrs. Farrington told her son to get out of the room, and for a moment Eden thought he was going to strike his mother, but he didn't. He smiled at Eden in a way that made the hair on the back of her neck stand up. Quietly, he left the room.

Eden didn't need to be told what she had to do. She looked at Mrs. Farrington, and there were tears in the old woman's eyes, but she nodded, then shoved Eden toward her bedroom. Eden jammed clothes into a suitcase, grabbed some boxes, and left with her daughter in the middle of the night. She'd had no contact with either of the Farringtons since that night twenty-two years ago.

Now, Eden walked to the bedroom window and looked out at the wet street lined with over-flowing garbage cans. She could hear the loud music from the bar across the street; a man was peeing into the gutter. She closed the curtain. Sometimes she wondered how she had ended up in New York City. She who loved trees and bird-song. She used to read gardening books as though they were novels. She used to memorize princi-ples of eighteenth-century gardening. Eden knew that the happiest time in her life had been those years with Mrs. Farrington. The people in town had thought Mrs. Farrington was an eccentric old woman, but all Eden had really known were her parents, whose great delight in life was meting out punishment. Compared to them, Mrs. Farrington was the sweetest, kindest—

Turning, Eden looked at her tiny room. She'd given the master bedroom in the apartment to her daughter and her new husband, thinking that they were going to be there only a few weeks. But the months had turned into years, and she'd had to put up with the man her daughter had chosen to love, a pompous man who coped with his inability to get ahead in the world by putting other people down. And his favorite punching bag seemed to be his mother-in-law. Stuart compensated for his failings by assuming an air of superiority, as if he were of a better class than Eden. He never said the words out loud, but still they hung in the air. Melissa made excuses for him, saying that he was on the verge of being promoted to partner, that they were going to live in a penthouse on Park Avenue. Melissa seemed to believe that when Stuart got the promotion that he'd been up for for four years he'd have an overnight personality change. He'd stop looking down his arrogant nose at people and would become the sweet, loving man she knew he really was.

Eden didn't want to disillusion her daughter, so she was determined to keep her nose out of it. There had been times when she'd tried to talk to her, but Melissa had a talent for hearing only what she wanted to hear. It was difficult for Eden to do, but she was going to have to let her child find out about life on her own. Was that like letting a child ride a motorcycle without a helmet, so he'd learn that he could get hurt?

Sighing, Eden went into her bathroom and stood there, looking at herself in the mirror. She had been told many times that she looked good "for her age," but she was still forty-five years old, and for a moment, a wave of self-pity ran through her. Since that night so long ago when she'd seen Mrs. Farrington's son looking down at Melissa asleep in her bed, Eden wondered if she'd had a moment to call her own. She'd had to raise her daughter alone. Most of the time she'd been too busy to think about herself, but there had been quiet evenings when she'd wondered how her life would have been different if she hadn't had a child so young. She'd had a couple of serious relationships, but in the end had chickened out on getting married. She'd always been too afraid of turning her life, and that of her daughter, over to a man.

When Melissa entered college on a partial scholarship, so had Eden. No scholarship, but she'd enrolled anyway. Eden had graduated with a degree in American history, with a minor in English lit. Melissa, giggling, had said that her degree in child development was actually an M.R.S. degree. As Eden got to know Stuart, she thought that a real diploma would have been much better.

After college, Melissa had taken a menial job in a law office in New York just to be near Stuart, telling her mother that if she "played her cards right" she was sure that Stuart would ask her to marry him. He did. After a year in the big city, Melissa had begged and pleaded with Eden to move to New York, get a job, and live near them. Since Eden had just broken up with a man and wanted to get away from him, she agreed. Within a week of arriving in New York, she got a job at a major publishing house. By what she called luck, and the publisher called "divine inspiration," she found a book in the pile of unagented manuscripts that had been turned down by six houses. With her heart pounding, Eden recommended that it be published. It was, and it spent thirty-two weeks on the *New York Times* best-seller list. In gratitude, the author requested that Eden be his editor. By the end of her second year she'd been promoted to senior editor. By the third year she was handling some very big names in the publishing world. But by that time, Melissa and Stuart were married and living with her, and she'd learned not to tell anyone when good things happened with her job. She didn't want to see the anger and jealousy on Stuart's thin face.

As Eden looked in the mirror, she could see herself as she was when she first met Mrs. Farrington. So young, so inexperienced in the world. Eden had never been anywhere, done anything. Her parents...The less said about them, the better. Eden had tried to contact them three times after Melissa was born, but each time she'd been rebuffed. She went to her father's funeral, but her mother had told her to get out.

But Mrs. Farrington saved me, Eden thought,

smiling. It had been difficult after she left Mrs. Farrington's house, but she and Melissa had had five whole years of warmth and love, so they made it. That house, which had taken her all those years to straighten up, was Eden's "happy place." When things got to be too much for her, from Melissa's hateful third grade teacher, to Steve, a man Eden had almost married, to all the years of financial terror she'd lived through, Eden's escape was to put herself back in that old house with Mrs. Farrington.

Closing her eyes for a moment, Eden could remember every inch of the place, every floorboard, every stick of furniture. What was the house like now? she wondered. Had it changed much? The letter said that she'd inherited house and contents. Was there any furniture left, or had Mrs. Farrington's son taken whatever they hadn't been able to hide?

Smiling, Eden remembered one day when they'd been burying a stack of plastic shoeboxes full of everything from old coins to children's wooden toys—actually, she buried, and Mrs. Farrington directed. They feared that the items would rot before they could dig them up, but there wasn't much choice. All the hiding space inside the house had been used. Mrs. Farrington leaned on her shovel handle and looked back at the house. "It ends with me."

At first Eden didn't know what she meant.

"Did you ever wonder how I kept the name Farrington? For centuries my family produced an eldest son, so the name stayed with us. But not my father. After being married for ten years he produced only one puny daughter, me. And don't give me that women's lib look. It *was* my father's fault. My mother was a widow and had had three kids by her first husband. She was twenty-six years old and had already produced three healthy boys. But she married my father and didn't conceive for ten years. When I was born I was so tiny they didn't think I was going to live."

Mrs. Farrington looked across the fence that enclosed her beloved flower garden. "Maybe I should have died," she said. "Maybe..."

"So how did you keep the name?" Eden asked, not wanting her friend to dwell on sadness.

"Married my cousin. He was a distant cousin, but he had the Farrington name. My mother begged me not to do it. She said that the strain of our family was already fragile and a cousin would further weaken it. But I didn't listen. If I had—if I hadn't been so enraptured with the Farrington legacy and hadn't felt as though I *had* to carry on the name—I would have married one of those great strapping Granville boys. My! But they were good-looking. Born ten months apart, strong as field hands, and smart. But I didn't listen to anyone."

"Haven't changed much, have you?" Eden asked, straightening up. They had six more boxes to bury before sundown.

"No. I've always done what I wanted to, when I wanted to do it. Spoiled. Always was. So I married a man who I thought was good enough for me, meaning I married another Farrington." She pointed at the next place Eden was to dig. "I was a fool. The man I married was a weak, foppish coward." She took a deep breath. "My husband was what you call today a bisexual."

Eden concentrated on the hole she was digging. Part of her wanted to tell Mrs. Farrington to stop remembering such dreadful things, but she knew that her friend had a point to make.

"My husband was an awful man, truly awful, and the only child we had together turned out to be worse than he was." She looked up at the sky again, her hands making fists so hard the knuckles turned white. "So I'm the last one. The Farringtons end with me."

"But your son could have children."

"No, he can't. The last time I got him out of jail, I only did so if he got fixed. Like a horse that's no good. The world doesn't want his seed spread around."

"Oh," Eden said, her head down, not knowing what to say. Vasectomy. As much as Mrs. Farrington cared about family, she had demanded that her only child be "fixed" so he could have no children.

"But the good news is that I found out that I'm bisexual too."

Eden's head came up as she looked at Mrs. Farrington in shock.

"I had affairs with *both* of those beautiful Granville boys."

Eden laughed so hard she had to sit down on the ground and hold her stomach.

Now, even thinking about it, she chuckled. Two days after that, she'd been in town and had seen one of the Granville "boys." He was ninety if he was a day, but he still stood up straight and still had a twinkle in his eye. When Eden stopped him to say hello, he asked after Mrs. Farrington, and Eden couldn't keep a straight face. "Why don't you visit her?" she asked, then a devil got into her. "Maybe you two could have lunch under the old willow tree down by the river." That's where Mrs. Farrington said that she'd made love with both boys, separately and together.

Mr. Granville laughed so hard that Eden began to fear for his heart. "Ah, Alice," he said. "Alice, Alice, Alice. What beautiful days those were. Give her my love," he said, then walked away, his shoulders back and his head up.

~

Yes, those days with Mrs. Farrington were good ones. The best days. The happiest of her life. And now Mrs. Farrington was gone and had left Eden that old house. She wondered if any of the boxes they'd buried were still there. Or had that son of hers taken them all? While it was true that Eden had had no direct contact with Mrs. Farrington after she left, she had kept in touch for a few years through Gracey. They'd exchanged a few letters, and Gracey had never asked why Eden left—in a small town everyone knew about everyone else, so they knew what the son was guilty of. Gracey had written Eden of the sale of pieces of furniture that had been in the Farrington family for centuries. One letter said Alester Farrington had gone to a Realtor and said the old house was for sale, but Mrs. Farrington went right down after him and said it wasn't. She owned the house, of course, so it wasn't put up for sale. For a while everyone in town feared for Mrs. Farrington's life, but her lawyer spread the word around town that if "anything" happened to Mrs. Farrington, the house would go to charity.

Eden had felt bad when she'd read those letters, but there was nothing she could do. She had Melissa to take care of, and she couldn't take her child back into that mess, not with Mrs. Farrington's son there. Eden was so afraid of him that she wouldn't even send a letter to Mrs. Farrington for fear her son would get her address.

Gracey died when Melissa was eleven, and after that Eden lost contact with the town. Over time she just assumed that dear Mrs. Farrington had died and that Alester had finally got his hands on the lovely old house. Yet, somehow, Mrs. Farrington had outlived him.

Eden looked down at the letter. It was short, stating only that Mrs. Farrington's son had died "a number of years ago" and had left no issue, so Mrs. Farrington was willing the house and contents to Eden Palmer. When Eden saw that the letter was signed by Mr. Braddon Granville, esquire, she smiled. The grandson of one of the "beautiful Granville boys."

Of course Eden couldn't possibly keep the house. Too much to maintain. Maybe she'd will it to a historical society so they could lead tours through it. Yes, that was a good idea. In the 1700s there had been hundreds of plantations along the river, but the houses had been pulled down, burned down, and bulldozed over the centuries. Now there were few houses like Farrington Manor left. It was, for the most part, an untouched house. Yes, there were two bathrooms in the house, and electricity too—but the paneling remained untouched from the time the house was built in 1720.

Or was it? Eden thought. Was the house the same now as it was those many years ago? What had been done to that beautiful old house in the past twenty-two years? Maybe she'd ask for some time off from work and go to North Carolina to see the house. Just see it, then fly right back to New York so she'd be here when Melissa had her baby. Heaven knew that Stuart wouldn't be any good in the delivery room. He'd leave Melissa by herself to sweat and cry and…

"If I weren't there, maybe he *would* go into the delivery room," Eden whispered aloud. Maybe if she wasn't there, always between the two of them, maybe they'd make themselves into a family. Maybe if Stuart had to support his wife and child he'd get the courage to go to his boss and ask for that promotion.

Eden sat down hard on the chair by her bed. The problem with being a single mother to an only child was that your lives got entwined with each other's in a very deep way. Right now, she couldn't believe what was going through her head. Leave Melissa? They'd been separated only once, and that was when Melissa went to New York to be near Stuart. During that year there had been endless phone calls, and Eden had flown to the city three times. Every extra penny she'd earned had gone to the airlines. Eden's attachment to Melissa was what had ultimately caused her breakup with Steve. "She's a grown woman," Steve had shouted. "Let her live her own life!" "She will always be my baby," Eden had answered. She'd returned his ring the next week.

But now Melissa was married and going to have her own child. And Melissa was caught between her love for her mother and for her husband.

Suddenly Eden could see her own part in what must be great stress to Melissa. Stuart tried to get his wife to eat healthy food while she was pregnant; Eden filled the refrigerator with pastries and chocolate. Did Stuart not look in the refrigerator because he knew what was in there?

Eden disliked Stuart because he made no effort to get them their own place to live, but now Eden remembered one night of hearing soft sobs from Melissa. Eden had been about to knock on their bedroom door when she heard Melissa say, "But she'd be so lonely if we left her. You don't understand that I'm all she has. I'm her whole life. And I owe everything to her."

At the time, Eden had smiled at what she'd heard and gone back to her own room. But now she didn't like the memory. Had it been Melissa who'd kept them from moving into their own apartment?

Epiphany. It was one of those blinding moments when people truly see themselves as they really are—and Eden didn't like what she saw. Yes, Melissa was her whole life. All of it. But now there was Stuart. Had Eden treated him as a usurper?

"The book!" Eden said aloud, the memory startling her. When she'd moved to New York, out of the back of a closet she'd pulled an old file box that she hadn't looked inside in years. In her frantic haste in leaving Mrs. Farrington's house on that night, she'd accidentally picked up the box she'd labeled PERTINENT INFORMATION. In her five and a half years of cataloging and listening to Mrs. Farrington, Eden had filled many notebooks with interesting facts about the family. There had been some beautiful letters written by a bride to her new husband who was serving in the Confederate Army. She wrote him one last letter after she found out he'd been killed, put it with their letters, and tied them up with ribbons. Even though she'd only been a teenager, Eden had realized that what she was reading could be made into a biography of the family, and she intended to write it, once the cataloging was done. She'd put all her notes and hundreds of photocopies into one box, which she'd accidentally taken when she'd left. But she never opened the box until many years later, when she got to New York. Eden had at last opened the box and started reading the notes she'd made, as well as looking over the huge pile of photocopies. Before she knew what she was doing, she was putting all the material in chronological order and writing introductions to each section. She spent several Saturdays in the New York Public Library, looking up facts so she could tell what was going on in the world at the time of the events in the lives of the Farringtons.

One day in her second year at the publishing house, Eden had stopped by the office of one of the nonfiction editors and asked her to have a look at what she'd written. Three days later the editor said she'd like to publish the book but couldn't because they'd all be sued. "You can't say those things about living people," she'd told Eden. "Wait until they're dead, then you can say anything."

Disappointed, Eden had taken the manuscript home with the intention of taking out all the things that could get her into trouble, such as Mrs. Farrington's love affairs. After hours of dulling the book down, she'd put her laptop aside and turned on the TV. The book was ruined, lifeless, and she knew it. But after Jay Leno's opening monologue, she had an idea. What about turning it into fiction? A novel? She picked up her laptop again and began a "search and replace" for the names and other identifying information. The sun came up, and she was still writing.

Six weeks later, she handed the manuscript to a fiction editor who had agreed to read it as a favor to Eden. Next morning the editor had burst into Eden's office to tell her she wanted to publish the book. Eden had acted cool, keeping her composure, but now she knew how people felt when she called them and asked to publish their books: screaming, crying, general hysterics.

The bad part was that Eden had no one to share the wonderful news with. She wanted to tell Melissa, but her daughter would tell Stuart, and his jealousy would ruin what should have been a wonderful event. And he would put Melissa between them.

The book was now due to come out in three months. Advance reader copies had already been printed and sent out to critics and libraries all over the United States. So far, the comments had been favorable. Actually, they were great. She told herself that the book would never hit the best-seller lists, but she hoped that it would do well. The few people in her publishing house who'd read the book had certainly liked it. If someone came into her office laughing, you could bet that he'd read it. "Bisexual lover" became a catchphrase around the publishing house.

It wouldn't be long before Eden would have to tell Melissa and Stuart about the book, and until this moment she had thought of her book as yet another triumph over Stuart's arrogance. But right now, Eden wasn't seeing it as a triumph. Right now she was seeing her success as another page in her daughter's divorce decree.

Standing up, Eden knew what she had to do. Mrs. Farrington had saved the life of Eden and her unborn child, and now it just might be possible

that Mrs. Farrington had saved a marriage and preserved a good mother-daughter relationship.

Eden took a deep breath and put on a brave face.
She had to prepare herself for the coming storm.
When she told them she was leaving, there'd be
tears from her daughter and triumph from Stuart.
Eden had to be strong.

Chapter Two

As Eden walked down King Street in Arundel, North Carolina, she thought that the best thing about historic towns was that they looked better the older they got. It was twenty-two years since she'd been here, yet the town had improved with age. The brick sidewalks were more bowed from the roots of the trees that had buckled them, and the old houses were even more precious and rare.

Smiling, feeling better than she had in years, Eden turned the heavy brass knob of the door to the law office of Mr. Braddon Granville and went inside. There was a small reception area, decorated in reproduction Colonial furniture, and a huge multipaned window that looked out on downtown

Arundel. No one was behind the desk, so Eden stood in front of the window and looked out at the pretty little town, the water of the sound glistening to her left.

She'd arrived in Raleigh last night, had rented a car and driven to Arundel. She was staying in the restored Tredwell house, one of the many bed-and-breakfasts in town. It had been a lovely, warm spring evening, and part of her had wanted to go outside and look around, but she hadn't. She was still in shock over the way the news of her leaving New York had been received by her daughter. Eden didn't like to think so, but Melissa had seemed almost glad that her mother was going. It seemed that all the things that had been a revelation to Eden had been part of her daughter's life for some time. Melissa, seemingly so young and still seeming to need her mother, had been quietly thrilled that she was at last going to be mistress of her own household. She was going to live alone with her husband, and *he* was going to start being her baby coach.

The minute Eden told them she was moving, Stuart got out pen, paper, and a calculator and started figuring out the rent they'd pay her for the apartment. There was no question that they'd remain. After an initial show of tears and some hugs, Melissa began to talk of curtains and wall paint.

Fifteen minutes after she had made her announcement, Eden crept back to her bedroom, feeling as though she was the only one who hadn't understood what was going on. After a restless night, she went to her publishing house the next morning and told them her news. As she'd known there would be, another editor was ready and more than willing to take over her stable of writers. It took only a week to sort things out. Eden would become a freelance reader for her publishing house, and a freelance copy editor too. They would send her manuscripts, and she'd comb through them to make sure the author didn't have someone wearing a wristwatch in 1610. Or, more likely, that a character went to a party wearing a red dress, then left wearing a green pantsuit.

It had all been amazingly easy. Eight days after she'd received the letter, Eden was packed and ready to leave. She'd called Braddon Granville's office to ask him if the house was livable.

"Yes, quite livable," he'd said in a deep, pleasant voice. "Mrs. Farrington did some major renovations after her son died. It seems that a teapot she owned had been made by Paul Revere, so she sold it for quite a lot of money. Sorry, but none of the proceeds are left. She spent every cent renovating the house. Between you and me, Ms. Palmer, I think she wanted to leave the house in good shape for *you*."

Eden had nearly started crying on the telephone. At least someone loved her! She could hear her daughter and Stuart in the living room talking in low whispers. They had four wallpaper books and eight fabric sample books on the floor and were planning what they were going to do to the apartment as soon as Eden left.

"Ms. Palmer?"

"Yes, I'm here. It's been an emotional time for

me to hear that my friend died. We didn't see each other for years, but I cared a great deal for her."

"She was a wonderful woman, but she'd had a full life. My grandfather cried like a baby at her funeral."

"He's still alive?" Eden asked, wiping at her eyes with a tissue.

"Yes and no. Alzheimer's. He can't remember yesterday, but he remembers fifty years ago quite well. Unfortunately, some of his memories are, well, of an embarrassing nature. We caught him telling his twelve-year-old great-granddaughter about his trysts with Alice Farrington under a weeping willow tree."

Eden couldn't help but laugh.

"So you heard the story too."

Eden could hear the smile in his voice. She also heard something else. Was he flirting? Just then one of Melissa's giggles came from the living room; Eden had never felt more unwanted in her life. "We'll have to compare notes of what we heard," she said, her voice lowered.

"I'd like that very much. Perhaps over dinner one night."

"That would be perfect," Eden said in her softest voice, just as she heard Melissa say, "Stuart, quit that! She'll hear us."

"I'll look forward to meeting you on the sixth," he said, and they hung up.

"Well, well, well," Eden said. One of the descendants of the beautiful Granville boys had asked her on a date. After a moment's elation, Eden sighed.

"He's probably married and has six kids," she mumbled. "And dinner is purely professional."

~

"Are you Ms. Palmer?" Eden turned to see a young woman, about Melissa's age, with a file folder in her hand. She looked Eden up and down hard, as though scrutinizing her.

"Yes, I'm Eden Palmer."

The girl held out her hand to shake. "I'm Camden Granville." She nodded toward the closed door behind her. "He's my father." Again she looked at Eden hard. "He's fifty-four, in perfect health, and he has been a widower for three years now. He has all his teeth, doesn't smoke, and he'd like to meet a woman who can talk about something outside this town."

Eden blinked for a moment, then laughed. "I'll see what I can do, about talking about something outside of this town, that is. Maybe I should mention Madison Avenue, or complain about taxi service. This jacket has a Bergdorf's label. Think I should show it to him?"

The girl didn't smile. "How are your teeth?"

"All mine, as is my hair."

"Good," the girl said, still not smiling, then she opened the door and motioned for Eden to go inside.

Behind the big mahogany desk sat a very good-looking man. He was broad-shouldered with a thick chest, and his suit fit him perfectly. He had a thick mane of salt-and-pepper hair. Very handsome indeed. He got up to shake her hand, then motioned her to a seat across from his desk.

"Did my daughter put you through it?" he asked.

"Completely. I'm to show you my teeth and the label inside my jacket."

"I can do without the jacket, but I'd like to get a much closer look at your teeth."

In spite of herself, Eden blushed. She'd meant to make a joke, not a sexual innuendo. It had been a long time since a man had made a pass at her. In New York, she'd had about three dates, each leading nowhere. The city was full of young, beautiful, young, gorgeous, young women. Eden felt that she'd never had a chance.

"So," he said, looking down at a file folder on his desk. "Mrs. Farrington left you everything. Did you know that it took me over a year to find you? You did a good job of disappearing. It was Henry Walters who said it was his guess that you were in publishing."

"Henry," Eden said, smiling. "He always was impressed with my ability to spell."

"Henry was impressed with everything about you. You were a young girl in a terrible situation, but you managed to make the best of it. He said you cataloged all the Farrington papers and became a good friend to cantankerous old Mrs. Farrington in the process."

"No, not cantankerous. She was kind and generous and easy to love." Eden looked down at her hands on her lap. This man's compliments and his open appraisal of her as a woman were making her feel shy. He really was *very* good-looking. And she was also cursed with her memories of what Mrs.

Farrington had told her about the Granville boys. Was this man as good a lover as his grandfather and great-uncle had been?

He was smiling. "I heard she used to greet trespassers with a shotgun."

Eden lost her smile. "She was a woman alone, and that house is well off the road. You can't imagine the number of drunken fishermen who would show up there at three on a Saturday morning, wanting to put their boats in the river at Mrs. Farrington's dock. And of course there were all those stupid stories about the sapphire necklace that was supposed to be hidden on the property somewhere. Mrs. Farrington had a lot to deal with."

Braddon Granville was looking at her with interest. "I see," he said, then smiled when Eden lowered her head, her face turning red. "Unfortunately, I didn't get to know her until after you had left."

When he reached into his desk and pulled out a set of keys, Eden felt her heart leap. There was the little silver angel that she'd seen in Mrs. Farrington's hands so often.

He held the keys for several moments, seeming to be reluctant to pass them on. "If I didn't have clients coming down from Virginia today, I'd drive you out to the house myself, just to make sure it's safe."

"Have things in Arundel changed that much?" She wasn't serious in her question. As far as she'd seen, very little had changed.

"You remember the cabin near the old house?"

Cabin? she thought, then smiled. "The wash-house?"

He smiled back. "Yes, the washhouse. You sound like one of the old-timers around here." All the buildings around the plantations kept the names of their original uses, no matter what had been done to them. "After Alester Farrington died—" He looked up when Eden drew in her breath.

"What happened to Mrs. Farrington after I left? I had to leave because..." She didn't finish her sentence. She didn't want to disparage Mrs. Farrington's son.

"Yes, I was told why you left. I think your daughter is a few years older than mine. Cammie is twenty-four."

"Melissa is twenty-seven and about to have a baby in a few months."

"Grandkids are wonderful."

"I'm looking forward to my first one. But what happened to Mrs. Farrington and her son?"

He looked down at his desk for a few moments. "It was all rather unpleasant. There was an incident in town. A child..."

Eden's mouth hardened.

"The child wasn't hurt, just scared. She had some scratches on her, and her clothes had been torn, but she was okay. She said she escaped from an old shack by pulling a board off the wall. She identified the man who took her from the street by his photograph."

"Alester Farrington?"

"Yes. The police went after him, but when they

got to Farrington Manor, they found out that he'd fallen off the pier at the back of the house, hit his head, and drowned." Mr. Granville lowered his voice. "I can tell you that there wasn't much investigation into that accident."

"No, there shouldn't have been," Eden said. She knew in her heart that Mrs. Farrington had stopped her son from ever hurting another child.

"She lived alone out there for years after that. Waiting to die, my grandfather said. She wouldn't see anyone. She hired someone to bring her groceries, but that was all. I used to go check on her every other week, but I can't say that we ever became friends. She was my client only because my father had retired." He smiled. "She said I wasn't nearly as handsome as my grandfather was."

"Yes, she'd say that." Eden wanted to change the subject or she'd start crying. "You said on the phone that the house is in good shape. What about the furniture? I'm afraid that what little furniture I own I left in New York with my daughter and her husband."

"Ah, the things we do for our children. The house is fully furnished, but I know that the son sold off the best pieces." He was still holding the keys, turning them around in his hands. "You wouldn't like to stay in town until this afternoon, would you? I could go out to the house with you then."

"No," she said, then leaned forward and took the keys out of his hands. Eden knew without a doubt that she was going to start crying as soon as she saw the place, and she didn't want anyone to see her. "What about tomorrow?" she asked. "I'll get groceries today and make some soup. How does homemade soup and some fresh bread sound?"

"Great," he said, smiling, and Eden smiled back. She gathered her things and stood up. "Tell me, Mr. Granville, is your daughter for or against your dating? I couldn't tell by her expression."

"Very much for it. She says that I'm a helpless man without a wife, so she wants to marry me off."

He looked at Eden so hard, with so much intention, that she blushed.

"Well, ah..." she said nervously. "Uh, I'll...come tomorrow at six. I'll probably have a hundred questions to ask you by then."

"Great," he said, standing and walking her to the door. "I look forward to it."

Eden thought that he wanted to say more, but there was someone waiting to see him, so he had to let them into his office. She gave a quick glance at the unsmiling Camden, then hurried from the office. She didn't want to give the young woman time to ask her any more questions.

Once outside, Eden got into her cheap rental car and headed toward the grocery store. But things had changed in twenty-two years, and the grocery she used to go to had been replaced by a car dealership. She thought she'd just stop in and ask for directions, but two hours later she'd leased a small SUV. By the time she'd had lunch (North Carolina barbecue) and had explored a few shops downtown, it was nearly four o'clock. After she'd filled her new car with groceries, it was growing dark. She wondered if she'd purposefully postponed seeing the house until late just so she wouldn't be able to spend much time there. She thought she'd put the groceries away, then go back to spend the night at the bed-and-breakfast. She'd not even asked if the electricity had been turned on in the house, so it would be better to postpone staying.

Even though Farrington Manor had once been the plantation house for a farm that covered over a thousand acres, the house was very close to downtown Arundel. Eden drove to the end of King Street, took a left onto Water Street, drove past the lush Braddon Park, then turned right over the narrow wooden bridge that took her to Farrington Manor. As she drove she saw two small houses on the left, built since she'd lived there and now pretty with flowers and ten-year-old trees. She saw that the old house that had once been the overseer's had been completely renovated.

On the left lay open fields that were leased to local farmers to grow peanuts, cotton, milo, or soybeans, but on the right was parkland of enormous, mature hardwood trees. Some of the trees that she'd come to know were now missing, felled by hurricanes. "God's way of pruning," Mrs. Farrington used to say. The high winds used to terrify Eden, but Mrs. Farrington and Melissa took them in stride, playing endless games of checkers by candlelight.

When Eden got close enough such that she knew in the next moment the house was going to come into view, she turned off her headlights and coasted forward, her arms on the steering wheel. First a chimney, then the roof came into view. Right away she saw that the house was in better repair than it had been years ago. Eden remembered the story of the silver teapot by Paul Revere. Had Mrs. Farrington known that she had such a teapot? Or had she pulled everything from under the floorboards and taken it all to a dealer?

Smiling with happy memories, Eden looked at the house in the moonlight. It was two stories, flat fronted, with two rows of seven eight-paned windows. At one point in its long history, the house had had double porches and a door out from the second story, but when a hurricane had badly damaged the top porch, Mrs. Farrington's father had removed it. Now there was one wide porch along the lower front.

Still smiling, Eden moved forward, her tires barely rolling. Suddenly, she stopped. There was a light moving about upstairs. A flashlight. Someone was inside the house!

So now what do I do? she wondered. Call the sheriff? And what if he comes out to the house, sirens blazing, only to find out that the person inside the house was a neighbor? Or maybe it was Braddon Granville. He'd had time enough to finish with his clients, so maybe he'd decided to visit her. The thought made Eden smile. She'd liked him and had been flattered by his frank admiration of her. In the years she'd lived in New York she'd spent many hours in a gym in order to give Melissa and Stuart time alone. Movies, the gym, and working on her book. Those things had taken up a lot of her time in the last years, but today Braddon Granville had made her glad of every sit-up and leg lift. She was proud of the fact that she was the same size as when she'd lived in Arundel so long ago. Having a baby when she was so young and her skin so elastic meant that she'd been able to regain her twenty-four-inch waist.

Eden parked her car under a tree, out of sight of the windows of the house, and quietly made her way to the front door. She tried the old door-knob. It was locked. Maybe he went in through the kitchen door, she thought as she used her key to silently unlock the door. She could call out to the person as she set her things down, but she well knew how isolated the house was. No, it would be better to be cautious. Above her head, a floorboard creaked then stopped, as though the person making the sound didn't want to be heard. That sneaking made her forget her good thoughts. Whoever was in the house shouldn't be there—and knew it.

Eden stepped out on the porch and pulled her cell phone out of her handbag. She didn't think about what she was doing when she called, not the sheriff, but Braddon Granville. He answered on the first ring.

"Eden!" he said, his voice full of pleasure at her call. "Did you change your mind about tonight? We could have dinner at—"

"Someone's in my house," she said.

"I'm sorry but I can't hear you."

Eden tiptoed down the porch steps and went toward her car. "Someone is in my house," she said louder so she could be heard above the frogs. "He's upstairs with a flashlight."

There was a pause on the phone, then the voice of a man in charge. "Get out of there right now," he said in a tone that was not to be disobeyed. "Get in your car and return to town. I'm going to call the sheriff, and he'll be there as fast as possible, but I want you out of there. Understand me?"

"Yes," she said, her heart pounding. She already had the door to the car open but then realized that she'd left her car keys inside the house. She started to tell Mr. Granville that, but he'd already hung up to call the sheriff.

Now what? Did she crouch in the bushes and wait in silence for the cavalry to come and save her? Or did she go back into the house, get her car keys, then roar away in a torrent of gravel?

Turning back to the house, Eden looked up at the windows and saw nothing. No moving light. What if all she'd seen had been a reflection of the moon? Had she been so spooked by Braddon Granville's story of Mrs. Farrington's evil son that she'd made something ordinary into something sinister? She called Mr. Granville's office again but got his machine. She was going to look really stupid when half a dozen police cars arrived and the only intruder was a reflection on the windows of a creaking old house.

Okay, better to face this on her own, she thought, or she was going to be the town's source of laughter for years to come. Taking a deep breath, she went up the stairs to the front porch and opened the door. She had intended to call out and ask if anyone was there, but as soon as she was inside she again heard the floorboards creak, only this time, the sound came from the living room.

On tiptoe, Eden crept toward the doorway. Thank heaven that most of the furniture had been sold or she never would have been able to make her way in silence. If the house were still as full of furniture as when Mrs. Farrington was alive, Eden would have had to crawl over and under surfaces to get there.

As it was, when she got to the doorway, she crouched down low, then looked around the doorframe. She could see a man's silhouette clearly outlined. He had a small flashlight, just a penlight really. If he were on the up and up he'd have a full-size flashlight, wouldn't he? Eden's intuition told her that this man was looking for something. For the silverware that she and Mrs. Farrington had hidden inside the walls? For that blasted necklace that had been in every *Lost Treasures* book ever written?

Suddenly, from some primitive instinct, she knew he was aware that she was there. In spite of all her precautions, she was sure he'd heard every sound she'd made. Had he come downstairs to greet her?

Truthfully, she didn't care why someone was in the house. Now all she wanted to do was get out of there and let the sheriff handle him. She just had to turn away, take three steps, get her car keys, then take another two steps to the front door. Once she was outside, she could run. And once she was inside her car, she'd be safe. But when she turned, she must have made a noise, because the man's head came up and he saw her. One minute he was on the other side of a couch and the next he was leaping toward her. "Wait a minute!" he said as his hand shot out in her direction.

Maybe he had a reason for being in the house. Maybe he was an innocent person. Maybe when he reached for her all he wanted to do was talk. But whatever his intentions, when Eden saw the hand come out of the dark and reach for her, she panicked. She wasn't forty-five years old with many years of life experience, she was seventeen, she was walking home from choir practice, and a man's hand was reaching out to grab her. Back then she'd been so innocent, so sheltered from what went on in the world that she didn't know what the man's intentions were until he tore her blouse and grabbed her breast. After that, she didn't clearly remember what was done to her.

For over twenty-seven years, Eden had been eaten with the thought, What if I'd fought back? What if she hadn't been such a frightened little ninny that all she'd done was cry and plead with him not to hurt her? When he'd told her he wasn't going to hurt her if she kept quiet and still, she'd been so young and innocent that she'd been reassured by his words. *What if I had fought?* was the question that had plagued her all these years.

Now, it was as though she was back in that park again and was being given a second chance.

This time she was going *to fight*. In an instant, she dropped her human persona and became a bundle of fighting fury. She kicked and she clawed; she bit and she hit with her fists. The man kept trying to hold her and he was saying things, but she couldn't hear him—and wouldn't have listened if she could. That other man on that night so long ago had talked to her too. He'd said that he wasn't going to hurt her. But he had hurt her. He'd hurt her in her mind, her body, and in her life. In one act of cruelty, he had taken away her future.

When the sirens sounded outside, the man didn't let go of her but kept trying to hold her to him, and Eden kept fighting him with all her might. She felt her teeth sink into skin and muscle. She heard his sounds of pain when her fists hit him. She felt her nails plow deep furrows into his skin.

She was still fighting when the front door burst open and men started yelling. The man was pulled away from her, but Eden was still too blind with memory and fear to stop fighting.

When Braddon Granville tried to touch her, she fought him too. She couldn't understand what he was saying when he called her name and told her his. She hit the man in the rescue uniform as he held her down so his partner could give her an injection. She fought until her body succumbed to the drug injected into it and couldn't fight anymore.

Chapter Three

When Eden awoke she knew she was in a hospital. The smell and the sounds were unmistakable. She looked around the small room at the picture of the seashells on a beach hanging on the wall, and at the machine next to her bed, to which she seemed to be hooked. She saw the hard gray chair by the bed, and the roses on the table at her side. Sunlight was coming through the window, so she knew it was morning.

She lay back against the bed and closed her eyes for a moment. Vaguely, she remembered what had happened.

"Good morning."

Eden looked up to see Braddon Granville standing beside her, a bouquet of spring flowers in his arms.

"Feeling better?" he asked, his voice full of concern.

"Better than what, Mr. Granville?" she asked, trying to sit up, but she hurt all over, so she lay back down.

"Brad, please. After what you and I went through last night, I think we're on a first-name basis."

"Who was he? What did he want?"

"Oh," Brad said, looking at the floor.

Instantly, Eden knew that whoever the man was he hadn't been a thief. She took a deep breath. "Okay, I'm ready. How big of a fool did I make of myself last night?"

"What do you remember?"

She turned her head away. Eden remembered the other attack, but that time she hadn't woken up in a hospital. Her parents had allowed her to miss school until her bruises healed, but nothing more. She looked back at Brad. All she seemed able to remember was hitting, biting, scratching, clawing. Who had she hurt? "I don't remember much about last night. I—"

She cut off because a police officer entered the room, smiling at her. He was young and strong-looking, and he seemed to be highly amused about something. "Is there really only one of you?"

"I beg your pardon?" Eden said.

"We were taking bets that there were at least three of you to do what you did to McBride. Brad, are you sure you want to tangle with this wildcat?"

"Come on, Clint," Brad said, chastising the young man but also enjoying his connection to Eden. "She's been through enough, so don't tease her. I'm not sure she remembers what happened last night."

"I can believe that," Clint said. "But I still need to ask her some questions. What time did you get home?"

"I don't know the exact time," Eden said. She felt as though she'd been thrown by a horse and trampled on. Every muscle hurt, and every molecule of her body was tired. "Could you please tell me what happened?"

Clint started to ask another question, but Brad stopped him. "I don't think there're going to be any charges."

"Charges? Are there charges against me?" Eden asked.

Brad put his hand over hers. "No, Eden, no one is going to charge *you* with anything. Young Clint here was wondering if you were going to press charges against McBride for trespassing and entering."

"I guess McBride is the man I...?"

"Nearly killed with your bare hands?" Clint said, chuckling. "Yeah, he's the one. Retired police. He said he'd fought two karate experts who didn't fight as hard as you did. Of course, between you and me, I don't think he fought back any. That's why he got so beat up. They had to give him a tetanus shot for the bites. You should see the one—"

"Clint!" Brad said sharply. "Would you mind your manners, please?"

"Yes, sir," Clint said, obviously speaking to a man he'd known all his life.

"Why don't you go get some coffee? I'd like to talk to Ms. Palmer now."

When they were alone, Brad sat down by the bed and took Eden's hand in his.

"What did I do to that man and who is he?"

"He's your next-door neighbor. I started to tell you about him yesterday, but we got sidetracked. He rented what used to be the washhouse."

"So why was he in *my* house?"

"Looking for the fuse box. I'd told him you'd be taking possession of the house soon, so he was on the lookout for you. There're a couple of outdoor lights on timers at your house and last night they'd come on. But just before you arrived, McBride was using his table saw and blew out all the breakers in his place. When he looked at your house and saw that it was dark, he knew that you must be on the same circuit, so he went over there to find the breaker box. He said the kitchen door was open, so he called out, but when no one answered, he used the little light on his keychain to try to find the electrical box. He was searching for a panel by the fireplace in the living room when he saw you. He said that when he walked toward you...well, you sort of went crazy."

Pausing, he looked at Eden for confirmation, but all she could do was turn away. She didn't want him to see her face.

Brad's voice lightened. "I think McBride was glad when we showed up. When you phoned me,

I panicked and called both the sheriff and the rescue people. I was afraid of what could happen, so I wanted to make a lot of noise when we arrived."

He squeezed her hand. She had her face turned away, still unable to look at him. "Eden, don't be embarrassed. It could have happened to anyone. After all, you've been living in New York and—"

She looked back at him. "Is that what everyone's saying?" She well knew that in a small town like Arundel this would be a big story. Everyone would be talking about it. "People are saying that because I lived in New York now I attack anyone who tries to help me?"

Brad looked like he was going to tell her that, no, no one thought that, but then he grinned and said, "Pretty much." When Eden groaned, he said, "Look on the bright side: No one within a hundred-mile radius is going to attack *you*. Hey! Maybe later you could give me a few pointers." He put his fists up like a boxer and made a few mock thrusts.

In spite of herself, Eden smiled and tried to sit up. Brad put a hand behind her back and helped her, then gave her a sip of water from the glass on the table. "How is Mr. McBride?" she asked.

Brad raised his eyebrows. "He'll live, but you banged him up pretty bad. As Clint said, he didn't fight back. He let you hit him—and claw and bite him—while he seemed to have mostly tried to keep you from hurting yourself." He gave her a crooked grin. "He's a real hero. But then, I think he's done that all his life. Clint said they received a fax of his record, and it showed that McBride was in a lot of fights when he was a cop. Shot, knifed. You name it. But he'd never met his match until he met you."

She narrowed her eyes at him. "Did your wife like your sense of humor?"

"Hated it," Brad said, grinning. "You know what the best thing about all this is? I was afraid that McBride was going to be my competition. You and him out there together. Alone. Him a big, virile-looking kind of guy, and you the best-looking thing to come to town since Susan Sarandon filmed a movie here. I was really worried."

"But not now?"

"I think he may ask for a restraining order against you."

"You are a truly horrible human being!" Eden said, but she couldn't help smiling.

"There, that's better." He looked at his watch. "Unfortunately, duty calls and I have to go. They're going to let you go home after the doctor sees you. You're just tired from the workout. There's not a dent on that pretty little body of yours."

"You're very fresh, aren't you?"

Brad laughed. "Fresh. I haven't heard that word in years. Don't you watch reality TV? Don't you know what people in the real world are saying to each other on the first date?"

"Not your generation and not mine," Eden said primly.

Brad took her hand in his again and for a moment looked as though he was going to kiss it, but then he put her hand back on top of the sheet. "Young Clint gets off duty in two hours so I'll make sure he drives you home. My housekeeper went out there this morning, gave the place a good cleaning, and"—he wiggled his eyebrows—"turned the breakers back on. I had to sign an affidavit swearing that you wouldn't be there if she touched your, uh, breaker box."

In spite of herself, Eden blushed. "You're incorrigible. Go on, get out of here. I'll be fine. It's Mr. McBride I'm concerned about."

"If I were you, I'd stay away from him. I doubt if he's your biggest fan. Gotta go. I'll see you at six tonight and I'll bring dinner. You take a bath, wash your hair, make yourself pretty, and await my arrival."

With that he was gone. As the door closed behind him, Eden grimaced. "'Await my arrival'?" she said. "Who does he think he is?" But she smiled anyway and rested against the pillow until she had to get up.

~

"So help me, Bill," Jared said into his cell phone, his teeth clenched, "if you don't stop laughing I'll remove two of your teeth the next time I see you— which will be soon."

Jared listened, but his temper didn't abate. "You didn't tell me she was insane. None of you happened to mention that fact, and it was nowhere in the papers you had me read. I thought she was some poor woman who'd had a hard life. I thought— No, I'm not going soft on you. So help me, Bill, if you start laughing again I'll..." Jared gave a nasty smile. "I'll tell the whole department where I saw you last summer."

Jared's smile returned to normal. "That's better. No, I'm fine. I've been a lot worse, but I look bad. No, I'm not being vain. I was sent here to seduce information out of a woman, wasn't I? So tell me how I'm supposed to wine and dine her when I have a black eye, an arm in a sling, and bruises all over. I tell you, I've never seen anybody fight like she did! She was blind! Crazy."

He listened for a few moments. "That's nice that the house shrink has a rationalization for why she attacked me, but it doesn't help any. I think you ought to send someone else out here to do this job. What about Lopez? He's great-looking. So what if he's fifteen years younger than she is?"

He paused. "I have no idea what she looks like! It was dark and she attacked me. I saw her snooping around, so I very calmly went to her, then she attacked me. I wasn't expecting it, and I couldn't very well attack her back, could I? I did everything I could to get away from her, but she's an agile little thing, I'll give her that. At one point, when I had almost scooted away from her, she bit me on the ankle. When I tried to push her head away, she bit my arm. And you should see the claw marks I have on me!"

Jared stopped talking and listened to his boss. He knew that Bill had been sent a full report of what had happened, but Jared wanted to exagger-

ate everything so, maybe, Bill would take him off
the case. It was one thing to try to sweet-talk information out of a woman he was attracted to, but
quite another to have to be around a woman whose
brain cords didn't connect properly. For all his undercover work, Jared was no actor. Maybe he could
play the tough-guy parts, but not the romantic
ones. That's why he liked women who were reformed bad girls. They didn't expect much from
him—which is just what he gave. His professional
life was difficult, so he didn't want the same in his
private life, what little there was of it.

"There's something else that wasn't in your reports on her," Jared said. "She's practically engaged
to some lawyer in town. Yeah, I know she just got
here, but they must have known each other before
because they're already a couple. Last night as I lay
bleeding on a gurney, being sewn up and swabbed
down, some kid of a deputy made it clear to me
that little Ms. Palmer belongs to one of the town's
founding families—or whatever they are down
here. Lord! Deliver me from the South. Everybody
knows who everybody's great-great-grandfather
was and what his rank was in the war. Civil War,
that is. No, I can't calm down!" Jared said. "I'm in
pain and I'm not the right man for this job. I think
you should send a woman to befriend her. Maybe
send an engaged couple, as I think Ms. Palmer is
about two seconds away from being engaged herself. They'll all talk to each other."

Jared took a breath to listen. "No, nothing. I
didn't see anything in the house that looked out of

place. Nothing. I only had about forty-five minutes and I had to use a penlight. I thought your people said she was spending the night in town."

Jared listened to Bill defend his information while he looked out the window at the river at the bottom of the hill. In the next second, he came alert as he saw someone coming through the cut in the hedge that separated "her" house from his. Yesterday he'd done some exploring of the two connecting properties, mainly looking for hiding places and avenues of exit. He planned to explore every inch of the place, probably at night while Ms. Palmer slept the sleep of the innocent—if she was innocent, that is. There were a couple of places outside that Jared thought might be good to stick some surveillance cameras. There were birdhouses and vines up the trees. He could hide the cords in the vines and the cameras in the birdhouses. No one would see anything.

Since last night he'd developed the opinion that Ms. Palmer was indeed guilty of something. He wasn't sure of what, but she was guilty. All the sympathy he'd built up when he'd read about her life had left him when she'd sunk her teeth into him for the third time.

Now he looked out the window and drew in his breath. Coming through the bushes was none other than the lady in question—and she was carrying a big ceramic dish, with a loaf of bread on top, pot holders covering her hands. While Bill was droning on and on about how Jared had to do the job and that if he were a good agent he could get it done in a matter of days, Jared got his first real look at Ms. Palmer. She wore jeans that were much looser than he liked on women and above that an oversize sweater that hid most of what was under it, but there was a breeze, and he could see the outline of a curvy little body that wasn't half bad. He'd read that in New York she often went to the gym after work, but the report hadn't said whether she went there to socialize or to sweat. From the look of her, she'd done a lot of sweating.

When the breeze lifted her hair and she moved her head to one side to get the hair out of her eyes, he saw her wince. Good! he thought. He hoped she was very sore from what she'd done to him last night.

Jared felt a tiny bit of guilt because he *had* been snooping through her house, and because his story about lights going off had been something he'd made up when the police arrived. And of course she had every right to call the sheriff or her boyfriend or anybody else, for that matter. And, yes, she was perfectly justified in thinking that he was a thief and therefore was probably going to attack her when he reached out to touch her arm. So, okay, maybe she'd been right on every count; but that didn't heal his body or his pride.

Jared listened to Bill and in an instant saw a way around all the obstacles. Her guilt. If he'd ever seen a human being with a sorrowful look on her face, the woman walking toward him with her peace offering was it. "I gotta go and don't call me back. She's here," he said quickly, then closed his cell phone. Jared ran to the chair in front of the empty fireplace. He hadn't had time to lay a fire on this cool spring morning because he'd been snooping inside the old house next door while she was still in the hospital. That she'd stayed longer than he had he was sure was due to her big-deal lawyer's word.

As Jared heard her walk up the front porch steps, he glanced at the coatrack by the door and saw three walking sticks, left, no doubt, by some previous tenant. He grabbed a stick, pulled a blanket off the back of the couch, then hurried across the room. By the time she knocked on the door, Jared was bundled up under what had to be the dustiest old blanket in the world, but he left his sling-bound arm outside so it would show. Beside him was the cane.

"Come in," he said in the voice of an old man in pain.

Slowly, the door opened to reveal a pretty woman with a hot casserole. Jared had seen worse sights in his life.

"I...I'm Eden Palmer," she said softly, looking at him with a combination of guilt and pity. Part of Jared wanted to jump up and show her that he was fine, that he looked worse than he was, but he made himself pull the blanket up around his chin in a protective way.

Eden took the few steps across the room to stand near him. "I don't know where to begin to apologize about last night. Until recently I've been living in New York and maybe I've come to think that everybody is…" She trailed off, not finishing her sentence. "Could I put this down somewhere?"

Weakly, Jared nodded toward the kitchen at the other end of the house. He watched her walk away and decided that under her big clothes was a mighty fine little tush. She disappeared through the doorway into the kitchen and he heard nothing but silence for several minutes. He knew why. The kitchen was a mess. Yesterday he'd thrown food into cabinets and the refrigerator as fast as possible so he could start scouting the area before the Palmer woman got there. He'd run in twice to make himself a sandwich and had left everything as it was. He figured that after she moved into the house he'd have plenty of time to straighten up.

A few minutes later, Ms. Palmer came out of the kitchen with a little tray filled with food. He could smell what seemed to be homemade vegetable beef soup. The women he liked were very understanding and tolerant of what he did for a living, but none of them were cooks. It seemed to be a law of life that women who took their clothes off for a living didn't cook, while women who went to church did.

"I, uh…" she said hesitantly. "I'll just leave you to, uh, heal, and, again, I'm sorry that I…" She looked at his eye, which he knew was huge and black and purple, and which distorted his face as though he'd had a stroke. On the other side of his face were two deep scratches from her nails.

Jared couldn't be sure, but he thought he saw tears form in Eden Palmer's eyes. "Could you put the food a little closer?" he whispered, as though talking was painful—which it was. "I think I can reach it if it's a bit closer."

"Yes, of course," Eden said quickly, then moved the tray to the table next to Jared's chair.

He pulled his uninjured arm from under the blanket and made a shaky attempt to get a spoonful of soup, but he dropped the spoon back into the bowl. He gave Ms. Palmer a look that said he was trying but couldn't quite make it.

In the next second, Eden had pulled up a chair and was feeding him. It was all Jared could do not to smile at such luxury. But he had to concentrate on playing the invalid, and that meant no smiling.

It took thirty long minutes to feed him all the food, and they didn't talk during that time. While he chewed, she scurried about the room, straightened up, and lit the logs in the fireplace.

"Thank you," Jared said, collapsing back against the chair. "I needed that. Since I got out of the hospital I haven't been able to do much for myself. I'm sorry the house is such a mess. You must think that I'm—"

"I don't think anything at all bad about you, Mr. McBride. It's me who's at fault. When I think about what you were doing for me last night and what I did to you, I…Well, I…"

Jared reached out for her hand. Nice, he thought. Soft. He started to move up her wrist but then remembered himself enough that he gave a tiny moan of pain and flopped back against the chair.

"Can you walk?"

"A bit," he said heavily. "I can get to the...you know, by myself."

Standing up, she put her hands on her hips, and when Jared groaned, it was for real. He hated that hands-on-hips stance that women put on. It was the Earth Mother pose, and it suited this woman much too well. Deliver me, thought Jared. He was about to throw back the blanket and tell her to go home when she spoke. "I insist that you stay in my guest room until you can take care of yourself," she said.

Jared wasn't sure that any woman had ever been able to take his breath away in the same way that she had just done. "No, Ms. Palmer," he said softly. "I couldn't move in with you."

"I'm not asking you to move in with me. It's just until you can take care of yourself."

He gave a sigh, then a wince as he moved in the chair. "This is a small town and people will talk."

"They'll talk more if they think I've left a man I've rendered helpless to fend for himself." She sat down on the chair in front of him. "I'm going to be honest with you. I feel very guilty about what I did. Someday, maybe, I'll tell you what happened inside my mind when you touched me in that dark room. It brought back some very unpleasant memories for me, and for a while I lost it. I apologize. But I can't go back and undo what I did, all I can do is try to make amends. I can't leave you in this dirty house to take care of yourself. I can't afford to hire a nurse to look after you, and I don't have the time to run back and forth to clean up your kitchen and keep fires going. This afternoon FedEx brought me a box of six manuscripts that have to be copyedited or critiqued within the next few weeks. Have you ever copyedited a manuscript, Mr. McBride?"

"I can't say that I have." He was watching her with amusement. She had put on an act of sternness, like a lady schoolmarm, but what she was saying was softness itself.

"They take a lot of time, so I need to have the time to give them. I really can't see any other way except that you move into my guest bedroom and let me take care of you there."

"And what about the lawyer?"

"Braddon Granville? Yes, he's my attorney," she said, puzzled, and the way she said it told Jared everything he needed to know. Maybe the lawyer and maybe the whole town thought that the Granville-Palmer wedding was a done deal, but it didn't seem that cute little Ms. Palmer thought so.

Chapter Four

Eden put down her cup of tea and glanced upward, as though she could see through the ceiling to what Mr. McBride was up to.

Why is it that men think all women are stupid? she wondered for the hundred thousandth time in her life. It seemed that a woman had to prove herself to every man she met before he believed that she had any brains. And after she'd shown him her intelligence, he still spent the rest of their time together seeing what he could get away with.

She'd been in Arundel just two days, but already she had two eligible, middle-aged bachelors who were coming on to her. She figured she had a choice. She could believe that, in their eyes, she was the sexiest thing since Marilyn Monroe, or she could believe that both of them were up to something.

Eden nibbled on a cookie that she'd just taken out of the oven. She had left Arundel by the time the old washhouse had been repaired, but Mrs. Farrington had often talked about her plans for renovating it. She was going to rent it to someone for a little money in return for working in the garden on summer evenings and weekends. Eden knew Mrs. Farrington well, and there was no way she'd connect the electricity between the washhouse and the main house. She'd insist on separate bills. Eden could almost hear the old woman now: "If they left all the lights on day and night, would *I* be required to pay for them? Absolutely not!" But now she had been told that the electricity of the two houses had been joined.

Today, Eden had had to spend most of the day in the hospital, and she felt sure it was on Brad's orders. She kept asking the hospital staff if she could go home, but every nurse and doctor had been evasive. Finally, at two o'clock, they'd said she could leave. Eden wondered if Brad had finally given permission for her dismissal.

The smiling, smirking deputy sheriff, Clint, was waiting for her, and Eden was glad for her sore muscles so she could use them to explain her angry red face. She'd had to sit in the police car on the ride back to Farrington Manor in silence as Clint made what he thought was one joke after another. According to him, Eden had lived too long in the

North and didn't understand how neighbors in
the South looked out for one another. They took
care of one another. Lent helping hands, that sort
of thing. Clint chuckled and smirked through the
entire ride. When they got to the house, he asked
her if she wanted him to get out his gun and go
through the house to check it for her. Eden was
about to tell him what he could do with his gun,
when his radio came on. He gave her a look that
said he had important work to do now, so she got
out of the car, somehow managing not to slam the
door.

Inside, Eden got her first real look at the magnificent old central hall. When she'd first laid eyes
on it years ago, it had been a mass of furniture and
papers; eventually the papers had been removed
and filed, but the furniture had stayed where it
was, even if the pieces were on top of each other.
There had simply been nowhere else to put it all.
Now, the hall was sparsely furnished, with two
small couches, a tall secretary (reproduction, not
original), and a few chairs and two little tables. For
the first time in her life, Eden could see the hall for
the grand size that it was.

"Magnificent" was all that she could say, and she
had to blink away tears that Mrs. Farrington had
renovated the house so beautifully and that she'd
left it to Eden. The walls had paneling to half their
height of twelve feet. The ceiling was surrounded
by tall, deep crown moldings. The doors at opposite ends were original, two hundred-plus years of
paint painstakingly removed so the dents and nicks

of centuries showed in a patina that only age could give.

"Beautiful," she whispered, twirling about and looking at everything.

She wanted to see the rest of the house, but she was sure that Brad was going to show up at any minute, so she got her cell phone out of her bag, then called the local electric company and told them she wanted her electricity and McBride's billed separately. "But it is," the girl at the electric company said. "Mr. McBride had all the electricity put in his name when he rented the house."

"Our two houses aren't on the same circuit?" Eden asked.

"No, ma'am."

"Thank you," Eden said, then hung up.

She sat down on one of the couches and looked at the beautiful molding around the room. Mrs. Farrington had had every bit of it restored. Brad had said that he believed Mrs. Farrington had had the house restored for her, for Eden. Yes, Eden could believe that, but she also knew that Mrs. Farrington had left the house to Eden so she could protect it. She went into the living room. Paneling covered the wall from the chair rail down, all around the ceiling. The fireplace was especially beautiful; even Thomas Jefferson would have liked it.

Eden leaned against the wall for a moment. What in the world was going on? she wondered. Brad had seemed to believe McBride completely, even to making Eden the butt of all the jokes. Dumb woman used to living in the city gets freaked out because a man is snooping around in her house in the middle of the night. "Let's see one of *them* find someone snooping around and see how *he* reacts," she said out loud, then pushed away from the wall with a moan of pain. It would take days to get over her soreness.

It seemed that the police had contacted someone, been told that Mr. McBride was one of them, and that was the end of it. No one had questioned his story. To them he was a man who'd been innocently using his table saw—male bonding *there!*—and when he'd seen that he'd blown out his female neighbor's lights, he had tried to repair them. Take care of the little lady, so to speak. Only Eden had thought it was odd that two separate houses were on the same circuit.

Trying to calm herself, she walked into the kitchen and saw that it was much as she'd left it all those years ago. She'd been the one to remove all the papers from the cabinets and the countertops. She'd read each piece, then carefully ordered them in one of the many file cabinets that Mrs. Farrington had purchased. Whenever Eden had found dishes buried among the papers, she'd washed them, then put them into the cabinets with the glass doors. As Eden looked around, she saw that the Wedgwood was missing. The expensive set. Mrs. Farrington's son had probably sold them.

Slowly, with each muscle aching, Eden went outside to her car. The groceries she'd bought the day before were still in there. Some of them were spoiled, but she could save most of what she'd bought. Limping, she managed to carry the bags inside. When she opened the side-by-side refrigerator, she saw that Brad had had his housekeeper fill it. There were three pounds of stewing beef inside, so Eden set to work making a pot of soup.

As she chopped, she thought about what had happened last night. Yes, she'd gone crazy. They'd all made her see that. From the doctor to the police boy, they'd let her know that she'd "overreacted." The only person who hadn't been "on their side" was one of the nurses, a large woman well into middle age. She was adjusting the machine that was monitoring Eden's heart rate and hadn't said a word when the doctor told Eden that she was fine. No real injuries, he'd said, then he'd given her a little smile and told her that the next time she should just run out the front door and not try to beat up a man twice as big as she was. The nurse waited until the doctor was out of the room, then she'd put her hand on Eden's wrist. "Honey, I know they're all giving you a hard time, but what you did was right. If you were a man you would have shot him. Snooping around your house like that at night! He shouldn't have been in there, I don't care who he was or what his intentions were. As for you, if other women reacted like that the morgue wouldn't be so crowded."

What the nurse said made Eden feel a lot better about herself, and when she was finally released, she could stand young Clint's smirking.

But as Eden made her soup she started to think

about what had happened to her in the past few days. Suddenly, there were two men in her life. A lawyer who seemed to already be assuming that the two of them were a couple, and another man who lived next door and had snooped around her house at night. What was going on?

When the soup was simmering, she went upstairs to the bedrooms. Technically, the house was just two bedrooms and two full baths, but the rooms were so big that they were disconcerting. Her bath was the size of a large bedroom, and the room on the other side of her bedroom was bigger than the average living room. Across the hall was a large bedroom with windows on three sides, and a bathroom in the corner. As Eden looked at the room, an idea came to her. If this man McBride was as beaten up as people said he was, maybe she should take care of him. Maybe she should move him into her house where she could be his nurse— or his jailer. If he was in the house she could see what he was doing. She was a light sleeper, so she'd hear him if he started snooping around again. Electrical box indeed! she thought.

As she went downstairs again, Eden thought how having someone live upstairs could also serve as a chaperone for her and Brad. That man was coming on too fast, too soon. That kind of thing happens when you're in your twenties, but not when you're forty-five. Eden's gut instincts were telling her that the two men were up to something—or wanted something. Could she use one man to protect her from the other?

When the food was ready, she had taken it to Mr. McBride's house—their first proper meeting. At her first sight of him, she felt bad that she'd done something so awful to another human being, but as she spent more time in his company, she knew that he was faking how badly he was injured. When Melissa had been in the third grade, she'd had a very hateful teacher, and every morning Melissa had come up with excuses as to why she couldn't go to school that day. Eden had learned how to distinguish between real pain and fake. When it had been extraordinarily easy to get Mr. McBride to move in with her, she knew she was right.

It had taken nearly thirty minutes to get Mr. McBride across the garden that separated their houses, then up the stairs to the guest bedroom. Eden knew that he was doing all that he could to slow their progress so he would have time to ask her lots of questions.

He seemed to want to know all about the history of Arundel and Farrington Manor in particular. On the surface, it seemed a normal bit of conversation, but something didn't ring true. If he knew absolutely nothing about the area, what had made him decide to come here?

And another thing: not only did he not ask her a single personal question, but he always deftly managed to change the subject when she asked him about himself. Eden grew suspicious.

"This is so very nice of you, Ms. Palmer," he said as he slipped into the bed in the guest room.

"I'm not used to Southern hospitality, but it seems to be all that people have said it is." Reaching out, he put his hand over her wrist, then lowered his voice. "You seem to be so nice."

"Mr. McBride," she said.

"Call me Jared," he answered, smiling at her in a way that she was sure had won the hearts of many women. In spite of a black eye and a deeply scratched cheek, he was still quite handsome.

"Mr. McBride," she said firmly, "I invited you to stay here out of a sense of guilt because of what I did to you. There's no more to it than that. Do I make myself clear?"

"Yes, ma'am," he said meekly, sliding down under the covers. "I could never hope that a woman as fine as you—"

She gave him a look that said, Cut out the bull.

With a little smile, he closed his eyes and pretended to rest.

Eden went downstairs to clean up the kitchen, and when she'd finished, she treated herself to a call to her daughter. "How are you feeling?" she asked.

"Fine," Melissa said quickly. "Oh, Mom, I don't mean to be rude, but could we talk later? Stuart took the afternoon off today and we're going shopping for our new apartment. I mean, your old apartment. Sorry, I don't mean to be throwing you out. So how is Arundel? Sleepy as always?"

Eden could hear the impatience in her daughter's voice. She wanted to get off the phone to be with her husband. Eden tried not to be hurt by this attitude, and she had to work hard not to try to get her daughter to focus attention on her. She wanted to say that she'd attacked a burglar, been rushed to the hospital in an ambulance, then had invited the burglar to move in with her. But she didn't. "Sure," Eden said. "Same ol' same ol'. Nothing ever changes here. Go with Stuart and have a good time. If you need any money, I—"

"Mother!" Melissa said stiffly. "Stuart can certainly support his own wife and child."

If I give him a furnished apartment for less than it costs me to rent it, Eden wanted to say. It seemed that after your children married, you did a lot of biting your tongue. "Of course he can, dear," she said. "Go, have a good time."

After Eden hung up the phone, she stood there for a few moments. She and her daughter had been everything to each other. Not even her daughter's marriage had been able to break the bond between them, but now...Eden didn't want to think what was happening, but she knew that the umbilical cord was at last being cut. "That's good," Eden said aloud. She and her daughter were too attached to each other. During the year they'd been separated they had barely been able to function, so now, at last, they were separating. And that was good. Wasn't it?

Eden took a deep breath and turned away from the phone. She had an urge to call her daughter back and say she was returning. She had an urge to call her publisher and ask for her job back. She had an urge to...

She stopped walking. She decided to go upstairs, wash her hair, and spend an hour and a half getting ready for Brad's visit tonight. He was moving much too fast, assuming too much too soon, and McBride...Truthfully, she didn't know what to make of that man. Both men wanted something, but until she found out what it was, maybe she could enjoy herself.

Chapter Five

D o you think that's wise?" Brad asked tightly. "I don't mean to criticize, but do you really think you should let a strange man move into your house?"

"He isn't strange, remember?" Eden said, her back to Brad so he wouldn't see her smile. "Your friends at the police station ran a check on him. I was told that Jared McBride is a full-fledged hero. Considering that I was *his* assailant I thought that the least I could do was put him into a place where I could take care of him." She turned to look at Brad, batting her mascaraed lashes. "Did I do wrong?"

Brad started to answer, then grinned. "Am I right in thinking that you're telling me to mind my own business and that it's your house."

"More or less," she said, pleased that he understood. She unwrapped the pecan-encrusted trout from the foil packages that Brad had brought from Soundside, the seafood restaurant that was steps from his office.

When Brad took plates out of the glass-doored cabinet, Eden noted that he seemed to know where everything was. He said he'd often visited Mrs. Farrington, but that they'd never become true friends; yet he seemed to have visited often enough that he knew his way around the house well. Had he been telling the truth?

He carried the dishes into the dining room and set the table. "So how long is McBride staying?"

Eden ignored his question as she put the fish onto the plates. She'd steamed green beans and made a salad. "Tell me everything that's happened in Arundel since I left here twenty-two years ago. Who got married, who died, who had babies? Any scandals?"

It took Brad a few moments to get his mind off the man Eden had invited into her home, but when he did, she found that he was a wonderful storyteller. As far as she could tell, Arundel hadn't changed much. But then, its residents fought hard against change. When Wal-Mart wanted to put in a store on the outskirts, the company met with so much protest that they slunk away in silence. The residents were quite willing to drive a hundred miles to buy goods, just so their pretty town wouldn't be polluted with ugly, modern stores. Brad's three last names were an example of the residents' dislike of change. All of his names came from the founding families of Arundel. Mrs. Farrington told Eden that there were certain names that were all over Arundel, on the street signs, on the buildings, on the businesses. The families had started the town and, for the most part, had never left it. The children still carried the old names, and they still left for college, but they returned to Arundel with spouses from good families to live in the family home, then bear children who were given three last names. Anywhere else it might be unusual to meet a girl named Haughton or Pembroke, but not in Arundel. The names were a permanent calling card, a way to let people know who they were and where they fit into history. Some people thought the whole idea was pretentious and snobbish, but others swooned over the historic continuity, which was so rare in the United States.

As Eden looked at Brad across the table, she thought how well he fit into the old house. It was as though he was a reincarnation of his ancestors who had often visited the place and had twice married into the Farrington family. When he poured her a glass of wine, she smiled at him and he smiled back. She felt comfortable with him.

"Okay," Brad said, "I know I'm too pushy and too forward, and I know that I've been taking liberties with you, but you have to realize how much Mrs. Farrington talked about you."

"Did she?" Eden said, smiling. "I think I missed her every day I was away from her."

"I don't know how! She was a demanding old woman. I can't tell you how many times she made me mow her lawn! I wasted two Saturdays a month here behind that hideous old push mower of hers. I used to..." He stopped and smiled at Eden. "If I hadn't had Alice Augusta Farrington while my wife was ill, I think I might have gone insane. My wife took nearly three years to die." He looked down at his plate, then back up at Eden. "In this light, at this table, I can almost see her, Mrs. Farrington, I mean. There are things about you that remind me of her."

When he pushed his food around on his plate, Eden felt that he had something to say but was afraid to say it. Silently, she waited for him to go on.

"You'll hear stories about me," he said softly.

"Will they be worse than the ones about me?"

"No," he said, then grinned and took a big bite of his fish. "After what you did to McBride, this town will have gossip for the next ten years. You're going to beat our resident clairvoyant for causing talk."

"A clairvoyant? Great! I can have my fortune told. Does this mean that Arundel is becoming New Age?"

"Far from it. She's a Pembroke."

"Ah," Eden said. That explained everything. While no one in Arundel would put up with eccentricity from an outsider, they tolerated pretty much anything from one of their own. "So tell me about your wife," she said.

"We weren't exactly a match made in heaven.

You're going to hear that. We'd already started divorce proceedings when she told me she had cancer."

"But you stayed with her."

"Yes, I did. I wasn't faithful, though. You'll hear that too. There was a woman…But it didn't last. After my wife died, I realized that I didn't want anything to do with her, not long-term, anyway. Mrs. Farrington made me see that."

"Really? But Mrs. Farrington was such a proponent of extramarital sex."

"Yeah, my grandfather and my great-uncle." Brad grinned. "But in between the Willow Stories, as I came to think of them, Mrs. Farrington told me about you."

Eden was flattered and curious. "What could she have told you about me?"

"What you liked to eat, what you wore, what you were good at, what you couldn't do. What interested you, what didn't. You name it and she told me about it. She said you liked the garden more than the house, so that's why she went to all the trouble of renovating this old house, but left the gardens a mess for you to have the pleasure of cleaning up."

Eden smiled. "I can hardly wait to get my hands on them. Know any muscular teenage boys who need summer jobs?"

"At least twenty of them. Mind if I help?"

"Don't tell me you're a gardener?"

"More or less. Well, actually, less. But I can dig holes with the best of them."

His look was so intense that Eden looked away for a moment. He seemed to want her to comment on what he'd told her about himself. "Brad, you don't have to confess your past sins to me," she said. "Really, at my age, I've committed a few of my own."

"You?" he said, one eyebrow raised. "What possible sins have *you* committed? According to Mrs. Farrington you were an angel come to earth."

"Didn't she tell you that I was lazy and daydreamy and all the other things that she complained about me?"

"She never said a bad word about you." His eyes were twinkling, and Eden was enjoying his teasing. "I got the impression that you worked nonstop and that you never said an unkind word about anyone in your life."

"She didn't tell you about all the horrible things I said about the youngest Camden boy? He decided he was going to marry me."

Brad groaned. "I know him well. Doing you a favor, was he?"

"Oh, yes. I think he had an idea that Mrs. Farrington would leave me the house, and he wanted it. There weren't enough old Camden houses for him to have one. I think he thought he'd die if he had to live in a new brick house. Whatever happened to that boy?"

"He moved up north where he got a Yankee wife, but when his brother had financial reverses, he moved back home. He lives in the Camden-Minton house now. He's good with money. He must have figured out that Mrs. Farrington couldn't leave the house to her son."

"Did everyone in town know about her son? About what he did?"

"Sure. We know about each other."

Eden looked down at her wineglass to hide her smile. To someone who'd never lived in Arundel, what Brad had just said was impossibly pompous. He was a member of a society that "knew" the others in that society. They would have known about Mrs. Farrington's son, but they would still have accepted him into their houses because he was one of them. But if an outsider had come into town and done what Alester Farrington had tried to do, they might have hanged him.

"When Mrs. Farrington died, you lost one of your families," Eden said, smiling at him. She had lived too many places and seen too much in her life to dislike "family" in any form. To her mind, that's what these people in Arundel were: a large family with a very long history.

"Yes, but as Mrs. Farrington said to me, perhaps it was for the better. Many bad things had happened in the Farrington family. She was of the old school and believed there was a bad 'strain,' as she called it, in her family. Genetics."

Eden started to say that she probably knew more about the Farrington family than anyone else on earth, since she'd spent years reading about them, but she said nothing. And she was tempted to tell him about her book, but again, decided to say nothing.

"What I really want to say is that if I seem a bit too familiar I ask your forgiveness. It's just that I feel as though I've known you for a long time. I know that we both share a fondness for cheesecake and that we both dislike hollyhocks. I know that you like rabbits but don't like dogs much. By the way, I own three dogs, all of them well mannered and polite, I might add. I know you aren't married, that you're beautiful, talented, and smart, and with those things added to owning this big house, you're going to have a lot of male interest. I'm concerned that in a sense of everything being fair in love and war, half a dozen people will rush to tell you all about how horrible I was while my wife was dying."

"Were you horrible?" Eden asked softly.

"No. I stayed with her, but I didn't love her. As I said, we'd already filed for divorce. I spent a lot of time here in this house during those years. I think I needed someone as bossy as Mrs. Farrington so I wouldn't have to think. It was the worst time of my life." He leaned back in his chair, and after a moment, he smiled. "Now that I've told you my deepest, darkest secret, what about your life? And I know about what happened to you to give you your daughter, so that doesn't count."

More questions, Eden thought. "Of course Mrs. Farrington would have told you about that," she said grimly. "But then I'm sure it was all over town from years before."

"Yes, she told all of us, but she did so because she didn't want people thinking you were just some hot pants teenager who'd fooled around with her boyfriend. She wanted people to understand." He smiled at her. "All of us did understand. I don't think anyone was discourteous to you while you were here, were they?"

"No," Eden said, looking at him. She realized that Mrs. Farrington had told the "family" about Eden and the word was sent out that, in spite of her unmarried-and-pregnant state, she was to be treated kindly, not snubbed. Even though Brad had not been in Arundel during those years, he included himself in the "we" of the people who understood.

Eden was about to say more when a movement at the doorway caught her eye. It was just a flash, then it was gone. A mouse? she wondered. But no, she didn't think so.

"How about if we take our wine outside?" Brad asked. "I'd like to see that lawn I worked so hard on, and maybe you could tell me of your garden plans."

"I haven't had time to really look at the outside," she said, thinking that the only time she'd been out was when she'd gone to McBride's house to take him soup. And with the thought of that man she knew what she'd seen in the doorway: McBride's foot. He was just outside the door, listening to her and Brad. How long had he been there? And, more important, *why* was he there? Just old-fashioned snooping? Prurient interest? Was that all it had been when he'd been snooping through her house at night?

"Yes!" Eden said. "Let's go outside." She said

this too loud and too fast. Part of her wanted to let McBride know that she knew he was there. She'd like to see his face when she caught him!

As she pushed away from the table, she glanced at the glass-doored cabinet and saw McBride's reflection in the glass. He didn't look guilty or embarrassed, just gave her a little nod and a smile, acknowledging that she'd seen him.

Her first instinct was to confront him, but she didn't. She didn't want to get Brad involved in this. She would deal with McBride on her own.

Standing, Eden tucked her arm in Brad's, and they left the house with their full wineglasses. Brad was telling her about the fenced garden that Eden had designed so many years ago, but it was difficult for her to concentrate on what he was saying. Somewhere in the back of her mind, she realized that Brad knew a great deal more about gardening and about Mrs. Farrington than he'd let on. Something he said made her give him her attention. "What did you say?"

Brad chuckled. "Didn't think I knew about that, did you? I said that I helped Mrs. Farrington pull the silver out of the floors and the walls. By that I mean that I used the crowbar and she criticized. I told you she made me work like a slave. Before the renovation could begin, she made me help clean out the inside of the walls and the floors. I must say that you ladies certainly did a lot of work when you put all those in there."

"And that's when you found the Paul Revere teapot."

"Not me, but yes, that's when it was found," Brad said. "I was the one who arranged the sale for her."

Eden looked at him. "I think she must have cared a great deal about you if she trusted you with a Farrington heirloom."

He leaned toward her so close that his lips were near her ear. "But she wouldn't show me what's buried in the garden. She told me about what you two had done, but she also said that whether or not those things were dug up was up to you."

Eden had to laugh. She was beginning to like this man a lot. Perhaps even beginning to trust him. Maybe she should tell him about McBride's snooping. Maybe Brad would go in there and beat him up for her. She didn't care if McBride was bleeding from every orifice, after Brad left she was going to tell McBride to get out of her house. Spying on her! Of all the ungrateful— "I'm sorry, what did you say?"

Brad was looking at her. "You suddenly seem distracted. And why do you keep looking at the house?"

"I saw someone at the window. I'm sure it was only Mr. McBride."

"I really do wish you hadn't moved him into your house."

"I didn't. The invitation was until he recovered from the wounds *I* gave him." Her tone let him know that it wasn't any of his business. She changed the subject. "Now, tell me, what would *you* do with this garden?" It was growing dark;

the warm air felt wonderful. She could smell the freshwater creek down the hill, and the night was so quiet that she was sure she could hear fish jumping.

They stopped when they reached the fenced garden. Many years ago, not long after Melissa was born, Eden had found some garden plans tucked inside a book. They were just crude sketches, but the paper was so old it had intrigued her. The book holding the papers was from the 1930s, but the drawings looked much older.

Mrs. Farrington had smiled when Eden showed them to her and said that her father had searched for those drawings for years. They were the original garden plans, drawn by Josiah Alester Farrington in 1720 when the house was built. Her father said the garden had stayed intact until the 1840s, when his grandfather had torn them up and put in what were called "carpet beds," designs created with annuals. The colorful gardens had been all the rage then but were extremely labor intensive. During the First World War, most of the grounds had been plowed up and put to cotton. After the war, paths were mowed through the weeds, and sometimes an industrious wife would put in a patch of vegetables and flowers, but with the decline in the family fortune, the gardens were mostly left on their own.

By the time Eden arrived, the gardens were a shadow of what they once were. After Melissa was born and Eden found the original eighteenth-century plan, it was Mrs. Farrington who suggested that she restore the gardens. Eden was young and restless, and Melissa was a good baby, so Eden had put her unused brain to studying the principles behind eighteenth-century gardening. After she'd nearly memorized the contents of the three books Mrs. Farrington owned, the woman had called the owner of the little bookstore in Arundel and told her to order "whatever Williamsburg had." When eleven brand-new books had arrived and Mrs. Farrington had told Eden they were a gift for her, Eden had sat down and cried—which had embarrassed Mrs. Farrington so much that she'd left the room.

The books had been the start of what became a passion with Eden. She read, sketched, ate, and drank eighteenth-century gardening until the day she and Melissa left Arundel.

Mrs. Farrington hired Toddy. He had worked for her family during the war when he was a boy, to help put the garden in, and when Eden saw him, ancient beyond belief, skin the color of a black walnut husk, she asked Mrs. Farrington if it had been the Civil War when he'd worked for them. But Toddy surprised her. He may have been old, but his brain was sharp, and he approved of what she was doing. Together, the two of them laid out the first of Josiah Alester Farrington's gardens.

It was fifty feet square, divided into four quarters by wide brick sidewalks. In the center was a circle containing a tall carriage lamp surrounded by a barrel full of jasmine that ran up the lamppost. Rosemary was planted at the base of the barrel, with dianthus around the edges. The four quarters of the garden were encased internally by a low boxwood hedge and externally by a three-rail cedar fence. Eden well remembered how the garden had once looked, but now it was mostly empty. A few shrubs were beginning to sprout in the early spring air, but for the most part it was a huge expanse of mulch.

"It took me over a month to clean it up," Brad said. "It had been allowed to grow into such a tangle that I had to chainsaw my way in."

She looked at him sharply and found that she rather liked the idea of him with a chain saw and sweat dripping off his forehead. The image aroused feelings in her that she hadn't felt in a long time.

Brad was watching her. "Fill it," he said succinctly, and when she said nothing, he continued. "You asked what I'd do, and I'd fill this garden with tall plants in the center and work outward. For those two sunny squares, I'd put buddleia there in the middle to draw butterflies, then I'd flank it with caryopteris, sedum, monarda, and coreopsis."

Eden's smile grew broader as he spoke. She hadn't heard those words in years, not since she'd gone to New York and lived amid concrete and steel. "You do like butterflies, don't you? What about fennel?"

He smiled broader, and it was a smile shared by gardeners. "Ah, yes, the swallowtails. I can't forget them. But we'd have to put the fennel in pots. Too invasive."

"Or a bottomless pot buried deep."

"Perfect. Now, that corner is under the pecan tree, so it's fairly shady."

"Astilbe and pulmonaria," she said. "Not hostas, too big."

"Exactly. Of course you could go wild with some native orchids."

"Orchids," Eden said, her breath drawn in. "But no monkshood. Grandchild coming."

"Yes," he said. "Nothing in the deadly night-shade family. Maybe my grandson could visit."

"You have a grandchild too?"

"Oh, yes, my daughter Camden's son. His name is—"

Eden put up her hand. "Let me guess. Granville Braddon Something."

"Nope," he said, smiling. "It's Farrington Granville Robicheaux. Robicheaux being the name of the man my daughter married."

"Farrington," Eden said, smiling. "Only in Arundel could that be a child's first name. I'm glad he was a boy." She stopped teasing. "Mrs. Farrington would be pleased. Maybe her name can be kept alive after all." They smiled at each other and she pointed to the fourth quarter. "Not that you know anything about gardening, but what would you put there? And I warn you that if you don't like dicentra, it's all over between us."

"Bleeding heart," Brad said. "My absolute favorite. Speaking of which, Friday is the annual Shrimp Festival. Would you go with me?"

"On a date?"

"Yes. I'll pick you up in my '57 Chevy, take you

to the festival, then later we can go to the local make-out hill." He wiggled his eyebrows at her.

"It sounds wonderful. I'll be ready. If only I had a poodle skirt to wear."

"I think poodle skirts were well before your time."

"One can only dream." Her head came up. "Where do you live?"

"Guess," he said, then they both laughed. The Granville house, of course. It was a big old monster of a house on the corner of Granville and Prince streets. Built in the eighteenth century, it had once been a small, elegant house, but it had burned down in the 1850s. The Granville who owned the land at that time had bought the four lots surrounding him, torn down the houses, and built a huge Queen Anne–style Victorian, complete with porches and a gazebo. There was a wisteria vine on a pergola in the front that was said to be the oldest wisteria in the state. Oldest or not, the trunk was as big as a tree.

"I want a tour," Eden said. "From basement to attic, I want to see every inch of that house."

His eyes were twinkling as he lifted her hand and kissed it. "A woman who owns an eighteenth-century house would never settle for a Victorian, would she?"

She wasn't sure what he meant, but she knew she didn't like it. Too much, too fast! She pulled her hand from his grasp, and just as she was about to speak, a movement made her glance up at a second-story window. She saw McBride watching her. She looked back at Brad. "Do you have a garden?"

"Of sorts," he said, smiling modestly. "A few Victorian things here and there that go with the house. Not much."

At that she laughed. She knew he was lying, and she imagined that he had a garden that had been in more than one magazine. She very much liked that he believed a garden should match the house. "Ever since I lived with Mrs. Farrington, my gardening mind has been pure eighteenth century. If I'd had the opportunity, I would have loved to study gardening." She looked at him. "I think that had my life been different I would have done anything I could to get to work for the Williamsburg foundation."

His eyes widened. "What do you know about Queen Anne?"

"Very sad woman. On the throne for a mere nine years, pregnant and drunk the entire time."

"Uh, yes, well," Brad said, blinking at her. "Major in history, did we?"

Eden laughed, a bit embarrassed. "Not the Queen Anne you meant?"

"I meant the new subdivision. They named it Queen Anne after the creek, which of course was named after your drunken pregnant lady. They're building two hundred houses on Route 32 by the water. Very high end. Preserving the wetlands, that sort of thing."

"I haven't heard a word about it," she said, trying hard not to glance up at the window to see if McBride was still spying on them.

"It's mainly a retirement community for rich people. There'll be boutiques and lots of services, such as a hair salon and a spa. And there'll be a purchased doctor or two."

"A what?"

"You haven't heard of those? I don't know what they're actually called, but a family pays a doctor a retainer, usually something like twenty grand a year, and for that they get personal service, such as house calls and checkups. Mainly, they get a doctor who remembers their name from one visit to the next."

"For twenty grand, I'd think so," Eden said.

"The point is that the houses in Queen Anne look as eighteenth century as we can make them. And the gardens surrounding them won't just be a few nasty evergreens along the driveway and the house foundations. They'll be structured gardens. Rooms. You know what I mean. Pure Williamsburg. We think they'll appeal to our clients." He hesitated, looking at her hard. "Maybe you'd like to help plan the gardens. Professionally, I mean."

"Who is 'we'?"

Brad gave her a sheepish grin. "I'm one of the investors, but that's because I believe in this. Our young people are leaving Arundel because there are so few jobs here. These new houses will create a lot of jobs and will run a lot of money through the town. Did you know that six months ago one of our only two grocery stores closed? If we don't do something soon, Arundel could turn into a ghost town."

She could see the passion in his eyes. She'd had no idea that Arundel was in trouble. To her, the place had always been paradise. It was true that the mosquitoes and chiggers were enough to drive a person mad, but a little clear fingernail polish over the spots stopped the itching. To Eden's mind, the warm weather and rampant growth of the plants more than made up for whatever problems the bugs caused. And made up for the snakes that found their way into everything. And for the muskrats in the ditches. And for the raccoons that ate anything you put in a decorative pond.

"Is that look a yes or a no?"

"It's an 'I don't know.' I never thought of designing gardens for a living. I didn't plan this one. I just followed the original design."

"Ha!" Brad said. "I know what you did and how you adjusted that plan to the modern world, and I know the way you studied the books Mrs. Farrington bought you. I even heard about the notebook of designs that you made. Most of all, I know how you loved doing it. Mrs. Farrington told me how you and Toddy were out here day after day, year after year."

Eden smiled at the memory. "Toddy was so old he remembered the eighteenth century. I just picked his brain."

Brad smiled at her so that his eyes crinkled at the corners. "You can't BS me. I was told the truth about you, remember? By the way, the books you accumulated on eighteenth-century gardening are in that big pine cabinet in Mrs. Farrington's bedroom. You must have every book ever published about eighteenth-century gardens."

For the first time since she'd arrived, Eden smiled—really smiled. It wasn't a polite little grin; it was a big wide smile that involved her entire face. She'd missed this in the years since she'd left Arundel. Someone who knew her. Someone who liked the same things she did. In the years since she'd been away, it seemed that all the men she'd met had wanted her for what she could give them. Their attitude toward Melissa had been one of tolerance. They were willing to put up with a child, but they hadn't really been interested in her. She'd been too quiet and withdrawn to interest them. In the end, it seemed that it always came down to having to choose between her daughter and some man. Eden had never hesitated in choosing her daughter.

But now, for the first time since she was a teenager, Eden was alone—free, actually. It was difficult for her to remember a time when she wasn't someone's mother. When she was still a teenager, she'd seen kids her age jumping into convertibles as they ran off to spend the day at the beach. Sometimes she'd been nearly overwhelmed with envy. Never in her life had she spent an entire day at the beach. Her parents hadn't believed in such frivolity, then she'd had the responsibility of a daughter. As for packing up Melissa and going by herself, that wasn't something that Eden could quite manage to do.

What she had done was throw herself into gardening. She'd spent her days in the garden, with Melissa never far away from her. Often, Mrs. Farrington had joined them, not to work (she couldn't contemplate using a hoe) but to sit under a tree in a pretty wrought-iron chair and read things like the Declaration of Independence (which one of her ancestors had signed) to Melissa, Eden, and Toddy.

Now, Brad was bringing back to Eden the memories of those wonderful days so vividly that she, well, she was feeling as though she was waking up. Design gardens? For a living? Get paid for doing something that she loved to do? When she'd put herself through college, it had been a small community college, and the choices of study had been limited. Garden design had not been offered. She'd taken courses that she thought would help her get a job as a teacher or in museum work or publishing. "Design gardens?" she said at last.

"Yes, something like what's at the Belltower House."

At that Eden's eyes widened. "The Belltower House," she said under her breath. It was one of the most beautiful houses ever built in the United States in the eighteenth century. In the 1950s it had been derelict but had been rescued by the local townspeople and restored beautifully. There had been a gasoline station in front of it, but that was torn down and in its place was put a reproduction of an eighteenth-century garden. No modern plants were allowed. It was gorgeous and accurate.

"The people we're aiming at with these houses are retired D.C. people. Power, brains, been everywhere and seen everything. We think that the historical aspect of the houses will appeal to them, and we thought that making the gardens look as historically accurate as the houses would also appeal to them. Of course the landscape company that's been formed by some of the local kids would put in the gardens and later maintain them, so you wouldn't have to do the digging."

"Local kids?"

"Okay, so they're adults and they're Drakes, Mintons, and one Granville by marriage, namely my daughter's worthless husband, but I think they can do the job. Maybe you could manage them. They all need direction."

She blinked at him. "If I'm understanding this clearly, you're asking me to take over a landscaping company that has a contract, more or less, for two hundred houses."

"That's about it."

She narrowed her eyes at him. "Did you just come up with this idea or did you develop it a while ago?"

His face lost its humor. "If you're asking me if I've been wining and dining you in an attempt to get you to help with my new subdivision, the answer is no. But I'll be honest with you: I am desperate for help. When you met my daughter, was she smiling?"

"No."

"Her life is a mess right now. She married some big, good-looking kid from Louisiana in her last year of college and got pregnant right away. Actually, I think she was pregnant before, but that's neither here nor there. She came home, and I saw right away that as soon as he saw the Granville house he planned to sit down and do nothing for the rest of his life. I gave him many lectures about how we all have to work for what we've managed to keep over the centuries, but nothing registered with him. He said that in Louisiana he helped his father do some landscaping. Between you and me I think he probably dug ditches. Anyway, at Camden's crying requests I talked my partners into letting this moron become involved in the landscaping. He went out and hired the blackest of the black sheep in this town to work for him, and now he expects *me* to buy him half a million dollars' worth of equipment and turn him loose on the gardens of all the houses. He doesn't know a daisy from a liatris, so how can he put in gardens that look like something Thomas Jefferson might have enjoyed?"

Brad put his hand over his eyes. "I tell you I'm caught in a three-way vise. I have my investors threatening me if Remi messes up. I have my daughter, who expects me to perform a miracle and make her talentless husband into a great businessman, and I have this kid telling me he can't do anything until I buy him half of John Deere."

Eden crossed her arms over her chest. "And just this minute you came up with the idea of turning this entire mess over to *me* and getting *me* to straighten it out?"

Brad grinned at her. "Actually, that's completely accurate. One hundred percent right on. I think you must be a mind reader."

In spite of herself, Eden laughed, and her body relaxed. "Your son-in-law is from Louisiana? Does he have one of 'those' accents?"

"Sometimes I can hardly understand him. You wouldn't *really* consider doing this, would you?" There was hope in his voice, but also a belief that it would never happen.

"Let me think about it. You say the books are in my bedroom?"

"With your notebooks. Do you think you could make up your mind by, say, ten o'clock tomorrow?"

"What happens at ten?"

"I'm to meet Remi at the John Deere dealer."

Again, Eden laughed. Family, she thought. All the problems of family. When she left Melissa and Stuart and the baby Melissa was about to have, Eden had thought she was saying good-bye to family. But here was an invitation to plunge into a family complete with squabbles and real problems. In this case, though, it looked a bit like diving headfirst into a swimming pool that she knew was empty.

"Is the John Deere dealer still on Berkshire?"

"Hasn't moved since 1954."

"I'll meet you there at ten tomorrow and talk to your son-in-law."

Brad grabbed both her hands in his. "I so appreciate this. You don't know…" He stopped and smiled at her. "I'm not yet sure, but I think maybe everything Mrs. Farrington said about you was right." He said the last very softly, and he had that unmistakable look on his face: he was about to kiss her.

As he bent his head toward her, Eden stepped back and the moment was lost. When he kissed her for the first time, she wanted it to be from passion, not gratitude. She took her hands from his. "You better go. I'll need to go through my books tonight and see…See what a fool I am if I even consider this."

"Yeah, okay," he said, stepping back. He took his car keys out of his pocket. "Tomorrow." He seemed to want to say more, but instead he turned and walked away. He looked back once and waved, then she heard his car start and saw the taillights as he drove down the driveway.

Standing alone in the moonlit garden, Eden shivered. Moments ago, it had seemed very warm, but now she was cold. Hurriedly, she ran up the stairs and back into the house.

It was utterly quiet inside, but she could feel the presence of another human being. McBride. Right now all she wanted to do was take a shower and settle down with her gardening books and think hard about Brad's offer of a job. Could she do it? It had been years since she'd even read a gardening book. Could she remember all that she'd learned? Had she even learned enough to be able to design gardens from scratch? Plant heights, pH levels, bloom time, pruning—they all had to be considered. And then there was the entire eighteenth-century philosophy of design. They were complicated gardens. And would she be able to get along with Brad's son-in-law, Remi? She'd never been able to get along with her own son-in-law, so how could she think of taking on someone else's?

She made herself a cup of tea and finished cleaning the kitchen while her thoughts tumbled on top of one another. When at last she was ready to go upstairs, she thought about staying downstairs and sleeping on the couch. Upstairs was Mr. McBride and the confrontation she wanted to avoid. When she'd moved him into her house she had good reasons, but right now she couldn't remember one of them. Had she really wanted protection from Brad? She smiled at that idea. She was beginning to think that being protected from Mr. Braddon Norfleet Granville was the last thing she wanted.

She stopped at the foot of the stairs and took a deep breath. Firm, she told herself. She had to be firm.

Chapter Six

Eden flung open Jared McBride's bedroom door. She didn't care if she caught him in the nude. On the way up the stairs, she'd put strength in her spine, and she wasn't going to waver in her resolve. "Mr. McBride," she said, with her mouth in a hard line, "I want you out of my house now. This minute."

He was sitting on his bed, his arm in the sling on top of the covers, the scratch on his cheek clearly visible. His blackened eye seemed to have grown bigger and darker in the last few hours. If she hadn't known differently, she would have thought he'd used makeup on it.

"Yes, of course," he said, then with grimaces of

pain, he moved the cover off his legs and slowly got out of bed. "So you think Granville is all right, then?"

"Of course he's all right!" she snapped. "Contrary to what you're insinuating, I don't hurt people who come to my house by invitation."

He paused, his bare feet on the floor, his sweatpants pulled up to his calf. He had a bandage around his right ankle, and she could see what was clearly the oval pattern of teeth marks on his ankle.

"I meant that you feel sure that there's no danger he'll hurt you," he said softly. "Sorry for spying on you, but it's the habit of an old policeman. Protection. I knew you didn't know Granville and he was here alone with you, so I was concerned. You're a beautiful woman and you wouldn't believe the things that I've seen men get up to when they're alone with a beautiful woman."

She knew he was lying; she could feel it in her bones. But no matter what was coming out of his mouth, his wounds were real—and they had been caused by her. As he stood up, the bite on his foot oozed blood. Closing her eyes for a moment, she tried to give herself strength, but it didn't work. "All right. Get back in bed. You can stay here tonight."

"No," he said tiredly. "You're right. I should get back to my own house. It's not right that a man should stay here alone with an unmarried woman."

At that she sat down on the chair by the wall. "Tell me, Mr. McBride, do you lie to everyone or is there something about me that brings out the worst in you?"

"I have no idea what you mean," he said as he hobbled toward the old dresser. She hadn't really looked at this room since the house had become hers, but she saw that Mrs. Farrington's son hadn't taken all the good pieces. The chest was pine and looked country, but she knew it was worth a lot of money. For a moment she could see Mrs. Farrington's smile. She'd managed to save some good pieces from the greed of her son, and Eden wondered what else was in the house.

But first she had to deal with the nuisance of McBride. "I would like to know the truth about what you're doing here in Arundel. Are you one of those treasure seekers? Are you looking for those lost jewels?"

"Sorry, but I don't know what you mean." He was on one foot now, hopping to the chair by the bed where his shoes and socks were.

"You're no more a fisherman or a hunter than I am. Everything in your house is brand-new, as though you don't want anyone to know who you are or where you came from."

"House fire. Burned everything," he said quickly, and Eden was sure he was smiling.

"The night I saw you in this house you were snooping around. You weren't looking for a fuse box. You were looking for something else. I called the electric company and they said that my lights are not on the same circuit as yours."

"It was a mistake. I thought they were together." He was sitting on the chair, his hands folded on his lap, and he was looking at her expectantly.

He's enjoying this, she thought. Cat and mouse. But who was the cat and who was the mouse? "Where's your table saw? I looked in your garage, and there's nothing in there but a pickup truck. Brand-new. No table saw."

"Power handsaw. The deputy must have mis-understood. The circular saw is under the work-bench."

"Shall we go look?"

Ostentatiously, as though in enormous pain, he stood up, using the chair as support. "Yes, of course. Let's go look now."

Eden threw up her hands in surrender. "Get back in bed," she ordered. She knew she was being a wimp, knew that he was exaggerating his pain, but his foot was bleeding, courtesy of her teeth. "I guess you're hungry," she said in disgust.

"No, ma'am, I can do without food," he said meekly as he hobbled to the bed. "But I will take you up on your offer of hospitality for another night, and I promise that I'll leave tomorrow."

"Good," she said, and she left the room.

Eden wanted to kick herself. The man had the ability to make her forget all that she'd planned to say to him. She went downstairs to the kitchen, got the soup out of the refrigerator, and heated a bowl of it. She put leftover salad into another bowl, poured a big glass of sweet tea, then also poured him a glass of wine. He was probably taking pain medications so the wine would knock him out. At least she'd have one night without his snooping.

She carried the tray up to him, cursing herself

every step of the way. He was back in bed, his head lolling around as though he were at death's door. She put the tray on the end of the bed and turned to leave.

"Did you have a nice night?"

"No thanks to you," she spat at him. Then, in spite of her best intentions, she turned on him. "How could you spy on us like that? Who do you think you are that you can snoop around my house with a flashlight, then lie to the police so that they believe every word you say? Do you know that they made fun of me? I come home to find a strange man in my house, I defend myself, yet *I* am made a laughingstock in this small town. I will never be able to live this down. Do you know what my life is going to be like because of you? I can't understand why they believed *you* and not *me*."

When he said nothing, she made her hands into fists and turned to leave the room.

"FBI," he said, his mouth full.

She stopped where she was, then slowly turned back to him. "What?"

"I'm FBI. The sheriff knows that. If he hadn't been told who I was, I'd have been thrown in jail until I rotted. People around here like you, something about your being 'one of them.' I hope that doesn't mean you're part of some cult that we'll eventually have to clean out. We lose too many men in those raids."

Eden was standing in the doorway, her mouth open, her eyes wide, too stunned to move.

"Your sheriff told me what he thought of me

before he put out the story that I was a great hero and that you were a dingbat Yankee. Do I have that right? It seems that down here being a Yankee is worse than being a serial killer. Certainly worse than being an FBI agent working on a case. I think that if it had been up to your sheriff he would have put a few bullet holes in me to add to the bite wounds. You better sit down before you faint. Here." He held up the glass of wine. "I think you need this. I can't drink this with those pills the doctor gave me or I'll pass out. Or was that your intention?" He took another slurp of soup and stopped talking.

Eyes wide, Eden walked across the room and took the wine from him, drinking it in one long chug. When she'd finished, she sat down on the end of his bed. "Why would the FBI be interested in me? There are no jewels."

He gestured with a piece of French bread. "I don't know anything about any jewels, but it sounds like a good story. Maybe you'll tell me about it sometime. If you can get away from lover boy, that is. How long have you known Granville?"

"None of your business," she said, looking at him. The wine was giving her courage. "I want to know why you're here and what you want."

"Do you know a man named Roger Applegate?"

"No."

"Sure?"

"Yes. If you don't tell me what's going on, I'm going to call the sheriff and tell him you're a liar."

Jared grinned. "He already knows that, but

you're right in that he'd love to have something to bring me in on. If he'd had his way he would have turned me over to the mob. If there'd been a mob, that is."

She glared at him.

He smiled at her. "So who is Granville?"

"Not that it's any of your business, but he's my lawyer—which I'm sure you know. Why are you here? What were you looking for in my house?"

"I don't know." He took another bite, then took an infuriatingly long time chewing it. "I've been in this bed for many hours now and I've had a lot of time to think. I didn't want this assignment, but my boss said I was the only one who could do it."

"Do what? What *is* your assignment?"

"To seduce you into telling me what you know."

"What?" Eden asked, aghast. "Seduce me?"

"Not necessarily seduce as you mean, just sweet-talk you, that sort of thing."

"To find out what I know," she said quietly. "Know about what?"

"That's just it, we have no idea. And, you know what, I don't think you do either. In the last hours I've had time to think and to listen. Yes, I sneaked down the stairs—at great pain, I might add—and I listened to every word that lover boy said to you. He's besotted, isn't he? But then I can understand him. Under different circumstances—" He looked her up and down until she glared at him. Smiling, he looked back at his soup.

"Anyway, after much thought, I decided that you didn't know anything and that what with your having a boyfriend, I wasn't going to be able to do this the way the boss wanted me to. I don't think I'm your type. Even when my face isn't black and blue, I don't think I'm your type. I think you like, well, boring men, like Granville."

"If that's supposed to make me tell you that I don't like men like Brad Granville and that I really like lying, snooping, creeping prevaricators like you, then it won't work."

Jared grinned at her and put his empty tray on the chair by the bed. "I've been watching you, Ms. Palmer, and I decided that you were going to be too difficult for me to put on an act of being the kind of man you liked just so I could find out about Applegate."

"Who is this man Applegate?" Eden asked, exasperated. She wanted this all to be a dream. Tonight she'd been offered what could be a wonderful job, something that would turn her life around in a way that she'd never imagined, but now she was being told that the FBI wanted something from her.

"He's a spy. Hand me my wallet, would you?" He motioned to the dresser.

Eden got up, got the wallet, handed it to him, then sat back down on the end of the bed. The way she was feeling she might faint, and she didn't want to fall out of a chair onto the hard floor.

He handed her a photo and pointed to one of three men. The man was frowning, as though he didn't want his photo taken. "Have you ever seen him before?"

She studied the picture. "No, at least not for

any length of time. I can't say that I never saw him on an elevator or working for someone or walking through my publishing house. But I've never known him in a way that would make me remember him." She handed the photo back to him, and he carefully put it in his wallet, then put the wallet on the chair.

He fluffed his pillows, leaned back against them, and put his arms behind his head. "That's what I thought, and I think you're telling the truth."

"Why would I lie? What does this man, this spy, have to do with *me*?"

"When he knew he was about to be caught, he ate a piece of paper with your name on it. We found it in his stomach after he was dead."

At that Eden stood up. She was going to her own bedroom and in the morning she would laugh about this. It had all been a hilarious dream.

Jared caught her arm and pulled her back to the bed, where she sat on the edge of it, facing straight ahead, her eyes glazed.

"Why?" she whispered.

"That's what we want to know. As you can imagine, you've been pretty thoroughly investigated, but we could find nothing in your past or your current life that would link you to a spy of Applegate's caliber."

She looked at him. "I was investigated by the FBI? And you found nothing? Am I supposed to be grateful for that?"

"Look, I know this is a shock to you, but I took a big chance when I told you about this. My telling you is a gesture of respect, actually. My boss wanted me to make you fall in love with me, then I was to try to get you to talk and tell me what you know. But I've read every word about you, and I've spent a whole day listening to you and watching you, and I've come to the conclusion that you don't know anything. Or don't know that you know it, that is. After much contemplation about this, I decided that I should just tell you what was going on and ask you to try to figure out what you know."

"Respect?" Eden whispered. "Respect? You have respect for me? You've snooped and spied on me, and you've pretended to be much more injured than you are so I'd feel sorry for you. Where's the respect in all that?"

"It worked, didn't it?" Jared said with a one-sided grin. "I'm here, aren't I?"

"No, it didn't work." She stood up. "I don't know anything about a spy, and I don't know anything that would cause a spy to know about me. Did it ever occur to any of you that I was an editor at a major publishing house? Maybe the man wanted to write a book and he was given my name as someone to send his manuscript to. Maybe a book editor is nothing in your world, but I can assure you that to a person who wants a book published we are only just below God."

He looked at her in surprise. "As far as I know, no one ever thought of that. It's a strong possibility." He smiled at her, but she didn't relent. "Look, Ms. Palmer, I didn't want this job. I pleaded with my boss to not assign me this. I said I'd rather deal with drug addicts and the underworld than with a church-going woman. 'Deliver me!' I told him."

With every word the man spoke, Eden's nails cut deeper into her palms. "Are you trying to make me feel *better*?"

"Not doing a good job of it, am I?" he said, obviously trying for humor.

"No, you're not doing well at it at all. I'm going to my own room now, Mr. McBride, and I want you to leave my house in the morning. In fact, I want you to vacate *your* house and leave Arundel. I don't know anything about a spy and I don't know anything that he'd want to know. My guess is that he believed that idiot jewel story and that's what he was after. I don't think that people spy for love of their own country. I think they do it for money, so the Farrington jewels would have appealed to a man like him."

"I have no idea what you're talking about."

"So much for the thoroughness of FBI research," Eden muttered as she glanced down at the bedside table. On the bottom shelf were several old paperbacks. Bending, she withdrew one and tossed it onto his lap. *Missing Treasures* was the title. "Since you're a big-shot FBI man, I'll tell you a little secret that not even the people of the other families in Arundel know. Mrs. Farrington's ancestor sold the jewels to pay his debts so he could keep this house. To save his pride, he spread the rumor that the jewels were stolen. The story is a myth. Now, Mr. McBride, I'm going to my own room to do some research for a new job. Tomorrow, I want you to leave. If you're not out of Arundel by six P.M., I'm going to the sheriff. I know the man. He used to play with my daughter when she was a baby. He'll listen to me. Have I made myself clear?"

"Completely," Jared said lightly. He was looking at the back of the book, which told about treasures that were missing around the United States, one of which was the Farrington sapphire necklace.

"I'll call my boss and I'll be out of here in the morning. No problem." He looked back at her. "See you in the morning."

~

When Eden got to her bedroom, she wanted to block out all that McBride had told her. How could such a lovely evening have turned so sour? FBI, indeed, she thought. Was she supposed to believe him? He had lied about everything else, so why was she expected to believe him now?

Obviously, the man was insane. That was the only explanation for what he'd told her. She was supposed to have been involved with a spy. When? was the first thing that came to her mind. When you're a single mother, you're father, mother, breadwinner. You're everything to one or more children. There had been days when Eden had craved a mere fifteen minutes of time alone, but she couldn't get it. She'd always had work to do, either the kind that earned money, or housework, or baby work. She'd always felt guilty that she hadn't been able to play with Melissa as much as she would have liked, but she'd never had enough energy or time.

Yet here was some man saying that he thought she'd somehow, some way, at some time, become involved with a spy. Too, too ridiculous.

She tried to clear her mind of McBride and was glad that he was going to leave her house and the town tomorrow. She went to the pine cabinet in the corner of the bedroom. That she hadn't even opened the cabinet reminded her that she needed to do a thorough exploration of the house and the attic. What was left and what was missing? Inside the cabinet were about half of the books that Mrs. Farrington had bought for her.

Smiling, Eden took out a book on Thomas Jefferson's gardening records. Opening it, she saw her notes in the margins. It seemed so long ago now. When she last held this book, Melissa had been a baby, and she'd spent most of the summer outside in the gardens. Only in inclement weather had she worked on cataloging. During the winters and the hottest summer days, she'd stayed inside and studied the history of the Farrington family.

She put the book back on the shelf and withdrew another one. It was a children's book about what it was like to live in the "Big House." She couldn't help herself as she sat down hard on the end of the bed and ran her hand over the book. How quickly children grew up! It seemed only days ago that she'd bought this book for her daughter. They'd read it together several times before that night when they'd had to run away and leave everything behind.

Eden looked at the old room, at the restored molding around the ceiling, at the fireplace surround that had been stripped of layers of paint, then perfectly repainted a classic off-white. Tears came to her eyes. Brad said that Mrs. Farrington had sold a valuable piece of family silver so she could have the house renovated for Eden. The love that went into that action made the tears run down her cheeks. Mrs. Farrington had not deserved the life she'd had. She deserved children who loved her and cared for her in her old age. Instead, she'd turned to strangers.

Wiping away her tears, Eden put the book back in the cabinet, glanced at the other titles, and wondered where the rest of the books were. Mrs. Farrington had purchased every book she thought Eden might possibly need. It had never been said, but Eden was sure that Mrs. Farrington's dream was for Eden to someday be the head of the Arundel Historical Society. To the outside world, it meant nothing, but to the people of Arundel, it was a job of high prestige. To be elected to it by members of the founding families, a person had to show extensive knowledge of restoration techniques and the history of the town. Historical gardening was part of that required knowledge. Eden remembered her one and only visit to Williamsburg, paid for by Mrs. Farrington. While Eden was away, Mrs. Farrington had hired three young girls to babysit Melissa (Mrs. Farrington was terrified that she'd be left alone with the child), all so Eden could go to a gardening symposium on eighteenth-century techniques. When she wasn't in class, she wandered about the old town and drank in the beauty of the buildings and the gardens.

Yawning, Eden closed the doors to the cabinet. "But then I was actually spying on my country," she muttered.

She was suddenly very sleepy, so sleepy that she could hardly make it to the bathroom to put on her nightgown. Ten minutes later, she was asleep in the bed that had once belonged to generations of Farringtons.

Chapter Seven

"Bill, calm down," Jared said into his cell phone. "Stop yelling so loud. She'll hear you. Yes, I did give her something to make her sleep. Poor thing, this has hit her hard. No, I'm not going soft on you." He listened for a moment. "If you'll calm down, I'll tell you why I told her who I am and what I want. Are you ready to listen?"

Jared took a deep breath. "Something is going on around here, but I can't figure out what it is. Some lawyer is acting like Ms. Palmer is the love of his life, but she only met him a couple of days ago. I don't trust him. Something isn't right. I think he wants something and he's planning to get it. But she's falling for him hook, line, and sinker.

She seems to believe every word out of his mouth. He even told her some cock-and-bull story about being unfaithful to his ex-wife while the woman was dying of cancer, and she swallowed it. It was all I could do to not step in and tell her a few home truths."

Pausing, he listened. "Yeah, I guess he could be on the up-and-up, but I doubt it. The point is that I saw that *I* didn't have a chance with her. She isn't what I thought she was going to be. She isn't some desperate, lonely woman who swoons every time a man makes a move toward her." He hesitated. "She's more of a no-nonsense type of woman, so I took the chance of telling her the truth. Besides, she'd already figured out that nearly everything I'd said or done was a lie. She should have worked for us."

Jared rolled his eyes and listened. "No, I'm not falling for her. It's just that I made a judgment call and decided that the best thing to do was to tell her who I am, what I want, and see if she can help figure out why Applegate swallowed her name and Social Security number. By the way, I want you to see if Applegate was writing a book, maybe a tell-all about his life undercover. Maybe he just wanted her as his editor." Jared smiled at the phone. "Yeah, she came up with that idea. She's not dumb. Look, I didn't call you to get yelled at. I need you to send someone here to do something for me. Ms. Palmer is a bit upset with me, so she's told me to get out of her house, to get out of town, actually. What I need is for you to send a man down here and maybe fire a few shots so she'll realize this is serious. No," Jared said patiently, "not at anyone, just fire a few shots around. I need to have a reason to stay near her. If she thinks she's in danger, she'll be more receptive to my hanging around her as a bodyguard, so to speak."

Jared listened, grimacing. "Yes, I know this is supposed to be an undercover assignment, and I know you think I shouldn't have told her anything, but I did. Now I want you to send a man out here right away. Put him in a car tonight. She's to meet Granville tomorrow at ten A.M., but I want her to miss that meeting. He's getting too close too fast, and I don't like it at all. Look, I gotta go. I put this red concoction on the cuts on my feet and it's burning. I have to take a shower, and I need to get a couple of hours sleep so I'll be ready for this man. Send somebody good, understand? I don't want any cock-ups. I'll call you tomorrow and let you know how everything went. Oh, and, Bill, thanks for doing this."

Smiling, Jared hung up the phone, turned it off so it wouldn't ring, then hid it under the bedsprings. Throwing back the covers, he got out of bed and pulled the sling off his arm. In the hospital they'd asked him if he thought he needed a sling, and he'd moaned that he did. Now he flexed his arm, made a fist of his hand, then dropped to the floor and did half a dozen one-arm push-ups. The arm was okay, but he was disgusted that so few push-ups could make him feel so sore.

He pulled off his clothes, dropped them on

the floor, then picked them up and put them on the chair by the bed. In the shower, he let the hot water run over him and wash away all the "wounds" that he'd colored his body with. He'd wanted Eden to think that he was bleeding and in pain. He hoped she didn't miss the red nail polish he'd taken from her bedroom. That, mixed with a little of her cocoa butter cream and some nail polish remover, had made a reddish mess that was burning his scabbed cuts.

He soaped himself and thought about how angry Bill had been when Jared told him that he'd told Eden the truth. But she'd made Jared feel like he had in the third grade when his teacher wouldn't believe a word he'd said. Other teachers had believed him. He'd made up elaborate stories about why he was late or where he'd been, and they'd all believed him. But not Mrs. Lancaster. She'd looked him in the eye and told him he had to write lines as punishment for lying.

Eden was like Mrs. Lancaster. She didn't believe him either. Clever girl! he thought. She'd seen that his clothes were too new, that there was no table saw in his garage, and she'd called the electric company about the houses being on the same circuit. If she knew he was a liar, how was he supposed to make her like him so much that she revealed secrets to him? And with Granville around, how could Jared get close to the woman as quickly as possible?

While he'd stood outside the dining room listening to her and Granville talk, Jared had thought about telling Eden the truth. No lying, just the facts of the case. He'd present it to her as a problem and let her help solve it.

As he'd hobbled up the stairs, he told himself that wouldn't work. If she was told about a spy, she'd throw him out, and he'd never find out anything. No, he thought, he'd better not do that. But then, he'd stood at the window and watched her and Granville in the moonlit garden, and he'd felt something that was rare for him: jealousy. Granville was older than Jared, not in as good shape, and had a boring office job, but it looked as though "the girl" was falling for *him.*

Jared had turned away from the window in disgust at himself for having such juvenile thoughts. This was a job, he told himself. It was the same as other jobs. But somehow it was already different. For one thing, he'd never before worked in a middle-class home situation. Gangsters, thugs, drug lords, the underworld had all been in his working life, but not this. This was a nice house, a nice woman, and a nice town—and they made thoughts of retirement and having a normal life come into his mind.

By the time Eden came up the stairs after Granville left, Jared was prepared for her. He had no doubt that she was going to tell him to get out, so he'd made his wounds look as though they were bleeding. She couldn't throw out someone dripping blood, could she?

She hadn't surprised him when she'd told him that she knew that everything he'd told her was a

lie. But he was surprised when, even knowing
that, she'd gone downstairs and made him a tray
of food. It was while she was downstairs that he
made the final decision to tell her the truth. He
was aware that part of him was hoping she'd be
so interested in what he told her that she'd spend
more time with him. But she told him to leave.
He was going to have to resort to other methods to
get close enough to her to find out what she knew.
By the time he got back into bed, he was smiling
again. When he'd first surveyed the place, before
Eden had arrived, he'd seen a cellar beneath the
house. It looked old enough to have petroglyphs on
the walls, and he didn't relish spending any time
down there, but it would do as a hideout for a few
hours. Still smiling, he went to sleep.

Chapter Eight

Eden awoke to the horror of someone's hand pressed firmly over her mouth. Her first impulse was to lash out, but a face and a warm breath were near her ear. "It's me, and please don't hurt me again," came the unmistakable voice of Jared McBride. "I'm still bleeding from the last time. There are people downstairs. If I take my hand away, will you be quiet?"

Eyes wide, Eden nodded. It was too dark to see his face, but McBride's tone of voice told her this wasn't serious. She first thought, What is he up to now? Slowly, he moved his hand away from her mouth, as though he didn't want to move. He was very close to her, leaning over her so that he was practically in bed with her. She rolled away from him and reached for the telephone by her bed, but Jared stopped her. Silently, he pointed to the cell phone in a case on his belt, letting her know it would be better to use that. He motioned to the door, gesturing that they should get out as soon as possible. As far as she could tell, he meant for her to leave the room as she was, which meant running off with this man who she didn't trust while wearing only her nightgown. She was glad that she'd been in too much of a hurry to put her clothes away the night before when she'd dressed to meet Brad. Draped across the end of the bed were her jeans, a sweater, and a T-shirt. She stuck her feet into her running shoes as she grabbed her clothes, then tiptoed out of the room behind McBride.

Since Eden had seen or heard nothing and had only McBride's word that anyone was in the house, Eden couldn't feel very cautious. In fact, she felt nothing but annoyance. What time was it anyway? She was glad to see that last night she'd been too tired to remove her watch. The house was dark, but the watch had a little button on the side that she pushed, and it lit up the dial. Ten minutes until five A.M.

McBride was crouching down like a character in an Xbox game and moving stealthily along the chair rail. Eden gave a yawn, then a shiver. Her nightgown had been fine under the covers, but now she was getting cold. She hugged her clothes to her and thought about stopping to put them on.

"Are you sure—?" she began, but McBride cut

her off. In an instant, he had grabbed her and put his hand over her mouth to keep her from talking. What she wanted to say was a very sarcastic "I see that you recovered well." But she said nothing. Last night she'd seen that the wounds she'd given him were bleeding. And he'd held his arm that was still in a sling as though it hurt him very much. She'd felt so sorry for him that she'd been tempted to spoon-feed him again.

But right now, he had one arm around her waist and the other around her head with his hand over her mouth. So where was his sling? Why wasn't he limping? If he was lying about his injuries, just as he'd lied about everything else, then he was probably lying about someone being in her house. She lifted her foot with the intention of slamming it down on his instep. Her plan was to run for the phone while he held his foot in pain. She figured she could punch the buttons for 911 before he could get to her.

But in the next moment she heard whispered voices from downstairs and became rigid with fear. McBride was still holding her, but Eden was no longer fighting him. He said one quiet word: "Cellar."

She nodded, and he dropped his hand from her mouth. At the end of the wide corridor upstairs was a door to what looked like a closet. It was true that there were brooms and mops in there, but behind them was a little door that opened to reveal an old staircase that was so narrow it was dangerous. It had been the fate of the poor overworked servants in centuries past to have to use those stairs, rather than the wide stairs in the front of the house.

As Eden pushed aside the handles of half a dozen old mops and a vacuum cleaner that was probably in use in 1910, she felt anger run through her. McBride had searched her house enough that he knew about the stairs down to the kitchen, which led to the other staircase down into the old cellar. Even when she'd lived here before, the narrow stairs to the kitchen had not been used. And only Eden had used the cellar. Mrs. Farrington had been accidentally locked in the cellar when she was nine, so she'd refused to ever go down there again. She'd wanted to fill the thing up with sand. But it seemed that Snooping McBride knew where the cellar was.

There was no light in the narrow staircase, so Eden went first and felt her way along the wall. Behind her, she heard McBride readjust the mops and brooms, then carefully close the little door. Eden had to repress a yelp when her face ran into a thick cobweb, a cobweb that made her realize that if McBride had seen the old staircase, he hadn't been down it. Gingerly, she felt each step before putting her foot on it. She didn't know if the staircase had been restored or was still made of rotting wood, as it had been when she lived there.

At the bottom of the stairs, McBride touched her shoulder, letting her know that he wanted to go first into the kitchen. When she stepped back into the tiny space, of necessity his body pressed against hers. She held the clothes over her arm

tightly between them. Cautiously, he opened the
door. Eden was relieved that the hinges didn't
squeak.

McBride stepped out into the dark kitchen and
looked around. For a moment he disappeared from
sight, then he came back. Putting his finger to his
lips, he motioned for her to follow him.

When Eden stepped into the kitchen, she
gasped. Outside a security light shone through the
curtainless windows and showed her that her clean,
tidy kitchen had been ransacked. Doors and drawers were open, canisters of food had been overturned. Through the window in the kitchen door
she could see what looked to be a flashlight moving
about on the screened porch. To her right, through
the dining room, she could see the glare of another
flashlight, and she could hear things being moved.
There were at least two of them, and they were
quietly shifting things around. She heard what
sounded to be a sofa cushion hitting the floor.

Why aren't they afraid of waking me? she wondered. She glanced up at McBride to see that he
was frowning so hard the furrows between his eyebrows were an inch deep. He didn't like what was
going on, and she had an idea that if she weren't
with him he'd confront the people in her house. In
a gun battle? she wondered.

He pointed to the door that led into the pantry.
It was a small room between the dining room and
the kitchen. Inside was a trapdoor in the floor that
led down into the cellar. Rarely did people see that
trapdoor, as it was usually covered with boxes of

cans. But Eden hadn't bought enough food to fill the kitchen cabinets, much less the pantry. As she reached for the ring that was flush with the floor, McBride caught her hand. She looked at him and he shook his head no.

When he reached for a bottle of cooking oil, Eden nodded and took it from him. Feeling her way along the dark floor, she felt for the rusty old hinges, then uncapped the oil and poured it on the tired old metal. Setting the bottle down, she turned to him and nodded, then he picked up the ring and lifted the door into the cellar. He wanted to go first, but Eden pushed him away. She knew the stairs better than he did. There were ten of them, and they had been replaced just before she left—which meant that they were now "only" twenty-plus years old.

Taking a deep breath, she started down the stairs, cautiously putting her foot down before she applied her full weight. They held. When she reached the bottom, she turned to McBride, who was right behind her. He'd lowered the door above their heads.

Eden felt along the damp walls of soft old bricks and tried not to shiver when she touched the dirty shelves. When she'd lived there she'd kept the cellar clean because she'd used it for what it had been built for: storing produce from the garden. She'd wrapped up green tomatoes, apples, potatoes, and carrots, and had kept them in the cellar for months. And even though one wall looked as though it had been rebuilt, the room was full of the nests of insects and rodents. Bath, she thought. When I get out of this I want a long, hot bath.

Finally, she found what she was looking for: candles and matches. Because of the dampness of the cellar, the matches were always kept in a tight metal box. Now she hoped that they'd kept dry for all these years. Holding her breath, she opened the box, withdrew a little box of matches, pulled one out, then struck it. It burst into a very welcome flame, and Eden lit three fat white candles. By the time this was done, McBride had his cell phone open.

"I hope you'll forgive me if I don't call your sheriff," he whispered, looking at her in the candlelight. "I think *my* people should handle this one," he said.

Eden started to say something but didn't. Instead, she watched him. She had no way of knowing what was going on, but she knew that something was making him very angry. He wasn't frightened, and didn't seem to be looking for a way to get them out of the house, which she thought was odd. Instead, he was calling "his" people. All things considered, she decided that Jared McBride knew a great deal more about what was going on upstairs than he was telling her.

Just as she heard his phone ring on the other end, they heard footsteps above their heads. In an instant, he had closed his phone and Eden had extinguished the candles. She could see nothing in the darkness, but she felt McBride's strong arm as he pushed her into a corner of the room while he stood at the foot of the stairs. She heard quiet noises from him, as though he'd bent and picked up something from the floor. She wondered what it was. Something he could use for a weapon if the men came down the stairs?

She heard footsteps over their heads, and when she heard voices she listened so hard her ears hurt, but all she heard was that one of them said something about a "jolly good time." They're English, she thought.

When the men moved away, Eden felt the full thrust of her fear. Who were these people? What did they want? Were they just more aggressive jewelry hunters? Twice while she'd lived with Mrs. Farrington they'd awakened on Saturday mornings to find people digging in the gardens, looking for those blasted jewels. Both times Mrs. Farrington had fired a shotgun over their heads, and they'd run away cursing her.

But why would they be here now? she wondered. What always triggered the jewel hunters was the publication of a new book that included the story of the stolen necklace. But there'd been no new book published recently. There was the Internet, though, and the Farrington story was always there for treasure seekers to find.

When she heard the unmistakable sound of the lock on the door overhead being latched, Eden drew in her breath sharply. They were locked inside the cellar!

She looked across the blackness and tried to see McBride. Why wasn't he upset that they'd just been locked in a cellar? But she heard nothing from him. He was silent. Eden was sure that she heard laughter as the people upstairs moved away.

McBride said nothing until there was no sound from upstairs, then he opened his cell phone and pushed a few buttons. In the silence, Eden heard the ringing on the other end, but he put the phone to his ear so she couldn't hear what was said and by whom. "Come get us," he said into the phone. "Now. We're in a room off the kitchen. Look on the floor for a door. We're locked in."

He held the phone open so she could use the light from it to relight the candles, and when they were lit, she looked at him. He didn't seem as angry as he had been, but maybe he was good at concealing it. "Turn 'round," she said to him, and he turned to face the wall while Eden pulled on her jeans, T-shirt, and sweater. She wished she had socks, as her feet were cold.

"Someone should be here in about an hour," he said softly, his back to her, then he held out his phone. "You could call someone else if you want. The sheriff or Granville."

As she dressed, Eden thought about what he was saying. No, she didn't want to call either of them. For all that she'd known him for years, the sheriff had a big mouth, and that deputy of his, Clint, would be sure to tell everyone in town what had happened. "Found her locked inside with that guy she beat up," she could hear Clint saying. "If you ask me, there's somethin' goin' on with those two." No, Eden didn't want Brad to hear that.

"Okay," she said, "you can turn around."

Leaning against the wall, his long legs out before him, he crossed his arms over his chest. "You want to tell me what's going on?"

"I'm part of a spy ring, remember? I have information to give to the enemy, and they came to get it. By the way, who *is* the enemy now? It's not still Russia, is it?"

McBride seemed unperturbed by her sarcasm. He moved away from the wall and picked up a big quart jar full of pickled beets.

"I wouldn't eat them if I were you. They're over twenty years old, and they'll probably explode if you open them."

"Do you mean that *you* canned them?"

"Not exactly rocket science."

He said nothing, just kept looking at the jar in wonder. "I never met a woman who could make pickles. That is what they are, aren't they?"

Eden squinted at him. "Why do I get the impression that you're glad that the two of us are locked in here together? I can't imagine that you did it for some sex-thing, so what is it that you want?"

He kept looking at the jar of beets, but Eden could see a tiny smile play at the corners of his mouth. "I don't know who those men up there are. I heard them and I got you out. I knew about the cellar, but I didn't know about that skinny staircase. That thing is a danger! I almost got stuck twice."

She didn't stop staring at him or lose her train

of thought. He was just too relaxed about all this for her taste. "What do you want? And how can I believe that you didn't send those men into the house?" She had the satisfaction of seeing him blink rapidly three times.

"I truly believe that the information I want is inside your head, not hidden away inside your house, so why should I send ransackers?"

"Does that mean that you've already been through every inch of my house and know there's nothing to find?"

"More or less," he said, putting the jar back on the shelf and giving her a crooked grin. "But I didn't get to see all that I wanted to because I was attacked by a wildcat."

"I see that you recovered well enough. Where's your sling?"

He didn't answer but went to the side wall and pulled four boxes out onto the floor. They were boxes full of big canning jars, and when stacked on top of one another, they made uncomfortable seats. He took one and motioned to Eden to take the other. After she'd moved her two boxes to the opposite wall, far away from him, she sat down.

"I don't know any spy and I have no idea why your spy would be interested in me," she said in the tone of a person who knew that a long night was coming. She wasn't sure if he'd set this up or not, but she had her suspicions. It wouldn't surprise her to be told that help would arrive only after she'd told him what he wanted to know— which she'd do in an instant if she only knew what it was. "Did you check out whether or not he was writing a book?"

"We're looking into it now. Are you warm enough?" He listened for a moment but could hear nothing.

"It's silent down here," Eden said. "You can't hear anything except what's going on on top of you. If I was going to be down here for more than fifteen minutes I had to get someone to watch my daughter. I wouldn't be able to hear her clearly, even if she was just in the dining room. Maybe you should call again. Are you sure they're sending someone for us?"

He looked at his watch. "It's only been ten minutes. You have somewhere you need to be?"

"Since you've listened in on my every conversation, you know that I'm meeting Brad at ten."

"Brad? The lawyer? Braddon Granville? Who names their kid Braddon?"

"I have no intention of explaining Arundel baby-naming policies to you. If we make chitchat you're never going to find out what you want to know. If you have questions to ask me, then do it."

"I would if I knew where to start. I was hoping that if I showed you Applegate's photo you'd say, 'Oh, that's so and so,' and the mystery would be solved. Are you sure you've never seen him before?"

"As I told you, I don't remember if I have seen him. I could have met him, yes, but then I'm an editor, so I meet thousands of people. When I go to writers' conferences I meet hundreds of people—

quickly. He could have been in one of those three-minute sessions where an author presents his ideas to me. I really don't remember him."

Jared looked at his shoe tips for a moment. "What you're saying makes sense, and maybe that's all this is about. Maybe the whole mystery is that Applegate was about to turn in a manuscript that told everything about everybody. You would have remembered a manuscript about a spy, wouldn't you?"

"Yes, and I would have turned it over to a non-fiction editor."

"Maybe you haven't come across the book yet." There was hope in Jared's voice.

"Maybe you should contact my publishing house and—" She broke off at a loud noise that came from upstairs.

Jared was on his feet in an instant, looking up at the ceiling of the cellar. In the next moment, they heard another noise, then silence.

Eden was standing beside him. "I hope they aren't destroying the house, and I really hope they didn't knock over the big secretary in the hall."

"Those were shots," he said, frowning. He ran up the stairs and tried the door. Locked. For a moment he looked as though he was studying the door, then he went back down. He opened his cell phone again and made another call. This time Eden realized that he was talking to a message machine. Again, he was calm, just saying that they were ready to get out.

"Nobody home?" she said, sitting back down.

"That gives me great confidence in the FBI. Aren't they supposed to always be on the alert? How come you don't have a firearm on you?"

"I figured you'd find it and use it on me," Jared said absently. He seemed to be thinking hard about something. "Is there any reason other than whatever the spy wanted you for that people would be ransacking your house?"

Eden gave a sigh. "Those blasted jewels!"

"Jewels?" Jared asked as he sat back down, then said, "Oh, yeah. In the book. You know, I didn't have time last night to read that, so why don't you tell me about it?"

"You don't think that spy was searching for those jewels, do you?"

"I have no idea. Could have been. We've always thought that maybe he swallowed your name to keep you from being thought to be part of his professional life." He leaned his head back against the damp wall. "So tell me about the jewels."

"How about if I tell you the *truth*?"

"I'd like that."

"I thought you would. It's been my experience that liars love to hear the truth from others."

Again, Jared gave a one-sided smile. "You have me pegged exactly. I took on this job of risking my life for my country just to have the opportunity to lie. It's what I live for."

Eden had to smile. "Okay, so maybe there is some truth in your story, but...Anyway, the jewels. You see, I'm cursed with knowing the truth through Mrs. Farrington, so I know there are no jewels to be found. How much do you want to know? From the beginning or just the facts, ma'am."

Jared looked at his watch again. "We have lots of time, so entertain me." He leaned his head back and closed his eyes. "Tell me every word of the story. Maybe there's something in there that could help me figure this thing out."

Eden couldn't resist saying "Once upon a time" and smiling. Except for genocide and murder and revenge, it was a great story. Or maybe because of those things it was a great story. She started to tell a cut-and-dried version about what had happened to the necklace, but then she thought, Why not tell all of it? She'd written the entire story in her fiction-alized version of the Farrington family, and she'd even told the truth, as revealed by Mrs. Farrington, of what happened at the end. She sincerely hoped that her telling of the family secret wouldn't cause any of the Farringtons to come back from the dead and haunt her.

"It was a necklace made for a French duchess," Eden began. "A stunningly beautiful necklace of three sapphires, each one the size of a quail's egg and surrounded by diamonds. It was said that the duchess's rich old husband bought the necklace for her, but she wore it—and nothing else—to bed with her lover. Her lover was the head gardener, and it was said that the son the old duke loved so much was actually the gardener's child."

Taking a breath, Eden leaned back against the wall. McBride still had his eyes closed, but she could tell that he was listening intently, and he was enjoying the story.

She continued. "A young Farrington son, on his Grand Tour, was traveling through the French countryside when the French Revolution broke out. By chance, he was staying in a small village on the very night when the villagers decided they'd had enough of the debauchery and greed of the old duke and were going to end it all. I don't know what the duke had done to make the villagers hate him so. There was something about a young boy in the village, but I don't know the details," Eden said. "And if Mrs. Farrington did, she didn't tell me, and I certainly didn't ask. I do know that they set the duke's great manor house on fire. As the villagers were celebrating his death, one of them paid a visit to the outhouse, and that's where he found the duke hiding.

"Of course they murdered the duke, then they went in search of his wife, who, I was told, was as bad as he was. But she had dressed as a peasant woman, so she escaped. She knew that a young, rich American man was staying in the village, so she went to him. Under her dirty clothes she was wearing all her jewels, which I was told were so many that she could hardly stand up under the weight of them.

"For all that the duchess was very beautiful and the young Farrington wasn't handsome at all, he was quite clever. The duchess offered him a pearl necklace if he'd get her out of the country, but he held out for the prize of her collection, the sapphire and diamond necklace. Since she was in no position to bargain, she agreed. He hid her under the seat of his carriage to get her to the coast, then he stowed her away in a trunk as they crossed the Channel. I can't imagine how horrible the trip must have been for the poor woman!

"When they reached England, she gave him the necklace, and they parted company. Unfortunately, no one knows what happened to the duchess after that, and since there's no record of her name, I couldn't research her. The young Farrington man went home to Arundel with the necklace sewn inside his coat. A few years later, when he got married, he had the necklace delivered to his bride an hour before the wedding, and that was the first time anyone in his family saw it.

"Mrs. Farrington told me that the necklace became what was most important in their family. They were called the Farrington Sapphires, and they would be taken out to be worn by the mistress of Farrington Manor only three times a year. People would come from miles around just to see them. The family developed traditions about who could wear the sapphires, and when. Each Farrington daughter could wear them on her wedding day, but only if the family approved of her husband. First cousins could wear the necklace once in her lifetime, but second cousins never. On and on it went. Mrs. Farrington said that it got to the point of being ludicrous, and many fights and long-standing feuds came about over that necklace.

"It stayed in the family until the late 1800s, and that's when the lies and the mystery began."

Pausing, Eden took a moment to get her breath. McBride was still listening intently. Smiling, she continued. "Mrs. Farrington told me that her great-grandfather, Minton, was a man cursed with bad luck. If he bought a racehorse, it broke a leg the next day. If he bought timberland, there would be a hurricane that turned all the trees into toothpicks. If he bought land for cotton, it would flood. Whatever the poor man planted, died. Mrs. Farrington said that if he'd just left things alone, he would have been fine financially, but he wanted to prove to his relatives that he could do as well as they had, so he tried to expand.

"I was told that the real reason he worked so hard to be a success was that he had a beautiful wife and that he was trying to win her love. But since he was as awkward and as socially inept as he was homely, he couldn't do it. It was said that she had married him for the Farrington Sapphires and that it broke his heart and his spirit because he knew that's what she truly loved.

"Now here's where the secret comes in. Because the poor man failed in everything, in the end he had to do the unthinkable and sell the necklace in order to pay the bills to keep Farrington Manor running. When he returned from the trip to New York, where he'd secretly sold the necklace, he found the safe open and empty, and his wife dead on the floor. She'd been strangled. That same day, a handsome young man who'd worked for the Farringtons for years—a notorious womanizer—was found dead in the swamp. Everyone said that he'd stolen the necklace, been interrupted by the wife, so he'd killed her, then he'd run off into the swamp, where he'd been bitten by a poisonous snake. When the necklace wasn't found on him, it was decided that he'd hidden it somewhere on the plantation, and that's how the story of the missing necklace got started. The story has been printed in a hundred books, and it's caused many years of problems with people searching for the Farrington Sapphires."

Jared opened his eyes and leaned forward. "The Farrington man either killed the wife or her lover or both."

"You've seen and done too many bad things," Eden said primly. "Unfortunately, though, you're right. On his deathbed, Minton Farrington told his eldest son the truth of what had happened. It seems that Minton had overheard his wife and her lover plotting to steal the necklace and run away together. Mrs. Farrington said that this was what made her great-grandfather want to get rid of the necklace. He decided that the sapphires were cursed and that his bad luck was caused by them, so he took the necklace to New York and sold it.

"When Minton returned to Farrington Manor, it was late at night, and there was his wife, dead on the library floor, the safe standing open and empty. He figured she'd been murdered by her lover when they discovered that the necklace was gone. Minton immediately got on a horse, took his two best hunting dogs, and went after her lover. He found the man the next day, hiding in a cabin in the swamp. Minton said he held a shotgun on the man and made him back up. What the man didn't see, but Minton did, was the big snake sunning itself on a rock. After his wife's lover was dead, Minton went back to Farrington Manor. By this time, his wife's body had been discovered, and in the confusion, people thought Minton was just returning from his trip, so the truth of what he'd done wasn't suspected.

"Minton never told anyone that he'd sold the jewels because he was afraid that people would figure out the truth about his wife. He'd rather it was said that she'd been killed during a robbery than that she'd been planning to run off with her lover. When the legend of the missing sapphires started, he didn't contradict it. In fact, he pretended to look for the necklace, even offering a reward.

"About six months after his wife's death, Minton met a plain-faced young woman who was said to adore him, and they got married and produced four healthy children. It was only on his deathbed that he told his eldest son the truth. The son told his eldest son, until it came down to Mrs. Farrington, who was an only child. As for Minton Farrington, he was glad he'd sold the necklace, because after it was gone, his luck changed. It seemed that everything he touched turned to gold, and when he died, the plantation was in the best shape that it had been in a century.

"And that's the end of the story," Eden said, rubbing her arms against the cold of the cellar. The candles were burning down, and she didn't see any more on the shelves. It wouldn't be long before they were in darkness.

"Great story," Jared said. "But I don't see any connection to Applegate. Jewels would be too hard to fence. He'd have to cut them."

"Pardon me, but I think you missed the point of the story. The jewels were sold, not stolen. By now they've been disassembled and sold to movie stars with big lips and artificial breasts. No one knows they were ever called the Farrington Sapphires, and certainly no one knows that they once belonged to an unfaithful French duchess."

"Hmmm," Jared said.

"And what is that supposed to mean?"

He put his elbows on his knees and looked at her. "It means that there are so many holes in that story that I don't know where to begin. Do you think that man overheard his wife and the gardener plotting to steal his family's pride and joy and run away together, and all he did was take the necklace to a pawnbroker? Do you want me to believe that he didn't want revenge? What was he planning to do when he got back from selling the necklace? Continue living with the woman? Give the gardener things to plant? You showed me that Minton was a man of revenge when you told me that he went after the gardener, held a gun on him, then watched him back into a deadly poisonous snake. You even said that 'after his wife's lover was dead' this Minton character went back to his house. What does that mean? That he stood there and watched the man die? If he did, don't you think he did it for his own enjoyment? And when Minton got back to his house he let people think that he'd just returned from his trip. Don't you think that there were men in the stables who knew that he'd jumped on a horse in the wee hours and gone off with a couple of dogs and a firearm or two? Did Minton bribe them or shoot them so they wouldn't tell his secret? I think your story tells the character of this man Minton very well. I think he killed both his wife and her lover. I think it's probable that the story of the trip to New York was just to give him an alibi, and I doubt if he went at all."

Eden sat there blinking at him. Every word he'd said made sense, but she'd never looked at the story as he was doing. "What about the jewels?"

"From your story, I agree that the first wife, the beautiful one, married the ugly man for the jewels. But then he probably married her for her beauty, so they had a bargain. I think what probably sent ol' Minton into a rage was that his wife broke their agreement. He knew she was having an affair. He was lord and master of the place, so he'd know what was going on. I think what sent him over the edge was that she thought she could leave him and take the jewels. That was a total breaking of their agreement. I think he strangled his adulterous wife, then killed her lover in a clever way, and wisely told the people the jewels had been stolen. With the jewels gone, a lot of the anger in the family was taken away, and he'd never again have to risk some woman marrying him for the sapphires. As for his bad luck, if he had a wife who hated him and was diddling the gardener, he was probably so stressed out that he couldn't make a decent decision. He took that accursed necklace out of the public's eye, found himself a faithful wife, had some kids, and he could think again, so his luck changed. That he committed two murders probably never bothered him any more than walking out of a bad land deal."

"Oh," Eden said, blinking. "Have you ever thought of writing? I think you could come up with some great plots."

"I've seen too much," he said. "I tend to think only the worst of people. They—" He broke off as he reached for his cell phone, which was vibrating. Opening the phone, he smiled. "Bill, where—" Jared paused. "Tell me that again slowly," he said, looking away from Eden. After a couple of minutes, Jared said, "Then who the hell are the men upstairs if they aren't ours?" As he said that, he glanced at Eden quickly. "Yeah, she's down here with me. Yeah, send some men. I think the guys upstairs are gone, but they knew this house well enough to know where the cellar door is, and they've locked us in. No, don't worry about it. I can shoot the lock off and get out." Again, he looked at Eden briefly. "Yeah, but go ahead and send them. Plainclothes. This town gossips about everything."

Closing the telephone, he looked at Eden as though preparing himself for a lecture.

She was calm. "Let me get this straight. I want my facts to be very clear. You staged all this just to get me alone so you could ask me what I know?

But then you've already asked me that and know that I know nothing. But still, you thought maybe I was lying, so you dragged me out of bed in my nightgown, and put on an elaborate charade about bad men being in the house. All the while you thought they were your own men—who *you* had arranged to be here—but now you've found out that the men up there really *are* bad guys. And, oh, yes, all along you've had a concealed weapon that you could have used to get us out of here."

Jared seemed to consider what she'd said. "You're pretty much right. But I hate to use firearms around civilians. Too often they panic and get in the way and get themselves shot."

"How considerate of you," Eden said nicely. "May I ask what the man on the telephone said?"

Jared ducked his head for a moment. "His son was hit in the head by a golf ball last night, so he's been in the hospital with his kid, and he forgot to send the men I requested. His son's doing fine, though."

"How nice. So who *are* the men who were tearing up my house?"

"I have no idea. You want to get out of here? It's getting a bit chilly. Besides, I'm hungry."

If there had been an instrument of destruction nearby, Eden would have used it on Jared McBride. As it was, all she could do was try to control her anger enough to keep herself from throwing jars of pickled beets at him. She took a deep, calming breath. "Mr. McBride, I would like for you to get me out of here this minute. I too am cold and hungry, and I have an appointment"—she looked at her watch—"in one hour and forty-six and a half minutes. I plan to make that appointment in spite of all that you're trying to do to stop me."

"You're still planning to meet with Granville?" he asked, but she didn't answer him.

Bending, Jared lifted his trouser leg and pulled a small pistol out of a holster strapped to his ankle. "Get in the corner and cover your ears," he said, and Eden did what he told her to. In the next minute, Jared shot the lock on the door in the ceiling, then pushed the door up. Eden shoved past him and into the pantry. She was so angry that she couldn't look at him.

Once she was in the kitchen, she blinked in the bright daylight and glanced around the room. The kitchen looked much worse in the daylight than it had at night. Someone had dumped out the freshly filled flour bin onto the floor, then walked in it. Flour was everywhere, including the countertops. It looked as though someone had climbed onto the counter and walked around. Eden looked up and saw that someone had cut a three-foot-square hole in the ceiling. So they could see into that part of the attic? she wondered.

Behind her she felt rather than saw or heard McBride. "Your agency is going to pay for this," she said through clenched teeth.

"Good luck on getting that," Jared said amiably, seeming to be unperturbed by what he saw. "Stay here," he said, then, with his gun drawn, headed toward the dining room.

Eden stormed past him, into the main hall, and nearly burst into tears. The big secretary was on its face, and the top ornamentation had broken off. She stood there for a few moments, fighting back tears, then she took off running to look at what had been done to the rest of the house. The living room was the biggest mess. The furniture had been overturned and the cushions on the couch cut. The pictures on the walls, painted by a Farrington ancestor who had no talent whatever, were in a heap by the fireplace. Had they been about to burn them? Why? To save their delicate sensibilities?

Jared came up behind her and put his gun away. There were no other people in the house and he knew it. When he put his hand on her shoulder, she jerked away from him and turned to go back into the hall. There was a powder room behind the main stairs. It had once been part of the master bedroom, but the big pecan tree outside had taken over the space. Rather than cut down the glorious tree, a Farrington had reduced the size of the bedroom so much that when the house had been plumbed, the room was made into a half bath. It was a smallish bedroom but an enormous powder room. In here, too, the ceiling had been cut and there were footprints on the counter of the sink.

"I'll get forensics in here," Jared said from behind her.

She whirled on him. "And what will they tell you? That some criminals did this to my house? That will be news, won't it?"

"I don't know why you're angry at *me*," he said

as he followed her out of the room. "These weren't *my* men."

"Not through any intent of yours!"

"That's true, I did try to..." He straightened his shoulders. "To keep you from throwing me out, I tried to make you see the seriousness of this situation. I didn't tell you this, but an agent was murdered here in Arundel just before you arrived."

At that she turned and looked back at him, her hands into fists, her eyes narrow with anger. "Now that's news! An FBI agent got killed. Isn't that what happens to you guys? Isn't the whole idea that you're supposed to fight trouble? So one of them was down here, in a small town, snooping around, no doubt asking a lot of questions about people's private business and he—"

"She."

"Oh," Eden said. "A woman."

"Go on. What were you going to say?"

"How did it happen?"

"Hit-and-run."

Eden gave a sigh. "A hit-and-run could have been an accident. She wasn't necessarily murdered." Her anger was returning. "And as for this today, did any of you think that those men were after *you*?"

He didn't answer her, and she didn't expect him to. She threw open the door to her bedroom and saw that it was exactly as she'd left it. Apparently, no one had been inside. The fact that no one had tried to find anything in her bedroom made her more sure that whoever had done this today had been after McBride, not her. With every minute that went by, she was more sure that his spy, this man Appleby or whatever his name was, had probably wanted her to publish his tell-all book, and, as McBride had said, maybe he'd not wanted the FBI to find out about it, so he'd tried to destroy Eden's name. Maybe he was afraid that the FBI would block the publication of his book. He, like everyone else who wrote, wanted that greatest of achievements: immortality, a book that lived forever.

Eden thought that after her meeting with Brad, she'd call her publishing house and see if any reader had read a book written by a man who'd been a spy. Or maybe he'd done what Eden had with the Farrington data and fictionalized his story. She glanced at the blue boxes stacked in the corner of her bedroom. Four of the manuscripts were by unknown authors. Eden was to read them and give a report. If the book was good, it would be given to an editor who had an in-house office to be read again, and perhaps published. If the book was no good, it would be sent back to the author with a polite thank-you. For all Eden knew—because she'd had no time to work—Applegate's book could be in that stack. Maybe the men who'd vandalized her house were looking for the manuscript but hadn't found it. But that made no sense, as the boxes were in plain sight.

Turning, she faced McBride. "As you can see, no one has searched my room. That's because they have no interest in me. If you look in *your* room, you'll probably find it's been torn apart. Now, Mr. McBride, I'm going to take a shower, then I'm going to meet a man I'm beginning to like a great deal. So if you'll excuse me, I'll—"

She wasn't prepared for Jared's lightning-fast movement. She had the door half closed when his arm reached out, grabbed her, and pulled her out of the room. He half threw her behind the door. "What—?" she began but didn't finish her sentence because McBride nearly leaped into her bedroom. Was someone hiding in there? She put her hand to her throat and her heart raced. When she heard no sound from him, her heart calmed down and she tiptoed around the door. McBride was standing in her room, staring at her bed. The covers had been thrown back, but as far as she could see, there was nothing unusual. Straightening, she walked into the room. "There's no one here," she said.

Jared held out his arm to keep her from getting any closer to the bed. "Go down to the end of the hall," he said quietly and calmly, "and get a broom. No, get two of them, then come back here. Don't make any noise and move slowly."

She wanted to ask questions, wanted to make him explain himself, but then she saw her bedcovers move. Something was alive and under the covers! She backed out of the room slowly, then ran down the hall to the closet that held the brooms and the stairs down. The door was open, and two brooms and an old mop were halfway out, but, as far as she could tell, no one but the two of them had been down the stairs. It was so unusual for a staircase to lead out of a broom closet that the intruders hadn't checked.

Grabbing two brooms with sturdy handles, she went back to the bedroom. McBride hadn't moved. In the middle of the bed was the head of a snake. It seemed to be warm and cozy under Eden's covers and in no hurry to leave. It was staring up at Mc-Bride as though it wanted to say hello.

Without looking at her, Jared reached out his hand for the brooms. "Would you please go to that far window, open it, then go downstairs?" he said in a quiet, even voice.

Eden walked slowly toward the window, her back against the armoire that was against the wall. The snake turned to look at her, but it didn't otherwise move. It seemed to have chosen McBride as its prey, and Eden was of little interest. At the window, she had to push upward hard. The wood in the windows had been replaced as was necessary to keep them from rotting, but they were still over two hundred years old—and they were a pain in the neck to work. More than once, years ago, Eden had looked at the ads for Pella and Andersen windows with longing.

Finally, the window was up. There were no weights inside it so it wouldn't stay up. She grabbed one of the blue boxes on the floor and stuck it in the window—she hoped it was the spy's manuscript. Once the window was open, she made her way back to the door, keeping against the wall and the furniture. As far as she could tell, McBride hadn't taken his eyes off the snake. They seemed to be hypnotized by each other.

Eden left the room but stayed just outside the door and watched. As though he were a snake charmer, McBride used a broom in his left hand to attract the snake's attention. With his right, he eased the second broom down under the snake's body, which had begun to emerge from under the warmth of the covers. It took time and patience, but soon he had the broom handle under the snake. When Jared lifted, the snake wrapped itself around the handle, and Jared quickly walked toward the open window. It was only a few steps but it seemed to take an hour. In one quick movement, he reached the window, then he dropped the enormous snake outside.

Relieved, Eden opened the door and started back into her bedroom, but McBride put his hand up to stop her. "Let me check the place out," he said, then began a slow, systematic search of her bedroom, then her bath.

He found a little copperhead inside the big armoire at the foot of her bed. It liked the warmth of the TV set and had curled up under it. Eden would never have seen it until she was bitten as she reached for something inside the cabinet. Under her bed, inside her gardening shoes, was a red-bellied moccasin. In her bathroom, behind a stack of towels in a cupboard, was a cottonmouth.

She stood at the door, growing weaker every time McBride pulled another poisonous snake out of her room. She figured a sack full of them had been released in her bedroom, then the door closed. She watched as he turned over chairs, stripped the bed, lifted the mattress and springs. He climbed on a chair and looked on top of the armoire, and on top of the mirror over the dresser. He lay down on the floor on his back and scooted under her bed, looking over every inch of it with a flashlight.

When he was sure that her room was clean, they went to his bedroom and he began to search it. There were no snakes in his room. Only in Eden's.

At last, she sat down on the old chest in the hallway and sighed. "Someone wants me dead."

"It would look that way," he said quietly, looking at her in speculation. "You and I have to figure out what you know or who you know. We have to—"

Everything that was happening to her was so out of everyday life, that she couldn't really deal with it. If she thought about what was happening now, she'd start thinking about what happened to her when she was just a girl, and that would lead to thinking about Mrs. Farrington's son. No, it was better to try to keep her life as normal as possible. She looked at her watch, then jumped up and started running for the stairs. "I have to meet Brad!"

"Ms. Palmer," Jared called out, running down the stairs after her. "You can't go anywhere. It's too dangerous. Eden! Wait!"

She paid no attention to him. As she ran through the hall downstairs, she grabbed her handbag and her car keys and kept running toward her car.

"I have to search your car. You can*not* go! Do you hear me?"

Eden unlocked her car door, then stood by it for a second. "Mr. McBride, I am forty-five years old and I've had to deal with loser men all my life. Now, at last, I think I may have possibly found a winner. If you think that the FBI, a bunch of murderers, and a few poisonous snakes are going to deter me, then all I can say is that you don't know *anything* about women."

Jared barely made it into the passenger seat before she spun out of the driveway and headed into Arundel.

Chapter Nine

"Y ou are a truly remarkable man," Eden said as she used the rearview mirror of the parked car to put on lipstick. Just down the road, she could see Brad's car at the John Deere dealership. She could also see a long-haired young man standing beside him, and from the stiffness of their bodies, she could tell they weren't having a good time. Eden had pulled off the road to take the cosmetics she always carried with her out of her bag and do her face. Her hair was a mess, but thanks to a good New York cut, she could make it look all right. She lined her eyes, curled her pale lashes, and coated them with mascara.

"It would be too much for me to hope that that

was a compliment," Jared said. "I want to know what you're going to tell Granville about why I'm with you—and planning to stay glued to you."

"You're remarkable because I've never heard anyone complain as much as you do. You've not taken a breath between your complaints since we left the house."

"I have to use words because my department frowns on their agents using force on a person they think might be an ordinary citizen."

"I am ordinary," Eden said, glancing from the mirror to the dealership down the road. Now Brad was gesturing at the young man. She'd better hurry before they resorted to fisticuffs.

Jared followed her glance. "Don't you know that men don't like to be chased?" he said.

She gave him a look. "Women do the choosing and every man knows that. You know, you're beginning to sound jealous."

"Not quite. It may surprise you to know that outside of work I have a private life. I even have a girlfriend."

"I'm so glad for you. Not for her, but for you." She gave herself one last look in the mirror, saw that it was the best she was going to be able to do, then turned the key in the ignition and started the car.

"What are you going to tell him about me?" Jared asked again. "And you'd better think of something, because I'm not going to leave your side. You get killed under my watch and I'll never get my pension."

She gave him a quick look to see if he was kidding. "Who could imagine that *you* have a girl-friend?" she muttered.

In seconds, she was at the tractor dealership. She parked the car at the far side of the lot and walked toward Brad. She was determined to ignore McBride and to forget all about what they'd been through that morning. She wasn't going to let Brad know anything about spies or the FBI or men who tore up her house. She knew the people of Arundel; they maybe had forgiven her for an illegitimate child, but whatever had happened in her life to make the FBI interested in her might be too much.

On the short ride into town, McBride hadn't shut up about how serious the matter was, and how they had to figure out what she knew and why Applegate had swallowed her name. He told her that she should stay away from Granville until this was settled. When he'd pointed out that if those sapphires were ever found, she, as Mrs. Farrington's heir, would be the owner of them, Eden's eyes sparked fire. "Are you hinting that Braddon Granville is after what I own—if it were even to be found, that is? Are you saying that he doesn't like *me* but what I may have inherited?"

Jared had backed down after that.

Now, as she walked toward Brad, wishing she'd thought to grab some clothes other than jeans, she was trying to think about how she was going to explain McBride's presence. What was she to say about why he was with her? That she felt so guilty about hurting him that she was adopting him? How was she to explain that he intended to follow

her everywhere? At least that's what he was saying
he was going to do. He said he was going to remain in her house and search her room every day,
and that he was going to set up surveillance equipment outside. He said he was determined that she
wasn't going to get killed while he was in charge
of her safety. She would have been flattered by his
concern if he hadn't said it in a way that made her
think that her death would be nothing more than a
blot on his record.

"I'm sorry I'm late," Eden said, holding out her
hand to shake Brad's. She was very aware of Mc-
Bride behind her and of Brad's questioning eyes on
him. Brad took her hand, but then he leaned forward and kissed her cheeks, one after the other in
the European way. Eden wanted to throw her arms
around his neck and tell him of all the horrible
things that had happened to her that morning. But
she didn't. She kept calm and looked past Brad at
the tall young man behind him. He was handsome,
but he also looked angry and sullen.

"You must be Mr. Robicheaux," Eden said, extending her hand.

"Yeah," he said, taking her hand but looking
confused as to who she was and why she was there.
He also looked at the man behind her.

"McBride, isn't it?" Brad said, extending his
hand to shake Jared's. "Are you looking for a tractor to buy?"

"Actually, I'm following Eden. We're cousins,"
McBride said.

Eden didn't look at him. She kept her eyes on

Brad and gave him a weak smile, and had no idea what to say.

But she didn't have to worry, as McBride took care of the explanation. She should have known that he was a fabulous liar in all aspects of life. "Third cousins, so we're not really close. On her mother's side, so the names are different. We were truly amazed to find the connection, but then I was told that I had relatives out this way, so that's why I came here in the first place. My mother's people knew Eden's mother, but our families weren't close. You know how that is." Halting, he gave Brad a huge smile.

Slowly, so she wouldn't erupt in anger, Eden turned to Jared. "I think we have other things to talk about than our, uh, relationship," she said calmly. "And I don't think Mr. Granville wants to hear about our family connection, such as it is. Mr., uh, Jared, why don't you go inside and get yourself a Coca-Cola? I'm sure there's a machine inside."

"Only if you go with me, cousin dear," he said, smiling at her. Taking a step toward her, he put his arm around her shoulders and squeezed. "Imagine my delight in finding my own cousin. After all these years apart, now I can't bear to be away from her for even a minute."

Eden, her eyes on Brad's, kicked sideways, knowing that she'd hit the pistol strapped to McBride's ankle and cause him pain. He covered his wince of pain well, but his fingers dug into Eden's shoulders until tears came to her eyes. Twisting, she got out from under his grasp. "Maybe we should talk about the business at hand," she said.

"Yes, well, uh," Brad said, looking from Eden to Jared and back again.

Eden turned to the young man who'd been watching all of this with the same sullenness, but now there seemed to be a hint of amusement in his eyes. He is one good-looking young man, she thought, and she could see why Camden Granville had fallen for him. The sullen, angry look wasn't something that would appeal to her, but she could imagine that some girls would like it. "What has Brad told you about me?" she asked, turning her back on Brad and McBride, who were glaring at each other like dogs about to fight.

Reluctantly, Remi took his eyes away from the men. He seemed to be enjoying his father-in-law's discomfort. "Not a word, ma'am," he said in that accent of deep Louisiana. Cajun.

Oh, yeah, Eden thought. She understood Camden completely. She headed toward the small tractors, away from the quarter-of-a-million-dollar combines, and Remi followed. Behind them, Brad and McBride walked slowly, side by side.

"I've had some experience in designing eighteenth-century–style gardens," she said to Remi. "So Brad thought that maybe you and I could work together. Do you think that's possible?"

"If you're willing to put up with my father-in-law's tightfistedness, and his constant complaining, yeah, sure. What do I know about designing fancy gardens? At home we let the Lord grow what we eat."

She smiled at him. "If I plant okra will you make me a pot of gumbo?"

"Why, shore, sugah," he said, drawling. "I'll cook you anythin' you want."

Yes, indeedy, Eden thought. Understand it well. "If you don't know about garden design, what do you know about landscaping?"

"If you ask my father-in-law, not a damned thing, but I know about the land and plants and about machines. What else do I need to know?"

"Nothing," Eden said and almost added "darlin'." "Can you set fence posts? Lay bricks in concrete? Most important, can you take orders from a woman?"

"Been doin' it all my life in one way or another," he said, smiling at her in that soft way that only Southern men can. "And if I don't know how to do it, I can learn. Maybe you'll teach me."

"Maybe I will," she said in the same tone. Oh! But it was good to be back in the South!

She had no way of knowing until she'd actually worked with him, but she thought that maybe she and Remi were going to get along well after all. Her worry had been that he'd want to interfere in the designing. What she needed were some strong young men and some machines, not budding designers. "I don't know about you, but don't you just love that tractor over there?"

He grinned at her. "Looks good to me. If you can get ol' man Granville to part with the money, that's more than I can do."

"Maybe he can't afford it," she said softly, remembering the evil that McBride had put into her head.

"He can afford it," Remi said. "He could buy everything on this lot with what's in his checking account. Remember when Compaq computers was going bust? He bought a lot of their stock then. When they came out with a new computer that outsold everything on the market, he sold his stock. He made millions. Multimillions. He can afford anything. He just thinks that I'm a lower class than he is, that's all. I'm an embarrassment to him."

Frowning, Eden turned to look back at Brad. He was standing beside McBride, and they were talking earnestly. She wondered what lies McBride was telling him. They were two very handsome men. Brad was an inch or two shorter, but he was built more powerfully, with a thick, broad chest that tapered down to a small waist and trim hips. McBride was leaner, darker. Brad had gray hair that made him look distinguished. You could see that he was a man of importance. McBride had dark hair and eyebrows, and he looked as though he'd be at home in a sports car with a model beside him. Two very different men.

She looked back at Remi. When she was his age, she too was disgusted at the unfairness of parents. When she was twenty-five, she'd had a boyfriend who was from a rich, educated family. He was sweet and kind and she'd liked him a lot—until she met his family. They'd quizzed her relentlessly, and she'd failed with every answer she gave. After that, it had only been a matter of time before the boy quit calling. At the time, Eden had hated the injustice of it all. The parents hadn't judged her on herself but on where she'd come from and what had happened to her to make her a mother at eighteen years old.

But as Melissa had grown up and started dating, Eden had changed. She'd wanted the best of the best for her daughter. When Melissa had dated a boy who rode a motorcycle and had tattoos, Eden had been nearly hysterical. Melissa had accused her of being a snob and a bigot.

Now, looking at Remi, she could see his side and Brad's. Brad had wanted what he thought was the best for his daughter, but she'd married a man who—Eden smiled to herself. "Made her bones rattle." That's what a coworker had said once, that she wanted a man who "made her bones rattle."

"Can you work that tractor?" Eden asked Remi.

He gave her a look that said, Just try me.

Coming toward them was a salesman, and Eden asked if Remi could test-drive the tractor, which had a front-end loader and what looked to be a half a dozen attachments sitting beside it. She glanced back at Brad and McBride. They were now talking in a relaxed, friendly manner. Their earlier animosity seemed to have gone, and they now had smiles on their faces. They looked as though they were planning to do something together. Play golf?

The salesman got the key to the tractor, and minutes later Remi was in the seat, giving a demonstration of what he could do. He knew the controls on the tractor as though he'd invented the machine. If he was half as good in other aspects of landscaping as he was on the tractor, she knew they weren't going to have a problem.

When Eden glanced at Brad, she saw that he'd given a cursory look at his son-in-law, but he seemed to be mostly interested in whatever he and McBride were discussing.

Suddenly, Brad looked at his watch, and an expression of panic crossed his face. He turned to Eden. "I have to go. The big meeting with the buyers is today. You'll go with me, won't you?"

It was all Eden could do to not look at McBride for permission. But the truth was that she wanted to do most anything in the world rather than go back to the house she loved so much. Visions of the secretary sprawled across the hall floor, and the snakes in her bedroom, ran across her mind. Part of her knew she should return to Farrington Manor and start going through those manuscripts piled in a corner in her bedroom. She needed to start on them for her publishing house's sake, but she also needed to start looking for anything she could find out about that spy who had eaten her name. Just the thought of it made her stomach turn. It was one thing to watch such things on *CSI,* but quite another to think that your name had been found inside a man's stomach. She was sure it was irresponsible of her, but right now she couldn't bear the thought of going back home.

Keeping her head turned so she couldn't see McBride, she smiled at Brad. "I'd love to go. Maybe I could get something to eat while you're in your meeting," she said.

Behind her, Jared said, "Me too. I'm starving. Maybe we'll see you after the meeting." Again, he put his arm possessively around Eden's shoulders.

Brad frowned slightly as he looked from one to the other. "It's the BIG EVENT, all capitals. Home buyers are flying in from all over the U.S., and we're meeting at the clubhouse. I shouldn't have left everything this morning for the others to take care of, but my daughter insisted." Pausing, he glanced at Remi, as though to say that if anything bad happened it would be his fault. Taking Eden's hand, Brad gently pulled her in an attempt to get her away from Jared.

But Jared didn't release his hold easily.

"I'd love to go with you," Eden said, forcibly pulling away from McBride and heading toward Brad's car.

As Brad got into the driver's seat, Jared took Eden's arm. "I don't want you around a lot of people," he said quietly. "Until this is sorted out, you need to be isolated."

"Isolated with *you*?" she asked, giving him a cold smile. "Mr. McBride, I'm beginning to wonder if your interest in me is purely professional. Perhaps you have other things in mind."

At that Jared stiffened and dropped his hold on her arm. "I'll have you know, Ms. Palmer, that I—"

He broke off when she quickly opened the passenger door and got into Brad's car. Jared slid into the backseat just as Remi took the seat beside him. For a moment Brad looked askance at Eden, but all she could do was shrug. She had an idea that if she said she didn't want McBride to go with them, he'd tell Brad the truth. And what would happen if it were found out that she was being investigated by the FBI? Or that men had broken into her house last night and searched it?

She gave Brad a weak smile as he started the engine.

Ten minutes later, he turned onto a wide road with a discreet sign that said QUEEN ANNE and nothing else. There were no words that shouted the number of houses being built, or that they offered water views and docking for boats. There was nothing but a small sign that by its very plainness declared elegance and wealth.

They drove through trees that had been saved from the builders' bulldozers, then had been pruned to be neat and tidy. To the right and left of them was empty land, with several trees, all of them of old growth. Someone had gone through the land, marked the best trees, then had the undergrowth cleared.

"Later in the spring, these meadows will start sprouting wildflowers. It all looks very natural, but it took years of work."

"Yes," Eden said, "get rid of the weeds first, then plant the wildflowers and nurture them until they take over."

"Exactly," Brad said, smiling at her.

As she looked out at both sides of the road, she saw no buildings anywhere. "So when do you start building?"

"What a compliment! Actually, we've sold eighty-two percent of the houses, and nearly sixty of them have been completed or at least started."

Eden twisted in her seat. "Where are they?"

At that moment, Brad drove over a little hill, and when they got to the top, he stopped the car. Below them was Arundel Sound, the huge body of water that connected the many freshwater lakes and rivers in the area to the ocean. The sound was part saltwater and part freshwater, and was great for boating and fishing. Between them and the sound was an enormous building, partly hidden by old-growth trees. Behind it was a parking lot, also nearly hidden. To the right and left of this building were houses facing the water.

"Beautiful," Eden said and meant it. Next to unspoiled wilderness, this was the best. It looked as though every big old tree that had been on the site had been preserved. Every subdivision of new houses that Eden had ever seen had started with land being bulldozed flat. Empty land was easier for the builders to get their trucks and machines onto. No one had to be careful with a backhoe when digging foundations if there were no trees in the way. No one had to think about concrete hurting roots. No one had to worry about harming anything if it was just barren land.

"Either you have an environment-loving builder or he hates you," she said.

"Both," Brad said, smiling at her. "By the end, though, it was hate. I even kept some natural shrubs, and to do that I had to have wooden barriers put around the plants. I wasn't popular."

"No, I can't imagine that you were." She raised her hand to indicate the coastline. "But it was worth it. So how many awards have you received for this?"

"A few," he said modestly, but Eden could see that he was pleased.

He parked in a space marked FOR THE DIRECTOR, and they got out of the car.

Jared caught her arm. "Stay near me," he said softly. "I don't want you out of my sight for even an instant."

All she could do was nod as Brad turned to her. "I'm sorry if I won't be able to spend much time with you today, but there are going to be a lot of people here. Do you mind if I introduce you?"

"No, of course not," she said, moving away from McBride and leaving him to follow beside Remi.

Once they were inside the building, she paused and looked about. Had she been told in advance about this she would have imagined one of those modern buildings with windows that almost reached heaven. The room would have dwarfed human beings by its size and grandeur. Rather like a cathedral that was meant to awe the occupants.

But this building wasn't like that. If she hadn't seen from the outside that it was huge, she wouldn't have known it from the inside. True, they were in a two-story lobby with huge windows that looked out to the sound with its picturesque sailboats, but the room didn't dwarf her or the furnishings—which, by the way, didn't look like the usual public building furniture. There was a mixture of chairs and couches and tables that looked as though someone's attic had been cleaned out. Standing in front of the windows, she looked at the furniture and knew without a doubt that not one piece of it was new. True, the couches had been reupholstered, but there was no mistaking the look of age. On the walls were pictures and framed pieces of fabric, and here and there was a quilt. There wasn't a single reproduction anywhere, and as a result the room had a cozy feel that made it welcoming and personal.

"Who did this?" she asked, and Brad knew what she meant.

"There wasn't an auction in North Carolina or southern Virginia that we didn't attend over the course of two years. By 'us' I mean my daughter and my assistant, Minnie. You'll meet her. She has the fastest auction hand in three states." Brad leaned toward Eden. "Want to know the truth? We started going to country auctions as a way to save money. We always planned to buy the couches and chairs new, then add a few old things as decoration. But Minnie found an old couch that she loved, had her friend's husband reupholster it, and that was that. Do you like the result?"

"Very much."

Smiling, Brad took her arm in his and squeezed it.

It made her feel good that he was pleased with her. Actually, the more she saw of him, the more she liked him. She glanced over her shoulder at McBride to see if he was impressed by the building, but he was looking about as though he was searching out hiding places. Remi had disappeared through a door as soon as they'd entered.

"Shall we go?" Brad asked just as a door at the end of a hall opened.

"There you are," said a young man, his face showing his obvious worry. "We thought maybe you'd run away and left us." Turning, he looked at Eden. "You must be Eden Palmer of Farrington Manor," he said, extending his hand. "I'm Drake Haughton, and I work with Brad on his project."

"He's being modest," Brad said. "He's the archi-tect."

"I merely draw whatever Brad envisions."

Smiling, Eden took the young man's hand. He was nice-looking in a pleasant way, rather like a young missionary. She had an idea that this was the type of man Brad had wanted his daughter to marry. That she'd instead married a man who was good on a tractor must have been a disappoint-ment. But Eden liked Remi. Maybe he didn't have the last names that were so important in Arundel, but he seemed like a good guy. At least his daugh-ter didn't marry someone like Stuart, Eden thought as she followed Brad and Drake into the next room, Jared just a step behind her.

They entered a room that again was of a scale that could have been intimidating, but the use of refurbished furniture brought it down to a human size. Through a wide doorway to the right was a large room filled with well-dressed people. They were milling about and munching on tidbits passed by waitpersons dressed in white and black.

"If you'll excuse me," Brad said, and his en-tire demeanor changed from laughing and warm to...well, laughing and warm. But the new version was like that of a salesman. He walked into the room full of people, smiling, his hand extended.

"Ah, Brad the salesman," Drake said, smiling at Brad's back, then he turned to Eden and looked at her again. "So you're the one."

Eden wasn't sure how to respond to that. Was she pleased that the gossip of Arundel was already matching her with Brad? Or was she annoyed that she was assumed to be a done deal?

Before she could reply, Jared cleared his throat, and Drake looked up at him, puzzled as to who he was. When he figured it out, he looked Jared up and down as though to ascertain his wounds. "The man looking for the circuit box," he said, extending his hand to shake.

"Jared McBride." He shook Drake's smaller, whiter, softer hand. "I take it you're of one of the 'families' of Arundel."

"That I am. Cursed with three last names. Shall I tell you my middle name?"

"No," Jared said, and for a moment Eden saw a frown cross Drake's handsome face. She knew that in that instant Jared had been cataloged and dismissed. "Mannerless Yankee" she could almost hear McBride being described as.

For a moment, the three of them seemed to have nothing to say to one another. Or at least Eden and Drake had nothing to say. McBride was still looking about the room and at the people through the doorway.

"Don't let us keep you," Eden said. She could

tell that Drake was waiting for her to explain why she was there with her rude neighbor, the man she'd put in the hospital. But Eden couldn't imagine repeating the story about McBride being her cousin, so she said nothing.

"Yes, Brad is to speak in a few minutes, then we'll have lunch. You're staying for lunch, aren't you?"

"She's doing the landscaping for all the houses," Jared said, looking at Drake with his eyes narrowed.

"Landscaping? But I thought you were..." He broke off, obviously having no idea what to say. "Yes, of course. Landscaping. I'll talk to Brad. Will you be all right here alone?"

"She's always all right when she's with me," Jared said.

Before he could put his arm around her shoulders for the third time that morning, Eden sidestepped him and reassured Drake that she'd be fine. When he was gone, she turned on McBride. "Where were you raised that you could be so vile to that young man? You were insufferable!"

"I hate snobs, and he was the pinnacle of snobbery. Right up there on the crest. Top of the garbage heap."

"You don't know that. He seemed quite nice. He—"

"'Shall I tell you my middle name?'" Jared mocked. "Who says 'shall' nowadays?"

"Certainly not any of the writers in the manuscripts that I'm given to edit. Are you jealous of that young man because he has an education? Is that something you never had? Please don't tell me that you quit school in the tenth grade so you could be an—"

She broke off at a look from McBride. He was so paranoid that he probably thought the entire clubhouse had been bugged and someone was dying to find out that he was an FBI agent. She threw up her hands in exasperation. "It's no use trying to talk to you." She lowered her voice. "I'm sick of people like you thinking that everyone who has an education and knows how to use a napkin is a snob. I wish my daughter had married someone like Drake Haughton instead of that useless man she did marry, and I bet that Brad wishes his daughter had married someone like Drake too."

"So what's wrong with the Cajun kid? I've never seen anybody handle a tractor the way he did. He moved that dirt around so there wasn't a crumb of it left behind. He could scoop out the ashes in a fireplace and not hurt the living room rug. But now you're telling me that that's not worth anything. No, a man needs to have lots of last names and—"

"For your information, I happen to like Remi. I have nothing whatever against him."

"Then it's just Granville who thinks he's above somebody who drives a tractor. He'd rather his daughter marry a prissy little—"

"Hello," said a voice behind Eden before she could answer McBride. She turned to see a young woman, not much taller than she was, with lots of crinkly red hair and blue eyes that were dancing with delight. "I hope I didn't interrupt anything. I'm Minton Norfleet, Minnie to everybody, and I'm Braddon's right-hand man."

Through this entire speech, Minnie's eyes had never left Jared. At first, he was looking only at Eden, but when Minnie kept staring at him, he drew his eyes away and looked at her.

When McBride's eyes softened as he looked at Minnie with what could have been thought of as a sexy look, Eden rolled her eyes in disgust. "Yes," she said too loudly, "Brad mentioned you."

"Did he?" Minnie said, her eyes still on Mc-Bride. "I hope he said good things, as there are lots of very good things about me."

"I bet there are," Jared said under his breath.

Eden stepped between the two of them and held out her hand to shake. "I'm Eden Palmer."

"Yes," Minnie said absently, shaking Eden's hand but not looking at her. "And this is?"

"I'm Jared McBride, Eden's cousin. I'm staying at her house. Farrington Manor. Would you like a map?"

"I know where it is, and I've always wanted to see the inside of that house," Minnie said.

"Come for dinner tonight," Jared said, looking over the top of Eden's head at Minnie and holding out his hand to shake.

"She can't," Eden said, looking up at McBride. Her eyes were telling him to remember that the house had been torn up, that there was furniture lying in the hallway, cut cushions in the living room—and who knew what was still in her bedroom? Besides that, what right did he have to invite people to *her* house?

"I'd love to," Minnie said. She was still holding Jared's hand.

He was the one to pull away. "I think you ladies have things to discuss. Ms.—uh, Eden, if you need me, I think you know that I'll always be close by." With that he walked away from them.

"Who is he?" Minnie asked, her eyes wide. "I mean, I know he's the man you beat up, everyone in Arundel heard about that, but I thought he must be a wimp. Obviously, I was wrong. So who is he?"

"Uh, cousin," Eden managed to mumble, then she brightened. Maybe Minnie could take McBride off her hands for a while. "He's a retired policeman, *very* early retirement, and he doesn't know what to do with himself."

"I could show him a few things to do," Minnie said, then waved her hand in dismissal. "Don't mind me. It's just that I haven't had a man in three months, and the bedposts are beginning to look good. Is he married?"

"No."

Minnie smiled at Eden, and Eden smiled back at her. It was an instant friendship. "You know, don't you, that Brad wants you to speak."

"Speak? What do you mean? Not, like in: Give a speech?"

"That's exactly what I mean. Oh, dear. Sometimes Braddon forgets the most important things. Last night he came home and—"

"You live with Brad?"

"Not like that. Utterly platonic. Like you lived with Mrs. Farrington."

"But she was an old woman, and Brad is..."

"A hunk?" Minnie smiled. "Maybe he is to you, but he's like a grandfather to me. Look, he lives alone in an enormous house, and I have a daughter to take care of by myself. I had the misfortune to fall madly in love with a man I met on a cruise ship and married him the next week. Two months after my daughter was born, my slimeball husband ran off with a woman who worked in his office, so I returned home to Arundel. Brad helped me get a divorce and child support from my ex's family. He helped me get full custody and my maiden name. You might have noticed that names are important here in Arundel. Anyway, after the divorce I was pretty stressed out with trying to raise a child alone."

"Been there, done that."

"Right. I'm not sure how it happened, but I ended up living in Braddon's big old house and taking care of everything in his life. Believe you me, if you want to marry him and let me move into some nice condo where the windows don't leak, let me know. Anyway, the point of all this is that I think Brad wants you to give a speech in about thirty minutes. Last night he was very happy about your taking over the landscaping. People can hire their own outside landscapers, of course, but Brad is afraid that they'll end up..." She hesitated as she searched for the right words.

"Letting some guy talk them into a Japanese garden with raked gravel, while the next-door neighbor has junipers in three colors, and the next house has gnomes in the flowerbeds."

"You sound just like Brad. Exactly like him, in fact. Are you sure you two aren't related?"

"Sure of it. Would you tell me what I'm supposed to speak on? And why didn't Braddon tell me himself that he wanted me to speak?"

"I have no way of knowing for sure, but my guess would be abject terror. He doesn't want to do anything to frighten you away. As for what you're to speak on, I think he just wants you to sell the people on whatever kind of gardens they're supposed to have. I'm sure it won't matter to them, because all they want to do is play golf and drink gin. As long as they don't have to pull weeds, they'll be okay."

"Maybe I could talk to Drake. He seemed to be Brad's second-in-command."

Minnie snorted in derision. "Don't believe Drake's smooth exterior. He went to architecture school because his father made him, and he's here because Brad is friends with his father."

Eden's mind was racing. She was going to have to do this by herself, but how to sell herself and her ideas in just a few minutes? Was this how new authors felt when they were given three minutes to present their ideas to her? Yes, of course it was. "I need a pen and paper and some time alone," she said, her voice frantic.

Minnie handed Eden a very pretty fake leather notepad holder. It was a dusky blue, a color some-

times called Williamsburg blue. On the front were
the words QUEEN ANNE. Eden took the pad, then
went to a quiet corner and tried to assemble her
thoughts. She didn't mind giving speeches when
she had time to prepare, but off-the-cuff like this
was going to be difficult. Eighteenth-century gardening, she told herself. What did she remember about it? Better yet, what did she *like* about it?
What made it so appealing to her that she wanted
to make other people like it too? It had been a long,
long time since she'd been involved in gardening. Holding down jobs, trying to get her child to
school and back, being frantic when her daughter had a fever for three weeks in a row, all these
things in life had driven the pleasure of gardening
from her mind. As for the last few days, all she'd
done was...

For a moment she chewed on the end of the
pen and remembered the last few days. Snakes,
two men who were no longer strangers to her,
her house ransacked. Closing her eyes, she tried
to clear her vision of the turbulence of the last few
days. Think eighteenth century, she thought. Not
the truth about the time, of fighting for independence, but the orderliness. What was that motto
she'd loved so much? How could she have forgotten that? It was what she'd based the garden she'd
designed for Mrs. Farrington on. Something about
nature being tamed. Yes, that was it. Smiling, she
began to write.

Chapter Ten

Standing in the doorway, Eden listened to Brad's welcome speech. The notebook with the few ideas she could dredge out of her memory was in her sweaty palm. When Brad had asked if he could introduce her, she hadn't known what he meant.

She came alert when he said that he wanted them to meet the new landscape designer, Eden Palmer, who was an expert in eighteenth-century gardens. Can he be sued for telling such a big lie? Eden wondered. How could she make these people want a garden that went against all modern-day ideas of gardening? How could she sell "difficult to maintain" and "wildly expensive"?

She looked back at Brad and willed him to say

they could meet Ms. Palmer another day, but he didn't.

"Now," Brad said, talking easily, as though he were born with a microphone in his hand, "we're not saying that you have to put in a garden that G.W. might have enjoyed. G.W. is what we call George Washington here in Arundel, because he came through here and slept around, so to speak. In fact, we're pretty sure that he slept in Ms. Palmer's house, Farrington Manor. Of course he was only twenty-three at the time, a long way from being president, and he was here surveying the Great Dismal Swamp. And we do not want to tell you what he said about the accommodations in North Carolina or we'd never sell you a house."

He paused while the audience laughed politely.

"Today, after lunch, you can consult with Ms. Palmer and decide what you want to do about your own garden. If you like her designs and want to put one in, then we have maintenance people to take care of it for you. By the way, the maintenance company happens to be run by my son-in-law, so let me know if he doesn't do his job and I'll tell his boss, my daughter."

More laughter, then Brad held out his hand to Eden, and she went to the podium.

~

Twenty minutes later Eden stepped down from the podium and followed Minnie into a long room where tables had been set up.

"That was good," Minnie said, referring to Eden's

speech. "Very good." There was a respect in her voice that hadn't been there before, and it made Eden feel good. She knew that in Minnie's eyes she'd gone from being just an extension of Braddon to being a woman with her own mind.

"You can sit here," Minnie said, walking to the far end of one table.

"I have nothing to show people," Eden said. Her heart was still pounding from her speech. Had she said the right things? Minnie had liked it, but did Brad?

"Don't worry about supplies. Brad has everything that was left by the two landscapers he fired."

"If I'd known I was to do this, I could have brought some books to show people what I would like to do." Eden grimaced. With the way her morning had gone, she should have done a presentation on poisonous snakes of North Carolina.

The tables had several seatings, each supplied with pencils, pens, pads, and notebooks, all with the name of Queen Anne on them. It was all very nice, elegant, even.

One side of the room was all windows, and just outside sat Jared McBride, half hidden under a shade tree. He had on dark glasses, and he was talking on his cell phone, but he nodded at Eden when she glanced at him.

The door to the room opened and a waiter brought in a tray of sandwiches and drinks.

"I told Brad you'd probably rather eat in here," Minnie said, glancing out the window at Jared. "But if you'd rather..."

"No, this is great. I need more time to think about what the heck I'm doing here."

"You can't kid me. I've seen the Farrington gardens, so I know what you can do. Just BS your way into it. Act like you know more than they do and they'll believe you. Besides, you're saving Brad's life. He was going to have to hire someone from outside Arundel or let his son-in-law do it. Brad would rather do it himself than let Remi have any responsibility."

"What in the world did Remi do to make Brad dislike him so?"

"Married his daughter," Minnie said. "Until she married, Brad and his daughter were very close. They traveled together, worked together. She ran that big house of his with an ease I'll never have. Between you and me, I'd like to burn it down. Termites and peeling paint! Ugh! Anyway, after Cammie got married, Brad was left alone. I doubt if any man could have pleased him as a son-in-law, but a blue-collar hunk like Remi never had a chance."

Once again, Eden could see both sides. Remi seemed to be a good person, but Eden knew what it was like to be ambitious for your child. She wondered if Brad would rather that his daughter had married someone like the clean, never-been-dirty young man Drake Haughton.

They had just started their lunch when Minnie said, "Everybody in town says that Braddon has the major hots for you."

Eden nearly choked. "I think it's much too soon to say that. And as for gossip—"

"Gossip, ha! It's hope. If you knew what that man has been through with women you too would want him to find someone!"

Eden couldn't help the little rush that went through her. She knew she shouldn't ask, but she couldn't help herself. "And what exactly has he been through?"

"Didn't anyone tell you about Braddon's wife?"

"Yes, but only quickly."

Minnie took a breath, ready to settle into her story. "They were married for over twenty years, but I don't think they ever loved each other—at least that's what Camden says." Minnie took a drink of her sweet tea. "Sourpuss, isn't she? She's married to the biggest hunk to hit this town since Brad Pitt, but to look at her, you'd think she was Woody Allen's new wife. Anyway, what did you hear about Braddon's marriage?"

Eden was cautious. "That they were about to separate when she was diagnosed with cancer."

"You were just told the bare bones. She was having an affair with a man who had been Braddon's best friend since they were kids. The boys were born just a few days apart and spent their whole lives together. Braddon had the brains, and Treddy had the brawn. His name—"

"Let me guess. Tredwell."

"Right. Tredwell Norfleet Pembroke. Anyway, they were a perfect match. When the boys left Arundel, they went to some school up north where Braddon could study law and Treddy could captain the football team. It was before my time so I never saw him play, but I was told that Treddy was headed toward being one of the all-time greatest football players in history. But in his freshman year he got in the sports car his father had given him for high school graduation and ran off the side of the road. He injured an elbow and a knee, and that was the end of his glorious career. He returned to Arundel to heal and try to help run the family businesses. But he wasn't any good at business. When Braddon came back to Arundel with a Yankee wife, ready to open his law practice, he tried to renew his friendship with Treddy, but by then Treddy was drinking too much and had a deep anger inside him. You know what I mean?"

"Yes, I do." Eden knew a lot about deep anger, and that knowledge was held in her voice.

Minnie looked at her sharply.

Eden looked down at her plate, not wanting to answer the questions that Minnie looked like she wanted to ask. "So what happened?"

"Treddy and Braddon's wife had a long-term affair. They managed to keep it secret for years, but Braddon finally found out about it and filed for divorce. Just days after he filed, she was diagnosed with terminal cancer, and Treddy hightailed it out of town pronto. Braddon stayed with her to the end, and three weeks after she died, Treddy came back to town married to some model half his age. There was a cocktail party to celebrate Treddy's marriage, and Braddon showed up. He didn't say a word, just walked up to Treddy and hit him in the face. He broke Treddy's jaw so bad it was wired together for months. Brad also broke two bones in his hand. He and Treddy aren't friends anymore."

"I should think not," Eden said, then lowered her voice even though they were alone in the room. "What I'm curious about is the woman Brad had an affair with while his wife was ill."

"That would be my mother," Minnie said, "but don't look shocked. I used Braddon's guilt feelings over not marrying her to get him to employ me and give my daughter and me a place to live. It's tough being a single mother."

"Yes, it is," Eden said, smiling at Minnie and understanding her "use of guilt feelings." "I'm a single mother too."

"That's great. Maybe our kids can play together sometime."

Eden started to explain, but then she laughed. She was sure Minnie knew all about her daughter and how she came to be. She also probably knew Melissa's birth date. "You're very kind," Eden said.

Before Minnie could reply, the door opened and people began pouring in. Within seconds, Eden was faced with her first client. She took a breath and did as Minnie had advised: she acted as though she knew what she was talking about.

Throughout the long afternoon, Jared sat outside, under the shade of the trees, always in view, now and then on his phone. A few times Eden saw him frowning and his conversation seemed to be angry.

Brad was at the far end of the room, talking and smiling at people, and seeming to do it all with ease. Once she looked up to see him watching her, and he gave her a look and gesture that said he was exhausted. Eden nodded in agreement. At five, Minnie efficiently and politely ushered everyone out of the room.

Brad collapsed on the chair beside Eden. "I don't know about you, but I need a drink. A large one."

"Me too."

He took her arm and they walked outside, where Jared was waiting for them. "Where we going?" he asked.

Eden felt Brad stiffen. "Eden and I are going to dinner," he said pointedly.

"Great idea. I hear there's a great seafood restaurant in town."

"McBride..." Brad began.

Minnie, coming up behind them, put her arm through Jared's and looked at her boss. "I'm famished. Where are we going for dinner?"

Brad was frowning, but Eden said, "I think we're outvoted."

They all looked at Brad, and after a moment he relaxed and smiled. When he started walking toward his car, his arm was still locked with Eden's. Behind them, Jared and Minnie were also walking with linked arms.

"Why do I feel like chanting, 'Lions, tigers, and bears'?" Eden asked. Brad laughed.

"We could make a mad dash for my car and escape them," he said.

"They'd find us. Arundel isn't that big."

"I know a few secret places." He leered at her in such an exaggerated way that she laughed.

"Actually," she said, "I want to spend some more time with Minnie. I want to hear more about why she and her child are living with you."

"Minton sometimes has a very big mouth. What else did she tell you? No, don't tell me. Let me have my innocence."

Eden smiled. "Did your broken hand heal all right?"

Brad groaned. "I'm going to strangle her." He glanced back at Minnie and Jared behind them. "You know, it's beginning to look like Minnie's setting her cap for your cousin. Maybe she'll keep him so busy that I can have you all to myself."

Eden looked at Minnie and Jared. She was talking ninety miles an hour, and Jared was listening, but he was also very aware of where Eden was. She had no doubt that Jared was directing Minnie's conversation toward whatever he wanted to know about anything that had ever happened in Arundel.

Chapter Eleven

I'm going to have it put on a brass plaque and framed," Brad said, leaning back in his chair and smiling across the table at Eden. "'Nature tamed, trained, and enclosed.' Marvelous. Perfect. What was the other one?"

"'Geometric symmetry within an enclosed space,'" Jared said, looking at Minnie.

"Not a word I said was original," Eden protested, but she was pleased with Brad's praise. She gave him a mock look of anger. "As for you, you owe me big time. An impromptu speech! On material I haven't looked at in twenty years."

"You were magnificent," Brad said, looking at her in awe. "If that's what you do off-the-cuff,

I can't imagine what you'd do if you had time to really prepare a speech. I want to hear everything that led up to that talk," he said as the waitress gave them their drinks. "From beginning to end. All of it. How did you figure out exactly which way to slant your speech?"

Eden played with the straw in her margarita. "It was the diamonds on the woman in the first row. The one with the streaked hair."

"Mrs. Wainwright. This is one of four houses she owns. She wants to be here because she's heard that some formerly famous people are buying into Queen Anne."

"Right. Rich. I stood at that podium and looked at the audience and thought, How can I sell the idea of gardens that are expensive to install and even more expensive to maintain to a bunch of people who, for the most part, couldn't care less what was planted in front of their houses? I'm sure they'd be happy with two paper bark birches and some petunias."

"You made it into a competition," Jared said, taking a drink of his McTarvit single malt whiskey.

"It was an excellent idea, and, judging by the response, it's going to work," Minnie said, her eyes never leaving Jared.

"What I had originally planned was to try to sell them on the idea that eighteenth-century gardens were pretty and practical, but they're not. They're a pain in the neck. Everything is enclosed and orderly, and you can't use a Weedwacker anywhere."

"You were brilliant," Brad said in admiration.

Eden sipped her drink and basked in the praise. As soon as she'd stood before that audience of rich people she'd known that the speech she'd planned was useless. She'd meant to try to persuade them that an eighteenth-century–style garden was as easy to take care of as an American lawn with a few trees stuck in it. But when she looked at them, she remembered what McBride had said about snobs, and she'd decided to play on that snobbery. Who in their right mind today would want a garden that was going to take an army of strong young men to take care of? Gardens such as no one outside of historical parks would want? They'd be expensive to install, what with adorable little outbuildings with lead roofs, bricked pathways, and trees that Thomas Jefferson would have known. No one in their right mind would want a garden that close to being historically accurate.

When Eden had seen the eyes of her audience as she said that no one would want such a garden, she knew she was on the right track. She hadn't been aware of it, but her fear in all this had been dealing with the clients. She didn't relish trying to please some woman who had too much money and too much time on her hands. She didn't want to think about trying to talk them into putting in a garden that was nothing like a modern American "yard." Worse, she didn't want to have to deal with them later when they found out that the gardens were only beautiful when they were well and carefully maintained.

But when she'd warned the audience that the

gardens were a pain, she saw eyebrows lift. For the most part, these were people who had achieved a lot in their lives. Senators, a former governor, two CEOs, men and women who'd been everywhere and seen everything, according to what Minnie had told her just before she went onstage. Yet they'd stepped down and were, for the most part, now retired. When Eden saw by their faces that she was challenging them, in essence dropping a red flag in front of them, she continued telling them that under no circumstances should they install an eighteenth-century–style garden.

After her speech, Eden had hoped for one or two people to stop at her table, but she got a line that ran out of the door and into the next room. She was handed cards of people whose names made her blink in recognition, and she was asked to call to make a date to talk about what she could do for them.

"Dolley Madison," one woman said. "Anything that Dolley liked, that's what I want. Can you do that?" Eden said she'd try.

"I want something that Mount Vernon will envy," another woman said. "Can you make me a greenhouse like the one they have?"

Eden stared at the woman. The Mount Vernon greenhouse, designed by George Washington, was magnificent—and very expensive. "I'm sure we could," Eden managed to say.

Another woman, with skin lined by years of sun, leaned forward and whispered, "The best. That's what I want. The best. I don't care what it costs, I just want the best in the whole place. Can you do that?" Eden opened her mouth to say that she could, then she closed it and smiled. "Every woman here has asked for the same thing from me. What I can promise you is that you will have a garden that is different from anyone else's on earth."

"I guess that'll have to do," the woman said, obviously disappointed.

By the end of the long session, Eden had made it appear that if she designed a garden for anyone she was doing that person a favor—and she hoped she could keep up the charade. She didn't want to be put in the position of having to argue with these people about what could and could not be put in the gardens.

Throughout her consultations Jared McBride had watched her and had continued talking on his cell phone. Twice he seemed to be arguing with someone, frowning and gesturing.

Now, at dinner, Brad said, "You were great," then he looked at Jared and Minnie for agreement.

"The best," Minnie said, looking at Jared adoringly.

Jared lifted his glass to Eden. "I was impressed," he said softly, and Eden blushed with the praise.

"To Eden," Brad said, lifting his glass.

"To the eighteenth century," she said.

"To Queen Anne, who gave her life so others could use her name," Jared said.

"To bringing in a profit," Minnie said, then they all laughed, clinked glasses, and drank.

~

It was a lovely dinner, Eden thought as she sat in the car beside Jared. Right now, Eden couldn't feel any anger toward him, as they'd all had such a good time. There'd been no animosity, no lightly veiled threats about who owned whom, no tension. They'd just talked and laughed all evening. There had been a heated discussion about Princess Diana's death in which Jared had said little, which made her think he knew more than he was telling. Twice, Brad had made halfhearted attempts to get McBride to talk about his experiences as a cop before he retired and moved to Arundel, but Jared wouldn't tell. He was good at skimming the issue and telling nothing.

It was Jared who brought up the story of the sapphires.

"That old saw?" Brad asked. "Everyone knows that old man Minton sold the necklace."

"I thought that was a secret!" Eden gasped. "Mrs. Farrington told me that only those in her family knew the truth."

"Yes, that's right," Brad said, confused. "Only the family knows."

"The family!" Minnie said, looking like she wanted to pull her hair out. "The family. I hate the thing! Marrying into one of 'the families' in Arundel is like being initiated into the Mafia."

"Being part of it got you a place to live," Brad said calmly. Obviously, he didn't take aspersions of the family lightly.

"Not fair," Eden cried. "I was given a place to live when I was desperate, but I'm not part of the family."

"I think you were," Brad said. "Everyone knew about Mrs. Farrington's son, so I think they looked on you as a gift from God. Your daughter became the grandchild that Mrs. Farrington was never going to have. And it worked out, since you inherited the house."

"And the story," Jared said. "And maybe the sapphires."

"They were sold," Brad said again.

Minnie had been looking at her food, thinking about what Eden had said. "Did they ever find him?" she asked softly.

Jared stopped bantering with Brad and looked at her. "Find who?"

Minnie looked up at Eden. "Did they ever find the man who, you know, gave you your daughter and made you desperate?"

Brad and Jared shifted uncomfortably in their chairs.

"They didn't need to find him," Eden began. "I always knew who he was. He had a stocking over his head, but I recognized his voice and the scar on his wrist. It was from a hunting accident. I used to stare at it when he passed the offering plate at church."

That information brought them all to a standstill.

"Wait a minute," Minnie said. "I'm confused. The story I was told, and I admit that by the time I heard it, it was old and had been through a lot of people, but I was told that you were raped, then thrown out by your horrible family. Oh! Sorry. I didn't mean that they were—"

"They were horrible," Eden said softly. "Truly horrible people. I didn't like what got me away from them, but I'm glad that I was able to escape them. If I'd stayed they might have married me off to someone repulsive."

Reaching across the table, Brad squeezed her hand. "Let's change the subject. Tell me about the first garden you plan to design. What—?"

But Jared didn't want to change the subject. "You know who the rapist was? I didn't hear that he was prosecuted."

"He wasn't," Eden said. "He had a wife and three kids, and he was the head deacon at our little stone church. My parents said that he was a good man and wouldn't have done what I was saying he did. They said that I was at fault."

"Yet another virgin birth," Minnie said, her mouth in a line.

"He should have been prosecuted," Brad said, his lawyer face on. "If he did it once, he'd do it again."

Eden looked at him, unsmiling. "You grew up in a different world than I did. If you were hurt you could go to your parents and they'd help you. I was what they call now a 'baby momma' and I had no one."

"Mrs. Farrington—" Brad began.

"Had her own problems," Eden shot at him.

Brad picked up his water glass and drank.

"There were places you could have asked for help and it would have been given," Jared said quietly, and smiled at Eden.

She knew he meant his agency. Or maybe he meant him. Smiling, she looked down at her plate. Sometimes he could be very nice.

Minnie was frowning, and when she spoke, her voice came out higher and faster than normal. "So how did we get onto this subject?" she asked as she raised her glass. "Let's make another toast. What is your deepest, most sincere wish in the world? As for me, I want my own: my own house, my own man." She looked up at Jared suggestively.

"To wipe the words *focal point* from the American vocabulary," Eden said.

"To kiss Angelina Jolie," Jared said, not looking at Minnie.

They all looked at Brad.

"To find the Love of My Life," he said with a look at Eden, then they all clinked glasses, laughing, and drank.

Yes, Eden thought. Except for Minnie sometimes flashing her looks of anger, it had been a very good evening, something she hadn't had in a long time.

"A penny," Jared said from beside her.

"I was thinking that even though my daughter is now grown, this is the first time that I've not been someone's mother since I was..." She hesitated.

"Since you were a kid yourself," he said.

"Exactly."

"You like this new freedom?"

"I don't know yet. So far, I still miss making sure that she's okay. I miss talking to her twenty times a day. I still worry that she's going to do something that I won't be there to see, and that she'll need me but I won't be there. Once a mother, et cetera." She turned to him. "Do you have children?"

"Nope. Not that I know of."

Eden groaned. "I guess that's supposed to be a titillating statement, but I've never liked irresponsibility."

"I never make any points with you, do I? Listen, I want to talk to you about something. That man who raped you, I could do something about him."

"Such as? Have him killed? Or just get him put in jail? No, Mr. McBride, I'm not into revenge. Besides, he gave me a beautiful daughter."

Glancing at her, Jared shook his head. "Okay, so no revenge. But I could do something."

"No," she said. "Nothing. It was a long time ago. There's nothing that needs to be done. I assume the man has grandchildren now and lives a normal life." When Jared started to speak, she raised her hand. "No, and I mean it. It was a long time ago and it's over. Maybe he had something bad happen to him that day and he took his anger out on me. Maybe—"

"I can't listen to this," Jared said fiercely. "I don't want to hear it. You should have—"

"Done what?" Eden said loudly. "I was seventeen years old, pregnant, and totally alone. I didn't even know how to earn money to feed myself, much less a child. But Mrs. Farrington took me in and took care of me and my daughter. You know what? I think that man did me a favor."

"What?"

"If I'd stayed with my parents I know they would have married me off to someone dreadful. You can't imagine what they were like. I've had years to think about this, and I'm glad that there was a reason for them to throw me out. It could have gone wrong, and I could have ended up on the street, but I didn't. I was taken in by a wonderful woman and given all the love and care I'd never had in my life."

"Then why did you fight *me*?"

"What?"

"If being attacked when you were a girl turned out to be good, then why did you attack *me*?"

"Instinct," she said, not liking what he was saying.

"I think that over the years you've told yourself some great big lies. As for not wanting revenge, what would you do if some man raped your daughter?"

"Kill him," Eden said softly, then looked at him. "Are you feeling sorry for me?"

They were in front of her house, and he turned off the car engine. "I think maybe I'd feel sorry for anyone in the world before I gave *you* any sympathy. And I mean that as a compliment."

Eden smiled at him. "Thank you." She looked out the windshield at her old house; she didn't want to go inside. Her beautiful house now had cut cushions and broken furniture. And, worse, it had memories of being unsafe.

"Come on," Jared said cheerfully. "I think you'll like what you see."

He got out of the car, then waited for her to get out. When she was slow going up the porch stairs, he took her arm in his and pulled her up to the front door. Jared took a big new key from his pocket and unlocked the door.

"Where did that come from?" she asked, wide-eyed. "And how did you get it? You haven't been out of my sight all day."

He smiled at her. "I do have a few secrets of my own," he said as he opened the door and went inside.

"What's that supposed to mean?" she asked, following him. "That *I* have secrets? I don't. I'm an open book. I—" She broke off because she'd entered the hall and was looking about her. The secretary was not only now standing upright, but had also been repaired. "Who—? How—? When—?"

"I made a few calls and the agency sent some people."

She narrowed her eyes at him. "You gave them permission to search my house, didn't you?"

"Saves having to get a warrant."

She knew she should be angry at him, but just then she saw a little camera in the corner of the ceiling. She whirled on him. "What have you done? And don't lie to me! I want to know all of it."

"I had some security put in, that's all. Cameras

inside and out. An alarm system. We're hooked up with my office."

Eden sat down on the little French couch against the wall. "Your office? You mean the FBI? I'm now directly connected to the FBI?"

"Yes," he said, not seeming to understand her problem.

Eden looked as though she wanted to cry. "You were on the phone most of the day and I saw you get angry more than once. That this house has been fitted out with security equipment, and that lots of money has been spent on my house, is important, isn't it? Why didn't the FBI send me away somewhere safe?" When she looked at him, he didn't meet her eyes. "They want to use me as bait, don't they? Like that goat with the T. rex in that movie."

"*Jurassic Park*," Jared said, looking away and avoiding her eyes. "I liked that movie. It was exciting. In my world too often really bad things happen to people, but in a movie you can make happy endings. It's nice." When she said nothing, he turned to look at her, then gave a sigh. "Yeah. You're to be the bait. This guy Applegate seems to have been involved in more than we thought he was. They just decoded his computer disks, and he was taking in information as well as giving it out. He was a sort of satellite to a lot of people, but we don't know who they were. There are no addresses, no names. He seems to have memorized most of the vital information."

"So the only name you have is mine."

"That's right."

"And your 'office,' as you call it, thinks that someone might come to me to find out what I know. Come here again, that is, like they came this morning. Of course you thought they were your own people because you'd arranged for them to scare me, but they turned out to be actual criminals, so now your office thinks I really *do* know something."

"You really are clever, you know that?" When she didn't smile, he sat down beside her. "Ms. Palmer...Eden, if it makes you feel any better, I don't think you know anything, and I said so today. I don't know why Applegate swallowed your name, but it's the only clue we have. I know I haven't known you for very long, but in this business if you don't learn to read people quickly, it could mean your life. I think you're an innocent in all this, but no one else believes that. I'm sorry for this, but you're going to have me inside the house and men on shifts outside. I don't think you'll ever see them, but they'll be there. Whether we like it or not, you either know something or have something that someone wants."

When she didn't say anything, he stood up. "Come on, we both need sleep. Tomorrow we'll start looking through this house to see what we can find."

"I have to meet Brad tomorrow."

"That's not until the afternoon."

"I need to research eighteenth-century gardens so I can start designing them. After I see the land, that is. And I have to get to those manuscripts from my publishing house. They have deadlines on them. And I need to call my daughter to see how she's doing. And I—"

"Tomorrow," Jared said. "Get a good night's sleep, then we'll take care of everything else, starting tomorrow. Tomorrow we'll—" He broke off when her phone rang.

"It's probably Brad," she said, just to annoy him, but it wasn't Brad. "It's for you. It's Minnie."

She handed McBride the phone, then started back up the stairs, but she couldn't help but overhear him. He didn't say much, just answered questions with "Yeah, sure" and "I think so" and "Love to," but his voice had lowered and was as soft as a kitten's. Eden couldn't control a tiny flash of jealousy that ran through her.

As she went up the stairs, her legs were heavy with fatigue and the responsibility of all that was going on around her. Tonight she'd had too much wine to be able to think clearly about anything, and that included McBride.

After he put down the phone, Jared walked up the stairs behind her. She didn't see him flash a tiny penlight off and on three times to signal the people outside. And an hour later when she was in bed, she slept so soundly that she didn't hear the footsteps in the attic above her head. All the records she'd filed so many years ago, all the Farrington furniture and mementos of the family that hadn't been sold, were being gone through slowly and carefully.

Chapter Twelve

Eden woke at five A.M. thinking, The sooner I solve this thing, the sooner it will go away. She lay in bed for thirty minutes as she explored the idea. Since McBride had appeared in her life, everything had been abnormal. Snakes in her bedroom, locked in a cellar, men prowling around outside. The list seemed to be endless. The worst part of it all was that, eventually, Brad was going to find out the truth. While it was true that, so far, Brad seemed to be an all-round great guy, she didn't relish the idea of telling him that she was being investigated by the FBI. For spying. Or being connected to a spy. Any way she told it, it sounded bad. Whatever happened between her and Brad, whether it became romantic or it was merely a working relationship, nothing would be helped by her being connected to the FBI.

Quietly, she got out of bed and walked to the window. Below, in her garden, the one she'd planned and installed, was a man. He was standing under the little arbor that she'd covered in confederate jasmine. She couldn't see all of him, but she could see enough to know he was there. She was being watched. Spied on.

Turning, she went into her bathroom and took a long, hot shower. Sometimes she did her best thinking while she was in the shower. McBride said that it was believed that she knew something. Or owned something. Since, until a few weeks ago, she'd owned next to nothing, she didn't think that was the problem. On the other hand, McBride said that an agent had been killed here in Arundel. It was a hit-and-run. Was it an accident, or did someone know the woman was an FBI agent? If an FBI agent was killed here in Arundel, maybe that meant this place had more to do with the spy than she, Eden, did.

She got out of the shower, dressed, partly blow-dried her hair, then stuck some fat Velcro rollers in the top of it. She applied enough makeup to keep her from looking as though her face had been erased (wasn't getting older wonderful?), then went to the manuscripts in the corner of her bedroom. Only one of them was urgent, meaning that it had a deadline to be copyedited. Eden opened it and found two grammar errors on one page. *Take* and *bring,* she thought. Why couldn't people get those right? She closed the manuscript box. Obviously, the book was going to require some time.

Setting that manuscript aside, she looked at the others. She was supposed to read them and decide whether or not they were worth publishing. With these books, grammar and punctuation didn't matter. Not even sentence structure mattered. Everything was about the story. If it was a ripping good yarn, some person, maybe Eden, would be told to fix the writing.

It took her an hour to determine that none of the manuscripts were about spies. There was only one murder mystery, but it was set in Victorian England and was about a man who surgically killed prostitutes. "That's original," she muttered to herself and closed the big box containing the 612 pages.

Smells coming from downstairs wafted up to her, so she uncurled her legs and went down to the kitchen. McBride had his back to her and was cooking pancakes. Beside him was a plate with a stack that had to be a foot and a half high.

"Expecting company?" she asked as she sat on a stool.

He didn't turn around but gave a nod toward the kitchen door.

"Oh, them," she said. "I thought they were going to be here in shifts, one at a time."

He put four pancakes on a plate, put it in front of her, then turned back to the stove. "Changing shifts, so there're two of them here right now."

She put her knife in the butter, then pulled it

out. Funny how being around good-looking men made you think about every bite you took. She put a small amount of syrup on the pancakes and cut. They were good! "Your own recipe?"

"Naw. It was on the package. I just added water."

"And bananas and strawberries. And what's the lumpy stuff?"

"Oatmeal." When he glanced back at her he was smiling. "Okay, so I added a little of this and that. Living alone, you learn some things."

She ate three more bites before she spoke. "Do you have a photo of the agent who was killed? The hit-and-run?"

Jared didn't say anything for a moment, then he turned to look at her, spatula in hand. "What do you have in mind? You wouldn't be thinking of helping me, would you? I mean, give up being hostile and fighting me at every turn, and actually *helping* me?"

She shook her head at him. "What is it that women see in you?"

"It would take me so long to tell you that we wouldn't have time to look for any clues."

"Spare me," Eden said, but she smiled. "You want me to take those pancakes out to the men?"

"No. You're not supposed to know they're there."

"Not even the man under my jasmine arch?"

"Especially not him." His face changed to serious. "I heard you up early. Did you think of anything that might have a bearing on the case?"

"If you mean, did I remember any spy meetings that I attended, no I didn't. I went through the manuscripts on the floor and there's nothing that makes me think any of them was written by an international spy. But then, what do you know about the man personally? What did he do as a hobby? A lot of romance novels are written by men so maybe he—"

"Wrote a bodice ripper?"

"Hey!" Eden said. "Don't disparage those novels to anyone in the publishing industry. They're our meat and potatoes. You know who's the most powerful person in publishing?" She didn't wait for him to answer. "It's the woman in the grocery store who throws a book into her cart. She decides everything."

Jared blinked at her a couple of times. "Two speeches in two days."

Smiling, Eden glanced down at her plate. "The point is that I didn't see anything in the manuscripts that might reveal the secrets of some spy. But maybe he didn't write about that. Maybe he wrote something else and he wanted me to edit the book."

"I don't think he wrote anything. And, no, I don't have any concrete reasons for thinking that, except for being in this business nearly thirty years. The writer-editor angle doesn't smell right to me."

"Thirty years. You're older than you look."

Jared started to defend himself, then smiled at her. She was teasing him. "More pancakes, or are you afraid Granville won't like you if you gain a pound or two?"

Eden ignored his jibe. "This morning I decided that the sooner this mystery is solved, the sooner you'll leave and I can fully participate in what is shaping up to be an interesting life."

Jared put his hand to his heart. "You've injured me, but, basically, I like that idea." He looked down at the pancakes on the griddle. "You know, don't you, that I could be thrown out of the bureau for telling you all this."

That statement made her angry. "I guess they just want a helpless victim who gets shot at, tied up, then rescued by the big strong hero."

"It's the way I usually work," he said solemnly. "I don't mind the rope burns but I hate the duct tape."

Eden laughed. "First of all," she said, "I want to know your theories on this. If you think this has nothing to do with Applegate wanting to get a book published, what do you think it does have to do with?"

"This house," he said quickly. "Maybe it's about those sapphires that I don't think were ever sold. Treasure hunters can be fanatical."

"I guess we can't very well show Applegate's photo around town, but maybe we could show a picture of the agent who was killed. Or at least ask questions about her."

"We," Jared said, smiling and looking at her, his eyes soft.

"So help me, McBride, if you start making passes at me, I'll…"

"You'll what?" he asked, his eyes teasing.

She grimaced. "I'm not going to play word games with you. Take the pancakes out to the men who aren't there, then come back in and we'll look at the documents you have."

For a moment Jared stood there, looking as if he was trying to decide whether or not to show her anything. "You're certainly a bossy little thing, aren't you?"

"When you're a single mother, you have to be. You can't say 'Wait until your father gets home.' You have to be mother and father to your child, so you learn to be the boss."

Jared looked at her for a moment, then turned away and picked up the pancakes. He put the plate and the butter and syrup on a tray, added some big glasses of orange juice, and went out the door.

As Eden turned toward the stairs, she caught sight of herself in the black glass door of the microwave. She still had rollers in her hair.

~

An hour later, Eden was in the dining room, surrounded by gardening books and grid paper. She'd told McBride that she thought that the best person to ask about the agent was Minnie and she was sure she'd see her this afternoon when she met with Brad. Between now and then, Eden planned to make some sketches for ideas for eighteenth-century–style gardens. "I don't need hours, I need days to do this," she said in a half whine.

"Good," McBride said, ignoring her plea for a

pep talk. "That'll give me time to do some things."
He didn't elaborate.

He helped her haul the books from the cabinet
in her bedroom downstairs to the dining room
where she could spread out. When he saw her pad
of twenty-year-old paper, he smiled but said nothing. Once everything she had—but not all that she
needed—was in place, he went upstairs. She could
hear him walking about now and then, and a few
times heard him on his cell phone. And Minnie
called him three times on Eden's house phone.
The first two times, Eden answered the phone, but
the third time it rang, she yelled for McBride to get
it. It was Minnie.

Eden went through books that were like old
friends to her. When she opened them, they vividly
reminded her of the time when she'd lived there
with Mrs. Farrington and Melissa. It was odd to so
clearly remember herself then and to think of herself now, and to look at all that had happened to
her in her life. When she'd lived there she'd never
thought much about the future. That's what happiness did to a person, she thought. It made them
content. If it had been left to Eden, she would have
stayed there forever.

She looked up from her book at the ceiling
molding. It had been repaired and now, except
for a couple hundred years of wear, was as good as
new. She looked about the room and could almost
feel Mrs. Farrington there, could hear her voice,
could see her smile as she held Melissa on her lap
and told her stories about the Farrington family.

Smiling, Eden looked about the room. As always, the late-nineteenth-century paintings of Tyrrell Farrington were on the wall. They weren't good, but they weren't bad either. Talent aside, Tyrrell had been as fanatical about his family as Mrs. Farrington was. He had painted a history of the family. There were ancestor portraits done from life and from the memories of old relatives, as well as four paintings of the house itself, each from a different angle. It was interesting to see how plants had grown. The pecan trees were still there, only much bigger. Tyrrell had never married and had lived in Farrington Manor all his life. When he was a young man he'd gone on a Grand Tour that lasted over three years. Mrs. Farrington said that if his mother hadn't faked a heart attack, and his father hadn't cut off his allowance, Tyrrell would have spent the rest of his life in Paris. Instead, he'd returned home, sulking and sullen, and had spent the rest of his life painting. Now the walls of the old house were covered with his work.

Eden looked back at her papers.

"How's it coming?"

She looked up at Jared. "I don't know. I designed one garden over twenty years ago, and since then I've done a thousand other jobs. It's hard for me to remember everything that I knew."

"It's not like you're not used to using your brain. You got your college degree while holding down a full-time job, remember?"

She looked at him suspiciously. "And what was my degree in?"

"American history, minor in English lit."

She looked at the eraser on her pencil. "I guess I have a file at the FBI."

"It's more like a whole cabinet."

Eden groaned.

"Come on, it's not that bad," Jared said, pulling out a dining-room chair and sitting down across from her. "I made a few calls and found out some things. Wanta hear?"

"Maybe," she said cautiously. "Is it bad?"

"Not to me," he said cheerfully.

She narrowed her eyes at him. "You found out something bad about Brad, didn't you? So help me, McBride, if you—"

"Did you know that McBride isn't my real name?"

"Whatever your real name is, I don't want to hear it. What did you find out? Other than everything there is to know about Minnie Norfleet, that is."

He ignored her remark. "Tess Brewster— that was the name of the agent who was killed— lived—"

"Did you know her?"

"Yes," Jared said succinctly, letting Eden know that he didn't want to talk about that. "Tess rented a house just down the road from here. A converted—"

"Overseer's house," Eden said. "I know the place well."

"Overseer?" he asked, one eyebrow raised. "Like in *Uncle Tom's Cabin*?"

"Don't give me that Yankee look," she said. "Nearly all the overseers for Farrington Manor were African-American, and I know. I did the research, remember? That house used to belong to Farrington Manor, but it was sold many years ago. Mrs. Farrington told me that at one point it was derelict and cows wandered through it, but one of the—" She opened her eyes wide.

"Right," he said. "One of the Granvilles bought it. It now belongs to your Mr. Slick."

"Brad," she said, ignoring the disparaging nickname. "That's good. I'll ask Brad about the woman and the accident this afternoon."

"Think he'll tell you anything?"

"No, of course not. I think Brad killed the woman and will want to cover it up. You're disgusting, you know that?"

"You're the first woman who has ever thought that."

"Why don't you go outside and talk to one of the men skulking out there? And if any of them smoke, tell them not to throw their butts in my garden. At least I think it's my garden," she said under her breath. "I don't seem to have time to go outside to even look at it. There are probably weeds taller than I am."

"That's easy," Jared said, smiling at her.

"Go! Get away from me! I have to work."

But Jared didn't move out of the chair across from her. He opened one of her books and looked at a photo of red tulips surrounded by a trim box-wood hedge. "I thought your idea of making those people beg you to create a garden for them was great. So what constitutes an eighteenth-century garden?"

"Pattern, symmetry. And they need outbuildings," she said, distracted.

"There are enough of those around here. I've never seen so many buildings falling down as there are here in North Carolina."

Looking up from her book, Eden stared at him in silence.

"What's that look for?"

"Maybe I could work with the Arundel Historical Society and Restoration North Carolina and move some of the smaller buildings into Queen Anne. The buildings could be restored."

"Good idea. Glad I thought of it."

She shook her head at him. "Your ego must reach the moon."

He smiled at her and didn't seem as though he planned to go away. "So tell me about all this," he said, motioning to the many books on the table. "It looks interesting."

She opened her favorite book, *The Gardens of Colonial Williamsburg* by Brinkley and Chappell, to the Benjamin Waller garden. "See," she said, "you need pattern and symmetry, and different plants are used together."

When Jared's face showed that he didn't understand but wanted to hear more, she warmed to her subject. "In America today, because we have so much land, we tend to plant one crop in one space. Modern American families will plant a quarter acre of corn, for instance. Or they'll put in a dozen tomato plants and make sure that nothing else is near their tomatoes. All very clean and sterile. The colonials lived in a dangerous world, so they lived close to one another, but they still had to grow a lot of their own food."

"Country in the city."

"More or less. In Williamsburg, the houses had half-acre lots, and it is amazing that they could fit so many plantings into that small space. Every inch of their lots was used. And nothing was barren. They didn't have the luxury of space."

Jared looked as though he wanted her to go on.

"Take herbs, for instance. Today, if an American wants to plant herbs, they put in an herb garden. They tend to separate everything. Herbs are here, fruit trees are there, vegetables are there, and flowers are over there. All separate. But the colonials mixed things up—which, today, we're rediscovering is a better idea."

"A cottage garden," Jared said, looking pleased with himself.

"No. A cottage garden prides itself on having twenty-five different species in one bed, and everything is free-form. The colonials couldn't have stood that. They wanted order and symmetry, so they'd make a design, architectural really, and each shape would be bordered by a hedge of one plant, such as boxwood, or lavender. Then, inside, they'd put their flowers or vegetables. And they would put plants together that helped each other."

"How do plants help each other?"

Eden opened a new book put out by her publishing house on companion gardening. "Certain plants like each other, and there's a theory that if you have problems with bugs on your crop, then you should plant something else nearby that the bugs like more than your crop. In the Middle Ages, no one would plant strawberries without planting borage next to it. Lovage goes near the tomatoes, and hyssop has to be with grapes. They're best friends. You grow catnip and use the branches as a mulch to repel the odious Japanese beetles—which, thankfully, the colonials didn't have. Valerian draws worms to the surface to aerate the soil, and it adds minerals to the compost pile. And marigolds should be everywhere. Bugs hate the smell of marigolds."

Jared blinked at her. "And you say you've forgotten what you knew."

Eden smiled at his praise. "I think I can remember most of it with some study, and of course there's so much more that's been published since I was gardening. Back then, people didn't even believe in mulch, and only a few people had any idea what a compost heap was."

"Imagine that."

Eden laughed. "It's a matter of what's old is new again. We're finally learning that nature and our ancestors knew what they were doing. They were organic gardeners out of necessity, and now a lot of people are looking into how they did it." She looked down at her paper. "Designing these gardens for other people is my problem. How do I do that? The colonials could get four gardens out of a half-acre lot."

"How big are the lots at Queen Anne?"

She looked at him. "Unfortunately, I don't know, but I assume the ones not on the water are from one to three acres."

"What would you do with three acres?"

"In colonial times it would have been pastureland, with sheep, cows, and horses, but now it could be a croquet lawn or a putting green. Just so it's not two and a half acres of lawn that has to be mowed." When she looked down at her pad and began to write, Jared leaned across the table and looked at the paper. "Must have," she'd written at the top of the page.

> must be enclosed
> must have outdoor structure(s)
> must have walkways
> must re-create the past

"So show me a hypothetical design," he said.

"Okay," she said, glad for his interest, because she needed someone to run her ideas past. "It's like this. Here's the house." She drew a rectangle near one end of the paper. "I'd bring in at least one old building and have it restored—and thank you for that idea. I'll be sure and give you credit." She drew a small square to the left of the page. "Now we connect the buildings with a walkway. Colonials didn't have a huge lawn where people could walk anywhere they pleased."

"And these were the guys fighting for freedom?"

"Before power mowers, having an acre of lawn to mow wasn't freedom."

"Point taken."

"Here, near the house, we enclose a place for a pleasure garden that would be used for picnics and just sitting outside on warm evenings." She drew a rectangle near the house, then surrounded it with what looked like rounded shrubs. "Trees at each corner, and over here a little gazebo, but you have to be careful of gazebos so you don't make it look Victorian."

"Then what?" Jared asked.

"The kitchen garden. Not too far from the house, but not too close either. A colonial kitchen garden was a thing of beauty and didn't need to be hidden." She drew six narrow rectangles, then a square with a diamond in the center. As Jared watched, she drew paths off the diamond.

"I see. You could put a fountain there in the middle. An authentic-looking fountain, of course."

She smiled at him. "Now, curving pathways to connect all the spaces, and they'd all be tree-lined, of course. This was before air-conditioning, so shade was important. And, depending on the size of the property…" She turned the pages in the book to the plan for the Governor's Palace and described the various "rooms." There was a "ballroom garden" filled with topiaries, a maze made from hedges of American holly, a canal stocked with fish, and a bowling green. It was a garden that nearly bankrupted the government, but Eden thought it was worth every cent.

Jared looked up from the book. "So where do the ATVs race?"

"On the highway, with the eighteen-wheelers," she said instantly, and he laughed.

"I'll take you on one for a spin one day, and you'll love it."

"I doubt it," she said, then looked at her watch. "I have to go meet Brad." Her eyes pleaded with him to not go with her.

"Sorry," he said, "but it's my duty to keep you safe. Tell Mr.—"

She gave him a look to cut it out.

"Granville," Jared said. "Tell him that I'm going to help you with the designing."

She started to protest but stopped herself. What good would it do? "You wouldn't happen to have a camera, would you?"

"Digital, five million pixels, with a one gigabyte card."

She raised her eyebrows, impressed. "Okay, you can take pictures of everything for me."

"Meant to do that anyway," he said softly. "I want you to get us into that house where Tess lived, okay?"

Eden nodded. She wasn't sure how she was going to ask Brad, but she'd figure out something. She smiled at McBride, and he smiled back. Maybe he wasn't so bad after all.

"So what's for lunch?" he asked, and she groaned.

Chapter Thirteen

W hen Eden saw Brad, she again marveled at how comfortable she felt with him. She wondered if it was because he was part of the Arundel family that Mrs. Farrington had been part of. For all that Brad was, more or less, a stranger, she felt as though she'd known him forever. Mrs. Farrington said that when you met the man, THE man, you started planning your wedding dress. So far in her life, every time Eden had dated a man for more than three months, she started planning how she was going to let him down easily. Never in her life had she been dropped by a man, but she'd had to tell several of them that it was over between them.

But Brad was different, and she knew it—and

so did he. When he saw her, his face lit up. Like a child at Christmas. Like she was a gift that he'd wanted all his life. We've had similar bad experiences, she thought, and we've never come close to finding that Great Love.

Brad hurried forward, took both her hands in his, and kissed her cheeks. He looked like he wanted to do more, but instead he just stood there, holding her hands and looking into her eyes.

"I hate to break this up," Jared said from behind them, "but the architect is waggling at you."

"Waggling?" Brad said, smiling at the old-fashioned word. Still holding Eden's hands, he turned to Drake Haughton, who looked exaggeratedly at his watch. "Sorry," Brad said to Eden, "but I'm on a strict timetable today. We have some buyers flying in from New York later this afternoon, and I have to be back here to meet with them. Shall we go?"

Eden followed Brad to his car, and after a look at Jared, he seemed resigned to his presence. As Brad held the door open for her, he said quietly, "I see Mother Superior is well." Eden giggled.

Eden thought she was to meet with clients, but Brad told her that the meetings would start tomorrow. "Today I'm going to show you everything. You can't go into a meeting without having seen the place."

"Of course not," she said, glad to be with him. If McBride weren't in the backseat, everything would have been perfect. Well, actually, perfect would mean that she wasn't being investigated by the FBI, and people weren't breaking into her house and filling it with poisonous snakes, and—

"Are you okay?" Brad asked, glancing away from the road to look at her.

"Fine. Just a little nervous about suddenly becoming a landscape designer. I spent the morning going over my gardening books and making a lot of notes. I hope people like the idea of these gardens. They're not what most people want."

"Something I've found out in this business is that people love restrictions. Covenants put on property make them feel safe. The guy next door can't park a boat in front of his house. They like that kind of thing. And I think they'll like the idea of everyone having to make gardens that aren't like the rest of the U.S."

"I hope so."

"You look nice. What did you do to make yourself look even better than you did yesterday?"

"She took a bath and put big yellow curlers in her hair," Jared said from the backseat, reminding them of his presence. "Eden wanted to ask you about a house you own."

Eden wanted to pinch McBride. She would have come to the house in time. Why did he have to rush things? And why did he have to remind Brad that they were living in the same house?

Brad looked at her questioningly.

"The overseer's house down the road. I, uh..."

"Her daughter is thinking of moving here to

Arundel, so Eden thought she might like that house. I called a Realtor, and imagine our surprise to find out that you own it."

Twisting in her seat, Eden glanced at McBride in disgust. What was inside of him that he could lie so easily?

"You'll have to fight Minnie for the place," Brad said. "She wants it very much, but I won't let her have it."

"Why not?" Eden asked.

"Maybe I should tell you now so you don't learn it from gossip, but I am utterly selfish. I won't let Minnie move into that house because I hate living alone. It's that simple. She hates my big old house and wants out of it, but if she and her daughter moved..." Trailing off, he shrugged at Eden. "I guess I should let her have the place, but Drake, my assistant, also wants it. I owe Drake's father and..." He trailed off.

Brad's eyes met Eden's, and she wondered if he was saying that he now hoped he was going to have a different person to live with. She had to look away from him so he wouldn't see what was in her eyes. She too hated living alone. The year that Melissa had been in New York and Eden had lived by herself had been the worst year of her life. Even now, although she'd never tell him so, she was glad McBride was in the house with her.

"How long has the house been empty?" Jared asked.

"Six weeks, I guess it is now," Brad said as he stopped the car.

Eden had been so intent on Brad that she hadn't looked outside the car. Now she saw that they were on a pretty, tree-lined street. Again, she saw that old-growth trees had been saved. Peeping through the trees and around the gently curving street, she could see houses that were all eighteenth century in design. Well-proportioned, simple rectangles, with beautiful, paned windows, she thought. No fancy, curved porches, no gingerbread trim, no witches' hat roofs. Nothing Victorian, and nothing modern anywhere.

"My goodness," she said. "They could all have been modeled after my house." And for the first time, Eden fully realized that Farrington Manor was *her* house.

"We were trying for perfection," Brad said, smiling at her as he got out of the car, then went around to open the door for her. "The owners of this house haven't moved in yet, so I thought we'd look around at the outside and you could see what you have to work with. Most of the lots are the same size."

"That's exactly what I need," she said, then turned to Jared. "How about if you take photos of everything?"

"I'll do my job if you do yours," Jared said pointedly.

Eden knew what he meant, and she nodded. In the next minute he walked around the back of the house and left her alone with Brad. Alone with Brad, she thought as she turned to look at him. Alone. From the look in his eyes, he was thinking the same thing.

"Too bad we don't have a key to the house."

His statement was so like a teenager's that she laughed.

He took her arm and walked her across the street. "Come on, I know a place where he can't find us."

"I doubt that," she said as they went across the street, through the side yard of another house, then through a gate to the back. It was a typical American backyard, with a couple of skinny new trees and about an acre of grass. Come summer, no one would step outdoors because they'd sizzle in the heat.

"Eden," Brad said, then started to pull her into his arms.

But she pulled away from him. She had no doubt in the world that at least one and maybe two FBI binoculars were on them now. She didn't relish having photos of her and Brad shown to McBride—or to anyone else, for that matter. "I..." she began. She couldn't think of a reason for not letting him kiss her.

"Right," he said, smiling. "Too public." He let go of her hand and gestured to the huge expanse of grass. "Think you can do something with this?"

That he was so understanding made her like him more. "Oh, yes. By the way, I wanted to ask you if there was a good nursery near here. I'm going to need a lot of plants."

"Raleigh. We have trucks you can use."

For a moment she looked about her and tried to think how to bring up the subject of the house.

"Is your daughter really thinking of moving to Arundel?"

"It's more that I'm wanting her to move here. You and I have something in common in that we bear little love for our sons-in-law."

"Don't get me started. Did Minnie tell you—"

She didn't want him to go in that direction. "You don't have a renter for the overseer's house? Or are you going to let Minnie or Drake have it?"

He looked at her for a moment. "No, I don't have a renter, and I own three other houses, any of which Minnie would like." He started walking toward the back fence, Eden beside him. "Did Minnie tell you what happened to the last tenant?"

"No, she didn't mention it."

"I can't believe she left out any gossip," he said as he opened the gate for her and they stepped out onto a service road. Right away, Eden liked the layout of the place. Instead of having the garages opening at the front of the house—and let's face it, a huge, blank garage door was ugly—the garages faced the back, and residents entered through small service roads that ran behind the houses. "I like this," she said, waving her hand. "So what gossip did Minnie leave out?"

"I rented the house to a woman who was a retired schoolteacher. She showed me some watercolors that I think she painted, but she was too shy to say so. They were nice but not great. She said she was interested in the old houses in this area. She was especially interested in Farrington Manor."

"You sound sad. What happened?"

"She was killed in a hit-and-run. It was a shock to the whole town. Her relatives came to claim the body, and..." He shrugged, not knowing what else to say.

"What happened to the woman's effects?"

Brad looked at her sharply.

Eden had to think fast. "Okay, so you caught me. I love watercolors and I thought that maybe she'd done a portrait of my house."

"Tyrrell Farrington's portraits aren't enough for you?"

"Puh-lease."

Brad smiled. "I could call and ask her family. I have the address and phone number her uncle gave me somewhere. When he came to get her body, he told me that if I heard anything about what happened to her, he'd like to know about it."

"A hit-and-run. That's so...cowardly. No one saw anything?"

"Nothing. The police think she was hit at about two in the morning. I can't imagine what she was doing walking on the roads at that time of night. Didn't she read the papers? Watch the news?"

"Where did it happen?"

Brad sighed, and she could tell that he was reluctant to answer her. "In front of your house. The police figured that someone was coming over the bridge, turned the curve too sharply, probably on the wrong side of the road, and there she was. You don't expect someone to be walking along the side of the road at two o'clock in the morning, so you get a bit lax."

"Not to mention drunk."

"Probably," Brad said. "It was all such a waste. Her uncle was pretty upset about her death. He looked like he wanted to hurt someone."

Eden wanted to stop asking questions, but she thought of what was becoming her secret life with the FBI and she continued. "Would you mind giving me the name and number that man gave you? I think I'll call him and see if she did a watercolor of my house."

For a moment, Brad just blinked at her.

"Is that too ghoulish of me?"

"No, actually, I think that's kind of you, and I think they might like that, but I just remembered something. I think Hank Smiley at the frame shop—you know, that room off the hardware store on Prince Street? I think he might have some of her watercolors. I forgot all about that. I was in there one day not long after she was found, buying some frames for photos of my grandson, and—"

"I can hardly wait to do that," Eden said, smiling.

"Grandkids are better than you can imagine. Anyway, Hank said something to me about pictures some woman had left in the store and he didn't know what to do with them. I was in a rush that day so I didn't pay much attention to him. I remember wondering why he was telling *me* about pictures left by some woman. I thought maybe he wanted my services as a lawyer to get his money for the framing job."

"But maybe he told you because the woman had been renting a house from you."

"Right. I bet her family would like to have those pictures."

"Would you mind if I went to the frame shop and asked about them? Maybe I could have Mr. Smiley call your office for verification of who I am."

"He knows."

"Of course," Eden said, half glad that people knew of her, and half annoyed.

For several moments Brad said nothing, just stared up at the house in front of them (brick with a wing with huge windows). Then he sighed, as though he had decided something. "So what's up with you and McBride?"

"He's my—" she began but broke off at the look on Brad's face.

"I've been a lawyer a long time and I know when someone's lying. He's good at it; you're not."

She took a deep breath. "How angry would you be if I told you that I can't tell you?"

"I'm flattered that you think I have the right to be angry, but the answer is, Not at all. Something's very wrong in your life, isn't it?"

Eden couldn't think what to say, and besides, she wasn't sure that she wasn't being taped.

"Does it have something to do with the woman who was killed?"

Eden looked down at her hands in answer.

"Long ago, I learned the true meaning of that old

cliché, that anything worth having is worth waiting for. Whatever is to happen between us can wait until you've solved what you need to in your life. Are those watercolors important to you?" Brad asked.

"Yes. Maybe. I don't know."

He put his hands on her shoulders and looked into her eyes. "I have a meeting in just a few minutes, and Drake and I have to be there, but afterward I'll go get that poor woman's watercolors—if that's what Hank has—and I'll take them out to your house."

"Couldn't Drake handle the meeting alone?"

"Not quite," he said quickly, "but don't get me started on *that*. The things we do for old friends, right?"

Smiling, she nodded.

"We'll have dinner together tonight at your house, if I can invite myself, that is."

"McBride will be there," Eden said heavily. His strong hands on her shoulders made her feel like falling forward and putting her face against his chest. He was so strongly built and looked so warm.

"Don't break down on me," Brad said, dipping his head down to look into her eyes. "Whatever is wrong, we'll fix it. Okay? Will you trust me?"

All she could do was nod. She'd held up so well since she'd been told that the FBI was investigating her, but now she wanted to collapse against Brad and turn everything over to him. A taken-care-of woman, she thought. A luxury she'd never had.

Brad slipped his arm around her shoulders and

pulled her close to him. "Come on, let's go back to the car. I'm sure McBride is hysterical by now, since you've been out of his sight for a whole fifteen minutes."

In spite of herself, Eden smiled and Brad tightened his grip on her.

"I just want to know one thing. Is he protecting you? Is that why he's always with you?"

She nodded. "But I can't—"

"I know. I mean, I don't know, but I sense that something is wrong. Ever since the first time I met him in the hospital, I've thought that there was something not right about him."

"That's just what he says about you."

"Does he? Well, at least I don't sneak around women's houses with a flashlight and try to make people think I was looking for a circuit box."

Eden stopped walking and looked at him in astonishment.

"Yeah, I knew," Brad said. "And I think the sheriff knew too, but he said he believed McBride. I played along with him. I was hoping that you'd come to trust me enough to tell me what's going on."

"I really can't."

"That's okay," he said. "I'll find out. I'm a lawyer, remember? I always find out the truth. And I keep to myself what I find out. I could tell you some truly ugly secrets about people in this town."

Eden lifted her head. "Such as?"

"Any secrets I tell you, you're going to have to kiss out of me."

"No, no, not that! Anything but that!"

Brad laughed, and for a moment she thought he was going to kiss her, but she looked up and there was McBride coming across the street, and he looked furious.

"Tonight," Brad whispered. "I'll be there at seven with wine, flowers, and chocolate cake. The rest is up to you."

He pulled his arm from around her and went forward to meet Jared McBride.

Chapter Fourteen

As soon as Eden said good-bye to Brad at the Queen Anne clubhouse, she felt a sense of panic. She was to cook a meal for a man who maybe, possibly, might become part of her life. What was she to cook? Words from Mrs. Farrington came back to her. "Honey, don't ever try to impress a man with your cooking, especially one you want to marry. If you spend all day in the kitchen making him the first meal you serve him, he'll expect you to spend exactly the same amount of time on *every* meal you cook for him."

As she got into the car with Jared behind the wheel, she put her hands to her temples. What would taste great but was easy to prepare? She didn't want it to seem that she was trying too hard. "I need to go to a grocery," she said, and Jared turned left.

"So what were you and Granville talking about while I was taking pictures?" he asked.

"We were exchanging spy information," she said as he pulled into the parking lot of the Food Lion. "Wait for me here while I get—"

She cut off as he got out of the car to go with her. Inside, he followed her around in silence, watching everyone who got near them while Eden shopped.

When they got home, Eden went to the kitchen to begin to cook. Her face looked as though she was trying to pass an exam that would get her into college.

"Mind if I...?" He motioned to her telephone, and she knew he was asking if he could check her messages. That he knew her PIN number didn't surprise her at all. He pushed buttons, listened, then hung up.

"Minnie?" she asked.

He raised his eyebrows in a way that made him look a bit like a trapped animal. "Four calls."

Eden waited a moment to see if he was going to call Minnie back, but he didn't. He sat on a stool on the far side of the Vermont soapstone–topped island and watched her moving from stove to sink to counter to refrigerator and tried to lighten the mood. "You've never cooked for me like that," he said in a false whine.

"I'm not trying to win your heart. Here, you can

chop the onions," she said as she pushed a cutting board, a knife, and a big Vidalia onion toward him.

"You know, don't you, that there's been research done on this. Women complain that men never help them in the kitchen, but studies have found that women always dump the most odious jobs on men when they do try to help. It makes men stop offering to help."

She didn't look up from the pot simmering on the stove. "And who says our tax dollars are unwisely spent?"

Jared gave a little smile as he started chopping an onion.

At exactly seven, Brad showed up at the screen door in the front, yellow and white daisies and mums in one arm, two bottles of white wine in the other, and a chocolate cake in a box at his feet.

"Am I early?" he asked.

Eden had taken a five-minute shower. She hoped she looked half as good to him as he did to her. He had on a tan cotton short-sleeve shirt, freshly ironed trousers, and he looked like he'd just stepped off a yacht. It was all she could do to keep her hands off of him.

But she knew that McBride was five feet away, so she behaved herself as he opened the door. She took the cake, the flowers, and the wine and handed them all to McBride. He grimaced, letting her know that he didn't like being a packhorse, but he turned away to take the things into the kitchen.

As soon as he was out of the room, Brad opened the screen door and reached down to pick up something else he'd brought. "It's a little house-warming gift," he said, and handed her a plant.

She looked at the plant, rubbed a leaf with her fingertips, and smelled it, then she looked into Brad's eyes. Slowly, she set the plant on the floor, then looked at him. Their minds were in accord. He put his arms around her, and as she knew they would, their bodies fit together perfectly. When his lips touched hers it was with a pent-up desire that seemed to have been held inside her for a lifetime. Whenever she'd kissed a man in her life, she had always been cautious. She didn't want to lead him on, didn't want him to think that she was going to give more than she was going to. But with Brad she didn't feel cautious. She didn't feel tentative. She felt that this man was the one she'd been searching for for a very long time.

She kissed him with passion and with promise. Their lips and tongues met; their bodies met. Perhaps it was Eden's imagination, but it seemed that their spirits met.

She wasn't sure what would have happened if McBride hadn't cleared his throat.

Brad pulled his lips from hers, and reluctantly, Eden moved her head down to rest on his shoulder. Her heart was pounding so hard that she couldn't allow her face to be seen. Brad stroked her hair and after a few moments she was able to pull away and look at McBride.

"Wow," Jared said in a falsely teasing voice. His expression looked as though he'd like to hit Brad.

"Do you react like that to anybody who gives you a plant?"

"This is lemon balm," Eden said, smiling lovingly at Brad.

"Is there something I'm missing?"

"Lemon balm's Latin name is *Melissa officinalis*. I named my daughter after this plant, and Brad knew it. It's just a thing between gardeners, that's all."

"Ah, right," Jared said, looking from one to the other of them, then he gave a false smile. "Maybe we should eat while it's still hot."

"Like me," Brad whispered as he followed Eden into the dining room, and again she giggled.

During dinner, Eden told herself that she had to stop acting like a teenager, but she was feeling as nervous as a girl on her first date. Brad and McBride talked about some things, but she wasn't sure what they were saying. Something about the house down the road, the one where the woman who had been hit by the car had lived. Eden cleared the plates after the appetizer (cold asparagus wrapped in paper-thin ham) and brought in the bowls of vegetables (spring peas, tiny new potatoes, itty-bitty carrots) and the roast chicken that she'd wrapped in rosemary from her garden.

Gradually, she was able to calm herself and began to listen to McBride and Brad and even to make a few comments. She had to give it to McBride that he never strayed from his job. His main concern was about the woman who had lived down the road, and he never left the subject. He had quickly secured Brad's permission to visit the house. To search it, she thought.

She served Brad's cake on a tall silver pedestal cake stand that Mrs. Farrington had loved.

"Ah, yes," Brad said, looking at the cake stand. "Pulled out of the walls," he said.

As they ate cake (from a bakery, not homemade) and had coffee, Eden said to Brad as she cleared the table, "Did you bring them?"

"They're in the car. I'll go get them."

"Get what?" Jared asked as soon as Brad left, and Eden told him about the watercolors.

Jared's face started turning red, looking as though he was about to explode. "You've known about these watercolors all afternoon, but you didn't tell *me* about them?"

"Yes, I knew about them, and, no, I didn't tell you. Do you plan to arrest me for withholding evidence?" She glared at him. "So help me, if you get angry I'll start keeping everything from you."

"You can't do that!"

"Oh, no? Try me."

Jared glared back at her. "If Granville knows about the watercolors, what else does he know? And *how* does he know about the watercolors? What did you tell him about *me*?"

"Don't look at me like that. I *told* him nothing, but he's figured out a lot. He says he knows that you're not what you say you are, and he knows that you were snooping in my house the night I beat you up. Right now I wish I'd used a weapon on you."

At that statement, Jared's face showed astonishment and disbelief, then he started to get angry. "If I hadn't been here, you'd be dead of snakebite by now."

"If you hadn't been here, I doubt very much if any snakes or men would have been inside my house."

"You think *I* caused all this?" Jared gasped out.

"You—" Eden began, then saw Brad.

"Did I miss something?" Brad asked.

"Nothing worth repeating," Eden said, smiling coldly at McBride as Brad put the box on the dining table.

"This has been a great evening," Jared said as he put himself between the box and Brad. "Lotta fun, but—" He yawned hugely. "I think it's time all of us hit the hay. Maybe we can do this again, Granville."

Brad didn't move, just stood there and stared at Jared. "I'm not leaving."

Jared took a step closer to him. "I think—"

"Stop it, both of you!" Eden said. "You! McBride, back off. Brad knows a lot about this and maybe he can help us."

"Help us with what?" Jared asked, glaring at her.

"Finding out whatever it is that you're trying to find out," Brad said, his lips in a line and staring at McBride.

"I'm not—"

"The two of you fighting like a couple of dogs isn't going to help anything," Eden said. She put her body between the two men, then put her hand on Brad's chest. "Mr. McBride believes that the woman who rented your house was murdered, that it wasn't an accident, and he's here trying to find out who killed her and why." Her eyes begged Brad to accept what she was telling him and to ask no more questions. Brad's lawyer-mind would, of course, see right away that what she was saying made no sense. A murder investigation didn't cause the investigator to move in with a person who'd not even been in town the same time as the victim. And, besides, earlier Eden had admitted that Mc-Bride was protecting Eden. From what?

Understanding, Brad picked up her hand and kissed her fingertips. "For you, anything."

Behind them, Jared rolled his eyes, then glanced at the box on the table. It seemed that wanting to see what his friend and colleague had left behind was overriding his common sense.

When the two men seemed to have silently agreed to back off, Eden turned to the box and opened it. Slowly, she withdrew nine framed watercolors, each nine by twelve, and put them on the table, one beside the other.

"Hank said he should charge me rent on them," Brad said into the heavy silence. "He was going to put them in an auction this weekend."

Jared set the box on the floor, and the three of them looked at the paintings. They were nice, what the English call "chocolate box" paintings, meaning they were like the romanticized house and garden paintings that are often seen on boxes of chocolates. Not great art, but charming, something you could easily look at every day and not get tired of. All the pictures were of Farrington Manor. Two were of the exterior, and the rest were of the interior.

Standing up straight, Brad looked at Eden. "I did not give her or anyone else permission to enter your house. It was kept locked, and I made sure that someone came by here *every day* to check on the place. I didn't want pipes freezing and not find out about it for a week."

Eden waved her hand to let Brad know that she wasn't concerned that the woman had illegally entered her house. "Maybe this is what she was doing when she was out at two A.M. These curtains are heavy, and there are blinds under them. She could have closed off the windows to block out enough light so that she could have worked in here at night. The question is why?"

Brad couldn't let go of his feeling of wrongdoing. "The truth is that if she'd asked for permission to paint the interiors I would have said yes. So why didn't she ask me?"

"Maybe she didn't trust you," Jared said. "You have a lot to gain with this house being inherited by an attractive woman like Ms. Palmer."

Turning, her face red, Eden opened her mouth to bawl McBride out for his insinuation, but then she heard Brad laugh.

"That's it, Eden, I'm after your money and this old house." He seemed to be truly amused by what Jared was implying. He looked at Eden. "You know, don't you, that if either of us had any sense we'd sell our old houses and buy one of those new brick things in Queen Anne. I could get us a real deal."

Eden smiled at the absurdity of the idea. "Trade an authentic Queen Anne for a fake one?"

Jared grimaced as he looked from one to the other. "All right," he said, "point taken. Now, could you two get back to these watercolors? What do you see in them? Anything different? Unusual?"

Brad looked down at the nine pictures, but Eden looked across the table at Jared. Was he asking for Brad's help? What was next? Would he tell Brad what was going on? *Trust* him? Looking at McBride, Eden raised her eyebrows in disbelief.

Understanding her completely, Jared pointed to the paintings, as though to tell her to get busy and stop trying to analyze things.

"Nothing," Brad said after a few minutes. "I don't see anything unusual. Eden, you haven't changed the house at all since you returned, and these pictures show the house just as it is now." He looked at Jared. "Of course it would help if I knew what I was looking for."

Jared didn't open his mouth and didn't look as though he was going to. He cast a glance at Eden as though to warn her, but she smiled coolly at him in return, then looked down at the paintings.

She had no idea what she was looking for either. Why had an FBI agent painted the interiors of her house? If she wanted to make a record of the place, why not photograph it? There was the living room with the pale green paneling and the furniture that nearly matched the color of the walls. The paintings were so detailed that they even showed six of Tyrrell Farrington's paintings, so familiar to Eden that she rarely looked at them anymore. The dining room showed the table and chairs, the windows with the tall burgundy velvet curtains drawn, and more of Tyrrell's paintings. There was the hall with the big secretary, and the master bedroom. There was even a painting of Eden's bathroom, with the big clawfooted tub in the corner. As far as she could tell, the pictures were photographically correct.

"I see nothing different," she said.

Straightening, Brad looked at Jared. "Me neither. What is it we're supposed to see?"

Jared put his hands in his pockets and stepped back. "I don't know." He stared at the fireplace for a moment and seemed to be trying to make a decision. When he looked back at them he seemed to have softened. Some of his animosity seemed to have left him. "I don't know," he repeated softly. "We're pretty sure Ms. Brewster's death was no accident, and we'd like to know who killed her and why."

"Can I assume that Brewster is the real name of my tenant? It's not the name I knew her by, but that's neither here nor there. And what do you mean by 'we'? Who are you affiliated with?"

Jared mumbled, "Yeah, Tess Brewster." Then he had a look on his face that said he'd told all that he was going to.

Brad looked back at the watercolors. "Think anything is written on the back of these pictures?"

Fifteen minutes later, they'd taken the pictures out of their frames, but there was nothing written on them. Nor was there a signature at the bottom. No proof that Ms. Brewster had painted them.

"There has to be something," Eden said, frustrated. "If all she'd wanted to do was record what was here, she could have taken a roll of film."

"Or a thousand photos on one disk," Jared said.

Brad sat down on a dining-room chair and kept looking at the pictures. "Murdered. She was run down in the wee hours of the morning, so someone knew she was in here night after night. Someone was watching her. I wonder if they had any idea what she was doing inside this house?"

"Obviously not," Eden said, "or they would have taken the paintings before she could get them to the framers."

Jared looked at her in amazement. "Good point. So someone was watching her, but they didn't know what she was doing."

"Maybe they thought she was doing something else," Brad said.

"Searching for those damned jewels," Jared said and sat down, his fingers on his temples. "Look, I knew Tess for years. Not well, but we were friendly enough, I guess, but I never knew she could paint."

"What if she was doing this just to kill time?" Eden asked. "No reason, but just waiting."

"For someone?" Brad asked. "Or for something to happen?"

"Very possible," Jared said, nodding.

"Like a watchdog," Brad said.

Eden walked to the far end of the room. "So Ms. Brewster sneaked into the house at night and waited for whatever, or watched for something, and to keep herself busy, she made watercolors of the house. It wouldn't take much light, a good flashlight would be enough. Then, one day, when she was leaving or just arriving, someone hit her with a car and ran off."

"So maybe the pictures she was doing had nothing to do with anything," Brad said.

Jared glanced at Brad but said nothing. He seemed to be determined to give nothing more away.

"I've never been on a stakeout," Brad said, looking at Jared, "but from what I've seen on TV, they're pretty boring."

"Yeah," Eden said. "In the movies, the men mostly seem to eat fried food. I think painting watercolors would be better than that. A watercolor box is quite portable."

Jared leaned forward, his arms on the table. "I'm not convinced. I feel that there's something in these pictures. She took them to the framer's for a reason."

"Yeah," Brad said. "I know what you mean. If you write something down, someone can read it. And if you make a call, someone can trace it. So how to leave a message that no one knows *is* a message?"

Jared looked at Brad with new respect.

"So what was the message she was trying to leave?" Eden asked, looking at the pictures. "She didn't take photos because—" She looked at the two men, then her eyes lit up. "Because something is different in these pictures. You know, like where they have two pictures and you're supposed to find out what's different."

The three of them looked at one another.

"I'll take the living room, you take the hall," Brad said.

"I'll take the dining room," Jared said.

"Bed and bath," Eden said.

In a flurry of motion, they grabbed their pictures and separated. Twenty minutes later, they met back in the dining room.

"Nothing," Jared said.

"Nothing," Brad and Eden echoed.

"I even checked ol' Tyrrell's paintings," Brad said.

"You mean these paintings that are all over the house?" Jared asked.

"Yeah. Painted by an angry son of the house," Eden said, smiling. "He wanted to live in Paris, but the family wouldn't allow it, so to get them back, he returned home and never left. He wouldn't marry and produce babies, wouldn't have anything to do with the running of the family businesses. He just painted night and day, and these are the results." Eden waved her hand about to indicate the paintings on the walls. "Mrs. Farrington always said that for talent, they'd make a good bonfire, but they're family, so they were kept. Personally, I rather like them."

"That's because you like families," Brad said.

"Yes, that's true," Eden said, smiling at him, and their hands inched toward each other's.

"At least he got to see that necklace that caused so much fuss," Jared said.

Eden's and Brad's hands stopped moving, and they looked at each other, then at Jared.

"What?" Eden asked.

"Here," Jared said, picking up the now-unframed watercolor. It was a picture of the big hallway in the center of the house. On the wall was a portrait of a woman with a little white dog. Due to the nature of the medium, it was blurry, but there was a blue and white necklace around the woman's neck.

After a moment's stunned hesitation, both Eden and Brad ran for the door of the dining room, Jared behind them. Two seconds later they were standing in front of the familiar portrait done by Tyrrell Farrington over a hundred years before. Around the woman's neck was indeed a sapphire necklace. Gaping, mouths open, Brad and Eden stared at the portrait.

"Somebody want to let me in on what's going on?" Jared asked from behind them.

"There was no picture of the necklace," Brad said softly. "The Farringtons said that if it was ever photographed or reproduced in any way, that..." Brad shook his head to clear it. "Who knows what they believed about that cursed necklace? All I know for sure is that the woman in that picture didn't have on a big, gaudy sapphire necklace when I used to visit Mrs. Farrington. She loved to keep me waiting, and I used to spend umpteen hours in this hallway. I could draw the wallpaper pattern by heart. *There was no necklace.*"

While Brad and Eden were standing there, immobile, staring at the painting, Jared stepped between them and lifted the big, heavy painting off the wall. "What do you say we see what's behind this frame?"

Jared carried the big painting into the dining room, moved the watercolors aside, and put it facedown on the table. Taking his pocket knife, he started to cut the backing, but Eden put her hand on his.

"It's new," she said. "The paper tape is new."

"And poorly applied," Brad said.

"So maybe it was put on recently," Jared said as he slit the tape around the edges.

Carefully, he pulled the painting out of the frame and saw that there was a flat, thin package taped to the back of it. On the outside, written in a shaky hand, was "Miss Eden Palmer, spinster."

"Puts you in your place, doesn't it?" Jared said to Eden, making a joke to lighten the air, but Brad and Eden were standing as stiff as statues, their eyes wide as they watched Jared cut the tape off the package.

Slowly, Jared cut the paper off the package, and even more slowly, torturously slowly, he began to unwrap it. "Sure you want to see what's in here?"

Eden didn't bother to answer him. Unblinking, her eyes were on that package. She well knew that it was Mrs. Farrington's handwriting on the outside.

When Jared had peeled back the paper, the three of them drew in their breaths. Inside, lying on top of a white envelope, was the necklace. It was the sapphire and diamond necklace that for over a century people had been looking for.

It was Eden who recovered first. She put out her hand and touched the big, round, deep blue sapphire in the center. Two other smaller, but still huge, diamond-surrounded sapphires flanked it. In the light of the dining room chandelier, the necklace sparkled, with lights dancing off it to send a million colors through the air. Slowly, reverently, Eden picked up the necklace and held it, turning it in the light. She was hardly aware when Jared picked up the white envelope. It too had Eden's name on it.

Brad took the letter and held it out to her. "It's something from Mrs. Farrington. It's private," he said softly, "so I'm sure you'll want to read it when you're alone."

Eden heard the tone in his voice and looked up. Both McBride and Brad were looking at her wistfully, like little children wanting her to read them a bedtime story. Smiling, Eden handed the necklace to Brad and took the letter, then carefully opened it. Mrs. Farrington had used her beloved sealing wax on the back. "The only thing the hippie culture ever did that was good was to bring back sealing wax, so it's easy for me to find," she used to say.

When Eden saw Mrs. Farrington's handwriting on the letter she pulled from the envelope, she had to sit back. This is going to be difficult, she thought. The last words of a woman she'd loved very much.

"'My dearest Eden and Melissa,'" Eden read aloud, then had to wait a moment for her eyes to clear and her voice to come back. She took a deep breath.

"'Eden, dear, if you're reading this letter, then you've found the necklace. Congratulations! You always were the cleverest person! I wonder how long it took before you saw that the necklace had been painted on one of Tyrrell's dreadful paintings. I painted the necklace on Great-Aunt Hester's neck and I think I did a damned fine job of it! Maybe I could have been a painter too. I certainly have as much talent as Tyrrell did.'"

Pausing, Eden chuckled before she continued. "'Oh! How I wish I could hear you laugh at that witticism. You always did laugh long and hard at my jokes. It was one of your most endearing qualities.

"'Now, on to business. I found the necklace—and the poor woman who was wearing it—when we renovated this old house. Toddy—you remember him, don't you?—helped me cover everything up. Or, in this case, bury it. My great-grandfather Minton said he'd gone to New York to sell the necklace and had returned to find his beautiful wife dead on the library floor. On his deathbed he admitted to his son that he'd killed her lover, but I think he killed his wife too. There's a stone for her in the family cemetery, but I think the grave is probably empty.

"'Toddy found a grisly sight when one of the walls of the cellar came down, and I had to go down there to see it. You know how much I loved doing *that*! Minton must have disinterred his wife because what we were sure was her body was in a little stone-lined closet. A wall had been hastily and poorly erected to conceal the entryway. Inside was a skeleton wearing the tatters of what had surely been her wedding dress. Around her neck was the necklace that has caused my family so much misery. It's my guess that Minton killed his wife when he discovered she was about to run off with her lover. Maybe he thought that a decent burial in a churchyard was too good for her, so he dug her up and hid her in the cellar. Or maybe he was so sick of all the unhappiness that necklace had caused that he let her have it for all eternity.

"'Whatever happened, Toddy found the poor woman's remains when the wall fell in. With the help of one of Toddy's strong young grandsons—who, of course, was sworn to secrecy—we buried her far away from my family, and *very* far away from Minton. I hope that she can at last rest forever.

"'As for the necklace that has caused my family so many problems, I spent several days thinking about what to do with it. Tell the world that it had been found? Then what? Have every shyster in the country show up here to try to sell me things? Would I have to tell the truth about Grandfather Minton? Would I have people wanting to write those nasty, hate-filled biographies about my family? Have the world know about the tears shed in my family over those stones? Know about the murders committed because of them? People would say the sapphires and my family had a curse on them. No, I didn't want any of that. After a dozen sleepless nights, I decided to turn the whole thing over to you, my dear, clever Eden. The necklace is now yours, and you can do with it what you want. Wear it out to dinner. It'll look good with your eyes.

"'Finding the necklace has caused me no happiness, but finding the teapot caused me nothing but joy. Toddy came to me one Sunday morning, very excited. He said he'd seen something on TV that was like something I owned. He'd seen the hallmark of a Paul Revere teapot and remembered seeing it when he used to polish the silver for me. I can tell you that the two of us old duffers had an awful time prying up loose floorboards and walls to find that particular pot. But we found it, and I sold it, and it paid for at last making my house into the beauty that it had once been. And it paid to send four of Toddy's grandchildren to college. The other two went on full scholarships, so they had no need of me.

"'Eden, my dear, I have missed you and your dear child every day since you left. That you had to leave and why you had to leave was the curse of my life. No matter what my ancestors had done, nothing compared to the evil that was in my son. I will not burden you with what happened at the last. That is between God and me, and I pray that He can forgive me.

"'The Farrington family that I sacrificed my happiness for in an attempt to keep the name going, is no more, and I think it's fitting that it ends. Too much hate and anger runs in our blood. There was too much bloodshed in our history. Maybe Minton's punishment for the murders he committed was that his seed should die out forever.

"'Dear, dear, Eden, I leave my beloved house to you. I know this is selfish of me, for I know that you'll take care of the house and love it as I did. I am glad that, in the end, I had the wherewithal to make it beautiful again. And I'm especially glad that I'm not leaving you a mummy in the basement.

"'I wish you and Melissa all the happiness in the world. I've tried to keep up with where you were and what you were doing. I cried on the day of Melissa's wedding. I hope she presents you with a dozen grandchildren.

"'I'm sorry that you have never found the right man for you. Have you become bisexual like me?

"'I want you to know that wherever you are, I'm looking down on you and sending you my love. If it's possible, I will be protecting you from heaven—if they let me in there, that is.

"'I must go now. I'm an old, old woman and I

don't have much strength left. I send you all my love. Kiss Melissa for me. And why don't you give one of the younger Granville boys a call? Maybe one of them is as good in the sack as my Granville boys were.

"'I will love you always,

"'Alice Augusta Farrington.'"

Chapter Fifteen

It wasn't until late that night that Jared got enough privacy to call Bill. Granville had stayed late, looking at the necklace as though it were the Holy Grail, and talking to Eden about what she should do with the jewels. Eden seemed to be more interested in the historical significance of the necklace than in any monetary value, so she'd talked about doing more research into the family history. Mostly, she just clutched Mrs. Farrington's letter. It was obvious that the letter meant more to her than the jewels.

As for Jared, all evening, he'd sat back and watched and listened to both of them. He liked that Eden hadn't had an attack of greed the second she realized that she owned a necklace that was worth...What? Millions? She hadn't started talking about all the things she was going to buy. Her only mention of money had been to say that she'd like to set up trust funds for all her grandchildren. "Which reminds me," she said, "I haven't talked to my daughter in days." Soon after that the party broke up and Granville went home. Jared knew that the two of them wanted time alone, probably to do more kissing, he thought, and was ashamed of himself at how jealous he felt at that thought. He'd given Eden a look, then glanced upward at the tiny cameras in the shadows of the corners of the ceiling. If Granville had noticed them, he hadn't shown it. But Jared was forming the opinion that Granville didn't let on to a lot of what he saw—or knew.

Eden had taken the hint and hadn't performed for the FBI cameras, but had given Brad cheek kisses when he left. As soon as the door closed, she held up the necklace to the cameras. "We found it," she said, addressing the lens. "So now all of you can go away and let me have a life."

Jared had started to say that they had no way of knowing that the necklace had anything to do with Applegate's swallowing of her name, but she wouldn't listen. "I don't want to hear it," she said. "I'm tired and I want to go to bed."

"Yeah, sure," he said. Truthfully, he wanted to sit up with her for a while and talk about finding the necklace. He'd had some experience with jewels, and he thought he might be able to help her make some decisions. But, mainly, he'd wanted to just sit and talk with her. Or watch TV together. It had been years since he'd just sat beside a woman and watched TV. Not since his marriage broke up had he done such an ordinary thing.

He nodded to the necklace that was in her hand. "You think—" He broke off when she tossed the necklace at him and he barely caught it. "Sure you don't want to wear it to bed?" he asked, teasing.

"That necklace caused the deaths of several people and rivers of tears. The sooner I get rid of it, the better. Look," she said, "could you please do what you have to do as quickly as possible so all of you can get out of here?"

Holding the necklace, Jared thought how it was still warm from her hand. "I'll do my best," he said, smiling, but Eden didn't smile back. Turning, she went up to her bedroom.

He stood at the foot of the stairs for a while, then walked into the kitchen, where he got a piece of cake to take outside to the agent on duty. He had seen nothing unusual, heard nothing.

"What about you?" the agent asked. "Find anything?"

Jared started to make a joke about finding millions in sapphires and diamonds but thought better of it. Years of training had taught him to trust no one. He bid the man good night, then walked to the far side of the house and called Bill Teasdale.

"So what has forensics found out about the men who ransacked the house?" Jared asked.

"Nothing yet. There were lots of hairs, but none

from strangers. And thanks for leaving that sample of Ms. Palmer's hair. You find out anything?"

Jared gave a snort. He wasn't fooled by Bill's faked ignorance. "Saw the tapes, did you?"

"Yeah, we watched the whole thing. Most exciting thing to happen around here in years. A real treasure hunt. So what's she going to do with that thing?"

"I don't know," Jared said, pulling the necklace out of his pocket to look at it in the moonlight. "I can't figure out if this necklace has anything to do with all this or not."

"You know what I think?" Bill asked but didn't wait for an answer. "I think that if Applegate stood up and said that he'd been looking for that necklace, you'd still come up with an excuse to stay there. If you could have seen your face when Ms. Palmer kissed Granville!"

"Had a good laugh at my expense, did you?" Jared said tightly.

"The best."

"If the necklace is what they've all wanted, then how was Applegate connected to the goons who ransacked this place and put the snakes in Eden's bedroom? It doesn't make sense to try to kill her."

"Her death would get her out of the picture, wouldn't it?" Bill said. "I'm sure her heirs would put that old house up for sale. Who'd want to live in Arundel if you weren't born there? No jobs, nothing to do."

"It's a nice place and the house is great," Jared said defensively, then had to listen to Bill chuckle.

"Okay, so I like her and I like this place. I admit it. But whether or not I like anything has nothing to do with this case. If you can get your mind out of the gutter for a moment, maybe you'll remember Tess's death and that someone tried to kill Ms. Palmer."

"All right," Bill said. "What do you have?"

"Nothing but instinct. Something isn't what it seems, but I don't know what it is. When Eden told me that story about old man Minton I knew that he'd killed his wife. If I figured it out, others can too. But who heard the story?"

"Anyone with an Internet hookup. I found it in three hundred and eighty-one sites. Lots of people are interested in missing treasure."

Jared groaned. "I want you to check out Braddon Granville."

"Ah," Bill said.

"Cut the crap!" Jared snapped. "This isn't personal. He knows too much, figures out too much. And it's been my experience that normal people aren't suspicious, but Granville is."

"He's a lawyer, isn't he?" Bill said. "What do you call ten thousand lawyers at the bottom of the ocean?"

"A good start," Jared said, bored. "I just want you to check this guy out. Anything you can find out about him, I want to know."

"You know what I think? I think you're falling for this Eden Palmer so hard that I'm beginning to wonder if we should put someone else on the case."

"What I feel for her isn't hindering my judgment," Jared said tightly.

"What about your vow to stay away from 'good' women?"

"Bill, you wanta cut this out? What I think of Ms. Palmer has nothing to do with anything. I want this guy Granville checked out."

"He broke a man's jaw."

Jared grimaced. "You've already done the research, haven't you?"

"Yeah, but I couldn't resist hassling you. I did some checking, and a few years back, Granville broke a man's jaw, but the guy didn't press charges."

Jared waited for Bill to continue.

"The police report said that Braddon Norfleet Granville walked into a party that was to celebrate the recent marriage of Tredwell Norfleet Pembroke...Norfleet in both names. Think they're cousins?"

"They're all cousins here. It's the South, remember? Go on."

"Granville walked into the party, hit Pembroke, and smashed his jaw. The man had to have it wired back together. The report doesn't say what they fought about, but it must have been something big."

"Granville broke the guy's jaw, but the man didn't press charges?"

"That's right. Maybe it was a family thing."

"Yeah, maybe," Jared said softly. "Send me all that you have, will you? I want to know everything there is to know about him."

"We don't have much. He's never even had a traffic ticket, but that town protects its own. You know what old lady Farrington did, don't you, and that was covered up. The police report of her son's death said 'accidental drowning.'"

Jared had his own ideas about justice, so he didn't comment on what Bill was saying. There had been more than once when Jared had played judge and jury. "Just send me what you have and I'll find out what I can from the locals. Nobody knows people like childhood friends." He changed the subject. "So what did you think of Tess's watercolors?"

"Threw me for a loop. She never struck me as being the watercolor type. No, Tess Brewster was more the pit bull type. If I'd been told she owned any paintings, I would have guessed they were on velvet."

"Find out about her painting, will you?"

"I've already sent out the order."

Jared hesitated before he asked his next question. "Bill, isn't your wife a member of some garden club?"

"Yeah, but that doesn't mean she can use a shovel. She and her sister like to visit gardens around the world—at my expense." There was disgust in Bill's voice, but Jared ignored it.

"Could you find out what kind of things a real gardener would like? Not some lady-gardener things, but for a serious gardener."

"Right. Something like that Melissa plant, maybe? Around here, we call that 'the kissing plant.'"

"Wasn't I sent here to woo her?" Jared asked, anger in his voice.

"Yeah, but it was supposed to be an act. And besides, you're doing a very bad job of it. She sure doesn't like you much, does she? And who is this woman who calls you every ten minutes?"

"Minnie Norfleet. She works for Granville. I don't have time for her now. Besides, she's not my type. As for Eden, she doesn't like me because she doesn't know me."

"She feeds you and does your laundry. What else is there to know?"

Jared started to reply, but Bill's chuckling stopped him. "Just get some gardening things, will you?"

"Are we talking a couple of plants or a twenty-thousand-dollar greenhouse?"

"Whatever is mobile. Tools, maybe. The old potting shed here is full of rusty shovels."

"Who pays?"

"Me. Put it all on my AmEx."

"If you'll just give me your number—" Bill began, but that was too much for Jared. Like the FBI didn't have the credit card numbers of pretty much everyone on the planet. When Jared didn't answer, Bill laughed. "By the way, your new girlfriend, the stripper, she's been out with some other men. I thought you might like to know that you're free."

Jared didn't say anything for a moment. Just days ago, Bill had acted as though he didn't know anything about Jared's new girlfriend, but now he was admitting that he knew all about her—and had had her watched. Jared didn't know if he should be grateful or offended. "I'm too old for this job," he muttered as he snapped the phone shut, then went back into the house. He saw the light on under Eden's bedroom door and started to knock and ask if everything was all right, but then he glanced up at the camera in the shadows and thought better of it. Everything that went on inside the house was now being watched by men at the agency, so he went to his own bedroom. As he put his hand on the knob, he heard the soft sounds of the washing machine and remembered what Bill had said: "She feeds you and does your laundry. What else is there to know?"

Jared told himself that Bill was right on one count: Jared needed to stand back from this case, distance himself. Did he really and truly like Eden Palmer, or was it just that he didn't like to lose? He was being out-courted by a slick small-town lawyer, and he didn't like it. Was his problem that he was losing or was his problem Ms. Palmer herself?

He ran his hand over his eyes. Maybe Granville was on the up-and-up. Maybe he was just what he seemed to be: a small-town lawyer who had been knocked over by the arrival of a beautiful woman like Eden Palmer. Jared well knew how few women like Eden there were out there. Sometimes it seemed to him that if you didn't find the right woman when you were in your twenties, then you lost your chance. It seemed that all the best women were claimed the moment they put on high heels.

But somehow, through circumstances, a grown-up woman like Eden was still unattached.

Bill was right: Jared was losing his perspective. He was getting to the point where he couldn't see clearly. He'd have to change that or he'd be taken off the case. First, he had to figure out who was doing what and why. Was it all for that damned necklace? Who else would know that it actually existed and that Mrs. Farrington had found it? The man who'd helped her find it, Toddy, knew, at least one of his grandchildren, and…Jared's eyes widened. Mrs. Farrington's lawyer would probably know. Did Eden have a copy of the will? Or had Granville not bothered to give her one?

In the next instant, Jared was outside Eden's bedroom door and knocking on it.

"Come in," she said.

She was sitting in bed, her face washed clean, reading glasses perched on her nose, and wearing an old pink nightgown. He didn't think he'd ever seen anything sexier in his life. She didn't look like a centerfold, but she looked like home, a place where food was in the oven, clean clothes were in the drawers, and the bills were paid. She looked like someone who'd wait up for a man when he was out late. And she'd forgive him when he screwed up. And she'd give him hell at the same time. She looked like a woman who…No, that was it. She looked like a *woman*. Not a girl, but a woman. He wanted to climb into bed with her and rest his head on her breast. Then he'd turn and touch her lips with his own and—

"You want to get that look off your face, Mc-Bride?" Eden said, taking off her glasses. "If I scream, all of the FBI will hear me."

Her words brought him back to reality. Without asking permission, he sat down on the end of her bed. "Did Granville give you a copy of Mrs. Farrington's will?"

"Yes," she said coolly. "It's there in the bottom drawer." She motioned toward the big TV cabinet across from the foot of her bed. When he went to it, she said, "Watch out for snakes."

"Funny," he said, opening the drawer and pulling out the document. It was in a dark blue folder with Granville's name on it in gold. "Fancy. Think he sends his stuff off to New York to be printed?"

When he looked back at her, she wasn't smiling. "Okay, sorry," he said, then sat back down on the end of her bed. She had to move her foot to keep him from sitting on it. Quickly, he read the document, then closed it. "Just as I thought, you get everything." He looked at her. "There were no other relatives?"

Eden didn't answer but narrowed her eyes at him.

With a half smile, he got off of her bed. Turning, he put his hands on the iron footboard. "Do you really and truly think that Granville is innocent in all this?"

"Are you asking me if I think he murdered a woman to get— What exactly *was* his reason for murdering Ms. Brewster? He didn't get the jewels, and I'm not even sure she knew they were behind the picture. Only someone familiar with the house and its furnishings would notice that the necklace had been painted onto Aunt Hester's scrawny neck."

"And Granville said that he'd spent so much time in that hall that he could draw the wallpaper."

"If you're hinting that he might have known, he took a year to find me, so why didn't he open the painting during that time?"

"Then what? Try to fence some rocks the size of chicken eggs?"

Eden threw up her hands. "So he waited until I got here, then he started courting me so he could get the jewels. If all he likes about me is the necklace, what's *your* excuse?"

"I like your left hook," Jared said, but she didn't smile. He stuck his hands in his pockets. He knew he should leave. The guys back at the office had probably set a stopwatch when he'd entered Eden's bedroom. But Jared didn't leave. "So what are you reading?"

"I happen to be earning a living. Remember that part of my life? My publishing house works on a schedule, and these books need to be edited and returned."

"So what's involved in editing a book?" he asked, moving toward her.

"One step closer and I yell for help," Eden said calmly. "Why don't you go back to your own room now?"

Jared didn't move. "Ever hear of a jelly beanie? Cranberry juice, gin, that sort of thing? Jelly beans in the bottom of the glass."

"Is this some form of seduction?"

"Yeah. I have to get a woman drunk before she'll go to bed with me."

Eden looked at him, at his dark eyes and hair, and his statement was so ridiculous that she smiled. "Okay, one jelly beanie. I'm so wound up from the excitement of tonight that I'll be awake all night. So what did you do with the necklace?"

Jared pulled it out of his pocket and tossed it onto the covers by her hip. "How about if you take everything off, put on the necklace, and wait for me?"

"Hold your breath," she said, and Jared grinned.

As he put his hand on the door, he said, "Honestly, is there anything I can do to help with those things?" He nodded toward the stack of manuscripts on the floor.

"One of them is a spy thriller, and I hate those things. All that techno-jargon bores me. You wouldn't want to read it and write a report, would you? My publishing house would love to have an expert's opinion."

"On one condition," he said.

She narrowed her eyes at him. "And what is that?"

"That you let me watch your TV while I read."

Eden had to laugh. "Sure. Just keep the sound down so I can edit."

"Great! One jelly beanie and one straight whiskey coming up."

An hour later, the manuscripts were on the floor and they were watching their third episode of

Fawlty Towers and laughing hilariously. Jared sat on the chair by the bed and Eden lay propped up in bed on her four fat pillows. It was well into the wee hours of the morning before Jared said good night and left the room.

Chapter Sixteen

The ringing of the telephone woke Eden. Groggily, she reached for it without opening her eyes.

"Mother!" came her daughter's irate voice. "I haven't heard from you in more than a week."

"I'm sorry, dear, but I've been very busy." Eden didn't want to open her eyes, didn't want to wake up. What in the world had McBride put in that drink last night? Some secret sedative that made people want to sleep for days? And what had been his motive? To put her out so he and his fellow agents could go through more of the house? They probably were embarrassed that they hadn't taken apart all of Tyrrell Farrington's paintings and looked inside them. Her eyes flew open. If they were now taking apart those paintings, so help her, she was going to—

"Mother, are you listening to me?"

"Sorry, sweetheart," Eden said guiltily. "I'm still a little sleepy. What time is it anyway?"

There was a long silence on the phone before Melissa said, "It is ten minutes after eleven A.M. Mother, are you ill?"

Eden slowly sat up in the bed, turned on the lamp, glanced at the clock, and saw that it was indeed midmorning. She didn't think she'd ever slept so late in her life. But then, single mothers didn't have time to sleep, did they? There was no husband to take the kids out for pancakes so Mom could sleep. "No, I'm not ill, it's just that it's been rather hectic since I got here and I guess I was rather tired last night."

"Hectic? In Arundel, North Carolina? Mother, I live in New York City. What could be more hectic than here?"

Being in the hospital, being investigated by the FBI, having a new job, meeting a couple of men, Eden wanted to say, but didn't. If Melissa was saying "Mother" every other word, then she was upset about something. "I wasn't comparing lives. What's wrong?"

"Nothing," Melissa said. "I just called to see how you were. You ran off to take possession of some old house, and it's only the second time we've ever been separated, but I didn't hear from you. I was just worried, that's all."

"So what's wrong?" Eden repeated. "And quit

lying to me. I'm your mother, remember? I know you."

At that, Melissa burst into tears and began pouring out a long list of complaints. It seemed that Stuart was working late and Melissa was by herself three nights a week. When he came home, he was too tired to even be interested in the baby's kicking. And then there was the kitchen. Stuart had said that they couldn't afford to eat out every night or even have delivery, so Melissa was supposed to cook dinner for them. "I have no idea how to cook," Melissa said.

Not that I didn't try to teach you, Eden wanted to say. "There are cookbooks in the cabinet over the refrig—"

"I know where the cookbooks are," Melissa said tightly. "Mother, is this going to be one of those fix-it conversations? I need some help here, not a pep talk."

Eden looked at the pile of manuscripts on the floor and knew she should have set her alarm for six. On the table was the sapphire necklace, and she picked it up. Was this why some man had swallowed her name? "I'm sorry," Eden said. "I know that starting a new life alone with your husband is difficult, but—"

"I want to be with you."

"Hmmm," Eden said, holding the necklace up to the light.

"Mother, are you listening to me?"

"Yes, of course I am. It's just that—" Frowning,

Eden held the phone to her shoulder, got out of bed, and went to the window. She pulled back the curtain, then raised the blind. Sunlight threatened to pierce her eyesight. "Damn you, McBride!" she muttered.

"Bride?" Melissa said. "Yes, I know I'm Stuart's bride, but I still have a mother and I want to be with you when the baby comes."

Eden looked at the necklace in the sunlight, turning it over in her hand. She'd once worked in a jewelry store and she'd seen some nice jewels. There was something wrong with this necklace. Was it just the old setting, or was it something else?

"Mother, did you hear what I said? If I get there tomorrow will you meet me at the train station?"

"Train?" Eden said distractedly. "Honey, there's no train here, except for freight trains, that is." She put the necklace down on the windowsill, took a breath, and gave her attention to her daughter. "Listen, sweetheart, I know that being pregnant is difficult, but you have Stuart now, and I think—"

"You don't have to tell me what you think," Melissa said quickly. "I know that your pregnancy was hell and I know that *you* were alone. And I know that having me has ruined your life."

"Melissa! What a thing to say! You've always been the best part of my life, and I've told you that often."

"Then why did you abandon me now when I need you so very much?"

Eden ran her hand over her eyes. "I didn't abandon you. You and Stuart were very excited to be on your own, remember? When I left, you were planning all the redecorating you were going to do."

"That's what I thought was going to happen, but it didn't. Stuart said we can't afford to do any decorating now that he has to pay for the whole apartment. You know what he said to me?"

Eden could smell food. The delightful aroma was wafting up the stairs and coming in under her door. She walked across the room, opened the door, and inhaled deeply. What in the world was McBride cooking this morning? "What did Stuart say to you?"

"He said that I should go downtown to one of those ragtag flea markets and get old, used furniture and refinish it. *Like you did!* Can you imagine that? Here I am, pregnant with *his* child, and he wants me to drive downtown, waddle through a bunch of dirty flea markets, and haul furniture back on top of your old station wagon. Have you ever heard of anything so impossible? Is that how a pregnant woman *should* be treated?"

Eden had a flash of her own pregnancy. Before she'd met Mrs. Farrington she'd gone without food for days at a time. After she met Mrs. Farrington, she'd been so scared she'd lose the job that she'd hauled huge boxes down from the attic by herself. She remembered one time when the dust made her sneeze eleven times in a row. "No, that's not how a pregnant woman should be treated," Eden said dutifully.

"Mother, am I boring you?"

"No, of course not." She heard McBride on the stairs; she knew his step.

"Food's on," he called. "You haven't lived until you've tasted my strawberry muffins."

"Be right there," Eden called back, her hand over the phone. She put it back to her ear.

"Mother, was that a man?" Melissa's voice was a combination of disbelief and disapproval.

"Yes, it was, but—"

"What is a man doing in your house at this hour of the morning?"

"Melissa, please don't sound like a prude, and besides, it's nearly time for lunch, remember?"

"I remember that when I called you this morning, I woke you up. Mother, did you spend the night with that man?"

Eden gritted her teeth. "Melissa, darling, my dearest daughter, that is none of your business. Now, if you can't talk to me in a civil manner, I suggest we cut this off. I also suggest that you make up to your husband and stop putting me between the two of you. And as for your visiting, might I remind you that you're a bit far along in your pregnancy to be taking long trips. Now, why don't you take a nice hot bath, then look through those cookbooks and make your husband a nice dinner? I'll call you when I can."

With that, Eden hung up. For about thirty seconds she felt great, like something out of a self-help book about standing up to your children. When Eden said she was leaving New York, Melissa had turned against her mother and chosen her husband's side—which she should have done. Eden again felt the hurt of it all, how her daughter and Stuart had been so glad when Eden told them she was moving out.

But her elation, her self-righteousness, and her did-the-right-thing vibes didn't survive a full minute. The next second Eden slumped down onto the chair, put her hands over her eyes, and started crying. She'd just told off her child, her daughter who she'd been with since she was born. Her daughter was now having her own child and was alone with a man Eden didn't like, and her mother had abandoned her. Should she have told Melissa to come here to Arundel? And get mixed up in some mistake with the FBI?

"Anything I can do to help?" came a soft voice from the doorway.

As Eden wiped her eyes with the back of her hand, Jared handed her a tissue. "Thanks," she murmured.

"That was your kid on the phone?"

"Yes," Eden said, blowing her nose. "My grown-up child now thinks I have abandoned her. And oh, yes, I'm a slut."

"You? You make nuns look promiscuous."

"I do not!" Eden said, sniffing.

"Sure you do. Last night I gave you my best seduction drink. If you knew how many women that drink has worked on . . . Well, maybe I shouldn't tell the total number, but I can tell you that it works. But not on you."

In spite of herself, Eden laughed. But in the next moment she looked down at her hands and her smile left her. "This isn't serious, is it? I mean, about the argument with my daughter."

"I don't have kids, but my guess is that it's not. And I think that what you said to her was the right thing. Okay, so maybe I was eavesdropping a little bit. Professional habit. But I think you were right on the money. If she runs home to Mom every time she has a fight with Hubby, she'll never learn."

"But Stuart, her husband...I can't stand him."

"He was a new husband and living with a mother-in-law who'd made a success of herself in spite of all that life had done to her. Do you know what usually happens to girls who get pregnant at seventeen?"

"Yes, of course I do, but I had help. I had Mrs. Farrington."

"Do you think she would have kept you if you hadn't worked yourself to the bone for her?"

Eden smiled. "No. She hated lazy people. She never did a lick of work herself, but she expected others to work from early until late."

"So maybe it was you and not Mrs. Farrington who made a success of the whole thing."

"Maybe," Eden said, smiling.

"All right, so I've done all my cheering-up for the day. As fetching as you look in that nightgown—which, by the way, is nearly transparent in the sunlight—why don't you get dressed and come downstairs and eat?"

"I—" Eden began. Her instinct was to grab a blanket off the chest at the foot of the bed and cover herself, but she didn't. Instead, she looked up at McBride.

"Oh, no, you don't. I want nothing given to me out of gratitude for my wisdom. Get dressed, and that's an order. I've already called Granville and told him that you don't feel well so you're staying home today. You won't be meeting any of his ego-maniacal clients and trying to design gardens that they'll never appreciate."

"You had no right to do that!" Eden said, standing up and glaring at him.

Jared looked at her standing in front of the sun-filled window, wearing just the old nightgown, thin from a hundred washings, and turned pale. He opened his mouth to say something, but then he turned on his heel and left the room. "Ten minutes, Palmer," he called back to her. "Take more than fifteen and I'll be back."

Eden couldn't help smiling as she closed her bedroom door and went to the shower. Men, and McBride in particular, were a pain in the neck, she thought, but sometimes they could make you feel great. In the shower, with the water turned on as hot as it would go, she washed her hair and lathered her face with a cleansing gel. Soap made her skin too dry, and the last thing she needed right now was flaking skin.

As the water washed over her, she replayed in her mind everything that she and Melissa had said. She hadn't been a good mother. She should have listened more, cared more, taken Melissa's complaints more seriously. On the other hand, she was a person as well as a mother, and it still hurt the way her daughter had let her leave New York so easily. When Eden had turned her apartment over to her daughter and the man she'd married, they'd been elated at the idea of being on their own. But it was one thing to dream about being someone's wife and another to be one.

"Not that I know anything about marriage," Eden said to herself. In the past, whenever she'd thought about marriage, her first consideration had been her daughter, and Eden had always feared what would happen if she let a third person into their lives.

But that was done, she thought. Now she was free. As she washed the conditioner out of her hair, she thought about Brad. In spite of all that McBride said against him, she liked Brad very much. He was kind, considerate, thoughtful. They liked the same things. She very much liked the subdivision he'd designed. What was it that Drake Haughton had said? That he drew what Brad imagined. Brad was creative and intelligent—and he liked Eden.

Where would we live? she thought, smiling. Here or his house? Here, of course, she thought. Who would want a Victorian house when they could have the eighteenth century? Yes, no question about it, they'd live here. Brad could let his daughter and her husband live in the oversize Granville house, and Minnie could move into the vacant overseer's house down the road. Yes, that was how it would be, and maybe her life would be perfect. Smiling, she imagined holding a cold drink as she and Brad showed guests around the garden.

By the time Eden got out of the shower, she was well over McBride's fifteen-minute limit, but she knew he'd only been kidding. Everything McBride said was a joke, wasn't it? He joked when he was a prisoner in a cellar, joked about death and about everything else. All the world was a joke to him.

As she dressed (this time blow-drying the curlers in her hair so she could take them out) she was glad that she didn't have to start seeing clients today. It seemed that ever since she'd arrived in Arundel, she'd been on a roller coaster. As she put in earrings (tiny frogs) she smiled at the thought of her daughter's reaction if she'd told Melissa the truth about why she hadn't called since she'd been here.

You see, dear, I'm under investigation by the FBI because some spy swallowed my name. In fact, I have a terribly good-looking agent living with me, and another man, or men, I don't know which, wander around my garden 24/7. No, dear, I'm not having an affair with the good-looking agent, but I am trying to have an affair with the good-looking lawyer Mrs. Farrington hired. But, you know how it is, with FBI cameras watching your every move, it inhibits you, although Braddon——that's the lawyer——and I have managed a few kisses. No, no, dear, I know that to you I'm old, but these men don't seem to think so, so

don't worry about me. And, by the way, Mr. Mc-
Bride—he's the FBI agent—didn't press charges
when I beat him up, so there'll be no assault and
battery charges on my record to embarrass my
grandchild. I think Stuart will appreciate that. And,
oh, yes, the FBI cleaned up the house after those
criminals nearly destroyed it. No, dearest, I don't
know what they wanted and neither does the FBI.
But we—that's McBride, Brad, and I—think it has
to do with the multimillion-dollar necklace that we
found last night. That's why I was sleeping so late
this morning. The excitement and all. No, dear, I
haven't gone senile on you. It's been a very event-
ful few days. Yes, very exciting, but also exhaust-
ing. That's why Mr. McBride is insisting that I stay
home today and not start the new job of designing
eighteenth-century–style gardens for Brad's new
subdivision. Oh? Didn't I tell you about my new
job? No, sorry, that's right, dear, I didn't call you,
but, yes, I have a new job. But I don't know if I'm
going to take it, because last night McBride looked
at the will and said I do own the necklace. We were
going to talk about that, but we started watching
Fawlty Towers and— What's that? Oh, it's only an
old English TV series. John Cleese and very funny.
Anyway, it was nearly three A.M. before McBride
went to his room— No, dear, I am *not* sleeping
with the FBI agent. Or the lawyer, for that matter. Anyway, McBride asked me what I was going
to do now that I'm going to be a multimillionaire,
you know, rather like I won the lottery, and I said I
have no idea. So today I think I'm going to work in

the garden and think about what I want to do with my life. Things have been happening so fast in the last few days that I haven't had time to figure out anything. But then, I'll tell you a little secret. I'm not sure, but I think the necklace is a fake. No, I'm not qualified to make such a judgment. I can tell that it's old, but I'm not sure if the stones are real or not. But don't worry. I'm sure the FBI has people who can tell a real jewel from a fake one. Uh-oh, dear, I have to go. Mr. McBride is calling me to breakfast. Or, by now, I guess it's lunch. See you when I can. Kiss the baby bump for me. Bye.

By the time Eden had finished the little play running through her mind, she was downstairs. McBride was standing by the stove and watching her.

"You don't get a bite until you tell me what's making you laugh. I could hear you chuckling all the way down the stairs."

"Nothing. I was just thinking of what I *should* have told my daughter."

"And?"

"Nothing," she said, looking away. The kitchen door was open. It was cooler than she liked, but it was great gardening weather. She could almost feel the soil in her hands. Too bad she had nothing to plant. Spring made her lust to dump plants out of pots and put them in the ground.

"Strawberry muffins, omelets with onions and green peppers, milk, coffee, tea, cranberry juice with no gin in it. But not one bite until you tell me what was making you laugh."

"Okay," Eden said, smiling, then she proceeded to run through the entire minidrama for him. She even held an imaginary telephone to her ear and pantomimed emotions.

As always, Jared was a good audience, and the more he listened, the more he laughed, so the more outrageous she got. By the end he was laughing with his mouth open, showing his strong, straight teeth. At the end, though, his face stilled.

"What?" he whispered when she'd finished.

For a moment, Eden blinked, realizing what she'd seen while she was on the phone to her daughter. At the time, Melissa's complaints had so distracted Eden that she hadn't fully registered what she was thinking. And since then, her thoughts had been on her daughter, not the necklace.

"Where is it?"

"Windowsill," Eden said, turning toward the stairs.

"You eat, I'll get the necklace, and I'll get someone out here as fast as they can to look at it."

Eden, starving, grabbed a muffin from under its cloth covering. "No helicopters," she called after him. "Everyone in Arundel will come out here to see what's going on if a helicopter lands in the fields." She went to the stove and lifted the lid to the skillet. "Helicopters," she muttered. "Two weeks ago I would never have thought of helicopters."

She slid the omelet onto the plate that Jared had placed on the counter and sat down to eat. What next? was her only thought. What monumental, dramatic thing could happen next?

When she heard the hydraulic brakes of a truck pulling into her driveway, she wasn't even surprised.

"What's that?" McBride asked from the doorway, the necklace in his hand.

"A SWAT team?" she asked, her mouth full.

Someone knocked on the door and Jared went to open it. Eden heard him exchange a few words with the driver, then they both went outside. She heard sounds of the truck door opening but didn't get up to look. By the time McBride came back into the room, she had finished eating.

"I think you better come look at this," he said.

"Is it good or bad?"

"Come and see what you think."

She put down her napkin, drained the last of her tea, and followed him to the front door.

Chapter Seventeen

All she could do was stare. Her mouth gaped open, and her eyes blinked several times, but she still couldn't believe what she was seeing.

On the oval lawn in front of the house was a little red truck, a Kawasaki Mule, cute beyond describing. It had a wide seat in front and a truck bed in back that was full of what looked to be top-of-the-line Spear and Jackson gardening tools from England. Behind the truck, on the ground, were hundreds of black plastic pots full of perennials. In front of them were annuals, and in back were boxes that bore the words LIVE TREES INSIDE OPEN IMMEDIATELY.

Slowly, Eden went down the stairs to stand beside McBride. She was too astonished to move.

Not so Jared. He stepped into the little truck, turned the key, and started the engine. "Look at this," he said, then flipped a switch and the bed moved upward. "It's a dump truck."

Shovels, rakes, a gardening fork, a three-pronged bulb planter, a soil aerator, and at least a dozen hand tools went tumbling out the back to the ground. "Look what you've done," Eden cried as she began to pick up the tools.

Jared turned off the engine, stepped out of the truck, and looked at her. "So what do you think of all this?"

"I think Braddon Granville is the most wonderful man in the world," she said softly as she put the tools against the big cypress tree. She went to the perennials to read the labels. Astilbe. For shade, she thought. Under the pecan trees. Heuchera and agastache.

"You think it was Granville who sent you all this?" Jared asked.

"Of course. Who else would do this?"

"Ah, yes, who else could it be?" he said.

"And what is that supposed to mean?"

"Are you going to accept gifts from a man you barely know?" Jared had his hands in his pockets and, for once, he wasn't wearing his isn't-life-funny look.

Eden looked at the plants, the truck, and the tools, then back at McBride. "Since I was eighteen years old, I've tried to set an example for my daughter. When a man liked me and offered me a gift, I didn't take it because I didn't want my daughter to grow up thinking that if a man gave her something she owed him something."

"Hard life to live."

"Yes, it was sometimes. I think I wanted to prove to myself and the world that even though I'd had a child when I was a child, I could still be a good mother."

Jared, with his hands still in his pockets, nodded toward all the things around them. "But now you have nothing to prove, so you're going to accept the gifts."

She put her hand on the fender of the little red truck. "I'd rather have these things than an engagement ring."

"Engagement ring?! So now you're *engaged* to Granville? When did this happen?"

"It hasn't, but a woman knows, and I know that I will be asked."

"Why not? You have nothing to lose," Jared muttered.

"Is that supposed to mean something?"

"Nothing. It means nothing," he said. "I'm sure that you and Granville will make a great couple. You can live together in your old houses, one week in his and one week in yours. You'll be the leading couple in town, and everyone will want to go to your parties. Young girls will make their husbands' lives hell if they aren't invited to your parties. In one generation you'll have gone from being a pregnant kid with nothing, to being Mrs. Astor of Arundel. Now, if you'll excuse me, I have work to do. Don't leave your property and you'll be safe."

Eden watched him go into the house, then sat down on the seat of the little truck. What a day! she thought. First Melissa and now McBride. She saw the thick stack of papers in the little cubbyhole to the right of the steering wheel and took them out. It was the instruction manual. As she opened the booklet, she told herself that she was going to enjoy the day no matter what anyone did to her.

Easier said than done. All of the hundreds of plants needed to be put into the ground, and something that usually relaxed her now seemed to be a monumental task. Her mind wouldn't stop working. *Had* she been horrible to her daughter? Should she have been more understanding? Should she have said that she'd known all along that Stuart was no good? Should she have jumped in her new car and driven to New York to be with her pregnant daughter?

That she'd done none of those things worried Eden, ate at her. She even wondered if she was jealous of her daughter. Melissa had everything while she was pregnant, but Eden had had so very little. As McBride said, Eden had worked herself half to death while she was pregnant. She'd climbed stairs carrying heavy boxes and stayed up late to read what was inside the boxes. Her only time "off" was when she was in the kitchen, trying to figure out how to cook something that Mrs. Farrington would like.

Brad had said that Mrs. Farrington was "cantankerous" and Eden had defended the woman.

It was true that Mrs. Farrington had treated Eden and Melissa well, but Eden had had to earn that good treatment. Before Melissa was born Mrs. Farrington had demanded a great deal of work. After the child was born, it had been better, but that Eden should sit down and rest were words that were never spoken.

Eden picked up her new hand shovel and looked at it. Damn McBride, she thought. He was as bad as those snakes that had been put into her bedroom. He was always spreading poison. The truth was that he had presented her with a picture of her future with Brad that she didn't like. And a truth that she didn't want to hear.

Was it possible that part of her attraction to Brad was that his family was so very prominent? Arundel, North Carolina, wasn't New York or Palm Beach, but, well…As Brad's wife, Eden would be accepted into social circles that had always been outside her world. When Mrs. Farrington had parties, Eden served drinks.

Eden knew from having lived with Mrs. Farrington that some of the families of Arundel were accepted in those "old money" worlds. Compared to the rest of the world, the United States was very young and had no aristocracy. By default, any family that had had money for over two hundred years was considered upper class. A Granville would be welcome anywhere.

Eden turned a bulb planter over in her hand. How much of her attraction to Brad was the man himself and how much was his name?

"Can't decide where to begin?" Jared asked from above her.

She didn't look up. "Get over your sulk?"

"I wasn't sulking," he said to the top of her head. "I was in a fury of jealousy."

"Oh?" she said, her head still down, but she was smiling. "Happen to you often?"

"Not even once before, I'm happy to say. Not even my wife—"

She looked at him. "You were married?"

"Long ago. And stop looking at me like that. The divorce wasn't any great traumatic thing that broke my heart."

When Eden just kept looking at him, he shrugged. "I was young, and marriage seemed like the thing to do, so we did it. Three years later I came home to find a note saying she'd left me. To tell you the truth, I was so tired that night that I was more angry that there was no beer in the refrigerator and that she'd taken the TV with her than I was that she'd left me. We didn't know each other very well and had never spent much time together, so I never really missed her."

Eden kept looking at him. "So how bad are you lying?" she asked softly.

Jared gave a laugh. "A hundred percent. I was mad about her, and I thought I was going to go crazy after she left me. The guy she ran off with came up to my shoulder and was bald at twenty-six. But he was home every night, they went to church on Sunday, and he coached Little League."

"Children?"

"Three. All of them smart, polite, and great athletes."

When he glanced back at her, Eden meant to give him a look of sympathy, but instead she laughed. "We're a pair, aren't we? School of Hard Knocks. So why don't you get a shovel and help me plant these trees?"

Jared looked aghast. "I've never planted anything in my life."

"Dig a hole, stick it in. It's not—"

"Yeah, I know, rocket science." His words were sarcastic, but he was grinning as he picked up a shovel. "So Granville sent you all of this?"

"Who else? The FBI? Maybe it's a new technique. Maybe instead of threatening people to make them talk, they're going to start using bribery. By the way, after you drugged me to sleep last night, did they do any more searching in my house? Tell me they didn't take the pictures apart."

"First of all, I didn't drug you. Is this shovel big enough?" he asked, holding up what could be used as a snow shovel.

"It's big enough to plant six trees. You should—" Eden started to explain about gardening equipment, but when she looked at him and saw that his eyes were twinkling, she knew he was teasing her. She had an idea that he knew more about gardening than he was letting on. "Could you open these boxes? We need to get the trees out, then we're going to the orchard to plant them."

He pulled a Swiss army knife out of his pocket and slit the plastic bands around the boxes. As they began to pull damp, shredded newspaper off the bare-root trees, she said, "So how did you get into the FBI?"

"I thought that was the way to save the world and that I could do it single-handedly. Great! A peach tree. My favorite."

"Why do I sense disappointment? Did you find out that you're not helping?"

Jared shrugged as he untangled three trees from one another. "I guess I've done some good, but the day-to-day bad you see gets you down. Sometimes things happen to make me realize that the average American man doesn't spend his days dealing with the lowlifes that I know. Drugs. Murder. Women with slashed faces. I once worked on a case where three women—" Cutting himself off, he looked at her quickly, then away. "I wish there really was a little machine that could make me forget what I've seen."

"Oh. You mean a machine like in *Men in Black*?"

"Exactly."

"So how many grown cockroaches have you had to deal with?"

"Hundreds."

Eden laughed. "So what's the future hold for you?"

"I have no idea. Retire and settle down, maybe. Or I could get out of the field and take a desk job, but that appeals to me about as much as..."

"As what?"

"As having a desk job, I guess."

Smiling, Eden looked toward the back of her

property. She could see the orchard—or what was left of it. Toddy and she had set the posts, and together they'd put in the three-rail fence. It had weathered to a beautiful gray, and by now her orchard should have been beautiful. But nearly all the trees were dead, or so overgrown that they looked as though they wished they were dead, and part of the fence had fallen down.

Jared followed her glance. "Bad, huh?"

"Very bad." She looked at him. "But thanks to the trees Brad sent, I can revive the orchard." She looked him up and down. "Are you up to some work? *Real* work? And you can't shoot anything."

"Not even Granvilles?" Jared asked without cracking a smile.

"Most certainly not Granvilles."

"I think I can handle it. But I have a bum leg and a couple of old wounds that—"

"Yeah, well, I had a baby. You want to compare pain?" Eden said as she turned toward the Mule. She needed to start making a plan of the whole garden, and what better way to survey her land than in the little truck?

Jared started to get into the driver's seat, but Eden glared at him, and, with a mock bow, he handed her the key. It took a minute for her to get the hang of starting it and keeping it started (choke out, neutral gear, choke off, brake off, forward gear), but once she got it going, she set off across the lawn. There was no windshield, and as the air ran cool and fast across her face, she felt young and free. She glanced at McBride and saw that he was enjoying it too. On impulse, Eden turned the wheel sharply, and since the truck was so small, it turned in a circle hardly bigger than an embroidery hoop. She headed toward the unplanted fields next to her house. There didn't seem to be any shock absorbers in the little truck because they could feel every bounce of the rough field. Again, she glanced at McBride and saw that he was smiling.

On impulse, Eden pushed the gas pedal to the floor and McBride almost fell out the open side. He grabbed the handle on the steel rod overhead, stuck his long legs under the dashboard, and held on. Eden raced across the bumpy fields, her teeth jarring and her breasts bouncing until they hurt. The air was cold on her face and blew her hair straight out, but the freedom of the ride felt wonderful. When she saw a leftover peanut bale, she hit it at full speed. When peanut stems flew up, she ducked her head, and McBride put up his arm to protect his face.

"All right!" he yelled joyously.

Eden turned the wheel sharply so they went in a circle, then she ran it toward another old peanut bale. When she hit it, the truck bounced them to the overhead canopy. Her head only touched it, but Jared yelled in pain—which made Eden throw back her head and laugh. Looking at her, he joined in the laughter.

It was on the fourth bale that they got stuck. The engine died and they stopped moving. Eden started the motor again, but the truck wouldn't move. She turned off the engine and looked at Mc-

Bride expectantly. Someone was going to have to push.

Jared threw a long leg out—and promptly sunk down to the middle of his calf. "What the—" he said.

"Swamp," Eden said succinctly, nodding toward the great barrier of trees at the end of the field. "Precisely, it's the Great Dismal Swamp. Did you know that George Washington surveyed the place?"

"Yeah, yeah, I know. And he stayed in your house."

Eden scooted to his side of the truck and looked over. The more McBride tried to get out, the deeper he became stuck. "Maybe. There's a bathtub that—"

"Could you stop with the history lessons and give me a hand here?"

When Eden raised her hands as though to clap, he narrowed his eyes at her.

"Come on," she said, teasing, "you're a big-deal FBI agent. What would you do if I were a drug dealer and about to escape?"

In the flash of an eye, Jared fell forward so that he landed on top of her. His feet and half of one leg were still buried in the mud, but the upper half of him was inside the truck and holding her down.

"Would you mind!" Eden said, looking up at him, utterly still beneath him.

"No, I don't mind at all," he said happily.

"The gearshift is sticking me and it hurts."

"Good try. The gearshift is on the side. So if you

were dealing drugs, how would you get away from an FBI agent who is handicapped with his legs pinned down?"

She glared up at him. "I'd get my gun out of the glove box and shoot you in the head."

"Try it."

Eden started to reach for the little black plastic glove box by her head, but she knew that if she moved, he'd love it. "Get off of me."

"Not good enough."

"I mean it. Get off of me!"

"No," he said, looking away, as though remembering. "I don't remember anybody saying that to me. I think they knew I'd not obey that command."

She squinted at him and didn't care that she was making wrinkles at the corners of her eyes. "If you don't get off of me, I'll go back to the house, stand in front of a camera, and tell whoever is watching that you are becoming emotionally involved with me."

Jared blinked at her a couple of times, then stood upright in the mud. "You sure know how to play dirty, don't you?"

"I've learned a lot since I was seventeen." Solemnly, she sat upright and turned the key in the engine. It started, but the truck wouldn't move in the deep mud. She looked at McBride. "Could you give me a push?"

Just before he moved, he had a glint in his eyes that made her eyes widen.

"Oh, no, you don't," she managed to say just before he gave her a push that sent her flying out the side of the truck to land on her fanny in the mud.

She pulled her hands out and tried to stand up, but fell back down. She looked up to see McBride, thick mud on him from the knee down, sitting behind the steering wheel of her brand-new Mule.

"You're getting it dirty," she wailed.

"A dirty machine to match the mind of its owner," he said as he started the engine, then tried to reverse it.

Eden grabbed a handful of mud and threw it at him. Her aim was perfect, and she hit him on the side of the face. When he turned to her, wiping mud out of his eyes, she grinned at him.

"I'll get you for that," he said, then leaped out of the truck.

She rolled, and he landed facedown. Eden let out a howl of laughter, and when he lifted his face and she saw the mud, she laughed more.

"You—" Jared began and made a grab for her ankle.

Eden tried to get away, but the mud was too deep and too slippery. Her head went back and the side of her face hit the mud. "Yuck!" she said as she scraped off two inches of it. Mud was crawling down the back of her neck to the inside of her shirt. "You are—"

She didn't finish telling him what he was because just then the sound of a helicopter came to them, and they both looked up. Eden knew without a doubt who the 'copter belonged to and where it was going to land. She also knew that she was going to have to meet whoever was inside while she was plastered in mud.

"At least it's not Brad," she muttered in disgust. She'd rather face the president of the United States like this than the man she was beginning to like so much.

When McBride removed enough mud off his face to give her a wicked grin, he pointed, and Eden didn't have to look to see what he was looking at. He was pointing toward the driveway, and she could hear gravel crunching.

"A car?" she asked over the noise of the helicopter.

McBride nodded vigorously.

"Brad?"

He nodded with such energy and enthusiasm that Eden wanted to hit him—if she could find her hand, that is.

"Girl in the car," he yelled. "Looks like you."

"Like me?" Twisting as best she could, Eden looked at the car that had stopped in the driveway. It was Brad's car, and he was driving. Beside him sat Melissa.

Eden thought maybe there were tears in her eyes under the mud, but she wasn't sure. She turned back to McBride. What other horrible, rotten, humiliating thing could happen to her?

In the next second the helicopter stopped to hover above them. In the noise and the wind, she looked up to see two men hanging out of the door with rifles aimed at her and McBride.

"Are you all right?" came a voice over a loudspeaker, and Eden was sure that everyone in Arundel heard it.

"Yes," Eden tried to shout up to the men over the noise of the helicopter.

"They mean me," Jared yelled, grinning. "I'm the good guy, remember? You're the suspect. They want to make sure you haven't hurt me—again."

Behind them, Eden heard a car door slam, then a wail that every mother on earth responded to. "Mother," came the voice, a high, plaintive wail that carried above the roar of the helicopter hovering over them.

"Kill me now," Eden said, and fell back into the mud.

Chapter Eighteen

I really don't know what to think," Melissa was saying as she held the hose on her mother. "I was already in Arundel when I called you. In the past, in normal circumstances, I would have gone straight to you, but you've been acting so strangely lately that I wasn't sure what to do, so that's why I called first and asked permission to visit my own mother."

The water from the hose was icy, and if Eden had had her way, she would have gone upstairs, peeled off her muddy clothing, and jumped in the shower, no matter how much mud she tracked in, but Melissa had been horrified at that idea. Eden thought maybe her daughter was enjoying spraying cold water on her mother. Eden bit down on her tongue to keep from talking and scrubbed off mud as quickly as she could. She glanced at Brad. He was standing under the big cypress tree in front of her house and looking at all the things he'd sent her. She'd have to thank him later—and that thought warmed her a bit.

Melissa was telling her story for the second time. "I had no idea what to do when my own mother told me I couldn't visit her, so I did the only thing I could think of and went to the office of Mrs. Farrington's lawyer. It was only by chance that I remembered his name. Really, Mother, you have been so secretive about all of this that I feel like I don't even know you. You can't imagine my surprise when I met the daughter of the lawyer and she informed me that her father and you were thinking about getting *married*."

"Melissa," Eden said, turning around to face her daughter, "could you please keep your voice down? I don't think—" She broke off because her daughter hit her in the side of the head with a freezing blast of water. The nozzle was set on "jet."

"Sorry," Melissa said, but she didn't sound sorry. "It has been almost more than I can bear. First you leave me in New York, then you don't call for weeks on end, then Stuart and I—" She paused to sniff. "Well, that's all over with. What with all the stress in my life, it's a wonder I'm not in labor."

"You look great," Eden said, rubbing mud off of her. "You look like a poster for a healthy pregnancy." She just managed to dodge the next blast of water. "I think that's enough hosing."

"No, you still have some mud in your hair. Bend down."

"I think—" When another jet shot past her ear, Eden gritted her teeth. This was punishment, pure and simple. Eden had never spanked her daughter but right now she was wondering if it was not too late to begin.

"I really don't think this is something to smile about," Melissa said just before her mother took the hose out of her hand.

"Neither do I," Eden said, pushing the arm down on the hose bib. "As soon as I get cleaned up and into some warm clothes, we'll talk about everything. But right now I'm wet and I'm cold."

"Alone, Mother," Melissa said. "I want to talk to you *alone*."

Eden looked around her garden. Three FBI agents were standing together, and she knew that McBride and some man named Teasdale had gone to the house where McBride was supposed to be living. Brad, looking forlorn and hurt and unable to understand what was going on, had moved to her front porch steps. Now and then he'd glance at Eden, his eyes begging her to talk to him and reassure him that everything was okay between them. Besides Brad's and Melissa's concerns, there was a murder to solve and a riddle to answer. "If I can," Eden answered at last.

"What does that mean?" Melissa asked, following her mother into the house. "Don't you think your daughter comes first? Your *pregnant* daughter?"

Eden was dripping water across the old wooden floorboards of the kitchen, through the hallway, and up the stairs. For all that Melissa kept saying that her pregnancy was hard on her, she was right behind her mother as Eden bounded up the stairs.

"Yes, of course, you come first in my life," Eden said. "But right now there are some things going on that—"

"I remember this place," Melissa said from behind her. "I remember these paintings."

On the wall, all the way up the stairs, were Tyrrell Farrington's watercolors. Two of them showed the creek, his family's boats lined up along the dock. The Farrington boats had all been sold, and the boathouse had fallen down long ago.

Pausing, Eden looked at the paintings. She opened her mouth to tell her daughter that a necklace had been painted on a family portrait and that had led them to solving the mystery of the Farrington Sapphires. But she didn't say anything, as she didn't think Melissa would be interested. Why was it that love took precedence over everything else in life? Eden hadn't been able to enjoy the beautiful gifts that Brad had sent her because of her love for her daughter. And now Melissa couldn't think of anything else except her love for her husband.

And, yes, Melissa did love him. Eden could hear it in every word out of her daughter's mouth. In between the complaints about having found her mother rolling about in the mud with a man Melissa had never met, her daughter told her everything about what Stuart had done—or not done. According to Melissa, Stuart had turned into a different person the second Eden left—and Melissa didn't like the new Stuart one bit!

However, from Eden's perspective, it looked as though Stuart had had a dose of reality after his mother-in-law left town. Since they'd married, Stuart had had Eden to depend on. She'd been there to make sure the rent was paid and food was on the table. Once Eden was gone, responsibilities had been dumped on Stuart. By necessity, he had gone from being a timid little man who was content to wait years for a promotion, to being a man who was making every effort to better himself. Eden thought she might like the new man Stuart had become much better than the old one.

But she couldn't tell Melissa that. Melissa was still a little girl, torn between being her mother's daughter and being a grown-up with a husband and soon a child to take care of.

If I had stayed, Eden thought, my daughter would never have grown up. She is so spoiled she would have turned the baby over to me. Eden shook her head to clear it. She didn't want to think that maybe she'd made some really big mistakes in raising her daughter. Oddly, it was as though she could hear McBride's voice in her head and he was telling her that it wasn't too late to start over.

Melissa followed her mother into her bedroom and would have gone into the bathroom with her, but Eden shut the doors. Once she was alone in her bathroom, Eden wanted to fill the tub and soak in it for hours. Truthfully, she wanted to tie the towels together and climb out the window and escape all of them. She didn't look forward to facing Brad, or trying to deal with her daughter's marital problems, or to talking to the FBI men who'd flown in.

"Being an adult is overrated," she muttered under her breath, then got into the shower for the second time that day. She was going to have to face all of them. What was she going to say to Brad about why she'd been rolling about in the mud with McBride? Smiling, she wondered what McBride was telling his boss about the way they'd been found.

Forty-five minutes was all that Eden could drag out for a shower and blow-drying her hair. Bracing herself, she opened the bathroom door and prepared to face her daughter. It was time to come up with explanations.

Eden nearly wept with joy when she saw her daughter, her big belly in front of her, stretched out on her mother's bed, sound asleep. She spread a cover over Melissa and offered a silent prayer of thanks. "One down and about fifty to go," she muttered.

As she stepped out of her bedroom, she almost ran into McBride. He had a duffel bag in his hand, so she knew he was moving out of her house. This is good, the intelligent side of her said, but the other side thought of omelets and pancakes and having someone to ride across the peanut fields with.

"Was it bad?" she asked softly, knowing he'd know what she meant.

"Yeah," he answered, glancing at the head of the stairs. He took Eden's arm and pulled her toward her bedroom. But when he opened the door, he saw Melissa just as she was turning over in her sleep, her belly so big it hid her face. "Should we call a doctor?" he asked, with almost fear in his voice.

"We should call her husband," Eden said as McBride pulled her into his bedroom.

He closed the door behind them and seemed not to know where to begin.

"Did you get in a *lot* of trouble?" she asked.

"More than you can imagine. There is no more cover. This town is going to know about us by evening, if they don't already know." He glanced quickly at her. "By us, I mean the agency."

She watched as he walked toward the window and looked out. She knew what was down there: at least three agents, and in the field sat a helicopter. If her tax dollars weren't paying for the thing, she'd wish it would sink in the mud.

He looked back at her. "No one any longer thinks you know anything. Someone remembered seeing a book about missing treasures in Applegate's apartment, so they think that searching for them was his hobby. They've decided that the paper he swallowed had a lot of other stuff on it, and it just happened to have your name at the bottom." He took a breath. "Anyway, they're pulling me off the case. Your part in this is over."

Eden sat down. "I see." It's what she'd wanted, but at the same time fear ran through her. "What about the men who ransacked my house?"

"They think it was some relative of Mrs. Farrington's who thinks he should have inherited this house rather than you. That makes it a domestic problem, not FBI."

"But Mrs. Farrington didn't have any relatives."

"Not that you know about," he said. "I've managed to persuade the agency to look into people who are related to her distantly. And"—he hesitated—"that son of hers knew a lot of very bad people. We think he made friends while he was in prison." Jared looked at her hard.

Eden pushed away the images that came into her mind of how a person made "friends" while in prison. "So you think that one of them..."

"Tried to find the treasure. I was told that the agency, as a favor, will splash it on the news about finding the necklace and its being a fake. We hope that will keep future treasure hunters away from you. They—we—think you'll be safe if no one thinks a valuable necklace is hidden inside your house. You'll have a bit of publicity for a while, but it'll blow over the first time a movie star gets a divorce."

"So the necklace isn't valuable?"

Jared lifted his eyebrows.

"Worth anything at all?"

"Historic value, and the gold is real." He shrugged.

Eden shook her head. "I wish I knew who that French duchess was who offered it to Mrs. Farrington's ancestor. I've wondered why she didn't hide the sapphires. The story was that she showed the greedy young man the pearls, but he turned them down and demanded the sapphires."

"Clever young woman. The pearls were probably real."

"Yes. He did just what she wanted him to do. He took the fake gems and left her with the real stuff."

"And later people were killed over that necklace."

Eden leaned back in the chair. "Irony," she whispered and thought about it all for a moment, then looked at McBride. "So you're leaving."

"Yes. I'm under orders, and, besides, things between you and me—"

She looked at him sharply.

"Okay, so maybe the attraction was one-sided. But I—"

"Don't," she said, turning her head away. She could feel him looking at her, but she wouldn't meet his eyes.

"Can't blame a man for trying," he said, and his voice changed, lightened. "I said good-bye to Minnie, and yes, I let her down easy. She was in a state over the gossip about us. And Granville's pretty broken up over what he saw this morning. I tried to talk to him, but he wouldn't listen."

"I'd better go to him," Eden said, getting up.

"He had to get back to his office, but if you

want to keep that going, you'd better come up with some good lies."

She glared at McBride. "I plan to tell him the truth. There was nothing, *is* nothing between you and me."

"And who's going to believe that?"

Eden stood up. "You really are despicable, you know that?"

"Yeah." He was grinning at her, and, suddenly, the heaviness between them was gone. Eden sat back down; they were friends again. "So how's it with you and your daughter?"

"She's okay. She thinks she's a mess and that her marriage is over, but she's okay. I figure Stuart will be here by tomorrow and demand that she return home with him."

"Will that work?"

"Probably. I think she just wants proof of love."

"Don't we all?" he said under his breath.

For a moment they looked at each other, their eyes locked. Eden was the first to look away. "I'm sure your boss is right and that this whole thing was about that horrible necklace." Her head came up. "Brad's daughter told mine that he wants to marry me."

"Is that supposed to be news?"

"No," she said as she looked down at her hands. "What am I going to tell my daughter about all this? FBI and spies, and snakes in my bed."

"*Snakes* in your bed! You and Granville have been *lovers*?!"

She glared at him.

"Sorry. Couldn't resist. I agree that the truth is too much, so maybe you should make up a few lies. After spending so much time with me you should have learned a thing or two about lying."

Eden smiled. "I should probably see a therapist about this, but I'm almost going to miss you."

"I could give you some great memories," he said, his eyes hot.

"Go on, get out of here." Standing up, she smiled at him. When he hesitated, she said, "If you make a pass at me, I'll tell my daughter that you're a great listener. I'll encourage her to tell you all the dreadful things her husband has done to her in the last week. In detail."

He groaned. "If the world had referees, you'd be thrown out of the game."

"No I wouldn't. I'd *win*!"

He smiled at her. "I think you would. Okay, so now I have to go. They're warming up the chopper for me."

"Look, I..."

"If you say one thing about it's having been fun, I'll—" He broke off and looked at her, and in that one second she saw the real man, not the man who joked and laughed and told lies to cover the truth of his life, but the *real* man. There was pain in his eyes, and a longing for a life that he couldn't have. It was gone as fast as it came. "I wish you and Granville the best in life. Send me an invitation to the wedding, will you?"

"Will you come?"

"And cry all over your wedding dress? No thanks."

She laughed.

"I'll send you a gift." He reached into his pocket and pulled out a piece of paper. "It's my cell number. Only three people in the world have that number."

She looked at the paper. "I assume that one's your boss, then me, so who's the other?"

"My mother, of course," he said, giving her a cocky, one-sided grin. In the next moment he grabbed his duffel bag, kissed her cheek, and left the room.

After he left, Eden sat down on his bed and looked at the paper. Why had he given her his cell number? Why not an address?

"Because telephones are instant, that's why," she whispered. "If I call, he'll be here quickly."

She looked up at the closed door, and she knew without a doubt that Jared McBride had been lying. About what, she wasn't sure, but she knew that he was lying. And she was sure that he wasn't going to be very far away.

Chapter Nineteen

Stuart," Eden said into the phone, her voice pleading, "please call Melissa. Please." It was the third message she'd left on his machine in the last hour. She'd lost count of the total number of messages she'd left for him in the last two days.

The evening of the day McBride left—that was the way she seemed to mark time now—she'd started calling Stuart. By the time Melissa had awakened from her nap that day, the house was quiet. All the FBI agents, along with McBride, had roared off in the helicopter, and for a few minutes, the house had been quiet. When Melissa came downstairs, in an instant Eden was cast back into the role of "mom." She tried to keep herself calm and not be resentful that she had gone from being a *femme fatale,* with two delicious men after her, to being plain ol' Mom in a single day.

Twice, Eden had interrupted Melissa's nonstop complaining about how rotten her life was to try to reason with her. But it was impossible. First of all, Eden soon saw that it was some modern taboo to not bring up the past. Bringing up the past was called "garbage bagging"—or something like that. "Mother," Melissa said impatiently, "you have to deal with the here and now, not a hundred years ago." According to Melissa's modern-day philosophy, what this meant was that Eden wasn't allowed to say "When I was your age..." or "When I was pregnant...." On the other hand, it seemed that Melissa was free to talk endlessly about *her* past. She said that Eden had "abandoned" her as a child in one day care after another. "I don't want what was done to me to be done to my child," Melissa said. "I want *my* child to have a father. Is that too much to ask? I remember too well my loneliness as a child. There were times when I thought I didn't have a mother *or* a father."

Eden had kept a sympathetic face, but it hadn't been easy. Part of her wanted to defend herself and point out that she had done the best she could. And, of course, she'd very much wanted to tell Melissa that she had no idea what a "bad childhood" was really like. Eden also wanted credit for all the Saturdays that she'd arranged all-day playdates for her daughter. And what about all the nights she'd stayed up after midnight cooking meals for the week so her daughter could live on something besides those hideous "chicken nuggets" that other children ate? Melissa was three before she'd ever eaten a french fry. Et cetera. There were thousands of good things that Melissa seemed to have forgotten.

But Eden knew that to defend herself would only anger Melissa more, and what good would that do? Right now her daughter was scared out of her mind about having a baby, and she was afraid that her husband was never going to come after her. Maybe Melissa's leaving of Stuart had been her daughter's last shot at being a romantic heroine. Maybe she'd wanted to run away and have the hero come after her. But, so far, it hadn't worked. No hero on a white horse—or in a silver Audi, for that matter—had shown up. Nor had he called.

With every minute that passed, Melissa grew more agitated and more determined to make herself believe that what she'd done was the right thing. She was fighting for her baby, wasn't she? She was trying to give him the best there was, wasn't she? She didn't want her child to grow up feeling alone, as his mother had, did she?

It was close to impossible for Eden to listen to what her daughter was saying without defending herself, but she did it. Every time she felt the blood shooting up the back of her neck, she'd look at Melissa's big belly and think how her daughter was going to learn. Melissa had all kinds of stories about bad mothers. She talked of seeing women in stores as they bawled out their children. "If those women would just take the time to reason with their children," Melissa said. "If they'd just *listen* to them." The hint was that Eden had never listened or reasoned with her daughter, but in spite of that, Melissa was going to give her child what he needed.

Eden turned away to hide her smile. She wanted to say, Wait until the kid says, "I'm not going to do that and you can't make me!" and wait until every secret you have is blabbed to the world. Eden would never forget one Sunday at church when the pastor asked the congregation if there was anyone who needed their prayers. Melissa, only three, said loud and clear that her mother needed prayers because she'd been raped. The child had no idea what "raped" meant, but she'd listened to the people who had whispered when they thought she couldn't hear them. All Melissa knew was that a bad thing had happened to her mother and she wanted God to help.

Just you wait, Eden thought. It was terrible to want to get back at her own daughter, but that's how she felt with every complaint that Melissa made.

Late that evening, Eden put in her first call to Stuart. Maybe *she* could patch up the problems between them. She didn't know how she was going to do it, and she greatly regretted every bad thought she'd ever had about her son-in-law, but she was going to try. If she had to grovel, she would. She'd apologize to Stuart, tell him she'd misjudged him, and say that she thought he was the finest son-in-law a woman could have.

But Stuart didn't call her back. Nor did he answer the next four calls that Eden made. She called him again at six the next morning, but there was no answer. It wasn't until later in the day that she thought of calling the superintendent of her building. By then Melissa's tears and complaints had so worn Eden down that she would have paid Stuart to come and get his wife. How about if I give you a fake sapphire necklace? she thought of saying to him. How about if I sign the apartment lease over to you? What if *I* pay the rent?

But Stuart didn't answer her calls, and when the super called back, he said that the doorman had helped Stuart into a taxi two days before and he'd had two big suitcases with him. Eden put down the phone and went to her daughter. Melissa was in McBride's bed—no, she was in Eden's guest room—and she was eating chocolate-covered marshmallows. Little brown papers littered the floor like dirty snowflakes.

"Was Stuart home when you left?"

Melissa looked up, surprised. "No. He'd just left for a trip to L.A."

"How long was he supposed to be gone?" Eden asked, keeping her anger under firm control.

"A week."

Eden blinked at her daughter. "Are you telling me that Stuart may not even know that you've left him?"

Melissa tried to roll over on her side, but her big belly kept her on her back. "Mother, haven't you been listening to me? I didn't leave Stuart, per se. I left an impossible situation. But of course he knows I'm not there. He always calls me from whatever hotel he's in, so when I don't answer the phone he'll know that I've left him. Or left that place, that is. You know something, Mother? I really like it here in Arundel. The fresh air. The land. The water. I like this big old house. I think Stuart and I should move in here with you. Wouldn't that be wonderful? You'd be around your grandchild every day. You'd like that, wouldn't you?"

Eden didn't say a word—she might start screaming and never stop. Silently, she closed the door, then called Stuart yet again. Didn't he pick up his messages? No, of course not. He thought he had a wife at home who would be answering the phone. But wait! What if Melissa had gone into labor? Surely Stuart had left a number where he could be reached.

Eden started to go back to Melissa's room to ask, but stopped. She very well knew that her daughter would never give her the phone number. Eden was so desperate that she felt no guilt when she made a thorough search of Melissa's handbag, but she found nothing.

Eden went to the kitchen, poured herself a big glass of wine, then took it and the bottle outside. It was still cool, and she shivered. How things in life could change in an instant, she thought. A few weeks ago she was living with her daughter and loving where she was. If it hadn't been for her son-in-law, she would have been quite happy. She was now ashamed of the thought, but if she'd been told that Stuart had been run over by a train, she would have been secretly glad. She would have had her daughter and her grandchild to herself.

But for the last few weeks she'd led a very different life, one that consisted of grown-up things, like…Well, like rolling in the mud with a man. Working on an interesting project with two men. She thought of the night she and Brad and McBride—Jared—had found the necklace. It had been exciting and scary at the same time. And she'd done it with two men. *Two* of them! Handsome men looking at her as though she was what they wanted most in life. Ah, yes. Exciting and scary at the same time.

But here she was now alone. Sitting in the garden alone, sipping wine alone. In the moonlight she could see her cute little red truck. The back of it had half a dozen brand-new tools in it. Was it true that it was easier to dig with a stainless steel shovel than one that was rusty and pitted? She'd sure like to find out. Near the truck, on the little bricked area by the potting shed, were nearly three hundred plants waiting, crying out, to be put into the soil. The perennials and annuals were in four-inch pots, the bulbs in bags, and she and Jared had put the bare-root trees in buckets of water to hold them until they could be planted. That should have been today, Eden thought, but she hadn't been able to get outside to do it.

She drank the rest of the wine and poured another glassful. Was she now going to get drunk alone? "Pathetic Palmer," she muttered.

She knew she had to make a plan. What if Stuart was hearing her messages and not responding because he didn't want to get back together with Melissa? If that was so, then Eden knew that she'd soon become grandmother-in-residence. When she thought of diapers and toilet-training and baby food, she took another deep drink of wine and wished she'd brought her cell phone outside with her so she could call Stuart again. Would it be too, too difficult to call every hotel in Los Angeles and ask if he was there?

Plan, she thought. She had to make a plan. Now that the fiasco about the necklace and that spy swallowing her name was over, she needed to think about her future. Had she ruined it with Brad? When Melissa had been hosing her down, Eden had looked at Brad's sad eyes and had wanted to go to him, but her duties of motherhood had kept her where she was.

Eden emptied the second glass of wine, then made herself stop. It would be nice to drink so much that she couldn't remember the last few days, but she wasn't going to do that. Brad and Jared. She missed them both already. Jared had been a temporary…What? Friend, she thought. Jared McBride had become her friend.

As for Brad…She wanted him to become more. When she stood up, she was dizzy, but she took a few deep breaths of cool night air and managed to get up the steps and inside the house. Tomorrow she was going to go to Brad and beg him to forgive her. In spite of what she'd told Jared, she knew she couldn't tell Brad the truth. "Well, you see," she'd say, "I told McBride to pretend that I was a drug dealer who was trying to get away, so he did what he could to stop me, which meant that he leaped on top of me and pinned me down. And when I said 'Push' he pushed me, not the truck. It was actually quite humorous. And I hit him with a fistful of mud because..." Even after two big glasses of wine none of that sounded like it would make him forgive her.

As she climbed the stairs, she resolved to find Brad and talk to him. Lie to him if she had to. Do whatever was necessary to get him to forgive her. When she reached her bed, she fell on it, facedown, fully clothed, and was asleep in seconds.

Outside, in a voice so quiet it could barely be heard, a man said into a radio, "Subject has turned in for the night. Soused." Chuckling, he put the radio in his pocket and leaned back against the post of the rose arbor. It was the last thing he ever did. A knotted rope was pulled across his throat.

~

"No," Bill said calmly, "you're not going to be allowed back on the case. That you're taking the death of an operative this hard shows me that you're too involved. You can't make unbiased decisions."

"If by that you mean that I will kill anyone who tries to hurt an innocent person, you're right."

Bill put his hands on his flat belly and looked at Jared pacing the room. "You want to sit down and quit this tantrum of yours? Your girlfriend is being well looked after."

Jared sat down but only to glare at Bill. "Last night a man was killed just outside her front door. Do you call that 'looking after'?"

"I call that verification of what we suspected. The woman is connected to a spy ring. She knows something, but *you* didn't find out what it was. I'm sure you found out that she likes to walk on the beach and loves those— What were they?" He looked at the stack of papers in front of him. "Jelly beanies. Drinks of seduction, I think you called them, but you didn't find out what she *knows*." Leaning across his desk, Bill returned Jared's glare. "But you've found out some things about her since you moved out, haven't you?"

"Snooping into my private e-mails and phone calls?" Jared asked, one eyebrow raised.

"Of course. So what did you find out?"

Jared got up again, trying not to pace but unable to sit still. When he'd heard that a man had been killed so close to Eden and her daughter, he thought he was going to go on a killing rampage himself. He'd wanted to gather guns and men and planes and take them to Arundel, North Carolina, and kill... That was the problem. They still had no idea who was behind whatever was going on. Two agents dead and no idea why. All they knew was that things centered around Ms. Eden Palmer and maybe around her old house. It had been with great reluctance that he'd agreed to physically remove himself from the case and give the impression that Eden was no longer being watched. But she *was* being watched. The cameras were still in place inside her house and out, and men were still stationed outside her house. Everything she did or said had been reported on. Jared had watched some of the hours of tapes, and had read some of the reports. The only thing he'd come up with is that if he were there he'd have let Eden's whining daughter have a piece of his mind.

Bill was still looking at him, waiting to hear what Jared had found out. That Bill didn't know the exact contents of what Jared was doing on his own time was reassuring. That meant that the blocks he'd put on his phone and computer were working.

"Something about Ohio," Bill said by way of encouragement.

"Yeah, one Walter K. Runkel."

"Let me guess. The whining brat's father."

Jared's mouth turned into a smirk. It seemed that Bill had also seen some of the tapes. "Exactly. Eden said he'd been the head deacon at her church, so I did a little digging, made a few calls, and found out who he was."

"And?"

"There was a big scandal at that church about four years after Eden was tossed out by her parents. The man who raped Eden got caught with another young girl."

"Another rape?"

"No. Seems that it was mutual. There was a lot

of commotion and accusations, but there were no charges and no arrests were made. Runkel and the girl were separated, then he went back to his wife and kids. As soon as the girl was of age, they were at it again. The wife packed up the kids and moved to California. As soon as the divorce was final, Runkel married the kid. Good thing, because by then she was seven months pregnant."

"You think Eden knows any of this?"

"Not a word of it. I think she's gone out of her way to not know any of it. When she left that town, she left it forever."

"So now Runkel is living with the kid? She's how old now?"

"He left her when she turned twenty. She took the kid and went back to her parents."

Bill gave a low whistle. "Where is he now?"

"Works in a carpet store. He's in the same town and everybody knows to keep their young girls away from him. He's no longer an active member of the church."

"What about Ms. Palmer's parents?"

"Both dead."

Bill looked at the files on his desk. "You don't think this Runkel had anything to do with what's going on here, do you? Maybe he plans to black-mail Ms. Palmer. I'm sure she'd pay him to make him stay away from her daughter and the grand-baby."

"I thought of that, but he hasn't left town in years, and I checked his phone records. No calls to North Carolina. I don't think he knows about Eden or her daughter."

Bill looked at Jared for a moment. "So what do you plan to do about him?"

"Except for Eden, he doesn't seem to have done anything that he can be prosecuted for. Or anything anyone knows about, that is."

"Any unsolved rapes on the books?" Bill asked, eyebrows raised.

"Three," Jared said with a half smile. "I checked into it, and I think he probably did it."

"Did they save DNA?"

"Yes." For a moment Bill and Jared looked at each other and nodded. Maybe Eden wasn't willing to go through the horror of a trial, but maybe the other victims were.

"Get on it," Bill said.

"I've already started."

"So what else?" Bill asked.

"Why didn't you tell me that Tess Brewster had never had a paintbrush in her hands in her life?"

"I knew you'd find it out. Besides, when you're around Ms. Palmer, you don't think about or see anything else. Just her."

Jared gave him a look that told him not to go there. "What do you know?" Jared asked.

"Only that Tess didn't paint those pictures. But she did take them to the frame shop."

Jared sat down. "Where did she get the pictures? You don't think she bought them, do you? Maybe this is a red herring and she bought them at a garage sale and had them framed. Maybe she was going to hang them in her apartment."

"Did she have an apartment? I thought she lived here at the agency. With you."

Jared smiled, and for the first time in days, he relaxed. "Like all of us. So what's the theory on the paintings?"

"I think Tess wanted to hide them. She got them somewhere and wanted to hide them where no one would look."

"Ah, yes, hide them in plain sight. So she took them to the frame shop and left them there, meaning to return and get them later."

"No, she sent us the claim ticket." Bill handed the piece of paper across the desk to Jared.

"You had this, but you didn't show it to me?"

"I didn't know we had it. It was mixed in with her reports, and—"

Jared looked at Bill in speculation. Was he telling the truth that they had overlooked something like this? Either Bill wasn't telling everything or he was flat out lying.

Bill wouldn't meet Jared's eyes. "I want you off the case," he said quietly. "Two agents are dead, and we still don't know anything."

Jared gave his boss, his friend, a half smile. "Afraid I'll bite the dust on this one?"

"Hoping for it," Bill said, but his face was serious.

"What are you doing to protect her?" Jared asked.

"We're just trying to watch her, that's all. She has no idea a man was killed outside her house last night. All she's concerned about is finding her son-in-law and getting him to take his wife home."

"So where is the son-in-law?"

"Busy," Bill said.

"I see. You're keeping him too busy to take his wife away. You don't want anything to mess up the bait, do you? You're dangling this innocent woman in front of the killer, so you might as well dangle the daughter too, is that it?"

"Maybe if *you* had found out what she knows this wouldn't be happening," Bill snapped.

"She doesn't know anything," Jared shot back. "At least not anything that would cause some spy to swallow her name."

"Yeah, well, maybe. I'm not convinced." He started to move the papers on his desk about, letting Jared know that his time was up. "You find out anything new, let me know."

"Yeah, sure," Jared said as he left the office. Outside the door, he leaned against the wall and thought for a moment. He needed to find out who painted those watercolors of Eden's old house. He needed to— Hell, there were a thousand things that needed to be done, and *he* was going to do them. He went back to his office and told his secretary that he wasn't feeling well. In fact, he felt a bout of stomach flu combined with bubonic plague coming on, and he thought he was going to be out of the office for at least a week, maybe two.

She smiled at him conspiratorially. "Call your

mom and she'll get in touch with you if there's an emergency?"

"Yeah," Jared said with a grin, then he grabbed a couple of firearms and was gone.

~

It took all of Eden's courage to get dressed and drive to the Queen Anne office the next morning. She wavered between fear and courage, then back again. What if Brad wouldn't see her? What if he ordered her out of his office and told her he never wanted to see her again? The next second she told herself that she was being absurd. They were adults. She and Brad hardly knew each other, so he had no claim on her and therefore no right to expect anything from her. In the next moment she was down again as she thought about what Minnie had told her about Brad's ex-wife and how she'd been unfaithful. "I am not his wife!" she said aloud as she pulled into the wide road that led to the clubhouse. "And I wasn't being unfaithful."

This morning with Melissa had been very bad. During the night her daughter seemed to have lost all her bravado. She'd stopped complaining and telling Eden that she was in the right and that she should be standing up to Stuart. Instead, Melissa had poked at her cereal and said that Stuart was working very hard to make a home for her and the baby.

Part of Eden thought she should stay at home and hold Melissa's hand. It was "mother's instinct." When Melissa had been a child Eden had stayed home from work whenever her daughter had even the slightest thing wrong with her—which is why Eden had lost job after job. "You do great work," her employers had told her. "It's just that you're absent too many days, so we're going to have to let you go."

As Melissa pushed her cereal around in her bowl, she looked up at Eden with sad eyes, the same eyes she'd turned on her mother when she was a child. But Eden looked at her hugely pregnant daughter and said, "I'm going. Melissa, dear, you have my cell number, the number of the doctor, and the hospital. If anything happens, let me know."

"But what if I go into labor?" Melissa said as she jumped down from the bar stool—and the dishes in the plate rack rattled.

"You haven't even dropped yet," Eden said, pulling on her cardigan. "I think you have at least six weeks before you deliver. Why don't you take a long, hot bath and watch a few movies on TV? I'll be back this afternoon, and I'll bring some fish. We'll wrap it in paper bags and bake it, like we did when you were a child."

"But, Mother—" Melissa began.

"You'll be fine," Eden said, then quickly kissed her daughter's cheek and hurried out the door.

Now, as she pulled into the parking lot of Queen Anne, her heart was pounding. How angry was Brad? And how did he express anger? Yelling? No, that didn't seem like him. Coldness? Did he just shut out a person and say nothing to them? Is that how it would be from now on?

Eden was sure her heart was in her throat as she walked into the office of Queen Anne. She'd already driven past his law office downtown and seen that his car wasn't there. She decided to go to Queen Anne, and if he wasn't there she was going to try his house.

When she knocked on his office door, no one answered, and when she tried the door, it was locked.

She felt as though someone was watching her. Turning, she looked into Minnie's office and saw the young woman staring at her. But the moment Eden looked, Minnie turned her head away. Eden didn't let that deter her. "Minnie!" she said brightly. "How are you?"

Standing behind her desk, Minnie gave Eden a look so cold that she wanted to run out the door.

"Is something wrong?" Eden asked, her voice close to breaking. Is this what she was going to get when she saw Brad?

"Wrong?" Minnie asked quietly, but in a deadly voice. "You were rolling around naked in the mud with *my* boyfriend, and you ask me if anything is wrong?"

"Your boyfriend?" Eden asked, eyes wide.

"Do you think he belonged to *you*? Do you think everything belongs to you?"

Eden thought her brain must be spinning around inside her head. She took a deep breath. "I think that Jared McBride belongs to himself. Minnie, I wasn't naked. No one was naked. The little truck got stuck in the mud, we were trying to push it out, and we fell. That's all."

"That's not what I heard," Minnie said as she opened a file drawer and jammed in a folder.

"I can assure you that—"

"Save it," Minnie said, turning to glare at Eden. "And here I thought you were different. You know what Brad went through with his wife. I told you the whole story as a warning. He can't handle another adulterous woman in his life."

"Now wait a minute!" Eden said. Maybe she couldn't stand up to her pregnant daughter, but this young woman was a whole other matter. "First of all, I am no one's *wife*, so adultery is impossible. And second, what's between Braddon and me, and even between Jared and me, is no concern of yours."

"Does that mean that you think you can walk into this town and suddenly *you* know what's best for everyone? Are those of us who love Brad to stand by in silence and see him get hurt again? Is that what you think?"

"Minnie," Eden said softly. "I haven't done anything to be ashamed of. If anyone thinks I have, then they are the ones who have the dirty minds."

"Then I guess that includes Brad."

"Brad thinks I—?"

"Brad thinks you're little better than his wife, that's what. You hurt him, Eden. You hurt him deeply. He got on a plane just hours after he saw you in the arms of another man, and no one has heard from him since. You know what he did? He called my mother."

At that Eden drew in her breath. Minnie's mother. The woman Brad had had an affair with.

"At least I'm glad to see you remember who she is. Brad will never marry her, but she won't believe that. You should see her now. She's giddy with happiness because she thinks Brad's going to ask her out again. I tried to talk to her, but she won't listen. I told her that Brad will probably forgive *you* and that he'll drop her again. But she won't listen. And I'm caught in the middle. My mother wants me to spy on Brad, and he needs me to clean up after him. If it weren't for my daughter needing her relatives, I'd leave this town forever."

"Minnie, I'm sorry," Eden said. "I never meant—"

"Right. You never meant to hurt anyone. You just loved having two men drooling over you, didn't you?"

"I think that's quite enough." Turning, Eden took a step to leave.

"You were a slut as a teenager and you haven't changed since, have you?"

Eden drew in her breath, then she turned to look back at Minnie. The young woman's face was so distorted with anger that Eden could hardly recognize her. There was nothing she could say to combat anger like that. She left the office.

Minnie sat down hard on her chair, and for a moment she wanted to burst into tears. With Eden Palmer's betrayal, all her plans for her future had been ruined. Brad would never marry Eden now. He'd had enough gossip about his first wife; he'd never set himself up for something like that again. And then there was Jared. Minnie felt betrayed by him too. She'd really felt as though they'd started something good, but it had all been an act. He'd only been in town because of Eden. Minnie wasn't sure why Jared McBride had been there, but she knew it had something to do with Eden's disgusting past. And as soon as he'd found out whatever he wanted to know, he'd left. So Minnie was right back where she'd started. She wasn't going to get a house of her own, and she wasn't going to get a gorgeous hunk of a man for herself. Instead, she was going to continue to be Braddon Granville's cleaning woman and gofer.

She put her head in her hands and thought how she'd like to make them all feel as bad as she was feeling right now. How could some girl who came to town pregnant and destitute have *two* men after her? And at *her* age!

Minnie's head came up. What was it Eden had said at that dinner about the man who raped her? He was head deacon at her church. Yes, that was it.

She jumped up from her chair, jerked open the second file drawer, and pulled out Eden's folder. She'd had to fill out an employment card, and on it was the name of her birth town in Ohio. It took only one phone call to the local library in Eden's hometown to find the name of a "little stone church," then she called the pastor and asked him if he could possibly find out who had been the head deacon in 1976.

"I don't have to look up the answer," the man said, "because you're not the only person to ask me that question. It was Walter K. Runkel."

Minnie didn't ask who else had called; she didn't care. "Mr. Runkel isn't by any chance still living, is he?"

"Yes, he is. He works at the local carpet store. Would you like to have the number?"

"Yes, I would," she said, smiling at the phone. "I'd like that very much." Minutes later, Minnie hung up, then she called Eden's house. Minnie and the rest of Arundel knew that Eden's pregnant daughter was staying with her.

"Is Eden Palmer there?" Minnie said in her most businesslike voice. "I have the information she requested."

"Information?" asked a sleepy Melissa. "She's not—"

Minnie cut her off. "I have the information she requested about her daughter's father."

"Her...?" Melissa asked slowly, coming awake. "Father? I don't understand. She doesn't know who the father is."

"I can only give the information about the father of her child to Ms. Eden Palmer herself. Are *you* Ms. Palmer?"

There was a hesitation on the phone, then the voice changed. "Yes, I'm Ms. Palmer. You can give the information to me."

"Do you have a pen and paper to write down the address and phone number?" Minnie heard a drawer being opened.

"Yes," Melissa said. "Go ahead."

Chapter Twenty

Eden couldn't sleep. She'd tried everything she could think of, but, still, she couldn't sleep. The over-the-counter pills had done nothing. She'd had two glasses of wine. She'd watched one of those sci-fi movies about giant ants attacking a town full of overly made-up people, but that hadn't put her to sleep either. Even the manuscript about the Jack the Ripper–like killer hadn't made her sleepy.

She wanted sleep more than anything in the world. She'd like to get into bed, close her eyes, and...What? Never wake up?

No, that was too dramatic, but at the moment, she felt as though her life had gone from being wonderful to horrible. Odd, she thought, that having her house ransacked and being locked in a cellar hadn't upset her much, but now she was truly miserable.

She'd left Minnie's office with her shoulders back, and her head high. She was innocent and Minnie was crazy. It was simple, wasn't it? And Eden was a hundred percent in the right, wasn't she?

So why was she feeling so bad?

She'd gone to the grocery, taking her time to choose foods that she knew her daughter loved. This will be all right, Eden told herself as she put lemons in a bag. Maybe she'd lost Brad, but it was better to find out that he was so jealous and unforgiving before she got serious about him. As she chose broccoli, she thought that her sympathy should go to Brad's wife. Maybe she'd had a reason to be unfaithful.

But Eden knew she was lying to herself. For a moment tears came to her eyes, but she blinked them away.

It will be okay, she told herself. She had her house and her garden—and maybe she was going to have her daughter and grandchild living with her. That would be fun, wouldn't it? She'd buy a big play set, one of those redwood things with a climbing wall. No, that would be too dangerous.

Maybe this time she'd be able to give the child a *good* childhood. No day care centers such as Melissa'd had. Yes, Eden told herself, she was being given a second chance. Melissa would, of course, get a job, and she'd leave the baby with Eden, so she'd get to raise a second child.

Eden conjured a vision of a lovely afternoon in the garden with her grandson, but unbidden to her came a TV commercial for a cruise line. A handsome couple, older, were standing at the rail of a cruise ship, arms about each other and looking at the sunset. There was another scene of dinners with wine and dancing. A couple laughing together. No children anywhere.

"Ow!" Eden said. She had an artichoke in her hand and had been clutching it so tightly the spines on the tip of the leaves had nearly punctured her skin.

Again, she blinked away tears of self-pity. She finished the grocery shopping, then drove home.

Melissa was sitting in the living room, and when she saw her mother, for a second, there was a look of anger on her face that almost made Eden's heart stop. But in the next second, the look was gone, replaced by a false cheerfulness that Eden almost found worse than the anger.

"Did you get the fish?" Melissa asked, heaving herself out of the chair.

"Yes," Eden said softly. "Melissa, has something happened?"

"Absolutely nothing. Why don't we make dinner together? Like we used to do when I was a child?"

Her daughter's tone was making Eden's hair stand on end. She put her hand on Melissa's shoulder. "What's wrong?"

"Nothing!" Melissa said, shrugging away from
other's touch.

Eden wanted to sit her daughter down and make her talk, but she couldn't do it. She knew that whatever was wrong with Melissa would be said to be her fault. "My fault," Eden whispered.

"Did you say something, Mother?" Melissa asked in a chilly voice.

Eden knew that right now she didn't have the emotional security to take on more complaints about herself. Minnie's angry words still haunted her.

It had been a cool dinner, with stilted conversation between them. Twice Melissa had shot Eden that look of anger—or was it hatred?

Immediately after dinner, Melissa had gone to her room and shut the door.

Slowly, trying not to think, Eden had cleaned up the kitchen, then gone to her room and tried to copyedit a manuscript. But she couldn't keep her mind on what she was reading. Instead, she kept asking herself, Now what? Now what was she to do with the rest of her life? Would Stuart never show up and take his wife away? If he didn't, would Melissa blame Eden for that too? "If you'd just been nicer to him," Eden could hear Melissa say. "If you'd just—" Was it a fact of motherhood that you got blamed for everything bad in your child's life?

At two A.M., Eden was still awake, still trying to not think about her future. What was she to do now? How did she make the best of what life was handing her?

At two-thirty, she got up, pulled on her jeans

and a sweatshirt, and tiptoed down the stairs. Maybe if she had something to eat she could sleep. Or maybe if she— She stopped thinking when she looked out the window and saw a tiny light. It was like a cigarette tip or a little flashlight. Whatever it was, it shouldn't be there.

Her cell phone was in its charger on the kitchen counter. She'd already programmed Jared McBride's number into it. Should she call him? He was probably back in D.C. by now, she thought. He was probably far away. He was— She picked up the phone and pushed the buttons to send the call through to him before she argued herself out of it.

He picked it up on the first ring, but he said nothing.

"There's someone outside my house," Eden whispered.

"I know. It's me," came Jared's voice. "I saw your light on. If you want to talk, I'm here."

Without thinking about what she was doing, Eden snapped the phone closed, then ran out the door into the night. She ran past the herb garden, then headed toward the orchard. There wasn't anything clearly in her mind about what she wanted to say, but the thought that there was someone nearby who she could talk to made her frantic. "Where are you?" she asked in a loud whisper, then felt a touch on her arm. Turning, she looked up into the dark blue eyes of Jared McBride.

"What's wrong?" he asked, and his face was that one she'd seen earlier: full of concern and ready to listen.

"I…" Eden began, meaning to sit down with him and talk over her problems, one adult to another. But the moment she looked at him, she collapsed. If Jared hadn't caught her in his arms she would have fallen to the ground.

"Hey, hey," he said softly, pulling her to him, holding her tightly and stroking her hair. "What's happened? Has someone hurt you?"

"No," she said as the tears began. "Yes, I…I…"

"Sssssh," he said, holding her tighter. Then he bent and put his arm under her legs and lifted her.

Eden sank into him, limp and helpless. Never in her life had she felt such a need to surrender to someone. When she'd been a pregnant teenager there had been a lot of fight in her, defiance. There was a streak in her that made her determined to win, no matter what she had to do. She was going to do anything she could for the child she was carrying.

But now the fight seemed to have gone out of her. Tears came that seemed to have been buried for years and years, maybe for all of her life. As he carried her across the lawn, she clung to him, tears pouring out of her so hard that her entire body was shaking.

After a while Jared stopped and put her down on something soft, but her arms were still around his neck. She tried to stop crying, but couldn't.

He sat down with her, still holding her, took out a handkerchief, and began to wipe her face.

"I'm making a fool of myself," she managed to say.

"Tell me what's happened," he said, ignoring her comment.

"It's just that...I mean..." Sniffing, she moved slightly away from him and looked around. "Where are we?"

"The well house," he said.

Blinking, she looked about her. A flashlight was pointed at the ceiling. The building, eighteenth century, and quite pretty, had once been the smokehouse to the plantation, so it had no windows. In the corner, inside an ugly plywood closet, were the tanks and pump necessary for piping well water to the house and the outside spigots. The rest of the small building had been used for storage, and it had always been filled to capacity. She saw that now it was clean and had what looked to be a mattress and blankets on the floor.

"The men used it," Jared said as he lit a fat candle and turned the flashlight off. He was sitting just inches from her on the mattress. "They were taking a chance that you'd find them, but a lock's been installed and..." Trailing off, he shrugged and looked away.

Outside, the rain began to sprinkle, making a pleasing noise when it hit the tin roof of the building. Eden wiped her eyes with the back of her hand. "I better get back inside. Melissa will—"

Jared caught her arm. "You're not going anywhere until you tell me everything that's been going on."

"Nothing," she said. "I need to get back inside. Melissa might need me."

"I think that girl needs to be turned over somebody's knee."

Eden smiled at him in the candlelight. "That's no longer done. Besides, Melissa is a grown woman."

"She's a little girl in a woman's body," Jared said, unsmiling, "and you let her stay a child. You ought to—"

At that, Eden's tears started again. She put her hands over her face and began to cry harder than before.

Stretching out on the mattress beside her, Jared pulled her into his arms. "Ssssh, baby, be quiet. I'm here," he whispered, stroking her hair.

The rain came down on the roof, isolating them in the beautiful old building. She clung to him, plastering her body against his. She so needed the comfort of another human being. She was sick of trying to be strong, of trying to be everything to everybody. She was worn out from being strong.

The harder the rain came down, and the harder she cried, the closer she wanted to be to the warmth of his body. He pulled her to him, but when her leg moved over his, he pulled back. "I can't do this," he said, his voice husky. "I can't hold you and not do anything else."

"It's okay," Eden said, her tears beginning to dry. "It's okay."

"I..." Jared began, but when he looked at Eden it was as though he'd made a decision. In the next moment, he was beside her, and pulled her into his arms.

"Yes," she murmured, her arms around him. "Yes."

He put his hand in her hair, clasped the back of her head, and turned her face to his. For a second he looked into her eyes, then put his lips on hers. He was tentative at first, giving her one last chance to back out, but her arms tightened about his neck, and his kiss deepened.

Eden knew that never in her life had she needed anyone as much as she needed this man at that moment. Lightning showed through the holes in the old walls of the little building, and in the next moment a clap of thunder echoed around them, making her move closer to Jared.

His hand went under her sweatshirt. She hadn't bothered with a bra, and when his hand touched her breast, she moaned under his lips.

After that, he didn't hold back. Within seconds, he had her shirt off and he was caressing her with his warm hands. His lips were on her neck and moving downward. It seemed that it had been forever since she'd been in a man's arms. Forever since she'd—

She cut off her thought and for a moment she pulled back to look at the man who was kissing her. His eyes were half closed and his lips were full and soft. He's in love with me, she thought. The Jared McBride she'd met such a short time ago was gone, and in his place was a man who had no defenses, no pretenses. What she was seeing was not covered under a mask of lies.

He opened his eyes to look at her, and in an instant, that guarded look was back. It was the face of a man who had been hurt and needed to protect himself. Like me, Eden thought. Pain beyond bearing.

Jared seemed to sense that something was different, and he started to roll away, his eyes hard, guarded, covered.

But she put her hand on his shoulder. He hesitated for a moment, then he looked back at her. She was on her side, naked from the waist up, her jeans unzipped and pulled low on her hips. She saw the desire in his eyes, and she saw the deep feeling there. She knew that if she had any sense, she'd stop this here and now, before it went any further, but she didn't. Smiling in invitation, she rolled onto her back and opened her arms to him.

There was a moment of hesitation from Jared, then with a small smile, he went to her and slipped the jeans down over her hips, giving a low laugh when he saw that she was wearing no underwear. She laughed too, then he turned slightly away from her. "Oh, no, you don't," she said. "I want to see the hand I'm being dealt."

He laughed, and when he disrobed in what had to be less than a quarter of a second, they laughed together. He stretched out beside her, and even though she could see and feel his rampant desire for her, he lay still so she could look at his body. Years of exercise had kept him in trim fit, but there were many scars on his body. She traced one with her fingertips and looked at him in question.

"Knife," he said, then kissed her neck.

Her hands on his back found another scar. "Bullet," he said.

There was another scar down by his hip. "You don't want to know," he said, then he put his mouth on hers and there was no more talking.

They made love for hours on the old mattress. There was the first frantic meeting of bodies, a bit awkward, but wonderfully pleasurable, and when they came together, Eden nearly laughed with the joy of it.

Jared collapsed on her, and for a second she thought he'd gone to sleep. She dug her heels into the mattress, then heaved him over onto his back and stretched herself out full length on top of him. "Come on, old man, you have work to do."

"No," he said, eyes closed. "I'm too tired. I want to sleep. I am an old man and I'll never be able to do this twice in one night."

"In that case..." Eden said as she made to roll off of him.

But his hand caught her and pulled her back on top of him. His eyes were still closed. "Maybe I could," he said tiredly. "Maybe you could bring me back to life."

"Me? And how would I do that?" Her hand moved downward.

"That's a start. I have a couple of other scars that you haven't found."

"Oh?" Her hand went lower. "Here? No, I feel nothing. What about here? No, no scars. What about here?"

Jared gasped as her hand closed over him. "Keep looking," he said huskily.

An hour later, they fell back on the mattress, not touching. Their skin glowed with sweat. The rain was slowing down, and at last Eden felt sleepy.

Rolling onto his side away from her, Jared reached under a cardboard box and withdrew a bottle of wine and two paper cups and filled them. "No sleeping," he said.

Eden turned onto her side, facing him, moved her legs up a bit and closed her eyes.

Jared pulled a blanket over her, then held out the cup of wine. "You're going to sit up and talk to me."

"In the morning," she murmured.

"Do you know the reading-out I got when I was pulled off your case?" he asked. "I was told that if I'd just talked to you more and—"

She opened one eye. "And what?"

"Drooled over you less," he said, tight-lipped.

"I like that," she said sleepily. "Not many men have drooled over me."

"You can't lie to me, Palmer, I've read your file, remember? As far as I can tell a whole lot of men have 'drooled' over you. You've always dumped them."

"Scared," she said, still smiling.

"In my opinion, I don't think you're afraid of anything in the world except your daughter."

That made her open her eyes. "Afraid of my own daughter? That's ridiculous."

Jared handed her the cup of wine, and reluctantly she sat up, pulling the blanket up under her arms. He was sitting there naked, seemingly oblivious to the fact that he was so exposed. But then, he did have a beautiful body. "How did you get—" she began, but a look from him cut her off. Sighing, she took a drink of the wine. "Okay, so what do you want to know?"

"I don't know," he said, an eyebrow raised. "When I saw you tonight you were crying like you'd rather not continue living, so maybe from that I guessed that something was wrong. But I saw the tapes of what your daughter was saying to you, so I know some of what's going on."

Eden looked down at her cup of wine and tried to compose herself. She tried to keep her face calm. "I assumed that the cameras had been disconnected. But if they haven't, that means the case is still open."

"One of the agents watching your house was strangled."

"Melissa," Eden said and started for the door.

Jared just managed to catch her wine before she dropped it. Setting both cups down, he pulled her into his arms, but she tried to push away from him. "There are two other agents out there," he said softly, his lips against her ear. "No radios, no sounds at all. And you can bet that they're on the lookout. Eden, sweetheart, someone wants something from you to the point that they'll do anything to get it. I need to find out who and what."

She pulled away to look at him. "Is that what

this is all about?" she asked. "You made love to me just so I'd tell you my secrets?"

The look on his face was enough of an answer.

"Okay, I apologize," she said, sitting back down and pulling on her clothes. When he gave her a questioning look, she motioned her head toward the outside. She didn't want a couple of FBI agents bursting in on them. "Are there any cameras in here?"

"What do you think?"

"Okay, again I apologize."

"I want you to tell me everything that's happened since I left. No matter how insignificant it is, I want to hear about it. Understand?"

"There's been nothing except some really hateful personal things." She turned away, not looking in his eyes. "No one has mentioned the necklace or...or anything that could remotely be something anyone would kill for. Except Minnie. She might kill me just for the pleasure of it."

"Minnie? Her beef is with me, not you."

Eden looked at him in astonishment. "She thought you were her boyfriend."

Jared shrugged. "Hazards of the business. Happens to me a lot."

His statement was so vain, yet at the same time so honest, that she laughed. "It's nothing to you, but Minnie wants a husband and a father for her child. And she wants a place to live. I think her deal with Brad is that..." Trailing off, she looked away.

"Go on," Jared said. "What happened?"

"I'm sorry, it's just that..."

"I know," he said, his jaw held tightly in position. "You can't think of Granville without what? Great pain? He dumped you, so you had a tumble with the second-best man. Thank you, I enjoyed it, and I can assure you that I won't tell him."

She looked at him for several seconds. "I see why your wife ran off with another man."

"I don't see anything bad about you at all," he snapped, "except your refusal to tell me what I need to know."

She looked down at her wine. Light was beginning to come in through the cracks between the old boards. Dawn was approaching. What was she going to think of herself when she was away from him? There was no future with a man like Jared McBride. He was a mover, a vagabond, a...a bum? He wasn't a man to settle down in one spot and plant fruit trees. And he certainly wasn't a man to elevate one's social position in a snobby town like Arundel. No, there was no future with a man like Jared McBride.

"You want to quit looking at me like that?" he asked as he pulled on his clothes. "I'm not something that you found under a rock."

"I'm sorry," she said. "I didn't mean—"

"It doesn't matter, and stop apologizing," he said as he buttoned his shirt. "I want to know what happened with Minnie."

Eden had to take a deep breath to give herself strength as she quickly told Jared the gist of what Minnie had said to her.

"I don't know about what she said about Granville, but she made everything about her and me up. I never gave her any encouragement."

She knew he was telling the truth, but that still didn't keep Minnie's anger from running around inside her head.

Eden took a deep drink of her wine. It was now morning, and she'd never had an alcoholic drink in the morning in her life. But then she'd never made love with a man she knew she had no future with. She'd never been a one-night-stand type of woman. She looked at Jared, remembering his hands on her body.

"Cut that out!" he snapped. "I can't concentrate when you look at me like that. Remember when I told you that that ancestor of Mrs. Farrington's had killed his wife and her lover? I was right, wasn't I?"

"Yes, but that was—"

"Human nature. It's something I've had to deal with a lot. Minnie is lying about Granville. If he called his former girlfriend, then it was for a reason other than getting back with her. What exactly did she say?"

"What does this have to do with some spy swallowing my name?"

"If Minnie lies about one thing, she'll lie about another. I can see that she might think I was interested in her. That could have been an honest mistake. Happens to me all the time. And too, I was trying to make you jealous so—"

"Why would you want to do that?"

Jared ignored her question. "Tell me again what she said, word for word."

Eden did the best she could, but it had been an emotionally charged conversation, so it was difficult to remember clearly.

Jared leaned back on the mattress, his hands behind his head. "Granville could have called the woman about something legal. It sounds to me as though Minnie's mother is as fanciful as her daughter. They've both made up men who are hot for them. What else did she say?"

Eden put down her empty cup and looked at her hands.

"That bad, huh?" Jared asked softly.

She lay down beside him, not touching him. "Minnie said that I was a slut when I was a teenager and I haven't changed since." She took a deep breath. "From the evidence of tonight, maybe she's right."

"Angels live in heaven, not on earth."

"What?" Turning her head, she looked at him.

"Did by chance your parents tell you that it was *your* fault that you were raped?"

"Oh, yeah," Eden said. "If I hadn't been wearing my ankle-length skirt, if I hadn't been walking in the woods, if I hadn't...et cetera. It was all my fault."

"So you've tried to prove them wrong, haven't you?"

"Am I going to have to pay you for this therapy session?"

"No, it's free," he said seriously. "I was curious why you let your daughter walk all over you."

"I do no such thing!" she said. "Under normal

circumstances, Melissa and I..." She took a breath. "Yeah, I invented Doormat Mom. Think I could get a trophy from somebody?"

"Maybe for sex, but not for being a doormat."

"Really?" she asked, turning toward him. "Have there been a lot of women to compare me to?"

"Do you think that now is the time to start in about my sex life?"

She lay back down. "Sorry. Okay, so Minnie is lying and Brad still loves me." Beside her, she felt Jared stiffen. "Sorry, I—"

Rolling away from her, he stood up. "This is getting nowhere. What else happened that's made you so upset?"

"Daughter, boyfriend, life. That about covers it." Yawning, she stretched, and when she opened her eyes, Jared was looking at her with interest. She blinked at him a couple of times.

"No, we can't. Besides," he said nastily, "your boyfriend might show up soon."

"Jared..." she began.

He put up his hand. "We can sort out our personal problems later. I need to do some checking on this Minnie. Give me her full name." He pulled a pen and a little pad of paper from under the box where the wine was.

"Minton Norfleet."

"If I stayed here awhile I think I could guess people's names."

"It's a custom around here."

"Yeah, made up in an attempt to exclude outsiders. Having one of *the* names lets you know who belongs and who doesn't." He closed the pad and looked at her. "Everyone in this town knows your history. Do you really think they'll accept you?"

"But they have. When I lived here before—"

"When you lived here before, you were protected by the Grande Dame of Arundel. No one would go against her. What will they think when you marry the prize catch of the town? Will they say what Minnie did?"

"It doesn't matter what anyone says because I don't think Brad will want me now," she said softly. She was looking down at her hands and didn't see the anger that flashed in Jared's eyes.

"Now that you've been sullied by me?"

"I didn't mean that," she said. "There were other things before all this happened." She waved her hand to mean their lovemaking.

"He dropped you so you were free to get off with the hired help. Is that it? But if he would take you back—"

"You're so right. All this was completely calculated. Preplanned. I knew you were skulking around out here, living in my well house like some feral cat, so I made up a reason to come out here and jump on you."

For a moment Jared looked as though he was going to get angry, then he grinned. "Just so we understand each other," he said. He started to say more, but his cell phone rang.

Eden grimaced. Was it his mother or his boss? Either way, it wouldn't be good for her.

As Jared listened to the person on the other end,

his face changed. His eyes widened and the color drained from his face. From the way he wouldn't look at Eden, she knew that it was something bad and that it concerned her.

"Okay," he said into the phone. "I'll do what I can." He closed the case, then took a step toward her. "Eden," he said softly, and his tone scared her.

Before he could reach her, she knew that whatever was wrong concerned her daughter. She stood up and put her hands in front of her face, as though to ward off an attack. "No," she whispered, backing up.

Jared took her hands in his. The candle had burned out, but there was enough light in the little building that she could see his face. Whatever he was about to tell her, she didn't want to hear. "Eden," he whispered, holding her hands tightly. "We'll solve this. I promise. On my life, I swear that we'll solve this."

She backed away from him until she was against the wall. She tried to pull her hands from his, but couldn't. "No, no, no" was all she could say.

In the next second, Jared unlocked the door. A man was silhouetted in the daylight, and he didn't see Eden in the dark interior. "McBride! Did you hear? They took the whining brat. Palmer's pregnant daughter has been kidnapped!"

In the next second, Eden fainted and Jared caught her.

Chapter Twenty-one

Braddon Granville rolled out of the luxurious bed and pulled on his trousers. A beautifully manicured hand touched his shoulder.

"Don't leave yet, darling," said a soft, sultry voice. "I'd like some more, please."

"Sorry," Brad said, "but I'm afraid that's all I have today. Age does that to a man."

Katlyn fell back against sheets of 1600-count cotton. "Age? What do *you* know about age? Now, Charley, he knows about age."

"You married him, dear," Brad said matter-of-factly.

"Please, no morality lectures today. It's been weeks since I saw you, so I don't want to fight.

What have you been doing? Other than the pretty heiress who just moved into town, that is."

"You do keep up, don't you?"

"With my hometown? Of course. Hate always makes one curious."

Brad rolled his eyes as he picked up his shirt. "Okay, so Arundel snubbed you. What can I say? You were born with the wrong name and in the wrong house. You weren't invited to *the* parties when you were growing up there. And, no, your beauty wasn't enough to get you inside, but you've made up the deficit, haven't you?"

Katlyn laughed as she reached for a cigarette from the gold box on the bedside table. She knew that Brad hated for her to smoke, but today she didn't care. She knew that she was losing him, and even though she pretended that it didn't hurt, it did. She had met him three years ago, when he was in New York for some convention in one of her husband's hotels. She'd been married to Charley Dunkirk for seven years, and she'd never been unfaithful to him. She didn't want Charley's greedy children to have any reason to try to take away the money after Charley died. And she didn't want to give her husband any reason not to leave her masses of it. He'd already lived five years longer than any doctor predicted when she saw Brad in a crowd of conventioning lawyers.

Instantly, she'd known who he was. He was a lot older than she was—well, less "lot" than Katlyn admitted to—and she'd seen him often in Arundel, where she'd grown up. But he'd been one of *those* people, the privileged families, "founding families" they liked to call themselves. Whatever the name, they were the ones who owned the town, and they were as impenetrable as a lead box. It hadn't mattered that little Susie Edwards had been the prettiest girl that town had produced in a century. She won every beauty contest there was—except Miss Arundel, of course. For that you had to have a pedigree, something that Susie didn't have. She didn't know her ancestors past her parents, and based on them, she didn't want to know them.

When she was eighteen, filled with anger and a deep sense of betrayal, she left Arundel and went to L.A., and then to New York. She got a job as a secretary to a man who was in an office two floors below Charley Dunkirk, an old and immensely wealthy man who was on his fourth wife. It had taken some doing and she suspected that Charley had seen through all her machinations, but she got him to notice her. But when he did, she would have nothing to do with him. She refused to have sex with him unless he married her. To a man used to having everything he wanted, Susie—by now renamed Katlyn—was a novelty. Eventually, he divorced his wife and married her, and Katlyn had kept her end of the bargain by being faithful to an old man who was nearly impotent.

But then she'd seen Brad across a room and knew that she had to have him. Not because she wanted him, but because he was from Arundel, and she'd always wanted what she couldn't have. Since Brad was a widower, it had been easy to seduce him. Afterward, when he'd called her "Susie" and let her know he knew who she was, she had laughed so hard she'd fallen off the bed. After that they'd remained lovers and had become friends.

Out of curiosity, and to protect herself, Katlyn supported the lazy son of the people who still lived next door to her father in Arundel. He looked after her father after her mother died, and, sporadically, he sent a badly written, misspelled report to Katlyn, telling her all the gossip around town. She'd read a lot about the woman who'd returned to town and had Braddon Granville chasing after her.

Katlyn had been surprised at how much jealousy she'd felt to think that Brad had fallen for someone else. Not that Katlyn was in love with him, but she rather liked to think that Brad was mad for her.

"All right, so I'm jealous," Katlyn said, inhaling deeply on the cigarette. Charley expected her to be an ornament, and smoking was the only way she could keep reed-thin. At least that was her excuse. "Are you planning to marry her?"

Brad paused in tucking his shirt in. "I was thinking about it. When I first saw her..." Pausing, he went to look out the window at Park Avenue. "It wasn't love at first sight, but it was a sense that I'd found someone who was like me."

"This is the girl who was raped and had a bastard when she was a kid?" Katlyn asked.

"Get your claws in. You got what you wanted."

"No, I wanted to marry into one of your families and give dinner parties that old Mrs. Farrington attended."

Brad snorted. "That's what you think you wanted, but you would have died under the load of charity meetings and dinner parties with cantankerous old women. No, you're much better off doing the nothing that you do now. Spending the days doing your nails. Eden has dirt under her nails most of the time. She doesn't know it, but it's there."

"She sounds delightful. Does she wear overalls?"

"No. Cotton. Ever hear of it?"

"It used to grow right up to my back door, remember?"

Brad didn't answer her but sat down to put on his shoes and socks.

Katlyn put out her cigarette, then stretched across the bed in what she knew was an alluring pose. "I do hope you aren't going to tell me that you're never going to see me again."

"Last week I would have said that I was going to send you a note to say that it was over."

She sat up. "This is beginning to sound interesting. You aren't going to tell me that this paragon of virtue has turned you down, are you?"

"Not yet."

"Is there another man? A Camden maybe?"

"He's not from Arundel."

This so startled Katlyn that she couldn't say anything.

Standing, Brad adjusted his pant cuffs, then looked at her. "I thought she and I were..." He grimaced. "Actually, I thought we were a done deal. I guess I was like the old maid who goes on a first date then picks out her wedding china."

"She didn't call you back?"

"Yes, she did." He took a breath. "We spent quite a bit of time together, and I thought there was nothing between her and the other man. I thought she didn't like him in that way, but I saw them laughing together."

"Ah," Katlyn said. She could understand that. She'd shared a few laughs with Brad, but none with her husband. "You think she's going to choose the other man?" she asked softly.

"Maybe. I don't think she knows what she wants. Right now, I think Ms. Eden Palmer could go either way."

"Palmer?" Katlyn said. She would have frowned if her forehead weren't so full of chemicals. "Eden Palmer. Where have I heard that name before?"

"Weren't you living in Arundel when she was? Or are you now too young to remember her?"

"My last surgeon says I now look young enough to be my own daughter," Katlyn said distractedly, then her face lit up. "The book!"

"Book? Yes, Eden was an editor here in New York for a while, and—"

Katlyn jumped off the bed, paying no attention to the fact that she was naked. She spent enough hours with a personal trainer to know she looked good with nothing on. She opened a little French cabinet and pulled out a paperback book with a plain blue cover. *To Die For,* the title read, by Eden Palmer.

"I didn't know Eden had written a book," he said, taking it and flipping through the pages. "When did it come out?"

"It hasn't yet," she said as she put on a silk robe. "It's an advance copy. Charley has things sent to me, and he asks my opinion sometimes, you know, for his movie studio." She shrugged, as though embarrassed by this confidence. "Anyway, this was sent to me. It's good. I told Charley the story had great potential."

"I had no idea you were a major force in the movie industry," he said, teasing her, and she looked as though she might blush. "What's it about?"

"Generations of a family in an old house," she said. "She takes them from the time they settled in America in the 1600s to the present. It's an old theme, but she does it well. There's a story of a duchess escaping the French Revolution and a—"

"Sapphire necklace," Brad said quietly.

"Yeah, right. A real whopper of a thing that leads to murder and lots of feuds."

Brad sat down on a chair and said, "I want you to tell me everything that's in the book."

"You can read it. It—"

"I don't have time to read it. Tell me everything. Are there any other mysteries in the book besides the necklace?"

"Who said the necklace was a mystery? The man who stole the necklace and then killed the mistress of the house died. Mystery solved."

"Right," Brad said quickly. "What *else* is in the book?"

Katlyn looked at him hard. "If you know about the necklace but don't know about the book, then is the story *true*?" Her eyes widened. "The Farringtons! Wasn't there some story about missing sapphires when I was a kid?"

He narrowed his eyes at her. In a second he went from lover to lawyer. "Tell me," he ordered.

"I can't think of any other mystery," she said, annoyed. "Oh! Wait! What about the riddle?"

"There's a riddle?" Brad asked softly.

Katlyn took the book from him, flipped the pages, then handed it back to him.

> *Five by five and three by three.*
> *Worth more than gold and married to thee.*
> *Ten times ten and legends of me.*
> *Look not where thou canst find me.*

He looked at her in question. "What does it say about this riddle in the book?"

"That it was always believed to be bad poetry written by someone in the family, but no one knew who. The main character, a woman from this generation, found it carved into the back of a door in the attic. She was told it was probably written by a kid and that it had no meaning, but she believed it was a riddle. She never found out anything about it, though."

"'Worth more than gold,'" Brad whispered. "'Legends of me.' 'Look not where thou canst find me.'" He looked at Katlyn. "There's only one person in the Farrington family who had an ego like that."

"Old Mrs. Farrington?"

"Not by a long shot." Brad grabbed his coat. "Mind if I keep this?" he asked, holding up the book.

"Sure, but—" She caught his arm. "Why do I feel like I'm never going to see you again?"

He frowned. "I don't have time for this right now. I have to get home. I think I have an idea of what they're after."

"Who is after what?"

Brad didn't answer her. He ran out of the room and didn't look back.

Chapter Twenty-two

Eden tried to open her eyes, but it wasn't easy. She didn't know where she was or what was wrong with her head. Her brain was fuzzy and didn't seem to be working properly. She sensed that there was something she should remember, but she didn't know what it was.

When she heard a low voice, she opened her eyes. Jared McBride was standing in front of her bedroom window, talking on his cell phone. He was frowning.

I must get up, Eden thought. It was daytime, and she never stayed in bed during the day. There was always work to be done. She had to get Melissa ready for school. She had to—

At the thought of Melissa, memory came back to her. Frantic, she tried to get out of bed, but her body wouldn't obey her.

"Gotta go," she heard Jared say, then he was leaning over her and moving her leg back onto the bed.

"Be quiet now," he said, his hand on her forehead. "Everything will be okay."

She clasped his wrist with both her hands. "What happened? Where is Melissa?"

He sat on the bed by her, her head by his thigh. "You're groggy because I gave you two of those sleeping pills you had in your bathroom. I need for you to keep calm right now."

"Tell me," Eden said, tears in her eyes.

"At three-thirty this morning, when it was raining hard, and while you and I..." He looked away, a muscle in his jaw working. "I didn't hear her. I should have, but I didn't." He turned away for a moment and she knew he was thinking that he had been lax in his duty, because if he hadn't been making love with Eden, he would have heard the car. "Your daughter got into your car and drove to the airport in Greenville."

"That's a long way." Eden was trying to keep her heart still as she listened.

"Yes, it is. One of our men was right behind her the entire way, but it was hard to see in the rain. She went to the airport where she met a man—"

"Stuart," Eden said, feeling some relief.

"No. We have photos of the man she met, and he wasn't your son-in-law. Besides, we know where Stuart is at every minute. He's under surveillance."

"Surveillance," she whispered. "You mean that he's being spied on. He's imprisoned. Like me."

Jared stroked her hair. "Yes, like you, he's being watched over. Taken care of. Anyway, your daughter met an older man. He's tall and thin. We're still trying to find out who he is and if he's the instigator of all this." Jared's calmness left him. "What the hell was your daughter doing out alone at that time of the night?" he snapped.

"She was never told anything about the danger surrounding her mother," Eden said. Her heart was beginning to race as she thought of the possible consequences of her daughter being kidnapped. Where was her baby right now? Was she safe? Warm and dry? Was she—?

"A man from the agency was right behind them every moment, but someone reported our man as having a gun, and you know what airports are like now. Before he knew what was happening, he was knocked to the floor and handcuffed. He looked up to see Melissa and the man hurrying away. That was the last our people saw of them."

Eden tried to sit up but managed only to get to her elbows. "Maybe the man she met is someone she knows. Stuart's father, maybe. I've never met him, so I don't know what he looks like. Maybe he—"

"A note was put on the seat of our agent's vehicle. It said that we would be contacted."

"Contacted? When? For what? By whom?"

Jared got up and went to the window. "We still

don't have any answers." He looked back at her. "I'm sorry. This is the most baffling case I've ever been on."

Eden collapsed against the pillows. "Why did you drug me? I can't think clearly. I can't—"

"I did it to calm you down and so you can't get into trouble. I'm going to send you somewhere safe."

"No!" she tried to shout, but it came out as a raspy whisper. "I want to be here. I want to be near my daughter."

"Your daughter—" Jared began, but stopped at a knock on the door. He stepped outside the room for a moment, and Eden could hear low voices. When Jared returned, he wouldn't meet her eyes, but before she could ask any questions, her cell phone rang and Jared picked it up. Answering it, he listened for a moment. "It's for you," he said. "It's Granville, and he wants to talk to you. He says he knows something."

Weakly, Eden took the phone. Jared plumped the pillows behind her head so she could sit up. "Brad?" she asked. When there were tears of relief in her eyes, Jared turned away for a moment, then he sat down beside her and motioned for her to let him listen. He put his face close to hers, the telephone between them.

"Eden, are you all right?" Brad asked. "You sound awful."

"I've been drugged," she said, her voice full of tears. "Did you hear? Melissa…" She couldn't go on as sobs overtook her.

Jared took the phone from her. "Granville? McBride here. What do you know?"

"What's wrong with Eden's daughter? Did she go into labor?"

"We can't tie up this line. If what you have to say isn't of vital importance—"

"I think it might be. Did you know that Eden wrote a book about the history of the Farrington family?"

Jared looked at her in astonishment. "Did you write a book about the Farringtons?"

"Yes. No. I mean it's a fictionalized version of their lives, but, yes, it's about them."

"You wrote a book but you didn't tell me?" he asked, staring at her in astonishment. "What else haven't you told me?"

"It's never been a secret. I hope that by now the sales department has made every bookseller in America know I've written a book. Why didn't your file tell you about my book?"

"I don't know but I'll find out. I'll—"

"McBride!" Brad shouted into the phone. "Ask Eden about the riddle. The one carved inside the door."

"He wants to know—"

"I can hear him," she said, sitting up straighter. "The door is in the attic, and yes, I copied it exactly as it is. He hasn't solved the riddle, has he?"

"She wants to know if you've solved the riddle, and I want to know *what* riddle."

"It's a mystery," Eden said, leaning back against the pillows. "No one knows who wrote it or what it means. None of the Farringtons were very interested in it."

"What do you know, Granville?" Jared asked into the phone.

"It's a hunch, that's all. I think Tyrrell Farrington wrote it, and I think it tells something about his dreadful paintings."

"Not dreadful," Eden said, her head lolling to one side.

"What do you think this riddle is about?" Jared asked. "Does it have anything to do with the kidnapping?"

"Kidnapping?!" Brad shouted. "What kidnapping? Who's been kidnapped?"

"I can't talk about that over the phone. Where are you?"

"On the way back to Arundel. Is Eden all right?" Brad's voice lowered. "Is it Melissa who's been kidnapped?"

"Yeah," Jared said succinctly. "What is it that you know?"

"If it's what I think it is, I may know why Melissa was taken. I'm not sure, but there may be millions involved. McBride, I want you to take one of Tyrrell Farrington's paintings off the wall, take it into the bathroom, and run water over it."

"Something's under his painting?"

"Maybe. I think it's a strong possibility. Just do it, then let me know, will you? I should be there in about two hours. And, McBride, take care of Eden, will you? You don't have kids, so you don't know what it means—"

Jared closed the phone before Brad could finish his sentence, and he was in the hall in two steps. Seconds later, he returned with one of Tyrrell's paintings.

"I want to see what you're going to do," Eden said, trying to get out of bed. Jared put an arm under hers and held the painting in the other. In her bathroom he sat her on the closed toilet and put the painting in the tub, then turned on the shower.

In silence, Eden and Jared watched as the water hit the old painting. At first nothing happened, but then Tyrrell's painting of the fields around Farrington Manor began to run. Underneath were oil colors of another painting.

Jared turned off the shower water, picked up the painting, and used a towel to wipe off what was left of Tyrrell Farrington's watercolors around the edges, then he handed it to Eden. "Recognize the signature?" he asked quietly.

The pills inside Eden were still making her dizzy and drowsy, but she thought she could have been dead and still recognized the signature at the corner. "Van Gogh," she whispered, looking up at Jared in disbelief.

"Yeah, ol' One Ear himself."

It was a picture of blue cornflowers in a field, the light swirling around the flowers. Beautiful and as bright and vibrant as the day it had been painted.

Putting his arm around Eden, he helped her back to bed. She fell back onto the pillows and closed her eyes. "Tyrrell was in Paris at the time

of the Impressionists. Their paintings were so unusual that they couldn't sell them. But then, most
of them just wanted to paint and didn't care if they
sold."

"Didn't you say that Tyrrell's family cut off his
money?"

"Yes." She opened her eyes. "They cut down
his allowance to try to force him to return home.
Maybe all he could afford was used canvases."

"Used by the other painters? The Impressionists?" Jared shook his head in awe as he looked at
the picture in his hands. "You think more of these
pictures have other paintings under them?"

"I don't know," Eden said, "but I do know that
not one of them is worth my daughter's life. How
do I trade them for her?"

"And for the man she met at the airport," he
said, his jaw clenched.

"If he isn't one of the people who took her,"
Eden said. "Have you found out yet who he is?"

When Jared didn't answer right away, Eden sat
up. Her head was beginning to clear somewhat.
"You know who he is, don't you?"

"I wish we did know who had taken her," Jared
said softly.

"That's not what I asked. Who did Melissa meet
at the airport?"

"I don't know," Jared said, looking into her eyes.

Eden knew he was lying, but she had come to
trust him enough to know that there was a reason
for the lie. Eden didn't care who her daughter had

gone to meet. It could be her daughter's lover, the true father of her child; Eden didn't care.

Between Eden and Jared passed silent communication. He was lying; she knew it, but she trusted him.

Sitting on the edge of the bed, Jared pulled Eden into his arms. "We're moving heaven and earth to find your daughter now, but no one has yet contacted us with a ransom demand. Where is this door with the riddle on it?"

"In the attic. There's a little closet on the left, under the eaves. I think some trunks are in front of it, so it'll be hard to find."

"I'll be back in seconds. Don't move," Jared said.

Eden closed her eyes. The drug inside her was lessening just enough that her fear was beginning to come to the surface. When her phone rang again, she grabbed it before the ring finished. "Yes?" she said quickly.

"You know what I want, don't you?" said a man's muffled voice.

"Yes. We just figured it out. Please don't hurt my daughter. She's going to have a baby. She's a good person. She doesn't deserve to—"

"No one will be hurt if you follow my instructions. There's a dirt road where Highway 580 crosses 45. It's easy to miss, but it's there. At the end of the road is an old house. Put the necklace in a paper bag and leave it inside the house. Do you think you can find the place?"

"Yes," Eden said, rubbing her eyes and trying

to clear the confusion from her brain. Necklace? What was he talking about? The necklace was worthless. It was just glass. Or was it? Had Mc-Bride lied to her about that too?

"Come alone," said the voice on the phone. "Anyone comes with you and your kid gets killed. Understand me?"

"Yes. When?" she asked quickly. She could hear Jared's footsteps on the stairs. "When?"

"At midnight tonight."

"Yes, I'll be there," she said, then snapped the phone shut just as Jared came into the room. He was carrying the little door with him.

"Were you talking on the phone?"

"I was trying to call Brad back to tell him what we found," she said, "but he didn't answer."

Jared nodded, then put the door on the bed. On the back of the door, the wood hardly faded since it had been in the dark for a couple hundred years, was a crudely carved four-line riddle.

Eden's head was clearing more with each second, but she didn't want Jared to know that, so she struggled when she tried to sit up.

"Tell me about this," he said.

"I found it when I was clearing up the attic, but Mrs. Farrington knew it was there. No one in the family knew who had written it or when. Mrs. Farrington said her father told her he thought it was put there when the house was built." She looked at Jared. "No one in the family thought anything about it. There's also a phrase written in Latin on a windowpane in one of the dormers. It says—"

"One mystery at a time. What do you think this one means?"

Eden didn't have to read it, as she knew it by heart. "I don't know. Ask Brad. He's the one who figured it out." Her mind was on her daughter and how she was going to slip away, alone, to deliver a worthless necklace to a kidnapper. And how was she going to sneak away from Jared to try to find Melissa?

"I need to sleep," she said in the most pathetic voice she could muster. She did need to sleep. She needed all the strength she could muster to face tonight.

Chapter Twenty-three

I wish you'd let me go with you," Brad said under his breath. "In a situation like this—"

"It's not a situation, it's my daughter," Eden said. "She's been captive for nearly twenty-four hours now, and I need to get her out. If somebody wants that worthless old necklace, he can have it."

"You aren't going to tell this person that it's worthless, are you? He probably needs to think that he's going to get the money to bail himself out of whatever problem he has in his life."

"No, of course not," Eden said slowly, looking at his profile in the dark car. "Brad, you sound as though you know something."

"Of course not," he said quickly as he swung the

car onto the dirt road and turned off the headlights. The dashboard clock said 11:32. It hadn't been easy to get Eden out of the house without McBride knowing, but they'd done it. When Eden had gone into a crying fit and McBride had given her a couple of pills to calm her, Brad thought Eden's plan was off. But her fit had been faked to create a distraction. Eden had spit out the pills, and when Jared thought she was asleep, she'd sneaked down the tiny, secret stairs to the kitchen and out the back door. The front of the house had been full of FBI agents, all of them waiting for a phone to ring, but the back had been clear.

As planned, Brad was waiting for her on the other side of the bridge.

Earlier in the day, after he'd returned from being with Katlyn, he'd been filled with remorse. He shouldn't have done that to Eden, he thought. But after he'd seen her in the mud with McBride, and after he'd seen the gifts of the little truck and gardening tools that he was sure McBride had bought for her, Brad had felt defeated. His pride and his ego had been cut in half. He knew he was considered the "prize catch" in Arundel, but when he'd at last found a woman he thought he might be able to share his life with, he was losing her. He needed something—someone—to make him feel like a man again.

But Katlyn hadn't made him feel good. Instead, she'd made him feel more alone than he had before he'd met Eden.

It was only by chance that Katlyn had told

him about the book Eden had written, and only by chance that Brad had seen the riddle for what it was. An ego trip of a bad painter, is what he thought at first. Who else in the Farrington family would write about "legends of me"? Once Brad realized who had written the riddle, all he'd thought about was the last line, but in the car on the way back to Arundel, he'd figured out the rest of the lines.

By the time he reached Arundel, Brad had changed his mind about Tyrrell Farrington. If the young man had openly returned to Farrington Manor with a stack of Impressionist paintings, his domineering father would have burned them. Brad had an idea that Tyrrell had had the foresight to see that the paintings would someday be worth something. But how did he insure that they would stay in the family and survive generations of tastelessness? If his father didn't destroy them, maybe the next generation would. How to save them?

Brad thought that Tyrrell knew his family well. He certainly understood their vanity. They'd never destroy pictures of what was theirs. So Tyrrell had reluctantly returned to the family, but he'd devoted the rest of his life to covering the wonderful Impressionist paintings with bad watercolors of his family and their possessions. And he had been right: the family vanity had saved them. After all these years, the paintings were still intact and waiting for someone to solve the riddle he'd left behind, and to discover the paintings under the watercolors.

~

Five by five and three by three. Quite simply, the size of the paintings. *Worth more than gold and married to thee.* Tyrrell had guessed that the paintings would someday be worth more than gold. He'd covered several of them with portraits of Farrington spouses. *Ten times ten and legends of me.* He left over a hundred paintings and knew—hoped—that the discovery of them would make a legend of him. *Look not where thou canst find me.* The easiest one: the real art had been painted over.

Brad had wanted to tell Eden all that he'd figured out the second he saw her, but the kidnapping of her daughter had taken precedence over everything else. And worse was when Brad saw the way McBride looked at Eden. Her only thoughts were about her daughter, but McBride couldn't take his eyes off her.

They've been lovers, Brad thought, and wanted to hang himself from the nearest tree for getting jealous and running off to the comfort of a woman he'd never really liked. His only hope of winning Eden was that figuring out the riddle would pull her back to his side.

When Brad first arrived at her house, he'd had to undergo a humiliating search by the FBI. McBride stood in the doorway, smirking, and enjoying Brad's discomfort. And McBride had enjoyed telling Brad that Eden was asleep and would be for hours. "She's been awake all night," he said, not meeting Brad's eyes.

Two minutes later, Brad was in a room with two FBI agents and telling them what he'd figured out about the riddle. As a result, they were flying in a couple of men who were art preservationists and would know how to extract the paintings in a way less violent than with the blast of a shower.

At four, Eden came downstairs. There were dark circles under her eyes, and she was inordinately quiet. She ate the food that was placed in front of her, but said nothing. She only nodded when she saw Brad, but she said nothing to him.

But later, when she passed him, she slipped a note into his hand, then she went up the stairs, her feet heavy and her body bent. Brad excused himself to go to the restroom to read the note. She wrote that she'd been contacted by Melissa's kidnapper, and she asked Brad to meet her at the far side of the bridge at eleven P.M. At the bottom, she'd drawn a map and written "deliver necklace here." Brad knew he should turn the note over to McBride, but at the same time, he saw it as a second chance with Eden. She trusted him, and he wasn't going to betray her trust. Before, when her daughter had arrived and Eden had needed him, when he should have stayed and fought for her, he'd abandoned her. He never wanted her to know how completely he'd abandoned her.

He tore the note into tiny pieces, then flushed it. He wasn't going to let Eden down a second time. He went home, emptied his gun cabinet, borrowed a couple of handguns from his cousin, then spent an hour hiding all of them inside his uncle's Jeep. He wanted four-wheel drive if he was going to be on a dirt road. He used his CDs of the North Carolina survey maps to bring up the area on his computer, then studied the old roads surrounding the abandoned house. He went to visit his great-uncle in the nursing home, and asked him a thousand questions about the house at the end of the dirt road. His uncle knew everything about everyone around Arundel and had a photographic memory. By the time Brad left, he knew the history of the house back four generations. Best of all, he had the phone number of a man who'd grown up in the house and knew the layout of it well. After Brad talked to him, he was almost ready. He had just one more call to make.

"Remi?" he said when his son-in-law answered. "I have something I want you to help me do. But I warn you that it could be dangerous."

"Anything," Remi said.

"I'm serious about the danger of this."

"Mr. Granville, I'm from Louisiana. We invented danger."

Brad rolled his eyes skyward. "Spare me," he said. "If you think you can do this, then get over here right away."

"Yes, sir."

Brad put down the phone and stood looking about him for a while. Inadvertently, in his hours of research about the abandoned house, he'd come across the name of someone. The name had come up twice, and as much as Brad hated the idea, he thought he knew who was behind the kidnapping.

All for a worthless necklace, he thought. And the irony was that the man had been alone inside Farrington Manor many times. He could have stolen the paintings at any time. Instead, he was risking everything for some colored glass.

Brad shook his head to clear it, slipped a tiny handgun into his pocket, then looked at his watch. It was after eight. Not much time left before he was to meet Eden. He picked up his Bible, opened it at random, and began to read.

Chapter Twenty-four

P lease don't try to stop me," Eden said to Brad. "It's something I have to do." Beside her, in his car, she was clutching the paper bag containing the necklace so tightly that her nails had cut through the top of it. "If he wants this thing, he can have it. All I want is my daughter."

Brad looked at the dashboard clock. It was now fourteen minutes to midnight. "I think I should go in your place," he said. "I brought a black sweat-shirt. If I pull up the hood, I—"

"No one would mistake you for me," she said, looking at the bag in her hand. "You'll stay here and wait for me? I don't know what will happen after I leave the necklace. Do you think he'll...?" She couldn't finish her sentence.

Brad put his hand on hers. "I think that once he gets the necklace he'll leave town immediately. I think he probably has a car waiting close by, and he probably has his plane tickets and his suitcases with him. I think he's already made arrangements to sell the necklace. Once he has the money in his hands, I think he plans to go to some country that has no extradition laws where he plans to spend the rest of his worthless life in a hut on a beach painting pictures that he thinks will make him the next Gauguin. I think he believes that his paintings will be so good that the world will forgive him for what he did to get the money to bankroll him."

Eden was looking at Brad with her mouth open. "What do you know?" she managed to gasp out.

"Enough to have an idea of what I'm dealing with. I don't think either you or your daughter are in much physical danger. I think he just wants the necklace."

"And after he gets it, will he release her?"

"We'll find her," Brad said. "You can count on that." He squeezed her hand again. "I've already alerted some people I know in New York. He won't be able to escape."

"Who is it?" she asked.

"Later," Brad said, looking again at the clock. "You'd better go. Oh, and Eden, if something should happen, I put a few weapons in this car. Under the seats, and in the glove box." He handed her a car key. "Just in case." As he closed his hands around hers, he said, "But I want you to know that I'll always be close by you."

"What if he hears you?" she said, panic in her voice. "He said I was to come alone. He said—"

"Trust me," Brad said. "Trust me to know what I'm doing as much as you'd trust McBride." To Brad's disgust, these words made Eden calm down immediately. He nodded toward the door, and she put her hand on the handle. He wanted to kiss her, but he couldn't bring himself to do it. Later, he thought, they'd sort out what was between them personally.

Eden took the big flashlight that Brad had given her and walked down the dirt road toward where she knew the old house awaited. She doubted that her daughter would be inside. Would her kidnapper get the necklace, then take it to an appraiser before he released Melissa? If he did that, he'd find out that the necklace was worth nothing. Then what would happen to her daughter?

There was no gravel on the old road and weeds had grown up in the center of it, but she could see that they'd recently been bent by a car running over them. With each step she took, her heart pounded harder and faster.

When the dark outline of the house came into view, she was sweating and shaking. What if—? she kept asking herself. What if he didn't keep his end of the bargain? But then, she hadn't kept her end of the deal, had she? She hadn't come alone; Brad was with her. At that thought she wanted to run back to the car and tell Brad he had to leave, but she didn't.

When she got close enough to see the house more clearly in the moonlight, she gasped. It was completely enveloped in blooming wisteria. She knew that most people in eastern North Carolina considered wisteria a noxious weed, but she couldn't see it that way. To her, it was one of the most beautiful plants on earth. She loved the way the trunks twisted about one another, loved the narrow, pointed leaves, and loved the drooping cluster of flowers that hung off it in the spring.

To the locals, wisteria "escaped." According to them, if you planted one stick of it, "soon" it would engulf everything in its path. The soon was about twenty years, and to Eden's gardener's mind, all it took was a bit of pruning each year to control it.

Where wisteria was most likely to "escape" was in old, abandoned houses like this one. Many years ago, someone had planted a wisteria bush and had probably kept it pruned. When the house was abandoned, the other plants, the magnolias and the snowball bushes, had been devoured by wild vegetation that was stronger than the modern, hybridized plants. But not the wisteria. Given the right climate, wisteria could cover the earth. Not even forests could overcome wisteria. The vine would grow right up the tree, keeping all sunlight from it, and eventually kill the tree.

In the moonlight, to Eden's eyes, the wisteria-draped house was ethereally beautiful. The old house was still strong enough to hold the heavy vines upright, and the flowers cascaded down it. It was a Hansel and Gretel cottage for gardeners, she thought.

The beauty of the old house made her calm down somewhat. She tentatively stepped onto the rotting porch, testing the boards before putting her whole weight on them. The boards creaked, and she paused, listening. She thought she heard something to her right, but it was probably only an animal. The door to the house was open and she walked inside, shining her light around the room. She saw nothing but a falling-down old house, a common sight in North Carolina. The wallpaper and the fireplace surround made her think the house was from the 1840s, maybe later.

A scurrying in the back made her jump. She put her hand to her throat, then turned out the light. "Melissa?" she whispered, but there was no answer. She stood still for a moment, listening, but heard nothing. But her instinct told her that she was being watched. With the light turned off, the house was pitch-black. The wisteria outside kept any moonlight from coming in; she couldn't see her hand.

"I'm leaving the bag now," she said too loudly. If anyone was there, he'd hear her. "I just want my daughter back. You can have the necklace. I won't even report that it's missing. Please," she said. "I just want my daughter."

There was no response, and she heard nothing—which made her sure that there was another human nearby. If she'd been the first person to enter the house, animals would have been scurrying everywhere. But someone else had disturbed them first, and now they were hiding and waiting for all the humans to leave.

"The necklace is here," she said, then started backing toward the door. She didn't want to turn the light back on. What if she saw who it was? That might make him refuse to release Melissa.

She backed into the wall, then had to feel her way to the door. When her hands touched the door, she backed through it. Only when she was outside in the cool air did she turn back around and start walking again. In her panic, she hit the step too hard and her ankle twisted under her. She went down, hitting the ground in front of the steps hard. An old board hit her in the side, making her gasp.

But the fall didn't frighten her as much as what she saw. Under the porch were two pinpoints of light: eyes. An animal? A person?

Fumbling, Eden tried to stand upright, but her hand caught on something, and she flailed about as she tried to get away. She didn't want to see who it was under the porch. To see, to know, would endanger Melissa.

When Eden finally managed to stand, she started running back toward the car. After the dark of the inside of the house, the moonlight was almost bright, so she didn't turn on the flashlight. When she saw the car, she breathed a sigh of relief—until she saw that Brad wasn't in it. Her first impulse was to call for him, but she couldn't do that. Her second thought was of anger for his not staying put, and anger at herself for asking him to help her. But she couldn't have done it by herself, she thought. She couldn't have secretly driven a car out from under the noses of McBride and the whole FBI force, could she?

She leaned against Brad's car. Now what? she wondered. Did she wait here for Brad like a good little girl, or did she go back into the dark woods surrounding the house and try to find...find what?

My daughter, she thought. Try to find my daughter.

Slowly, she moved away from the car and slipped into the woods that were closing in on the house. There had to be outbuildings still standing. Maybe— She didn't have any plans or concrete thoughts about what she was doing, but maybe she could see something or find out something.

As a gardener, she knew something about the way plants grew. From the way the wisteria was draping over the house, it grew from the side. Most people planted wisteria by a door, where it could drape over a porch roof. If that was the case, then there was a door on the east side of the building— and there would be a thick trunk to the vine. Eden could hide there and, in secret, see who came out of the building. She could even follow him, or if he got in a car, she could get a license number.

Hurrying, in case she missed him, Eden made her way around to the side of the building, then slipped through the darkness toward where she thought the trunk to the huge vine might be. It was easy to find, and she thought that if she clung to it and stayed very still, she would look like part of the gnarled, twisted trunk. If he aimed a light directly on her, she'd never fool him, but she doubted that he'd do that. If she had any luck at all, he'd walk right past her.

In the distance she heard a car start, heard it crunch on the rocky surface of the drive. Had Brad returned and driven away? Without her? No, she had an idea that he was the type of man who'd never leave a "lady" to fend for herself.

So who was in the car? she wondered. Who was driving away? After a few moments, the sound of the car faded, and all was again silent, but, still, there were no sounds from inside the house. The animals didn't start making their noises; they knew that a human was there.

Eden stayed very still, willing her heart to slow down and stop making so much noise. After what seemed like an hour, she heard a sound from inside the house. Within seconds she heard footsteps. Someone was walking inside the house.

She waited, staying utterly still. She heard the noise of the paper of the bag she'd put the necklace in. Was he opening it? Or did he trust her? She saw no light, so maybe he was just feeling it rather than looking at it. She held her breath when the footsteps came toward her. Yes, he was going to use the side door. He was coming toward her!

When he got to the door, she saw the silhouette of a tall man. In his hand was the bag, but she couldn't see his face. She watched in silence as he walked within two feet of her and headed toward the back of the house.

When he was about fifty feet away, she moved from her hiding place and started to follow him. She stepped on a twig, and the man started to turn around. Eden drew in her breath. He was going to see her!

Before the man could turn his head, a hand clasped over her mouth and she was pulled back into a thicket of pyracantha—the barbed wire of the plant world. At least twenty thorns sank into her flesh, but she couldn't move to get away from them for fear of making noise.

The hand was still over her mouth, the thorns were sticking into her, and she was jammed up to a body that she'd come to know well. Through the bushes she could see the silhouette of the man with the bag in his hand. He was looking back toward them and listening, but he saw nothing, heard nothing.

There were tears in Eden's eyes from the pain of the thorns. When the man with the bag turned away and started walking again, she shook her head to get McBride's hand off her mouth. Frowning, she looked at him. She wanted to bawl him out for lying, sneaking, and tricking her, but he had on his FBI face, with no hint that there was anything personal between them. Besides, she was glad to see him. If he hadn't shown up, she would have been seen by the man.

Jared was dressed all in black, and his face had been darkened, so she could hardly see him in the shadow of the bush. Silently, he motioned for her to move back into the open, and she readily obeyed. Once she was free of the bushes, she started twisting about to remove the thorns from her skin.

Stepping ahead of her, Jared looked toward where the man had gone. She could see nothing. Turning back to her, he motioned for her to go back toward Brad's car. It was only when he turned that she saw that he had night-vision goggles on his head, and that there was a large pistol in his hand. Around his waist was a belt that held more weapons.

Eden obeyed him. Silently, she turned toward the driveway and headed toward the car Brad had borrowed. But the second she was out of sight of Jared, she turned back. For one thing, she didn't think it was safe for her to be near a car, and for another, Jared's presence made her believe that Melissa was somewhere nearby.

"Eden!" She heard an urgent whisper that she knew was Brad's.

Putting out her hands, she went forward. He caught her hand in his and pulled her down to the ground beside him.

"Where have you been?" he asked, worry in his voice.

"I went back to the car and you weren't here, so I—"

"I think I know where Melissa might be."

"Take me there," she said. "Now."

"Remi is here, so don't get frightened if you see someone."

"Remi? The son-in-law you don't trust?" She looked at him. "Was he hiding under the porch of the house?"

"Yeah," Brad said, and she could see his smile in the darkness. "Clever, aren't you?"

She started to say that she'd discovered him by clumsiness, not clever deduction, but didn't. Brad took her hand and turned to his left, away from the house, and away from the car.

"Icehouse," he said over his shoulder, but then said no more. They unclasped hands, but she could follow him easily. He walked slowly, always waiting for her to catch up. They used no light, and they were as silent as possible.

An icehouse, Eden thought, and knew that it was a good choice for a hiding place. Icehouses were nearly always underground, so no lights would show on the outside. And no screams could be heard, Eden involuntarily thought, then shivered.

As she watched Brad moving through the woods, she thought maybe she should tell him that McBride was there, and that the woods were probably full of FBI agents, but Eden said nothing. She was at the point where she wasn't sure of anything or anyone.

It took nearly twenty minutes to find the old icehouse, and Eden knew that Brad had to have done a lot of research to know where it was. Or had he played there as a child?

There was an artificially created hill, and on the north side was a heavy oak door. Brad ran his hands down it, feeling for the lock. There was none.

When Brad reached to pull the door open, Eden grabbed his arm, her expression telling him to be careful. Smiling at her, he patted her hand, then he pulled a pistol out of the holster at his side. He hadn't been wearing a gun earlier. He motioned for Eden to go into the trees to safety, but she shook her head. She'd stand outside, but she wasn't leaving.

Brad pulled the door open, and when it made no sound on its hinges, Eden knew that they had been oiled recently. The inside was darker than the house had been. She heard insects scuttling across the floor, but no other sound.

"Melissa?" Eden said into the darkness, and in the next second, she heard whimpering. Her daughter!

Stumbling over her feet, Eden ran toward the sound. She could see nothing, but her hands felt warmth. Frantically, she reached out and touched her daughter's big, hard belly. In seconds, she found Melissa's face and pulled down the gag from her mouth.

"Oh, Mommy!" Melissa cried. "I knew you'd come. It's been horrible, Mommy. It's been—"

"I know, sweetheart," Eden said as she felt down Melissa's arms. Her daughter was in a chair, her hands taped together behind her. Brad turned on his flashlight, and the little room flooded with pale light. Eden went to her knees behind her daughter and tried to tear the duct tape off. When her fingers couldn't do it, she used her teeth.

"Here," Brad said from above her, and handed her a knife.

"Mommy, Mommy," was about all Melissa could say.

"I'm sorry," Eden said, sawing at the tape to free her daughter. "He wanted the necklace, so he took you. It was all my fault." She got the tape off her daughter's wrists, then moved to the front of her to release her ankles.

Brad helped Eden stand up, as her knees were shaking.

"Could you help me up?" Melissa said to Brad.

He had to put his arms under hers to lift her, as her legs and arms had lost their circulation. "I think we should get out of here."

"Too late for that," said a man from the doorway. He was a heavyset man, with thick eyebrows, and Eden had never in her life seen a man with so little life in his eyes. There was no emotion there, no feelings.

"Who are you?" Eden whispered.

"Somebody that don't want no trouble," the man said, looking Eden up and down, then looking at Melissa. When Brad moved his foot, the man turned quickly and shot him in the leg. The sound inside the earth-encased room was deafening.

With a scream, Melissa collapsed back onto the chair. Eden ran to Brad as he fell to the floor.

"He's all right," the man in the doorway said. "I just wounded him. You." He pointed his gun at Eden. "I want you to come with me."

"You have the necklace," she said.

"Yeah, I got it," he said, pulling it out of his jacket pocket. "I didn't plan on that. That skinny guy held on to it so tight I had to pry it out of his hands."

Eden looked at the man, trying to understand what was going on. If he didn't want the necklace, what did he want? And if he hadn't taken the necklace, who was he?

"You gonna get up or am I gonna have to shoot the kid?" He pointed his gun at Melissa.

"You want the paintings, don't you?" Eden said softly as she walked toward him.

"Yeah, sure. What else would I want?"

She glanced down at Brad on the floor. The bullet had grazed his thigh. He was bleeding and in pain, but she knew that he'd be all right. She walked slowly, so the man in the doorway could see that she wasn't going to cause any problems.

"My house is full of FBI agents," she said calmly. "It will be difficult to get the paintings out of the house."

"Your house used to be full of agents," the man said, "but I got rid of a lot of them, including the ones around here."

Eden tried to keep from gasping out loud. Was Jared one of the agents he'd rid himself of? She couldn't keep the blood from draining from her face.

"Yeah, missy," the man said, an ugly half grin on his face. "I got rid of your boyfriend too." He glanced at Brad on the floor, who was wrapping the sleeves of his windbreaker around the wound in his leg. "One of 'em, anyway. So which one are you plannin' to stay with?" he asked Eden, smirking like a dirty little schoolboy. He waved his gun at Brad. "He know what you and McBride did in that shed?" He looked at Brad. "And she know what you did with your fancy dame? You three are why I never wanted to settle down and have a family. Ever'body in bed with ever'body else."

"If you're insinuating that my mother—" Melissa began, trying to heave herself up out of the chair.

"No!" Eden shouted when the man pointed his gun at Melissa. Eden leaped to put her own body between the path of the bullet and her daughter.

"Ain't that sweet?" the man said. "But I ain't never killed no pregnant woman and I don't plan to. Now you," he said, motioning to Eden, "you come with me. I got a couple of men waitin' to load up the paintin's, then we'll get out of your way."

"Mother," Melissa said from behind her. "Please—"

"I'll be all right, won't I?" she said to the man.

"You behave yourself and you'll be fine." He stepped back in the doorway to let Eden pass him, then glanced back at the two people in the icehouse before he shut the door, leaving them in the dark.

Eden walked through the night, trying not to trip on anything. She had an idea that if she fell, the man would shoot her. In fact, she couldn't see why he hadn't just stolen the paintings in the first place.

Far ahead of them, behind the house, she saw the outline of a car. His? Or did it belong to the

FBI? She glanced back at the man, and he motioned for her to go toward the car. She took another step, then tripped over something and fell to
the ground. She braced herself, expecting death.

The man behind her pulled a flashlight out of
his pocket and flicked it on. Eden had to work to
keep from screaming. Lying on the ground, his
nose inches from hers, was a man whose dead
eyes were staring into hers. She put her hand
in her mouth and bit her knuckles to keep from
screaming.

"He a friend of yours?" the man asked, humor
in his voice.

"I—" Eden began, trying hard to keep herself together. The man behind her shone his light on the
dead body.

"I asked if you know him," the man said, this
time with no humor in his voice.

"He's—" She went to her knees to try to get up.
She thought that perhaps she had been hurt when
she fell down the steps in front of the house, and she
knew that there were thorns in her body from when
Jared— She blinked to keep from remembering
him. He couldn't be dead, could he?

"He worked for Brad," she said when she was
standing. When the man looked puzzled, she said,
"Brad is the man you shot in the leg."

"Oh, him. I'm too nice. Anybody else would
have killed him."

Eden gave him a weak smile that seemed to
please him. He motioned for her to step over the
body and go to the waiting car. Eden put her head

up and tried not to think about what she was doing as she stepped over the legs of Drake Haughton, the young man who was Brad's architect for Queen Anne. She remembered what Brad had said in the car about the man who was demanding the necklace wanting to go somewhere to paint. Had Drake been a frustrated artist? Had he been the one to paint the watercolors that Tess Brewster had sent to the frame shop?

"I tell you," the man behind her said, "I don't know what the world's comin' to. With just plain, ordinary people kidnappin' and robbin' their friends, what's left for us professionals to do?"

"You're a professional criminal?" Eden asked, sounding as though she was asking him if he was a plumber.

"Yeah. Been one for years now. Most of my life, really."

"Do you enjoy your work?"

"Was that one of them veiled things?"

At first Eden didn't know what he meant. "A veiled insult? No. I was just curious. How did you find out about the paintings?"

"Applegate. Or whatever he called hisself. Did you know he was a spy? I might have to kill a few people now and then, but I'd never betray my country. But he did."

"Was the U.S. his country?"

"I don't know. Hey! Whose side are you on?"

"My daughter's," Eden said quickly. "Did you kill Mr. Applegate?"

"Yeah. But he didn't do nothin' for my country.

He played the ponies and owed my boss a lot. He sold some info and paid some debts, but he'd just rack 'em up again. When my boss got sick of him, I went to see him. He said he knew where millions of dollars in paintin's were."

"I see," Eden said, looking ahead toward the car. She was walking very slowly, but the man didn't seem to mind. She had an idea that he thought it was a nice night for a stroll. "How did he find out about the paintings?"

"He said he figured out a riddle. That's what he told my boss. Applegate said he was good at solving riddles and he figured out the one in some book. You read that book?"

"I think perhaps I wrote it," Eden said softly.

"Not the smartest thing you ever done, was it?"

"No, it wasn't." She didn't add that she'd had no idea the riddle had anything to do with millions of dollars' worth of paintings. "He told you where the paintings were, but you killed him anyway."

"That's what I was told to do," the man said, shrugging. "But I made him eat the paper he wrote down your name on. I thought that would get rid of it. Who knew they'd find it inside him? It's amazin' what they can do nowadays."

Eden was beginning to understand. A man with an addiction to gambling had for years paid off his debts by selling government secrets. But when the debts overwhelmed him, he'd been ordered killed. He'd tried to save his life by telling what he'd figured out about a riddle in a book that had yet to be published. But it hadn't worked. He'd been made to eat what he'd written down, then was killed.

"I guess your boss was interested in the riddle," Eden said, walking even more slowly, trying to give Melissa and Brad time to get away.

"Yeah," the man said. "Real interested. But by the time we got here, the FBI was already here— and some man was stayin' in your old house and paintin' ever' night. It was Grand Central Station in here. I had to get rid of the agent, and I had to ask that man what he wanted."

"Drake."

"Yeah, the necklace guy. When I found out that he was crazy and didn't know nothin' I let him go."

"Crazy?" Eden asked. The car was close now.

"Yeah. Said he was plannin' to be a great painter. I thought his stuff was good, but not great. I used to watch him paint while I was waitin' for you to show up. The FBI took a long time to get you here."

"I was important?" she whispered. "You could have taken the paintings at any time."

"Naw. Boss said it had to be legal or he'd get only about twenty percent of their worth. He wanted you to show up so you could sell 'em to him, but, I tell you, it wasn't easy. You got more men around you than a pop star."

"But you killed them off. What about the men who ransacked my house?"

"To make you want to leave. You would be gone too, except for that FBI guy."

"And the snakes?" she asked softly.

The man's eyes brightened. "That was my idea. McBride and I go way back. I was supposed to keep you alive, but I knew he'd take care of you, so to speak, so I could afford to give him a little trouble. Payback for all the trouble he's given me over the years."

Eden started to ask about Jared but couldn't bring herself to do it. "You told Drake that we'd found the necklace."

"Yeah. I was watchin' and listenin'. Seein' as it was his paintin's that led you to the necklace, he thought it should be his. He said it was his chance to prove his talent to the world. I helped him arrange the kidnappin'."

"Who did my daughter meet at the airport?"

"Don't know. Ugly little creep. He ran off as soon as I showed up."

"So what happens now?"

"You're gonna sell me the paintin's," he said. "I got papers for you to sign. You don't like 'em, so you're gonna sell 'em to me. And after I buy 'em I'm gonna find out, by accident like, that they have other paintin's underneath 'em. All done legal-like and all sold on the open market. No tryin' to find secret buyers for 'em. My boss wants all this to be legal."

It was on the tip of her tongue to ask who his boss was, but she thought better of it.

"'Course the funny part is that if you tell anybody what happened tonight, I'll come back and do whatever I have to."

"Yes, I understand," Eden said quietly. She wasn't sure, but she thought she saw a shadow move. Was someone there? Had someone survived this man's slaughter? "I assume that you're getting a good cut for doing this. If it's to be your name on the papers, legally, you will own them."

"Are you tryin' to turn me against my boss? He won't like that."

"No, Mr.—"

"Jolly. Ever'body calls me Jolly. Counta I don't laugh a lot. But the name ain't fair 'cause I got a good sense of humor. It's just that it don't match anybody else's."

When he said the name, Eden froze in place. She'd heard his name when she'd been locked in the cellar, but she hadn't told Jared. If she had, maybe—

She stopped her thoughts because she heard a shot in the direction they had come from. In Melissa's direction. She turned, and so did the man. It ran through her head that she should use his turned back to try to escape, but she didn't. He might take his anger out on Melissa.

"You stay right there," Jolly ordered. "If you don't I'll—"

"I know," she murmured, then watched him retreat into the dark woods.

In the next second she was on her back, tackled from the side by a heavy body and flattened to the ground. On top of her was Jared McBride.

"Please tell me you weren't going to just stand there and wait for him to come back and kill you."

"I can't breathe! I thought you were dead." There was relief in her voice.

"You can mourn me later." He rolled off of her, stood up, then pulled her up with him. "Stay low," he whispered, "and stay close to me. Jolly has two other goons with him."

"What about Melissa?" Eden said into his back as she did her best to keep up with him.

"I don't know. I'm the only one here."

"Remi is here," she said.

Halting, Jared looked at her. "That big Cajun is here?"

"Somewhere. I saw him hiding under the porch of the house."

Jared shook his head in disbelief. "Why didn't we just send out invitations? It was bad enough having to act like we didn't know what you and Granville were up to. I had to fish pieces of a note out of the toilet pipe." He made a noise of exasperation. "Stay with me and keep quiet. Can you use a gun?"

"Never shot one in my life."

"That's a help. Get down!" He put his hand over the top of her head and pushed her down into a circle of tree trunks. They could hear male voices near them, but the voices didn't seem upset, so maybe they hadn't found out that Eden was missing. She was the only one who could sign the papers, so they needed her.

"Hands up!" came a voice near them. "Drop your weapons! Do it or we'll shoot."

"Who the hell is that?" Jared said under his breath. "And who is he talking to?"

Eden thought she was going to be sick. She recognized the voice. "He's my son-in-law," she said. "Stuart."

Jared leaned back against the tree trunk, then with a grunt of pain, turned his back to Eden. "Could you...?" She knew what he meant. There were still pyracantha thorns in his back, as there were in hers. While he reloaded two guns, she ran her hands over his back and pulled out all the thorns she could find.

"Thanks, honey," he said, making a joke. "Wish me luck," he said as he started to leave their dark little nest.

But Eden caught his head in her hands and kissed him hard. "Save everyone," she whispered, "including yourself."

He removed the pistol from his ankle holster and handed it to her. "Aim, then pull." He kissed her again, then he was gone into the night.

Chapter Twenty-five

Eden waited as long as she could stand to. She heard no sounds, not even animals. Nothing slithered or scurried. After what seemed like hours but was probably only minutes, she heard the sound of a car being started. Whose car? she wondered. And where was it going?

And what about Stuart? Who had he been telling to drop his gun? The scary Mr. Jolly?

As quietly as she could, Eden left the relative safety of the trees and made her way back to the icehouse. Silently, she went inside. It was dark, so she had to feel her way around. She nearly slipped on a puddle of blood from Brad's leg, but no one was in the icehouse.

She went outside and stood still, listening, but she heard nothing. She took two steps and tripped over a body. Cautiously, wishing she had a light, she bent down to the body. When it groaned, she reached into her pocket and pulled out the gun Jared had given her. She'd heard of safety catches. Was there one on this gun? If there was, was it on or off?

The person on the ground groaned again, and she recognized the voice. "Stuart? It's me, Eden." She put the gun back in her pocket and bent down to her son-in-law. "Are you all right?"

"My head hurts. Someone hit me. Where's Missy?"

"*Melissa* is—" Eden said pointedly, then made herself stop. She'd always hated that nickname. "I don't know where anyone is or what they're doing. I heard you tell a man to stick his hands up. Who was he?"

"I don't know. He'd been shot in the leg."

"Oh," Eden said flatly. "That was Brad. I was hoping—"

"That I'd rescue everyone and be a hero?" Stuart asked sarcastically. "Wouldn't that foil your plans of getting my wife and child to leave me and live with *you*?"

"I don't want them to live with me," Eden said as she took his arm and pulled him upright.

"That's what you've always wanted. You've done everything you can to make Missy think that I'm incompetent and that I can't support my own family. You've—"

"Stuart, do you think it's possible that you could tell me what's wrong with me *after* everyone's life is safe? What happened to Brad? Where is Melissa?"

"I don't know. I flew from New York to Raleigh, then drove a rental car to Arundel. My intention was to pick up my wife and take her home. You can imagine my surprise when I saw my mother-in-law inside a car beside some strange man at eleven o'clock at night. I did the natural thing and followed her—you. When I saw you turn into a dirt road, I parked just off the highway and walked in. I saw the light and got here just in time to see…"

"See what?" she asked gently.

"See that man get shot in the head. Who was he?"

"Drake Haughton. He worked for Brad, the man who was shot in the leg," Eden said. "Stuart, I think we should go. I have a feeling that everyone has gone back to my house and they're waiting for me."

"For you?" Stuart asked, and Eden couldn't help grimacing. Stuart made it sound as though he couldn't believe anyone would want *her*.

"Stuart," she said, her teeth together and her hands made into fists. "Yes, my daughter does want to leave you, and, yes, she wants her and the baby to live with me. As you know, I have a lot of influence over my daughter, so it's up to me what she does with her future. If you don't cut out your snide, catty, jealous remarks, so help me I will do everything in my power to get her to leave you. Do I make myself clear?"

"Yes," he said softly. "What do you want me to do?"

"Can you drive a car?"

She could tell that he was fighting back a sarcastic remark, but all he said was "Yes."

"Then follow me. We're going to get Brad's car and go back to Farrington Manor."

Eden nearly ran through the woods, listening to the sounds, but she heard nothing that made her think that people were hiding nearby. What had happened? Where was Melissa? she thought, and her entire body started to shake, but she got it under control. Where were Jared and Brad? Remi?

Eden pulled the key Brad had given her from inside her pocket and handed it to Stuart. As soon as he started the car, she climbed into the backseat. She was going to search for the weapons that Brad had told her were hidden in the car.

"What are you looking for?" Stuart asked as he turned the car around and headed for the highway.

"Guns. Knives. Explosives. Whatever I can find," Eden said. Her head was hanging over the backseat as she searched the floor. She found a pistol taped under the driver's seat. There was a rifle under the overhang of the backseat.

"I think I'm lying on one," came a voice from the back.

Stuart slammed on the brakes so hard that Eden's face hit the back of the seat. She felt blood begin to run from her nose.

In a second, Stuart had jumped out of the car

and run to the back, where he threw open the big back door. Eden, dripping blood, hung over the seat. Her daughter, her beautiful daughter, was lying on her side, curled up in the back of the Jeep.

Eden reached for her daughter, but Stuart beat her to Melissa. He pulled his wife from the car and was kissing her face all over.

"I was crazy with worry," Stuart was saying between kisses. "Don't you know that I wouldn't have a life without you? You're my very breath. You're everything to me."

"I thought you didn't care about me anymore," Melissa was saying, crying and kissing Stuart back.

Eden turned away from them and sat down in the backseat. There was a box of tissues on the floor, and she pressed a handful to her bleeding nose. In her lap was a pistol, a rifle across her legs. Did every mother have this moment? she thought. This moment when she realized that she'd lost her child?

"I think we better go," she said softly, but no one heard her. She was tempted to climb over the seat and drive away. If she was sure Melissa—and, okay, Stuart—would be safe, she'd do it. But Eden didn't know who or what was still outside.

"Let's go!" she said, louder, making them hear her. Holding hands, not wanting to separate, Stuart and Melissa sat side by side in the backseat and Eden drove back to Arundel. When she stopped the car in front of the sheriff's house it didn't take much persuasion to get them to get out.

"Mother," Melissa said. "I don't think you should

go back there. I think you should stay with us and talk to the sheriff."

Eden didn't bother to explain her motives, but she knew that by the time she waited for the sheriff to get out of bed, have a couple of cups of coffee to wake himself up, then take forty-five minutes or so to understand what Eden was saying, there'd probably be half a dozen more people dead. She had an idea that Mr. Jolly was waiting for her to return to the house to sign the papers before he left. And he's welcome to the paintings, Eden thought as she sped away, leaving her daughter and son-in-law standing on the sidewalk.

The streets of Arundel were empty at that time of the morning, so Eden ran the red lights and made her way to the bridge as fast as she could. She went over the bridge at sixty, twice hitting her head on the roof of the car. I won't sign anything until he releases everyone, she thought.

She stopped the car on the road, jumped out, grabbed the two weapons, and started running toward her house. Standing on the side of a wooden flower bed, she looked into the living room window. She could see a light in the center hall and she thought she could see the silhouettes of at least three people. Who were they?

"Where the hell did you come from?" came Jared McBride's voice close to her ear. "I thought you were inside."

"Who *is* in there?" she asked as she handed him the rifle and the pistol. She still had the little gun in her trouser pocket.

"Granville and his son-in-law are taped up and on the floor in the hall. Jolly and his goons are moving around."

"I guess you know that man Jolly."

"Oh, yeah. We've never been able to get him on anything before because he leaves no witnesses. Where's your daughter?"

"With her husband at the sheriff's."

"When Jolly hears the sirens, he'll shoot Granville and the kid."

Eden swallowed. "What do we do?"

"*We* do nothing. Now that I know you're safe, I plan to go in there, and—"

"And save everyone? All by yourself?"

"If you think that *you* are going with me, I'll tie you up first."

"Sex later. Right now we have to think about business."

Jared gave a snort of laughter. "You can't go in there. There'll be gunfire."

Eden swallowed again. "How about if I go in there, sign his papers, and he leaves with the paintings?"

"You think he'll leave after he gets them? Wave good-bye? Say thank you? No, he intends to kill anyone who's seen him."

"But Melissa is already at the sheriff's house."

"He'll get her later."

Eden pulled the little gun from her pocket. "Show me how to work this thing."

Jared hesitated, then took the gun from her. "I want you to know that I'm only doing this because I have no other choice. I want you to go in the back, up those little stairs, then come down the big stairs. Just wait there and do nothing. When the time is right, I'll shout, 'Look out!' then I want you to fire this. Don't try to hit anyone because you'll miss. Just shoot in the air. The noise will create a diversion and that'll be enough. Understand me?"

All Eden could do was nod, then she followed him to the back of the house. He climbed on the giant air conditioner on the ground, lifted the window up, then bent down to help Eden to climb up. She started to climb through the window, but he stopped her, and for a moment she thought he was going to kiss her, but he didn't. Instead, he just looked into her eyes, and the look said that he'd die to save her. Chills ran up her spine, and she leaned toward him, but he gently pushed her toward the window.

She knew the old house well. No one else could have sneaked around on the old floors in silence, but she could. She knew to lift up on the door to the stairs so its hinges wouldn't make noise, and she knew that she had to step over steps six and nine or they would creak. When she reached the top of the stairs, she put her ear to the door and listened, but she heard nothing. Slowly, she opened the door and peered out. Tyrrell Farrington's paintings had been stacked on the floor, ready to be taken out of the house. When she heard a sound outside, she tiptoed to the window. Two men were loading a paneled truck with the paintings. They were taking their time and seemed to be arguing about how to get all the paintings into the truck, but Eden knew that soon they'd return to the house, to this hall, to get the paintings stacked there.

There are too few of us and too many of them, she thought. Bad men were outside and in, and it was only her and Jared. If only she could create a *big* diversion, she thought.

On her bedside table was her ring of keys, the one Brad had given her when he'd turned the house over to her. Her first thought was, What are they doing there? They should have been in her handbag.

In the next second a ray of moonlight came through the window and landed on the little silver angel on the ring. Mrs. Farrington's angel. Eden looked at the angel, and she could hear Mrs. Farrington's voice. She'd always hated the cellar, and one of her many reasons was that she was afraid that everything in it would explode. Eden smiled. She knew what to do and how to do it.

A second later, she was running down the stairs, leaping over the creaking steps as she whispered "Thank you" to what she knew was Mrs. Farrington's watching spirit.

In the dark kitchen she could hear the voices of the men in the hall. The two men from outside had come back in. She heard Jolly's voice, and he sounded agitated. The thought of Brad and Remi tied up on the floor gave her new courage. She hurried across the room to the pantry. First, she lifted the window that led to the side porch. She'd read that a thief always planned his exit first. When the window was open, she lifted the door in the floor, then she took out the gun Jared had given her. She knew she couldn't shoot something small, but maybe she could hit a wall full of jars of twenty-two-year-old pickled fruit. They'd had time to ferment by now.

Turning her head away, she aimed at the wall she couldn't see in the dark and shot. She was rewarded with an explosion—and the exploding jar set off a chain reaction. As Eden dove through the open window, she heard men running. She hid behind an overturned chair, her breath held, as she heard men shouting. The next second, she heard a door slam and knew that Jared had locked the men in the pantry. When one of them started to come out the window, Eden fired a shot in his general direction and he went back inside. Two minutes later, she heard sirens, and in the distance, she heard a helicopter. Eden stayed where she was, the gun aimed at the open window, ready to shoot at anyone who tried to leave the pantry. There were tears running down her cheeks.

It was over.

Chapter Twenty-six

E den," Brad said, reaching for her hand. He was half reclining on the cushioned swing in front of his house, a cane propped against the wall. Summer had finally come to Arundel, and the unusually cool spring was over.

Eden didn't take his hand, acting as though she didn't see it. Holding on to her glass of sweet tea, she looked out at Arundel. She now had absolutely everything that she'd ever dreamed of having. It was as though she'd spent her entire life as a tightly wrapped flower bud, and now she was at last blossoming. When she was a child and had lived with her repressive parents who told her that everything in life was bad, she'd looked at the other children at her school with longing. She used to listen to them talk about their parties and their dates, and she imagined what it would be like to be one of them.

When she'd become pregnant and had been discarded by her parents, thrown out, tossed aside like so much rubbish, she'd been terrified beyond comprehension. She'd been too young to think clearly, but the question Why me? had filled her mind.

Mrs. Farrington had been the first person who had really cared about her, and Eden used to imagine what it would be like to be Mrs. Farrington. She daydreamed about growing up in that beautiful house, with that beautiful garden, and belonging to a group of people whose friendship extended back hundreds of years. To belong! she thought. To belong to a group of people who never threw you out.

In the last weeks since Melissa had been kidnapped, Eden had found out that a lot of people knew about Drake Haughton's mental instability. The young man hadn't been kidding when he said that all he'd done was draw Brad's ideas. Eden found out that Drake had never wanted to be an architect. Just like Tyrrell Farrington, Drake had wanted to study fine art. But Drake's father, like Tyrrell's father a century before, had forbidden his son to do something so bohemian. If Drake wanted his father to pay for his education, if Drake wanted to receive his inheritance, then he'd have to get a proper degree in a proper subject, and use his education. Out of friendship, Brad had given Drake a job, but the young man had been driven nearly insane with longing for a different life.

Now Eden looked out at the perfect little town
of Arundel, and it seemed different to her. In the
years that she'd had to raise a child by herself,
memories of this pretty little town had kept her
going. It was what she strove to achieve. She'd
never had much money, but she'd taught her
daughter the good manners that Mrs. Farrington
had taught Eden. Melissa knew how to converse,
how to say please and thank you. She knew how
to act at a party. No, Eden thought, her daughter
hadn't been raised to be a kid who wore blue jeans
and ate fast food. Her daughter—

"Eden?" Brad asked again. "Are you here with
me?"

She took a sip of her tea and smiled. "Of course
I am. I'm just thinking, that's all."

"You've been through a lot," he said.

"We have." She drank more of her tea and
looked back at the town. Yes, she'd been through
a lot in the short time that she'd been back here
in Arundel. She'd returned to a town that she'd
known as a child, but now she was an adult. And as
an adult, she saw things that she hadn't seen before.

"Want to talk to me about anything?" Brad asked.

"Not yet," she said, still smiling. She knew what
he meant. Two days after the FBI had taken Jolly
and his men away, Brad had asked her to marry
him. "You were magnificent," he'd said.

Eden had wanted to explain about her and Jared
and what that odious Jolly had said in the icehouse, but Brad had put a finger to her lips. "We're
adults," he said. "We've both made mistakes. We've

hurt each other. I think we should start over, don't you?"

At the time, Eden had agreed with him, but later she thought that she didn't want to start over. It wasn't right to go through what they had and learn so much, then discard it and pretend that it hadn't happened.

In the last weeks, Eden had seen that it was at last time to let go of her daughter. No more tug-of-war. No more tearing Melissa down in the middle and making her choose between her husband and her mother.

After everything had calmed down, Eden had sat down with her daughter and a huge bowl of popcorn and they'd talked. Not with all the boundaries that mother-daughter placed on them, but as woman to woman. Eden was shocked to hear what had been going on among her and Stuart and Eden. Eden realized that she'd caused her daughter many tears by not letting her grow up, by not letting her leave. "But you're all I have," Eden said.

"Don't you think I know that? I am your entire *life*! You have nothing else but *me*! And all I've ever had is *you*!"

Melissa told her mother about the call from Minnie and the information about her father. Melissa had called him immediately and had paid for his plane ticket to fly to Greenville.

"But all he wanted was money," Melissa said. "And he tried to make me believe that you had seduced him." With tears running down her face, Melissa told what the man had said, that Eden had ruined his marriage, ruined his whole life. "He blamed *you* for all his problems. He..." At the end, Walter Runkel had run his hand up Melissa's arm in a way that had made her flee the airport and run into Drake Haughton's arms.

That talk changed them. Melissa said she wanted her husband and child, but she was afraid to leave her mother alone. After much hesitation, Eden at last admitted that she had no idea in the world what *she* wanted.

"But you're a rich woman now," Melissa said. "You have this house and this town that you've always loved, and Brad adores you. You could marry him and live here forever. I can see you as the Grande Dame of the whole town." She was teasing her mother. "I can see that ambitious young women would fight to be invited to *your* parties. What you wear will be reported in the local newspaper." She waved her hand about the house. "You could have a New York interior designer come here and drape this place in silk. You could get into *Architectural Digest*. Wouldn't that be something for a little girl who was thrown into the streets? Mother! Maybe you could get on *Oprah* and tell your story."

Eden didn't smile at Melissa's vision. It was nearly the same vision Jared had given her, except that this time it was presented in a way meant to entice. "Mrs. Farrington said that this house was dead until I put a baby in it."

Melissa clasped her mother's hand. "Stuart and I and the baby will visit you often. Every long weekend and every holiday. Did you know that Remi has asked Stuart to handle the books for his new landscaping business?"

Eden smiled. After the police and the FBI arrived, Brad told them that Remi had saved his life. One of Jolly's men had wanted to kill Brad, but Remi had quickly said that he knew where all of the paintings were and he'd tell if they didn't hurt Brad. In the end, Remi had hoisted his wounded father-in-law across his shoulder and carried him to the car.

When Brad was in the hospital and thanking Remi, the young man said, "I want my own landscaping company. I don't want to work for you or anyone else." His eyes were defiant and he was standing up to his full height, his shoulders back.

"You have it," Brad said, "and if you need—"

"I have everything else that I need," Remi said, his arm around Cammie's shoulders.

Since that day, Eden had seen Brad's morose daughter smile a whole two times.

"Somebody's gettin' some," Minnie had said, and poked Eden in the ribs.

Minnie had spent quite a bit of time begging Eden to forgive her. Eden was sure it was small of her, but she couldn't forgive Minnie for what she'd done. Minnie had hurt people over her imagined involvement with Jared McBride.

Eden didn't answer her, but she'd told Brad that he had to free Minnie from her obligation to him. "I don't care if you do hate living alone, we all do, but you must give that girl her freedom." He deeded the overseer's house to Minnie, and now she was Eden's neighbor.

Minnie liked to pretend that nothing had happened between her and Eden, but Eden couldn't do it. She spoke to Minnie, but she wasn't warm, wasn't friendly.

And then there was Jared. She hadn't seen or heard from him since he went off in a helicopter with Mr. Jolly and his men. That night he'd been angry at her. "I told you to stay put," he said, his eyes blazing, "but you went up and down the stairs. You could have been killed!"

His tone said he was furious with her, but his eyes looked as though he wanted to pull her into his arms and cry in happiness that she wasn't hurt. But he hadn't touched her. By then they were surrounded by people, all of them wanting to ask a thousand questions.

Jared had raised his hand in farewell to her as the helicopter lifted off the ground. She didn't know if she'd ever see him again.

The next day some art experts arrived and they wanted to take all the paintings away with them, but Eden wouldn't let them. They'd already lost one of Tyrrell's paintings in the shower. She wasn't going to lose the rest of them. She wouldn't release the paintings until a document, written by Brad, was signed by them saying that they'd make a complete photographic recording of Tyrrell's family pictures before the underlying paintings were uncovered.

In the end, only four of the paintings turned

out to be valuable. One minor, three major. But, historically, the paintings that Tyrrell had preserved were worth a fortune. She'd already been approached by two authors who wanted to write about what the paintings told about the time of the Impressionists.

As Melissa said, Eden was now very wealthy, or would be as soon as the paintings were restored and sold. The art world was excited about the find, and Christie's auction house expected two of the paintings to go for millions.

"Eden?" Brad asked again. "You don't look well. Is it the heat? Would you like to go inside to the air-conditioning?"

"No," she said. "I like it out here." She looked at him. "Have you ever wanted something so much that you thought you'd die without it, then when you got it, it wasn't as good as you thought it was?"

"Of course. Anyone over the age of three has experienced that." His face was serious. "What is it you wanted so much?"

"Mrs. Farrington's life," she said. "I thought that if I'd had what she was given, I wouldn't have made a mess of it. She married the wrong man and had the wrong child. She conducted herself in some very unladylike ways. I didn't realize it, but I was always criticizing her in my mind. I was thinking that if *I* had had loving parents and *I* had had a good school and birthday parties and—" She looked at him. "Did you know that I've never had a birthday party in my life? It's been something that I've fantasized about all my life. Whenever I watch

TV, see a movie, or read a book, and someone gives a birthday party for someone else, even a child, I get teary-eyed. Isn't that silly?"

"I don't think wanting affection and celebration is silly," he said seriously. "Eden, you're trying to tell me something, but I don't know what it is."

She set down her glass of tea. "I wanted Mrs. Farrington's life, but now that I can have it, I find that I don't want it. I don't want to live in that old house alone—" She put up her hand when he started to speak. "I don't want to live in it with a man and 'drape it in silk,' as my daughter says. That house deserves life. *Young* life." She didn't add that her daughter had the "wrong" name, so she'd be safe from all that Eden had grown to dislike about Arundel.

When she started to stand up, Brad caught her arm. His leg was still in bandages and it hurt him a lot. He grabbed his cane and tried to stand, but Eden gently pushed him down in the swing.

"No," she said. "Don't get up." She walked to the edge of the porch. "You know something, Brad? I don't know anything about myself. I lived as a prisoner when I was a child, and went from childhood to motherhood in one night." She turned back to face him. "I've worked hard at giving my daughter all that I could. I gave up my life for her."

"But she's grown-up now," Brad said.

"Yes, she's grown now and about to be a mother herself. She went to dances as a teenager and she—" Eden waved her hand. "What I'm trying to say is that I want to find out about myself. I want to find out what I'm good at, what I can do, and what I like. I don't want to be Mrs. Farrington. I want to be *me*. It's just that I've experienced so little in my life that I don't know who I am."

Sitting on the swing, Brad looked at her. "You want to leave here, don't you?" He didn't wait for her to answer. "I'll go with you. I'll live on a sailboat, if it means that I can be near you."

"No," Eden answered. "You belong here. This is *your* town. And you know something? It's my daughter's town too. I'm going to give her and Stuart and my grandchild Farrington Manor. They belong there. Stuart can open an accounting firm here in Arundel. It's a good place to raise a child."

"It's a good place to *live*," Brad said, his voice pleading with her, his eyes near to tears.

"Brad, you're a wonderful man, a little controlling for someone as independent as I am, but a good man. But I need to try out my wings. I need to . . . to see some of the world before I get to be too old to enjoy it."

"Wherever you want to go, I'll go with you," Brad said, struggling to stand up.

She stepped down a step. "Give me a year," she said. "One year."

"A year," he said in agreement. "Then I'm going after you wherever you are in the world."

"A deal," she said, then she turned and ran down the porch steps before she could change her mind.

Epilogue

Eden Palmer looked up from the book she was reading. A man was standing over her. The sun was behind his head so she couldn't see his face. But she knew who he was.

"This seat taken?" he asked, motioning to the beach chair next to her.

"No," she answered and put down her book. She twirled around in the chair, presenting her almost naked back to him, and handed him the suntan lotion.

"I hear you've been busy," Jared McBride said as he massaged oil into her skin. Since she was lying completely in the shade of a huge umbrella, and her skin was perfectly white, he knew she didn't need the lotion.

"Very busy," she said, turning her head toward the ocean where Melissa and Stuart and her grandson were playing.

"You didn't stay in Arundel?"

"No, as I'm sure you know."

"I might have checked out a few things about you. Now and then. I hear you're writing a book about gardens around the world."

"It gets me into the gardens," she said.

"I stopped by Arundel about a month after the trial."

"Trials," Eden said.

"Yeah, right. Your testimony helped put Runkel away. And we got Jolly's boss. You were great!" He grinned at Eden, but she didn't smile back, just kept looking at him solemnly. "Sorry you had to go through that, but the agency appreciates it a lot."

"Tell them they're welcome." She didn't say any more, just let Jared continue caressing her back. She saw Stuart start toward her, but Melissa stopped him.

"I saw Granville."

"Oh?"

"You can imagine my surprise when I found out that you two weren't married. I thought that was a done deal. Money change your mind?"

"Being so close to death changed my mind. How was Braddon?"

"Full of confidence. He said that when you got back you two would be married. He told me...Well, actually, I had to get him drunk first, but he told me that you'd asked for a year to make up your mind. He seemed to think that was a normal thing. He said that in Victorian times it was ordinary for a young woman to take a year to make up her mind about who to marry."

"Ah," Eden said.

"What does that mean?"

"Nothing. Just ah."

"I did a little checking and it's been over a year since you asked him for a year to make up your mind."

"Ah."

"Have you made up your mind yet?"

"Maybe," she said, then turned and took the lotion from him. "I don't have access to every person on earth's intimate files, nor do I get people drunk, so I haven't been able to keep track of you. What have you been doing in the last year?"

"One year, six weeks, and two days," he said. "Not that I've been counting. I quit the agency."

"Get another job?"

"Don't want one."

"What do you plan to do with the rest of your life?"

"I thought I'd take it one day at a time. Not plan anything. You wouldn't like to go on a safari with me, would you?"

"Photos, not shooting?"

"No shooting anything. I gave that up. I think they have some gardens in Africa."

"Really?"

There was a shout and Jared looked toward the water. "That your grandchild?"

"Yes," Eden said, and her voice nearly melted.

"Handsome kid."

"Yes, he is."

He turned back to her. "Eden, I've lived my whole life alone. Even when I was married, I was alone. I made a real cock-up of that, but I'd like to try something different. Maybe—"

She put her fingertips over his lips. "I've been alone too, so let's see how we get along. I'd like to go on a safari."

Melissa, Stuart, and dear little Cody were walking toward them. Stuart was frowning at Eden in a protective way.

"By the way," Eden said, not taking her eyes off her approaching family. "What's your real name?"

"Montgomery. Jared Montgomery."